PROPHET OF PATHWAYS

PROPHET OF PATHWAYS

TONY PEAK

Prophet of Pathways

This book is published on behalf of the author by the Ethan Ellenberg Literary Agency.
You can reach the author at:
Author website: www.tonypeak.net
Facebook: https://www.facebook.com/tonypeak78
Twitter: @tonypeak78
Amazon Author Page: https://www.amazon.com/Tony-Peak/e/B00H70H7IE/ref=dp_byline_cont_all_1

Prophet of Pathways

Tagen awakens in a grimy, rain-slicked cityscape after committing suicide. The otherworldly city of Meridian, surrounded by the endless waters of the Styx, is filled with people with no memory of their pasts and ruled by the bloodthirsty cult of Clowns and their High Priestess, who denies the truth that everyone in the city is dead. Tagen remembers nothing of his past, except that he came to Meridian on purpose, in search of his wife Alexis.

When a fortune teller named Sveta gives Tagen a Tarot card reading, she draws the Magician, a sign that he has an important role to play in the fate of Meridian—but drawing the forbidden card condemns them both to death for heresy before the High Priestess. They are saved by Andromeda, who once led a failed rebellion and means to use Tagen's powers to overthrow the High Priestess. Even as they are pursued by the Clowns through clockwork spires and abandoned ruins, Tagen causes the memories of those around him to awaken, inspiring hope in the lost souls of Meridian. But he must recall his own memories to understand why he is there and how to escape, and facing his past may be the most daunting part of his journey.

BOOKS BY TONY PEAK

Beethoven's Tenth
Inherit the Stars
Prophet of Pathways
Signal
Wages of Cinn

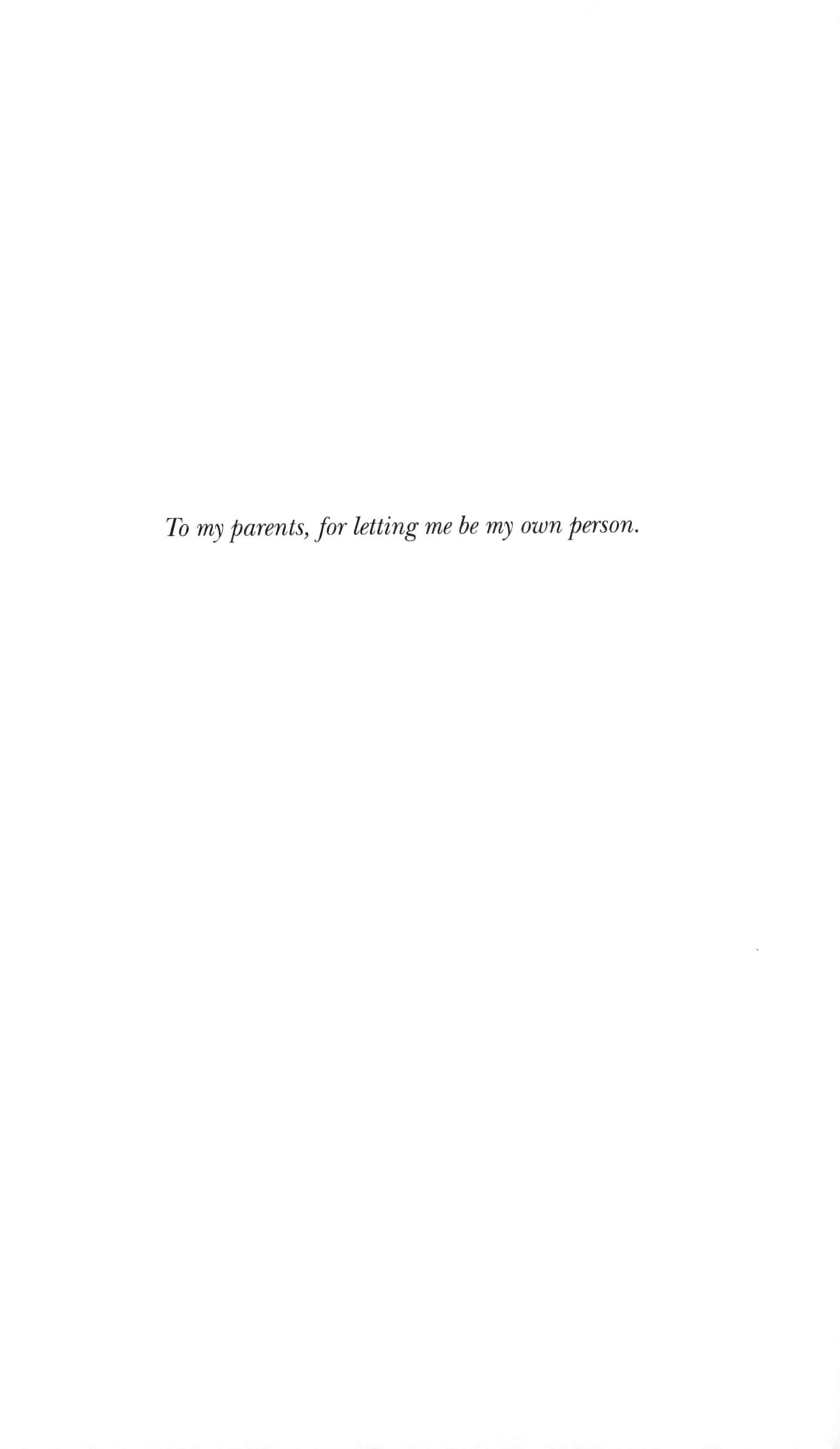

To my parents, for letting me be my own person.

Table of Contents

Acknowledgment

I'd like to express my thanks my agent Ethan Ellenberg, who graciously published this novel. Many thanks to my beta readers, who took time from their own writing to critique this novel: Ian Welke, Josh Vogt, Gregory Clifford, and Michael Pignatella. Though I never knew her, I'd like to acknowledge the late Pamela Coleman Smith for designing her world-famous Waite-Smith Tarot; its imagery was a definite influence on this story and the Meridian setting. Finally, I want to thank my family for always being there for me.

0.

THE FOOL

1: Prince of the Other World

Tagen stared at his slit wrists. The cuts were scarred over but it felt like he had sliced them only moments before. Though he recalled every second the knife had sawed into his flesh, every ruby drop of lifeblood pooling at his feet, he remembered little else.

Except that his wife had killed herself and he had followed suit. He couldn't remember her name, either.

Cool rain dribbled over Tagen. Harsh yellow light illuminated the trash-filled alley around him. It came from a tall streetlight, which emitted a small jet of steam every few seconds. The sky above the alleyway swelled into darkness. Sheet-metal posters hung along the alley walls of a voluptuous woman painted like a clown. She held a deck of cards. A halo radiated from her.

Was he really dead? Tagen studied his wrists again. The streets around him didn't look like Hell. No flames, no pointy-eared shits stabbing him with pitchforks.

Maybe he'd survived and the local hospital released him as a John Doe. That had to be it. Besides, the dead didn't heal. And he'd never heard of rain in Hell.

Rubbing his head, Tagen tried to figure out where he was. He fumbled in his jeans pocket for his phone but it was gone. Maybe he'd left it in…no, wait…

Damn it. He couldn't remember anything about his house, the street he lived on, why Alexis had committed suicide—

"Alexis?" It felt good to say her name. To finally remember it. Afraid that he might forget it again, he shouted it until he coughed.

Tagen hacked and winced. Every nerve was raw and inflamed. Hunger roiled in his stomach. He rose from the dank puddle he'd been sitting in. The alley's dampness penetrated his shirt and he shivered. Patches of mildew covered his clothing.

How long had he sat there? Minutes, days? Years? It felt like centuries.

"Shit...oh shit…" He stared all around. If he were dead, where was Alexis? How long had she waited for him? His breaths quickened. Nausea overtook his hunger.

She'd once told him about a city in that deck of cards.

"Alexis?" Tagen sloshed past garbage piles and clumps of decayed blackness containing humanoid shapes. The stench made him gag. He hurried through the alley, toward the street. "Alexis!"

A hand grabbed his sleeve.

"Look lost." Strong arms hauled him back into the alley and slammed him against the wall. People walked past the alleyway, ignoring him. One was dressed like a clown from a nightmare with full-body grease paint, filthy wig, and wild eyes. An even more horrid figure stepped before him.

"New to Meridian, yes?" The speaker patted Tagen's cheek with oily fingers. "Fetch good trade from Bone Guild."

The man wore a hodgepodge of metal plates and bones, resembling armor. His features were stitched together from numerous bodies: different skin tones warred over a brutish face. Gold, silver, and bronze teeth comprised the man's smile.

"Let go of me, asshole!" Tagen struggled but four others pressed him against the wall. They were dressed like the speaker, with similar flesh and teeth.

"Name's Radomir. None will know yours." The armored man's grin widened.

"Wait!" Tagen cried. "Where am I? Is this Hell? Is this my punishment?"

"Nothing personal, yes?" Radomir asked. "Just Gutter Knight business. Right, Lezzek?" One of the others nodded and produced a blood-stained sack.

Tagen's palms itched and he tried pulling away,but their eager fingers burrowed into his flesh. Radomir drew a slim dagger from his belt and stepped closer.

"Oh God—somebody help me!" Tagen shouted.

Radomir's chuckle possessed a metallic timbre. "No god here, unless High Priestess. Gutter Knights don't serve her. Relax, won't take long, yes?"

Shaking, Tagen sucked in a breath. Did he lie in his bed dreaming? This couldn't be the city in Alexis's cards. That had been a happy place, one where—

Radomir's blade touched his neck. Tagen's palms grew hot.

An image flashed in his mind: *a man on a hill fended off seven stave-wielding attackers.* He remembered the card from Alexis's deck: the Seven of Staves. Clenching his fists, Tagen seethed. Why think about that now, he needed to fight!

A violet flash filled the alleyway.

Radomir grunted and hesitated. Tagen's palms cooled.

In his mind, the seven staves shattered.

The Gutter Knights fell over, wheezing as if something had knocked the wind from their lungs. Drained of energy, Tagen sagged against the wall.

"Very stupid, yes." Radomir stood over him. The other Knights fled.

"Please…" Tagen lifted his right hand to ward off Radomir's dagger.

A poster rattled though no wind stirred. Dark inky shapes reflected in the alley's puddles and disappeared. For an instant Tagen visualized Radomir in a suit and tie, his face whole and clean.

Radomir's albino-like gaze filled with shame. He fell against the opposite wall, knocking down one of the clown posters. The dagger slipped from his grasp and splashed into a puddle.

Tagen stood and rubbed his hands. A card lay face-down in his palm. It glowed purple for a moment, lighting the alleyway in a brief violet sheen.

"Where the hell am I?" Tagen stumbled toward Radomir. Anger and hunger tangled his guts. "Where, you son of a bitch?"

Cringing, Radomir raised his gauntleted hands. "Meridian. Sorry, didn't mean—" He stopped as if staring into some other world.

Tagen snatched the dagger from the puddle and held it below Radomir's chin. "What place is this? How did I get here?"

Several clowns strolled past the alley. Their painted bodies glistened in the streetlight as they juggled skulls. One blew a kiss at Tagen and the others laughed.

Radomir pushed past Tagen from the alley.

"Hey!" Tagen pursued the rat-like man, then halted in the middle of the street.

A dim, corroded city surrounded him. Rain dampened everything. Towering buildings leaned against each other in disrepair. Runoff coursed down gutters into grimy sewer grates. Regularly spaced steam-powered lights lit the steep, garbage-lined streets. Green mildew tinted the city's walls and curbs. An abandoned dock gave way to an endless expanse of black water beneath a horizon without sun, moon, or stars. Only the city lights prevented total black void.

Glancing at the card in his hand, Tagen stopped breathing. It showed the Ten of Cups. He raised it closer to his face but the card vanished.

What was happening to him? Things appearing from thin air, these weird scenes in his mind—

Something bumped into Tagen.

"Outta my way, fuckface!" A man glared at him, then walked on. Steam hissed from vents in his back and his body creaked on metal legs ending in clawed feet.

Tagen stumbled backward. "I..."

Two female clowns brushed past, their nudity obscured only by grease paint swirls. Their eyes fluttered in drugged stupor. Three children robbed a beggar in a different alley, beating him with femur bones.

There were no flames or winged devils. No 'lake of fire' or any of that bullshit. Nothing like he'd heard from those weirdos going door to door, passing out pamphlets.

"Meridian," Tagen whispered.

Another passerby bumped into him. Hot fury shot through Tagen and he brandished the dagger. Where the hell was Alexis, why couldn't these people leave him alone? Was there any food around? Stiff with tension, he took a deep breath and stuck the dagger into his pocket.

Why had Alexis killed herself to come here?

Afraid to stand still, Tagen ambled along with the crowd. People of every age and ethnicity occupied Meridian. Many dressed like semi-nude clowns or possessed metallic, steam-powered additions such as claws, clockwork hands, or chest grills. Others genuflected before images of the clown woman he'd seen on the poster.

Rubbing his hands again, he wondered what had happened in the alley with the Gutter Knights. His fingertips encountered pits along both palms so he stopped and examined them. Dark lines were carved there, ending with the cut across either wrist. Like he had mutilated his hand and slit his veins in one uninterrupted cut.

Pacing in a circle, Tagen tried to control his frustrated breaths. He'd committed suicide to find Alexis! The memory was spotty— she'd lain on the floor, blood spreading from her body, drowning the Tarot cards scattered around her.

Yes, Tarot cards. The one in her stiff hand had showed a city of light. She'd wanted to come here, where only the dead could go—but why?

Try as he might, nothing came to mind. He blinked against the rain drizzle.

The people around him all acted alive. He knew he was dead.

"We're all dead!" His laughter petered off into a whimper. "Don't you know?"

People shoved past him.

"Where's your devils?" He clawed at his eyes. "Where's your fire? Goddamnit, answer me!"

Everyone ignored him.

"Alexis?" he asked no one in particular. As more people walked past, Tagen sought her face among them.

"Alexis? Alexis!" He pushed through the crowd, eliciting curses. Shaking with desperation, Tagen turned in a circle and wrung his damp hair.

"Alexis—?"

"Shut the hell up." A large man shoved Tagen into a gutter. Brackish water sloshed over him. A sob crept up his throat.

He'd known what he would face once the blade had opened his wrists. He'd been prepared. But this place was beyond any nightmare, any—

"You should watch where you're going, 'dead man'," a female voice said.

Tagen stared up at a slim woman covered in white grease paint. Purple diamonds were drawn under her eyes, resembling tears. A torsolette hugged her body, colored in a faded purple diamond pattern. A three-pointed jester's cap dangled from her head with a shock of blonde hair beneath it. She held a rusted square box in both hands.

"Who are you?" He tried to focus on her blue eyes and not her fishnet-clad legs.

"Andromeda. What's your pitch?" The box in her hands transformed into a floating head. It had glowing green eyes, a copper jester's cap, and a clockwork jaw. Small steam jets kept it aloft.

"Um, Tagen. What's that?" Looking Andromeda over, he flinched when she caught him ogling. What was wrong with him? Alexis needed him, not this person.

"Khyran, a Mecho jack-in-the-box." Andromeda studied him. "You're not a regular kinker 'round here, are you?"

"What?"

"Let's find a food joint, and we'll talk," she said. "I know you're starved."

"Why should I trust you?" Tagen asked.

Her eyes hardened. "Because you're new. And you don't know the take."

Licking his lips, he followed. Andromeda and her disembodied friend led him to a kiosk down the street. It stood seven feet, covered in rusty tin. Steam jetted from a pipe in its roof. A red neon sign of a skull and cleaver flickered above the window. An emaciated man sat inside, selling slimy food to hungry customers. Tagen's stomach growled.

Andromeda ordered them both a handful of dark green tendrils filled with pink chunks, then paid the vendor two copper shards. Khyran hovered above them as if keeping watch.

"Here you go—"

No sooner did she hand Tagen the food, than he gulped it down with ravenous bites. The dark tendrils exploded with a salty taste and slid down his throat. He crushed the pink chunks between his teeth, releasing juices sweeter than any pork chop he'd eaten. After a brief moment of satisfaction he licked his palms, having eaten it all.

"Easy, Jackpot. Meridian's urges are strong. Some new kinkers go mad and eat their hands and feet." She ate the tendrils but not the meat.

The vendor watched them with a flat, machine-like stare. Tagen glanced at the flashing sign. It displayed the skull and cleaver one moment, then a logo reading 'Bone Guild' the next.

He stopped licking his fingers. Radomir had mentioned the Bone Guild. Had planned to kill and sell Tagen to them.

A burning tremor traveled up from Tagen's gut to his throat. He turned to vomit in the gutter.

"There's hope for you yet." Andromeda nudged his shoulder. "It's all most troupers eat in Meridian. Kelp harvested in the waters of the Styx and…"

"Shit." Tagen didn't know what sickened him more: eating human meat, or the fact he'd enjoyed it. If Radomir had taken him, someone might be eating him right now.

"Even the dead must eat," Andromeda whispered. "Hey, you listening? I told you, urges are harder to resist here. Now that you've eaten, maybe you'll pay attention."

Tagen caught himself ogling her petite form again. Shiny grease paint along her thigh, the hint of a nipple poking through her torsolette...

"My eyes are up here, Jackpot."

Face flushed, he looked away. "Then...I'm really dead? Is this Hell? Purgatory?"

Andromeda took his arm, walking with a dancer's grace. "It's Meridian. Most kinkers don't know they're dead and the city's surrounded by the endless Styx. Only the steamlamps give us light. Only the Tarot gives us hope."

"Tarot? But I saw this city in those cards before I..." Tagen ran a hand down his face. "Before I ended my life."

"You saw Meridian in the cards? In your former life?" A strained look passed over her face. "Memory is a gift most here don't have."

"I came here to find someone, goddamnit..." He stopped, realizing he'd stepped toward Andromeda with his fists clenched. Though her eyes narrowed, she stood her ground. Her warning about urges came back to him.

"I'm sorry," Tagen said. "This place isn't what I saw. Hell, I'm not even sure what I saw. But I know I died. How can I leave Meridian?"

"You'd better keep that to yourself." She gripped his hand for a moment, then continued. "Look, Tagen, you need to take special care. There's not many of us left who remember what came before."

"You're not making sense. Can I leave Meridian or not?" Fresh rain pattered down on them.

"You got itchy feet? No one can escape Meridian." Andromeda pressed him into a trash-filled alcove and waited until a few people passed. "There's nothing beyond this city. The Clowns kill anyone trying to leave. It's the decree of the High Priestess. Yes, the dead can die again. And dying here is worse."

"How?"

"The city takes you," she said. "Forever."

"But aren't you a Clown?" He still had Radomir's dagger in his pocket but didn't want to use it on her.

"No." She glanced around. "We're in Vagrant's Row, the roughest part of this joint. You must get to the Bazaar. I have loyal kinkers there. You'll reach it by following this street. It's an open, round area full of stalls."

"Hold it. I'm looking for someone. Another new arrival." He frowned. "Could I find this person in the Bazaar?"

She looked away. "Wait for me there and we'll see. But avoid the painted freaks. I know someone who might help you."

"Why can't you take me there?"

"If you're seen with me that close to the Circus…it's too dangerous. The Clowns might catch on."

Tagen grabbed her wrist and ignored Khyran as he hovered close. Perhaps the floating head protected her. "Catch on to what? You buy me food, tell me to hide, promise help…why?"

"You got floss for brains? Let go."

He shook his head. "Tell me."

They stared at each other as the downpour smudged her face paint. Her skin was warm but her eyes were colder than the rain. Tagen didn't relent. Her gaze softened.

"Because I want to," Andromeda finally said. "I'll find you before the Alueryic Clock in the Mecho District tolls seven times. We'll meet in the Bazaar. Keep a low profile, Jackpot. And keep your damn hands to yourself."

Before he could ask anything else she jerked her hand away and left. Khyran watched him for a moment, jetted steam, and followed her.

Tagen tried to calm himself. Why would the Clowns want him? What was Andromeda withholding? He recalled the incident with the Gutter Knights. Something had happened to make them fall and release him. He studied his palms again.

Again, just dark carvings on each palm.

He left the alcove and hurried down the street, avoiding eye contact with anyone. More Clowns, steam-enhanced individuals, and other miserable denizens went by in a blur of forbidden humanity. None of them were Alexis. Or were they?

Would she even know him?

2: Blind Ambition

After ensuring that Tagen hadn't followed her, Andromeda clambered atop a headless statue of the Gorgon on an ancient curb. Studying Meridian's decrepit urban wasteland, she grunted with frustration. Never had she felt so much power in a newcomer. Not even when she'd first met Khyran.

She'd almost given up patrolling the Row for new arrivals. Ever since the High Priestess had taken over, fewer people remembered their past life. That meant fewer could escape Meridian. But there'd been no time to tell Tagen. Not yet.

Damn, he was stupid. Shouting in a crowd like that. If the Clowns had heard…

By Charon, though…she hoped Tagen made it. Touching the glyphs on his hand had stirred the deepest part of herself. A part that was all but expired, a smoldering vengeance. One that the city's perpetual rain could never extinguish.

The old Tarot prophecy…was he the one?

She somersaulted off the two-story statue and landed on her feet. She was ready.

But was he? Tagen had to fend for himself. Until she reached a safer area or had certain things in hand, the High Priestess would sense Andromeda's every move. Tagen wouldn't stand a chance.

She didn't want to attract attention to what he might be. Not until everything was in place.

To think he'd seen Meridian in his past life, in a deck of cards! Then killed himself to get here, to find someone? That kind of insight…it might to be the prophecy. Strolling through the Row,

Andromeda hummed a few notes to herself. Notes from a happy tune, from a happier time.

Her own former life was a collection of foggy memories. Tightropes, juggling, laughter from an adoring audience. Choosing the sobriquet of a mythological princess for her stage name. Performing act after death-defying act until her confidence turned to arrogance, her shows into challenges to authority.

Andromeda gazed past the streets while rain poured over her. More than anything she remembered the card she'd drawn in the fortuneteller's tent right before her death.

A figure with one hand pointing at the sky, the other at the earth. The face had changed many times. Once it'd been Khyran's but now she wasn't sure. Like everything else in Meridian, memories became coated with grime. Twisted by the city's power.

"I sensed him, despite the cards shunning me for so long. Like I felt you enter Meridian, long ago." She caressed Khyran's metallic cheek. It had been flesh once. Andromeda missed his lips brushing her stomach, her fingers in his hair. Holding each other during the city's heartless downpours.

Meridian had been tolerable then. Before the High Priestess discovered Khyran's power. Before Andromeda bathed her shame in grease paint.

Steam misted from Khyran's bronze lips. She remembered him wandering the streets as a new arrival just like Tagen. She wanted to envelop the possibilities that Tagen heralded, use him against her rival…but her guilt over Khyran remained too strong. Not even Meridian's temptations could overcome it.

She wouldn't let them.

"Jackpot has the markings on his palm; I felt them. Maybe he can read the Stygian deck for us. You did, once." Khyran's green eyes flashed as she kissed his bronze cheek. "Now we must alert the others."

3: Reckless Desire

The rain grew colder. Though Tagen's stomach rumbled, he avoided the next Bone Guild kiosk. He had no copper shards anyway. Instead, he focused on the various Tarot trappings pervasive to Meridian. Doing so lessened his hunger, helped him ignore people's challenging stares. Took his mind off Alexis.

Metal posters advertised Tarot readings at the Circus or the beneficial care of the High Priestess. Clown children held similar placards on street corners or character icons from the gaudy Clown Tarot. With so many residents wearing grease paint, Andromeda's advice about avoiding 'painted freaks' was laughable.

No vehicles traveled the Row's hilly, grubby streets, and no visible force kept order. A man chewed stringy muscle from a severed arm nearby...it looked so juicy and filling. Tagen swallowed but hurried on. He quelled the casual anger a stare or a bump would elicit from contact with others. All the near-naked Clown women fired his blood. Damn, they were so sexy and willing. Twice he had to stop and close his eyes until the throbbing passions abated.

Nothing was forbidden. No taboo kept desires in check.

He yearned for demons to jump out and punish him or these people. Boiling pools of lava ready to incinerate them. Anything to make it all stop.

Bereft of purpose or design, Meridian was worse than any Hell.

Near the sheet-metal posters and lacquered icons, however, people acted less angry or lustful. Seductive Clown smiles were angelic alongside the hellish misery he'd witnessed so far. Everywhere he went the eyes of this pure, lovely High Priestess figure were always on him.

Those eyes...no, they weren't Alexis's. Where would Alexis be if she were here? She'd never cared for the rain. He remembered that much.

He lifted his coat above their heads as the rain fell. They ran down the street trying to hail a cab. Alexis laughed, clinging to him, her dress sodden despite his erstwhile chivalry. It didn't matter if the gun in his shoulder holster got wet, he was glad to shield her, glad to...

The memory ended. He wiped his eyes, happy to recall that moment. But a gun?

Maybe he'd been a cop or a detective. Something better than this city.

As the drizzle increased Tagen hurried into a crumbling building. People lined the floors in various states of dress and rest. Stilling himself, Tagen eased past two women feasting on someone's leg. Neither of them was Alexis, thankfully. On the next landing three men indulged their sexual appetites with each other. Sounds of chewed gristle mixed with thighs slapping against a bottom.

He forced himself not to join either party. It was as if he lacked any restraint.

Stopping before a window, he gaped. Viewed from higher up, the tattered spires of the rainy panorama, filled with the dead, commanded his attention.

Meridian stretched far and wide with huge arching structures deteriorating on cracked foundations. A millennium's worth of rot and mildew coated each skyscraper. And yet, the city's languorous, steam-lit refulgence was as seductive as a lover's whisper.

"Where are you?" he murmured, chest tight and throat dry. "I found this place. Why can't I find you?"

A collection of gaudy tents ruled central Meridian, key among them a huge red and white-striped one. Beside it sprawled a shiny region of angular buildings emitting steam vapors. No ships plied the waters of the Styx near the empty quays and rotten docks. Hadn't Andromeda mentioned the Bazaar was round and open... yes, there it was.

The two women smacked their lips as they finished their macabre meal.

To hell with following that street through Vagrant's Row. He plotted a new course from his location to the round amphitheater-like area nearby.

The meandering streets reminded him of the snaking crimson lines leaking from Alexis's body at the moment he'd killed himself. There had been a card in her other hand, depicting a figure in a golden mask. Why couldn't he remember everything else?

Tagen wiped his eyes again. It hurt not knowing how much he'd loved her.

Wetness touched his ankle, then something sharp plunged into it. He jumped back. One of the women had bit him.

"Mmm-mmm." She smiled. "So fresh. So firm. The Clowns say we shouldn't be afraid of what we feel."

The other woman stood, her shirt ripped open. Her breasts bore bloody teeth marks and she lacked a right hand. In its place was a stump affixed with a serrated blade.

He forced down his anger and revulsion. "I don't want any trouble—"

"I'm hungry. Why the fuck am I always hungry?" The handless woman lunged at Tagen. Her blade grazed his left arm. Blood dripped from the gash. The other woman supped up the crimson droplets from the dirty floor until the handless one kicked her.

"Mine, bitch," she said. Both giggled like girls stealing candy from a busted machine.

Tagen swallowed, wanting to fuck the women, thrash them, devour them…

They came at him again. He drew the dagger from his pocket but in his clumsy fright it clanged onto the floor.

"Ah, he gives us something to help with the carving," the crawling woman said.

Tagen ran. In the adjacent hallway, people lying in heaps tripped him. He tumbled over a pile of gnawed bones. Two invalids rose from the bones and held him. Both cannibal women rushed in, faces alight with killing glee.

"You don't have to do this! I just want my wife!" He held up both hands.

The eyes of every assailant contained a deep pain, a forgotten longing for something better. Feet jabbed into his stomach and ribs. Hands clasped his arms and legs. The serrated knife neared his neck. Blood-caked lips glided up his thigh to his crotch.

He just wanted to escape, didn't wish these people harm—

His palms itched as an image coalesced in his thoughts: *a figure carrying five swords fled the people assaulting him, who focused on two other swords. The Seven of Swords. The card shone in the raindrops outside the window, reflected in the eyes of his attackers.* He blinked and the vision ended.

"Catch him, assholes! I'm still hungry!" The handless woman stabbed at the air while the others pummeled the floor beside Tagen. He stared while they ignored him and attacked a nonexistent foe. His right palm stung. One of the marks on it darkened.

Tagen fled the building while his attackers continued their crazed actions. Limping from where that crazy bitch had bit him, he tried to remember the path he'd plotted from the window.

I.

THE MAGICIAN

1: Caster of the Dice

Tagen finally stumbled from Vagrant's Row into the amphitheater area. Defaced statues of robed figures lined it. A neon sign hung from a busted steamlamp with 'Bazaar' flashing in green letters. Merchant lean-tos and threadbare tents covered the quarter, which bustled with customers. Unlike the previous district, people didn't feast on each other in darkened corners or assault their fellow citizens. Stern-looking Clowns with swords or clubs policed the area.

Other Clowns in colorful tents sold grease paint, wigs, and Tarot trinkets. Bone Guild kiosks sold human meat and sewer kelp. Mechanical people—Mechos, he overheard someone say—traded in precious metals, spare parts, and paid copper shards for salvage. Their entire bodies were coated in pure bronze or silver, streamlined to fit every muscle, each curve.

"Ah, would you like to upgrade that measly body of yours?" a bronze-coated man asked. "Through the steam-powered science of mechanis, you will never hunger, lust, or frown again!"

Tagen pushed on. No way would he look and sound like a machine.

A few Gutter Knights scurried past, carrying junk parts or scrap metal. Tagen tensed and slipped behind a tent. Though they talked among themselves in a guttural cant and carried slimy leather bags, all merchants traded with them, no questions asked. What did dead people want or need? The items and services available, through barter or bought with copper shards, shocked him. Plastic doll parts, clockwork jewelry, tattoo artists, prostitutes, mechanis accordions and music boxes, even leashed humans sold as pets.

One man with a self-turning, clockwork hurdy-gurdy in his chest accepted payment while a young woman danced to the device's trite music. Armed, stony-eyed children hired themselves out as mercenaries. Shaking his head, Tagen moved on.

A fenced-off pen contained naked shackled humans with drugged stares. Signs reading 'thief', 'invalid', or 'heretic' hung from their necks. A neon Bone Guild logo flashed above the pen.

Fists clenched, Tagen stomped past.

Books sealed in metal boxes or scrolls dipped in thick musky oil were highly priced. Tagen guessed the city's moisture rotted such items. With no apparent livestock or forests around, he didn't want to know where the paper came from, nor the oil.

Tagen's frown hurt his face. How much cheaper could life become in Meridian?

He leaned against a steamlamp post and caught his breath. Neon mechanis signs showed him heading toward Nomad Way. Hunger already plagued him again despite his aversion to Bone Guild meals. The sleek, painted Clown women still summoned other cravings. They sought converts by singing raucous songs or performing lewd dances. New believers were baptized in hot grease paint and given a ragged wig.

It would be so easy, surrendering to them. Find out why they smiled all the time. Tagen flexed his fingers and inhaled the grease paint's oily smell. They looked so sultry and delectable. Eager for his lust. Maybe Alexis had joined them and he'd find her naked, painted form waiting for him. Then he would—

An orange-painted Clown batted aside a nervous convert with his club. The other Clowns laughed, spat, and groped their genitals in the poor bastard's direction. Andromeda's warning came to mind: what would they do to him? Tagen hurried on.

Several beggar children clustered near a sewer grate, picking cast-off food from the grills and eating it. A Clown strutted by and threw a full Guild dish into the grate.

Tagen snatched the plate before it washed away and handed it to a small girl. She mouthed her thanks, then inhaled the steaming meat chunks. Other children punched her.

Nauseous, Tagen limped away. He wanted to throttle the assholes who ruled this place. He wanted to puke. He wanted to cry.

Why was he here? Was this punishment for his suicide?

Someone bumped into him and cursed. Scowling, Tagen reached for something under his left armpit. When he gripped nothing, he stumbled and blinked.

He'd reached for the gun in the shoulder holster. From that memory.

Tagen smiled with grim satisfaction. He hadn't been a victim in that life. Nor would he be in this one. He kept walking.

Near the Bazaar's edge, people in blue clothing traded from canvas shelters. Tattoos of stars, moons, and suns decorated their bodies. All wore silver jewelry. Their finely tooled leather goods and hand-worked pottery attracted fewer customers than the Clown or Mecho offerings.

A violin's slow, haunting strains drew him toward the shelters. It made him think of a wingless bird singing in stormy twilight.

"Vases fashioned from Elysian clay dipped in the Styx," a woman called to him.

"Sky Nomad boots will keep your feet dry," another vendor said.

Tagen continued until he found the violin player: a brawny man sporting a gray ponytail, with matching beard and mustache. His blue eyes regarded Tagen with mild curiosity. The man sat on a stool beside a booth painted with silver stars and moons.

Inside the booth a young woman shuffled a thin metal Tarot deck. She stopped, stared at Tagen, then looked away.

Alexis had used the Tarot. She might have come here.

Breathing deep, he approached the booth. He resisted the scrumptious aromas wafting from Bone Guild kiosks, refrained from staring at the Clown women's painted bottoms. Meridian brimmed with temptations he wanted no part of. None of them would lead him to Alexis.

Tarot cards might.

The man ceased playing and Tagen missed the sound instantly.

"Greetings. Perchance, a Sky Nomad tale might enlighten you?" The old man smiled. "I am Georgio. My words are cheap for a copper shard."

Tagen hesitated. Was this man a friend of Andromeda's?

"The knave's tongue, the sting of lies, beyond dark waters are blue, blue skies." Georgio touched his silver half-moon earring. "Would you care to hear more?"

Several Clown warriors walked by. Tagen tugged at his collar. He didn't have time or money for stories.

"I'm looking for…" Tagen lacked any description, not recalling Alexis's face.

"Care to have your fortune told, sir?" the woman in the booth asked, her smooth voice cutting through the Bazaar's clamor. Her dark brown hair hung in braids held with silver clasps, framing a face with full lips. Calm green eyes regarded him with professional nonchalance. She wore a small blue vest and short skirt, showing ample skin. Flowing, amorphous tattoos, unlike those of other Nomads, covered her limbs. A silver medallion resembling a compass hung from her neck.

Tagen could wait for Andromeda and risk getting caught by the Clowns, or he could get a Tarot reading. He'd found his way to Meridian through the cards. Maybe he could find Alexis—and a way out.

"Yes, I'm Tagen—"

She beckoned him closer. "What is it you seek, sir?"

As he leaned into the booth, her scent made him step nearer. Fresh rain, budding flowers, and sharp spice. Where had she found such a fragrance in Meridian?

Tagen glanced to either side. No one stood in line behind him. "I…I want to know why I'm here."

A brief look of pity crossed the woman's face, then she reshuffled her deck. The thin metal sheets were embossed with images. The reverse of each card bore a smiling Clown face.

"Is that the Clown Tarot?" he asked.

"Yes, the only Tarot sanctioned by the High Priestess," she said. "Now pay attention. I will do a three card spread."

Before she drew the first card Tagen touched her wrist. Her jaw clenched but he didn't withdraw. Blue fingerless gloves covered her hands.

"What's your name? I mean, you are going to tell my fortune." With his old memories still in stasis, he wanted to know the name of such a woman. She glittered like a jewel among Meridian's filth.

Several Clowns guffawed nearby as a new recruit choked during a grease paint baptismal. Clown warriors watched in silence. Heart beating faster, Tagen ignored them.

"Sveta." She tugged her wrist free, drew the first card, and laid it on the counter.

"The Six of Swords," Sveta said. The card showed a Mecho poling a boat over rough waters to a distant shore. A Clown woman and child sat in the boat.

"You come from strife seeking a new beginning." The curtness left Sveta's tone.

Georgio said something as the Clown warriors drew near. Tagen gripped the counter and held his breath.

Sveta drew and lay down the second card. It showed two Clowns cringing beneath a full moon. Two clockwork towers loomed in the distance.

"The Moon. You follow your instincts but the time has not yet come to act. Perhaps you should practice patience." She glanced at him and Tagen leaned back.

A few feet away a Clown warrior slapped a Nomad woman's rump with the flat of his sword. Tagen's teeth ground together.

"The final card shows the result of your endeavors." Sveta drew the third card and laid it down. Looking from him to the final card, she gasped.

It was made of paper, not metal.

She didn't need to tell him the card's title. Somehow he knew it. A figure standing on a dock where a cup, stave, sword, and pentacle coin lay. His right hand pointed skyward; his left, to the Styx below.

The Magician.

"Pay me and leave." Sveta's hands shook as she reached for the cards. Dark shadows reflected in a puddle beside the booth.

"I don't have any money," Tagen said. "Hey, what's the matter? What does this card mean, the Magician?" His last word carried over the noise around them.

Sveta shot him a cold stare. The Clown warriors outside her booth fell silent. Several customers hurried to another part of the Bazaar. Even some Nomads ceased hawking their wares and watched. Georgio gazed at Tagen.

"Just leave," Sveta whispered, desperation in her eyes. "You don't know what you've done."

A Clown warrior blew a steam horn. People tossed aside items they'd considered buying. Merchants shuttered their stalls. Every customer in the Nomad section left.

"What's the big deal?" Tagen asked.

A circle of mirthless Clowns gathered around Sveta's booth. They carried clubs with sharp nails or nicked swords.

"Shit, Clowns of Staves and Swords." Sveta reached for the three cards again but a red-painted Clown grabbed her hand.

Taut and sinewy, the Clown smirked at them. His hair rose in purple and green spikes. Ragged pants were his only apparel. He lifted a blood-stained sword.

"That's right, Sky Nomad." The Clown's voice sounded as if he'd gargled fingernail clippings. A large scar showed through the paint around his neck.

"What do you want? I've told fortunes here for—" Sveta managed before the Clown clamped a hand around her throat. Tagen stepped forward only to find sharp blades at his own neck.

"Name's Darwick, Nomad," the red Clown said. "I heard what your customer said. Get your ass out here."

Sveta obeyed and left the booth. Clasping his violin tight, Georgio rose from the stool. More customers and merchants left the Bazaar as if a plague had broken out.

Darwick shoved her into Tagen, knocking them both against the tent. Sveta pushed herself away from Tagen and stood straight. She looked more afraid of him and the paper card than the Clowns.

Studying the Magician card on the counter, Darwick's smirk contorted into a bestial expression of bared teeth and flared nostrils.

"Where'd you get this? No deck in Meridian should have this fucking card. Tell me or I'll carve out your guts, Nomad slut." He nicked her vest with the tip of his sword.

Though his palms burned, Tagen remained still. If he moved, they'd both die.

"He wanted a reading. I drew it." Sveta's eyes were like cold emeralds.

"The Sky Nomads are allowed to tell fortunes by the High Priestess's edict," Georgio said. Tagen couldn't tell if sweat or rain glistened on the old man's brow.

"You ain't allowed to spread blasphemy, bitch. The Magician prophecy is lies. When will you fuckers realize that Meridian's all there is?" Darwick ripped the paper card in Tagen's face. "For you, huh? Who the hell are you?"

"Tagen. I think—"

Darwick gestured. Clowns grabbed Tagen and forced his fists open. In Tagen's right palm was a dark, half-moon shaped mark. Until now it had been a scar.

"He has the glyphs." Darwick said. "Fuck. What about her?"

Two Clowns forced Sveta to her knees and yanked her gloves off. She had similar glyphs on each hand.

"So you're a cartomancer, too. Fucking Sky Nomads. The High Priestess should have burned you all with your airships. Tie 'em together, we're taking 'em to the Circus." Darwick slashed Sveta's booth with his sword. It collapsed in on itself. "You're done telling fortunes. Hurry, get 'em tied!"

The Clowns trussed Tagen and Sveta face to face with bronze wire. It bit into their skin. Sveta met his eyes with accusation and resolve.

Tagen shook his head. "I didn't mean to involve you—"

Darwick slapped Tagen's cheek with the flat of his sword. "Shut that shit up or I'll only take your hands to the High Priestess. Let's go."

As the Clowns hefted the pair over their shoulders the movement caused the bronze wire to lacerate the captives' arms and legs. Tagen winced and bit his lip. Sveta grunted and tears filled her eyes. People scurried from the Clowns' path as they toted the pair from the Bazaar. Behind them, Georgio glared in helpless anger.

While they traveled back through Vagrant's Row some people scurried from sight. Others held up icons of the High Priestess and cheered. Several tossed gutter filth at Tagen and Sveta. What had he done?

A few blocks ahead, the collection of tents Tagen had spotted earlier loomed like garish monoliths.

Tagen caught Sveta's eyes again and mouthed, 'I'm sorry'.

Something in her stare brought an image to his mind: *a Clown woman wrestled a clockwork lion, holding it down in victory*. The Strength Tarot card.

Warmth flowed through Tagen's limbs and the bronze wire didn't sting as much. No blood seeped from their cuts. Sveta gaped at him in wonder.

2: The Way Implied

Radomir ducked behind a corner until the Clowns shuffled past with their prisoners. He'd watched the entire incident in the Bazaar after following the newcomer from Vagrant's Row.

Ever since that encounter in the alley, Radomir had imagined himself in a different world, yes. *A clean, ordered one, filled with sunlight, smiling friends, and an infant in his arms.* These were more vivid than his memories of living in Meridian. He'd visualized them over and over since meeting the newcomer in that accursed alley.

What had that man done to him?

"What gives, Radomir?" Lezzek asked. "I have a golden jawbone with new mechanis apertures to trade."

Three other Gutter Knights unloaded various parts at a Mecho booth nearby. Radomir clutched a copper coil he'd planned trading for a clockwork pistol. For all the bartering and merchandise around him, though, he couldn't take his eyes from the Clowns and their prisoners.

"Good trade. Yes." The words exited his mouth in a monotone.

All his time in Meridian, Radomir had never considered his past life. Even doubted such a thing, yes. The very idea of being dead was ludicrous. He stole and scavenged to survive, to avoid serving either the Clowns and their painted goddess, or the Mechos and their copper-plated savior. He'd never felt guilty about selling corpses to the Bone Guild nor robbing Mechos of their copper organs. Not until meeting the newcomer.

The coil in his hand weighed him down with its empty materialism. What did things like this matter when he now recalled what he'd lost?

Radomir knew Darwick and his cronies would take the pair to the Circus. The High Priestess would probably kill them like she did all her enemies. Maybe the images of a baby boy, or a clean desk in a high-rise building, would disappear from his mind with the newcomer's death. Then he'd concentrate on finding easy loot, weak victims.

But...he didn't want the images to fade from his mind. In one recollection the baby boy giggled and spoke.

"Da," Radomir whispered. His son's first word in the life before this one.

"Huh? Listen, I'm pawning this before they close the damn Mecho booths." Lezzek walked back into the Bazaar.

Radomir hid the copper coil beneath his armor and trailed after the Clowns.

3: Chicanery

Lips tight, Andromeda picked up one half of the paper card. Darwick's vandalism hadn't ruined the Magician's image on it. She held it up for Khyran to see as he transformed from a box to a floating head.

"Why couldn't that floss head have kept out of sight? Goddamn those painted freaks." She scanned the square. No one would return here for business until the Alueryic Clock tolled ten times. Andromeda shoved the card's remnants into her torsolette.

"I've never seen a paper card in Meridian. Not even when you read the Tarot." She patted Khyran's cheek as he flew near her face. That was so long ago now. Most in Meridian had forgotten their names, the sacrifices she and Khyran had made. Few remembered anything now, trapped in Meridian's decadence. But she remembered.

When they overthrew the Clowns...Andromeda would enjoy those times again.

"No surprise, seeing you trail another cartomancer," Georgio said behind her.

Andromeda whirled, hands near the blades beneath her torsolette's skirt.

"And I'm not surprised you hid one among your natives." Andromeda held her breath but no other Sky Nomads appeared. "Still seeking a path from Meridian, then? I thought you'd outgrown those old Nomad tales."

Georgio's blue gaze hinted at a loss separate than what she'd done to him. "Sveta is dear to me. She cannot show such a path— but that man Tagen might. Why else would you have followed him here?"

"It's my sideshow, not yours. I've seen enough victims go to Clown Alley." She glanced at Khyran's head and shivered.

"How many will suffer in your quest for vengeance?" Georgio pointed at her skirt. "You keep steel closer to you than people. Meridian has poisoned you, Andromeda. The Blades of Charon cut you as much as your enemies."

She stiffened. "Some of my kinkers trail Darwick even now. Jackpot and the girl will both be freed. My pitch is, we should be working together."

"The last time we tried that you betrayed me," Georgio said.

"Stop bowing to the High Priestess!" Andromeda cried. "With the Stygian Tarot, I can defeat her."

"I don't know where that deck is. You gave it to Khyran, just like you gave Azibar the secrets of Nomad mechanis. Besides, you can't read the cards anymore. The High Priestess would crush you." Georgio turned to leave but she touched his shoulder.

"The deck wasn't on Khyran when the High Priestess defeated him."

"As you sit in the steamlight glow, her name is written in the dark Tarot," Georgio muttered.

"Please, Georgio. You're one of the few who remembers. Don't fold the show."

"Khyran was a good man. I'm sorry what happened to him… but you'll just use Tagen the same way. I have to help Sveta." Georgio hurried from the Bazaar, followed by several other Nomads.

"Damn you," Andromeda whispered, then ran though the empty aisles toward Vagrant's Row. Georgio was wrong—Tagen was different. Her heart thudded in time with her rushing footsteps.

By Charon's eyes, Georgio was wrong.

4: As Above, So Below

The Clowns set Tagen and Sveta down. He tensed. A circle of people blocked the street ahead. Sidewalks and alleys in the vicinity looked deserted. Darwick motioned over two Clowns, a man and woman.

"Keep an eye on 'em while the rest of us break this shit up." Darwick and the other warriors hurried down the street.

The circle of people raced past the Clowns. Darwick cursed in confusion. A low whistle carried on the air. A chill traveled up Tagen's spine.

Three people sprang from an alley, tossing daggers. One Clown collapsed with a blade in her eye.

"Ambush!" Darwick sprinted after the attackers. They wore black leather outfits and masks, with dagger-filled bandoleers strapped across their chests. Another Clown went down with a dagger in his throat.

Two black-clad figures assailed the Clowns guarding Tagen and Sveta. While one fended off both Clowns the other cut into the bronze wire imprisoning them.

"Hurry, Saissa! I can't hold—" the attacker's words ended as a Clown club brained him. The one trying to free them bolted and her dagger clattered beside Tagen's face. It was curved with block-like lettering engraved along the onyx-colored blade.

Up ahead the other attackers fared no better. One squealed as a Clown sword pierced his stomach. Darwick slashed another of them down and bellowed. The last figure turned to run but the Clowns, trim and eager for slaughter, pounced on her with relish. Swords and clubs rose in bloody arcs. Crimson stained the street's puddles.

A violent churning erupted in Tagen's stomach and cold sweat beaded his skin. Those people had just died trying to save him and Sveta. Why? The Clowns' laughter stung his ears and kindled rage in his heart. A curse came to his lips but the sound of moist scraping gave him pause.

Several citizens carried away the attacker's bodies, saliva dripping from their mouths. One man, steam venting from his neck, knelt on hands and knees and lapped up blood from the street. Darwick and the rest laughed at him.

"Holy shit," Tagen murmured, trying to hold back the sickness in his stomach.

"You're not helping," Sveta whispered. "Be quiet!"

"What the hell was that about?" Tagen whispered back, heart pounding as he squirmed after the dagger.

"The Blades of Charon, a secret faction," Sveta said. "They strive for the High Priestess's downfall."

"Why did they help us?"

"Who knows? Crazy fools. Almost as crazy as the Magician—" she hesitated.

Tagen craned his neck to face her. "What is the Magician prophecy?"

"The High Priestess fears the Magician. He's supposed to change—" Sveta stopped as the Clowns lifted them up again.

Tagen grimaced. The dagger was out of his reach.

Darwick flung blood from his sword. "See that, asshole? The High Priestess don't tolerate unbelievers. Can't fucking wait to see what she'll do with two cartomancers."

His laughter sounded worse than spikes scraping over coals. That throat scar must have something to do with his voice…

"How'd you get that scar on your neck?" Tagen asked. Sveta eyed him with a dangerous expression but he didn't care. These Clowns made him sick. He'd already killed himself…fear should mean little now.

Darwick stuck his face beside Tagen's while the warriors hoisted the pair over their shoulders. "I was born with it. Want one to match it?" He brandished his sword. The other Clowns laughed.

Shapes moved in Tagen's peripheral vision. Sensations of wind blowing the branches of a tree, of a form swinging on a rope, crept into his thoughts.

"I think someone hung you," Tagen said. Sveta nudged him but he strained at his bonds, anger flooding him. "Hung you like the piece of shit dog you are."

Darwick wrenched them both down from his compatriot's shoulders and punched Tagen in the face. Tagen tasted blood.

"What do you fucking know about it? I've only lived one life, you hear? Ain't never lived outside Meridian. Never!" He kicked Tagen in the stomach then spat in his face. "That's what's wrong with you fuckers. The High Priestess gives you everything, and you still bitch. I see through your attempts to fuck with our heads. Get 'em back up!"

After the Clowns lifted them again Sveta shook her head at Tagen. His taunting had produced a harsher reaction than he'd guessed. Why did some in Meridian deny a past life so strongly? These people must have arrived here, just like him. Maybe not as suicides, but dead all the same.

Would Alexis remember him if he found her? He refused to consider that.

Andromeda had warned him not to speak of a past life. Shit, he should have listened. But where was she? Where were these friends she'd mentioned?

Tagen remained alert while the congressman smiled with the patients in the children's hospital. The press loved it, snapping photos. Alexis had wanted to come but security concerns were too much and he—

He coughed and Sveta regarded him with scorn. The fleeting memory was gone.

While they all trotted past, Tagen looked away as a small boy bit into one of the Blade's decapitated heads. Youthful lips gorged on a geyser of blood.

Tagen fought back a sob as madness gnawed at his mind. Meridian was worse than any Hell. Worse still, because he knew it could be him, eating that corpse's face.

Why had Alexis entered this rage-filled, forsaken cauldron of misery?

II.

The High Priestess

1: Queen of the Borrowed Light

A profusion of shabby tents awaited Tagen and Sveta as the Clowns carried them inside the Circus. Some stood like half-deflated balloons while others were covered in dark stains. Past the tents, hundreds of Clowns busied themselves with myriad distractions, their combined voices a wall of noise.

New recruits knelt under grease paint baptismals like Tagen saw in the Bazaar but these rituals were far cruder. Converts screamed as scalding paint washed over them amid clouds of steam in a wide, neck-deep pit. Other Clowns smeared designs on the new adherents with brutal slaps. The stench of unwashed humanity took Tagen's breath.

Clowns puffed from hookahs, the brass coils throbbing inside painted lips. Some ate sugar-coated human meat in a dizzying array of culinary dishes—all gaudily colored, all eaten in excess. Musicians performed on a stage of melded skulls. Their trumpets and horns sounded flat and warbling. A steam accordion accompanied the ensemble along with a wailing Clown chanteuse. A floating neon sign read 'Rhapsody in Noir'.

Other Clowns in carnival wagons tendered copper shards to devotees from all over Meridian. Payees bowed and kissed an icon of the High Priestess before receiving the simple currency. Those who asked for more were beaten.

A long line of nude, shackled figures waited before a Clown dressed like the figure on the Justice Tarot card. He wore blood-stained robes and held up a set of scales, meting out sentences while waving a rusty sword. Those found guilty were ushered into Bone Guild wagons waiting nearby.

After a few moments Tagen had to look away from the condemned. Their eyes pleaded for mercy, justice, revenge…things he couldn't give them.

"This is what all Meridian will turn into." Darwick beamed. "All you dumb shit heretics will either bathe or drown in Clown paint."

Many non-Clowns waited in lines at prostitute wagons. Through open tent flaps and wagon doors, displays of uninhibited lust stabbed Tagen's eyes. Bodies writhed in pools of filth. Grunts and moans drifted from behind beaded curtains.

Tagen wanted to turn his head or close his eyes but the activities possessed a frightening magnetism. The voyeuristic sense of inclusion by watching sickened him.

"Behold the deliverer of pain, of hunger! Behold the only true light in Meridian!" yelled a Clown carrying a glowing neon banner of the High Priestess. Tagen resisted his rumbling stomach or the warmth in his groin. Instead of containing Meridian's primitive urges the Clowns reveled in them. They didn't want to remember the past.

Darwick's warriors shouldered them further into the Circus, approaching the huge red and white tent. Various fortunetellers along the way preached the Clown Tarot's virtues: take what you want, nothing is forbidden, life is happy as long as you believe in the High Priestess.

"See?" Darwick wrenched Tagen's head around. "We don't need your bullshit lies. Everything we need or want is here."

"Then why do you need us?" Sveta asked.

Darwick backhanded her. "Keep your fucking mouth shut."

Shaking with rage, Tagen forced himself to focus on anything but the red handprint on Sveta's cheek.

The various castes within the Circus provided a grease-painted spectacle. Smeared in purple and blue, Clowns of Cups lost themselves in drugs and song. Clowns of Pentacles indulged epicurean or carnal hungers. They had lathered themselves in green, pink, and yellow paint. Clown Fools dressed like jesters from some infernal court, wearing bells and caps. The faithful bowed and begged after these figures.

None dressed like the Magician. No iconography displayed his image or name.

"Have you been here before?" Tagen whispered in Sveta's ear.

"Of course not." She edged away from him. So that's how it was going to be.

Several armed Clowns stood at attention, watchdogs in a carnival gone mad. Those with clubs wore orange paint while those with swords were covered in red. Unlike their boisterous fellows, these Clowns displayed nothing but restrained violence. Darwick and his companions belonged to these warrior castes, Tagen realized. Clowns of Swords or Staves, like Sveta had said.

Ahead, dozens of Clowns lay around the base of the largest tent like corpses ringing a graveyard. Some sung wordless laments. Others mewled the cards of the Tarot in monotonous chants. Maybe they sought the same release he had when he'd slit his wrists. Where would such release take them?

What had Andromeda meant, that the city claimed those who died here?

Unlike the Tarot faithful in Vagrant's Row, few Clowns paid him or Sveta any heed. The wanton sex, drug use, and gluttony occupied these people as if nothing else existed. He feared whatever controlled this motley assemblage. What it wanted with him.

Darwick stopped before the large tent. "Untie 'em."

They dumped Tagen and Sveta onto the muddy ground then yanked the bronze wire from their bodies. Gripping his shoulders, Sveta gritted her teeth against the pain. He grunted and helped her rise. Fresh terror shone in her eyes. Tagen wanted to comfort her but the Clowns guarded them with cruel smiles and eager fists.

"The High Priestess awaits." Darwick gestured into the tent with mock courtesy.

Tagen brushed aside the blood-stained tent flap and Sveta followed. Darwick entered behind them while the other warriors stood guard.

A long, dark aisle led toward the tent's center. Despite the clamoring throng outside, the structure's interior remained as silent as a cathedral. Rain drizzled on the stretched tent fabric. He made out shapes sticking from the ground on long poles either side of the aisle.

A reek worse than Vagrant's Row stung Tagen's nostrils. The aisle brightened the closer he neared the tent's center.

Sveta gasped behind him.

The light revealed what was on the long poles: heads impaled on metal stakes. Hundreds of men, women, and children. Though none had decayed, no life shone in their glazed stares.

Tagen wanted to curse, yell, or express his revulsion, but nothing came out. All he could do was stare, the eyes of the dead burning into his mind.

"Hurry the fuck up." Darwick shoved Sveta into Tagen and they bumped into the horrific collection. Tagen scrambled away from the heads, bile burning his throat.

Over and over he hoped Alexis's head wasn't among them.

After he helped Sveta regain her feet they continued. A shaft of light shone down on the center ring. Darkness ruled the rest of the tent. A trapeze swung back and forth over the ring, bearing a steam lantern. It flashed with a strobe effect.

Tagen jumped, his heart clawing up into his throat.

Scores of Clown warriors waited like statues in the shadows outside the ring.

"Enter." The feminine voice compelled Tagen to walk closer.

A young voluptuous woman sat in a high-backed chair at a small table in the ring. She wore nothing save for a red cape and a ruby-encrusted crown. Pure white grease paint covered her skin from head to toe. A scarlet topknot hung from her head in wet tendrils. Red-tinted eyes regarded him with interest. Hands with crimson fingernails shuffled a gold-sheet Tarot deck.

Darwick shoved past Tagen and bowed. "High Priestess, I bring you—"

"Two cartomancers." The High Priestess's domineering voice dripped with seductive undertones.

Tagen glanced sidelong at Sveta. Her eyes shared his trepidation.

As the High Priestess rose her cards floated onto the table. She flung the cape over her shoulder and allowed Tagen to study her alabaster nudity. Her smile shone like a wolf's before the kill.

"A newcomer and a Sky Nomad. The cards did not lie." She swept an arm out before her. As one the Clowns knelt and Darwick kissed her hand. She shoved him away and stood before Tagen and Sveta.

"Quite the pair, you two. But I am the only prophet, the only seer, of Meridian. All other cartomancers are false, leading the citizens of this city into heresy."

The Clowns rose and shouted their agreement. Maws spat out mindless words.

"Tell me, what else is their crime, besides cartomancy?" The High Priestess sauntered over and fingered Sveta's braided hair. Staring ahead, Sveta stood resolute though her neck muscles tensed. For the tenth time Tagen regretted asking her for a reading. His curiosity had condemned them both.

Darwick glared at Tagen. "The Nomad slut did a reading for this fucker. She drew the Magician card."

The High Priestess flung Sveta to the ground and slapped Tagen's cheek. Her nails scratched his skin. "Infidels! Have I not told you the Magician prophecy is a lie? How many more pretenders will try to destroy what I've built?"

"What is the—?" Tagen started but the High Priestess placed a finger to his lips. Her flesh smelled like cloying talc powder.

"What is the prophecy? I can sense your naiveté like a Gutter Knight scents newly minted copper. You're not the first who thought to test my power. Emrys, Khyran, and others have failed." Lips curled in malice, the High Priestess circled around him.

"Can I execute 'em?" Darwick raised his jagged sword.

"Not yet." The High Priestess walked back to her table and sat. Though her perfect ivory figure glistened in the light from above,

Tagen thought her a pale maggot in Meridian's guts. He helped Sveta up but she brushed his hand away. While he didn't blame her for resenting him, he hadn't asked for any of this. He just wanted Alexis—and his memories—back.

"Show me their hands," the High Priestess said in a bored voice. Darwick and another Clown forced Tagen and Sveta to their knees before the table.

"Open your fists, shitheads," Darwick said. Tagen and Sveta both lifted their hands, palms up.

For an instant the High Priestess's confidence faltered as she looked at their palms. Tagen sensed fear in her, something painful, buried deep. Recovering her haughtiness, she studied Sveta's hands first. Tagen glimpsed odd markings on her palms, akin to scars.

"You have the Sun and Moon glyphs. The symbols of emotion and divination. No wonder you've been telling fortunes. How is it you drew the Magician when no Tarot deck in all Meridian has that card? You know it is forbidden."

Sveta met the High Priestess's gaze. "He wanted a reading. I gave him a three card spread. The Magician was the final card I drew. I don't know how it happened."

The High Priestess sniffed. "A lie meant to stir unrest against me."

"Some Blades ambushed us on the way here," Darwick said.

"Blades of Charon?" The High Priestess grinned. "Andromeda is still in love with a lie, then."

"What is the Magician supposed to do?" As soon as Tagen asked Darwick shoved a knee into Tagen's back and pulled on his neck. He coughed and grunted.

"She ain't addressed you, asshole," Darwick whispered in his ear.

The High Priestess stared at Tagen. "The Magician will cast Meridian into ruin. I have seen it in my cards. Only my deck contains that card and I have drawn it only once, during that reading. I protect my people and this city from his coming. He will not win against the righteous."

All the other Clowns shouted once in unison.

"No one can interpret the Tarot as I can. Only I know the true path." The High Priestess yanked Tagen's hands forward while Darwick maintained his excruciating hold.

Tagen held his breath but blinked when she tenderly studied his palms. That soft touch, those wide, concerned eyes…what did she see? What did she want?

After rubbing her fingers over Tagen's palms once more, the High Priestess gestured at Darwick. He released Tagen, who coughed and winced while his back popped back into place.

"You had these branded on you, didn't you? No cartomancer has ever had black palm glyphs of the Sun, Moon and the Star. The Star gifts perception, the ability to see beyond. None have it but me! You flaunt your heresy?" Her golden cards floated around her head like a halo.

Tagen shook his head. "I don't know what the hell you're talking about! I've just arrived here after following the path I saw in the cards…"

A hush fell over the tent. Darwick's face pinched with annoyed disbelief.

The High Priestess sat back. "Arrived? From where? There is no place but Meridian, you fool. Everyone knows that."

Tagen's voice rose. "You're wrong. I killed myself to get here." He ignored Darwick's fingers biting into his shoulder, or Sveta's amazed look.

The High Priestess laughed. "This heresy of a past life amuses me. You truly think everyone here has died already? Nonsense. Emrys thought as you do. He was slain by my servants. Khyran died a heretic's death. But you interest me. I shall do a reading."

Four more Clowns hurried over and held Tagen and Sveta down. The High Priestess cast off her cape and pushed the table aside. The Clowns shoved the pair against their leader's knees, so close Tagen could have licked the woman's skin. Her powder scent stifled him.

As the golden cards drifted into the High Priestess's palm, Tagen glimpsed a Star glyph there. "What is your name?" She ran a fingernail down Sveta's neck to the mounds of her breasts.

"Sveta."

"Lovely. Let us see what the cards say about you, shall we?" The High Priestess drew a card and smiled. It showed a Clown woman in a lush garden with exotic birds.

"Nine of Pentacles. You carry great gifts within you, Sveta." She drew the next card. On it a Clown sat beneath a steamlamp with three cups. From a gout of steam a clockwork hand held a fourth cup which the Clown ignored.

"Four of Cups. You resist something, my beautiful Sveta. You must make a choice. Of course, by giving this man a reading, you made a very bad decision." The High Priestess scowled. "Last card."

The Star card hit the table. On it a naked Clown woman knelt at Meridian's docks, pouring water into the Styx with one hand, and into a gutter with the other. A silver, eight-pointed star shone above her. An airship floated over the city in the distance.

"You show great promise. The gifts from the first card will blossom in you, once you reconcile with your true nature. But this is a future that shall never come to pass." The High Priestess's smile dripped with spite but Tagen understood why the Clowns followed her.

Part of him wanted to worship her, believe her. Adore her. So beautiful, so pure. How would her lips taste, how soft would her breasts feel crushed against him? He imagined thrusting his cock inside her, yanking her hair as he came, and her cooing him asleep afterward. She equaled his salvation from the trash and pain outside the Circus. Lowering his head, Tagen pursed his lips near her bared thigh.

His palms warmed.

The image of woman wearing a golden mask invaded his thoughts. She was faltering in a sea of corpses but he offered a hand. She reached for him...

The vision ended. His palms hurt. Shadows lurked in his peripheral sight again.

Lips curling back in revulsion, Tagen stared up at her. "No."

The High Priestess glowered down at him. "So you deny me? No matter. I shall show you the path. What is your name?"

Tagen recalled his ID before setting the knife to his wrist. Twenty-seven years old. An organ donor. Born on the sixteenth of some winter month. Damn it, why couldn't he remember the rest? He'd had two names but only one exited his lips.

"Tagen."

Instead of rebuilding his memories, Meridian was eradicating them. He feared becoming like all these others, ignorant of their past and identity.

A card floated from the High Priestess's hand and lay on the table. On it, a Clown raced down a street on a unicycle, with sword upraised. Severed heads lay in his wake.

"Knight of Swords," the High Priestess said. "You charge into a situation you think you can fix. Impetuous and unwise." Eyes smoldering, she flicked the card aside with a fingernail. It faded into nothingness and she drew the next card: a Clown carrying a bundle of staves. The staves dripped with blood which the Clown was about to slip in.

"Ten of Staves. What you fight for will bring you down and drown your spirit. I like your reading so far, Tagen." She caressed his cheek. "Your head will look wonderful on a stake, with those blue eyes of yours, and this long black hair."

"Draw the last card." Tagen surprised himself with his flat tone. At his side, Sveta regarded him with fresh respect.

The High Priestess spread her legs, insulting him with her splayed sexuality. She fingered her crotch before drawing the third card.

"This reading is my final word on you. I am the ultimate decider of your fate, Tagen. I am Meridian." The card floated from her hand to the table.

Tagen sucked in a breath and waited.

The High Priestess recoiled as if a snake had appeared on the table.

"No," she whispered, her lips trembling. Her breasts heaved with nervous breaths.

On the table lay the Magician Card: embossed on thin gold, but similar to the paper one Sveta had drawn.

"High Priestess?" Darwick asked in a worried voice.

The High Priestess grabbed her cape and covered herself with it. "So you have come for me at last. Do you think I'm afraid? Do you?"

Tagen slowly shook his head. "I don't—"

"Do you?" she shouted.

Pity replaced his anger. Something in her eyes crumbled. No one moved or spoke. Her hands shook in her white-painted lap.

"I remember." He reached out with his left hand. She flinched.

"Take him! Take them both, damn you!" The High Priestess's words shocked Darwick and the others into action. Tagen cried out as they jerked him and Sveta to their feet then dragged them to two empty metal stakes. Darwick raised his blade, shaking with intense anger. Tagen had frightened their goddess. Only one penalty existed.

"Wait!" The High Priestess rose from the chair and collected herself, arrogance returning. She tossed the red cape over her shoulder and placed hands on hips. The trapeze strobe light kept swinging. Darkness haunted the tent one moment, painted demons the next.

"Do not execute them yet. I won't add them to my collection until I have learned more." She smiled at her gallery of gaping mouths and sightless gazes.

Tagen shivered. The crazed woman had killed any threat to her power, anyone who remembered. It sickened and angered him. Even though he remembered little of his past life it meant a great deal to him. He'd come here to find the rest of it in Alexis but the High Priestess outlawed such personal rights as memory and individuality.

"They've blasphemed, High Priestess," Darwick said. "How can we let these fuckers live?"

The High Priestess chuckled. "They shall be punished. But first I must discover if they have any allies in Meridian. Put them both in the Funhouse."

All the Clowns in the tent whooped, drowning out Sveta's screams and Tagen's curses as their captors dragged them out by the hair. The High Priestess remained in the shaft of light, kneading her left breast and sneering.

2: Unveiling

Radomir paced back and forth outside the Circus. He pretended to make deals with Clowns for fresh meat or mechanis parts whenever they approached him but in truth he awaited an opening. The newcomer and the Sky Nomad had been taken inside and an emotion he'd never felt before gnawed at him: concern for another human being.

"Sell man to Bone Guild," he muttered to himself. "Mechos might want Nomad woman for new copper goddess."

That's what a Gutter Knight would do with them but…he wanted more than simple bartering. More memories, more images of his baby boy, of the people he'd worked with in the office building.

Who but Tagen could give it to him?

Someone else wanted the newcomer, yes. Radomir fingered the curved dagger he'd picked up after the Clowns had been ambushed in Vagrant's Row. He'd always sold such daggers to the Clowns but now he wondered at the rebels' motives. If they took Tagen, Radomir would never get to speak with him—the Blades despised Gutter Knights.

As he walked along the curb he passed several Clown mirrors. While most showed the viewer as too tall or too fat, one appeared normal. He stopped and tried to still his rising breaths. How many times had he passed by here and not noticed?

Radomir touched his stitched together face, his trash-heap armor. How ugly, yes. He opened his mouth to laugh it off but the teeth in the mirror gave him pause. So many he'd killed to build his set, prying silver molars or golden incisors from dead jaws.

What memories from a life outside Meridian had his victims possessed?

Scowling, Radomir wiped his eyes. The teardrop on his finger reflected his image in a microcosm of disgrace. It bothered him that his tears ran down a cheek from someone else's face and not his own.

3: Plague of Secrets

Shaking with anger, Andromeda entered the street outside the Circus. Her team had been crushed in Vagrant's Row and Tagen carried into the High Priestess's den. Which of her friends still lived? She touched her eyes though no tears came. Meridian had wrung them from her long ago.

Despite her disguise, she hadn't planned to enter the Circus and rescue Tagen. Memories of Khyran's execution inside that ring of tents chilled her skin more than the rain. His floating head hadn't returned from the Mecho District yet. Perhaps Azibar couldn't be lured into helping her this time.

A low whistle caught her ear. She reached toward her skirt. None of the nearby Clowns noticed but a lone Gutter Knight at the Circus entrance looked her way. His pinkish eyes widened and he walked in the opposite direction. Georgio and several Sky Nomads waited at the curb but they had no hope of infiltrating the Circus.

Andromeda tensed. Would that old Nomad fool reveal her to the Clowns?

The whistle came again. A slim, dusky woman exited an alley across the street.

Relief flooded Andromeda. It was Saissa, a fellow Blade of Charon. She wore a black leather corset and a dagger bandoleer. A caul embroidered with block-like Charonic sigils covered her hair. While Andromeda pretended not to see her, Saissa hurried to a Bone Guild kiosk and dug out a copper shard.

"Kelp with extra chunks," Saissa said in a husky voice.

Andromeda ambled up to the kiosk and leaned on it.

"Wanna share that?" Andromeda asked in her silkiest tone. "My legs go all the way up to my ass, bally girl."

The Bone Guild vendor stared with dumb muteness.

"Aye there, I shall." A note of anxiety rang in Saissa's voice.

Andromeda linked arms with her and they entered an alley filled with clumped refuse and a busted gutter. Water sloshed past their feet into a clogged grate. Andromeda hoped it shielded their voices. As soon as they were clear she grimaced at Saissa.

"Goddamnit, you know better than to give the whistle this close to the Circus! The natives said six bodies went to the Guild for meat." Andromeda slapped the kelp and flesh meal from Saissa's hand. "That might be one of our kinkers already. Tell me."

Exhaling, Saissa leaned against the alley wall. "We ambushed 'em. Got two with daggers, but the team up front acted too soon. I tell ye, I barely escaped. It couldn't be helped, that is."

Andromeda bit the inside of her cheek. Ever since losing the city, she'd recruited many discontents in her fight against the High Priestess. And many had died. Without her old cartomantic magic they fought a hopeless war. Tagen's arrival might change all that... but how many Magicians could she pin her hopes on?

"It's done, with no after show." Andromeda squeezed Saissa's shoulder. "I need you to gather the rest."

"Jaabir, he wants to know why you risk so much," Saissa said. "Aye, and me too."

"My pitch is that I can get Jackpot out of the Circus. The Mechos might help us, so I'll take him to their joint. I'll leave a message at Doll House that will convince Jaabir and the others. Until then we have to stay separate."

"Why?" Saissa asked.

"Georgio may red light me." Andromeda crossed her arms.

"He'd never tell on ye, ya spunky tart." Saissa arched an eyebrow. "Figure we should ally with him, rather than that copper choad bucket, aye?"

Andromeda frowned. "A Blade of Charon never makes new kinkers. Only contacts. We'll grandstand in Lotus Station, below the Row."

Saissa removed her cap and scratched her short black hair. "I do this 'cause ye my friend, Andromeda. 'Cause I've seen ya suffer all too often, and no salve but Meridian's rain. Aye, I love ye like a sister, that is." Her dark eyes still contained questions.

"I know you're no sellout." Andromeda hugged Saissa tight and whispered in her ear. "Please trust me. One more time."

She remembered buying Saissa from a pet dealer in the Bazaar and setting her free. Thankful, the young woman had joined her cause, then excelled in dagger and stealth training. Andromeda refused to think she sacrificed such friendships for her own vanity and longing.

"Aye, then, I'll tell 'em. Charon be with ye." Saissa put her cap back on and exited the alley. After counting to twenty Andromeda entered the opposite street.

The usual mob flooded her sight. Dirty, horny, angry individuals looking for something to fill the darkness inside them. Once she might have sung to them or danced between the rain puddles. Anything to provide cheer and joy. Now she didn't want to see these people any more. She needed Meridian back…before she became one of them.

Khyran hovered toward her, eyes flashing. He always knew where to find her.

Andromeda took a tin sheet from his mouth and read its embossed words. Due to Meridian's incessant drizzle and dampness, no one used paper for anything.

"You have proven a valuable ally in the past," she read. "You know I only keep what you want so that others in Meridian may have hope. Yet, I am willing to trade one cartomancer for another."

Valuable ally. The words caused Andromeda to shake her head and close her eyes. Georgio was right: she had betrayed the Sky Nomads to Azibar long ago. She'd turned over their mechanical secrets in exchange that he would help her overthrow the High Priestess. It had gained her nothing but Georgio's enmity. How much farther would she fall from grace? Her grip tightened on the tin sheet, denting it.

Khyran hissed steam and nudged her shoulder.

"Yes. Azibar still trusts us." Andromeda touched his cheek, wishing his lips could form a smile or his glowing eyes show more expression. She tucked the sheet into a small compartment beneath Khyran's chin but he vented steam from his back vent.

"Come now, no fuss. We may need that." Andromeda ducked into another alley and pulled out the torn Magician card. "This will buy us a pass. Maybe even your body."

She hesitated. A card reading once said she would fall in love with the Magician.

Though Andromeda had loved Khyran, she'd used him. If Tagen was the real Magician, who did her heart beat for? Just imagining the touch of his palms electrified her as the city's power flowed in him. Power that she could use. It wasn't fair but he wasn't the only one who could remember.

She hugged Khyran's head, staring at the garish tents.

"A whisper of love, a whisper of hate…show no mercy at the Circus gate."

4: Touching the Curtain

Darwick slammed the Funhouse door and stalked back into the High Priestess's tent. Those two heretics had insulted the woman he adored and loved. Fuckers.

After the other warrior Clowns left he waited at the back of the tent. The High Priestess lay on her silken bed, not even wearing her cape. Beds were rare in the Circus since most Clowns slept where they fell after a day of revelry.

But revelry had always eluded Darwick in Meridian. Doping and fucking mattered little to him since he wanted to ensure that the guilty received their due.

Except when he saw her like this.

Her breasts rose up and down with each breath. Her hands glided over her painted thighs and stomach.

Darwick preferred these visions over the faint ones plaguing his subconscious. *Hot sun. Stinking horses. Prickly hemp rope around his neck. The jerk of the gallows, the cheers of the executioners.* None of these thoughts had ever troubled him. Not until Tagen had to be an asshole and say something about Darwick's scarred neck. Were they lies placed in his head by this new Magician?

Were they genuine?

His jaw clenched. No, he couldn't betray the High Priestess. She said nothing existed outside Meridian or beyond the Styx's black waters. The city was all there ever was or had ever been. Her word was fucking law. He wanted to believe her.

No, he did believe her, he was no shit-faced heretic! Darwick was her guardian, her captain, her…king?

Yes, the honor would be his. She wanted him to hold her in the bed. Hold, caress, and kiss those perfect limbs. Fuck that milky white body. Saliva flooded Darwick's mouth and he swallowed. A hot, eager stiffness rose in his crotch.

He reached inside his pants and gripped, tugged. A tight gasp exited his lips. With every breath she took, he replied with taut fondling.

"Ain't nobody going to take you from me," he muttered, tugging faster. Soon she would do this for him herself, with those delicate ivory hands.

The Magician wouldn't threaten his precious alabaster beauty. Only she ruled Meridian, only she offered salvation from the city's decay and hopelessness. Darwick would butcher any asshole that denied her.

He clasped his hat tight. "Listen, I know this ain't the best place to homestead—

"I like it." She hopped off the wagon and flung off her bonnet. "No; I love it!"

Laughing, he swung her around under the hot prairie sun.

His thighs clenched. Boiling dampness oozed over his hands. He sucked in air then released it in a ragged sigh. Staring at the High Priestess's feminine splendor, Darwick lost himself in supple folds of painted flesh. Something other than lust swelled in his heart, and his eyes grew hot with tears.

Swaying back and forth on the rope, while they laughed at him.

"I love you, darlin'," he whispered.

III.

THE EMPRESS

1: Clothed with the Sun

The Funhouse door slammed shut. Tagen helped Sveta up. Unlike the rest of the Circus, metal walls and steaming vents made up the structure. Exhaust and shadow obscured everything else. Red, green, and orange lamps flashed from a high ceiling. Acidic steam vapors made them both cough. Sweat ran down Tagen's face.

"What the hell is this place?" he asked but Sveta pushed him away.

"Would that I have never met you! Do you know how long I've evaded—?"

A large Clown face shot out at them, laughing with mechanical repetitiveness. It was connected to the wall by a sliding metal bar. Another Clown face thrust from the left, its steel jaws snapping. The teeth just missed Tagen's ear.

"Damn! Listen, I'm sorry. You think I wanted this? This isn't why I came to Meridian—oh shit!" He grabbed Sveta as another Clown head lurched from the darkness. It spat scalding steam where they'd been standing.

A dozen other faces, pincer arms, and oversized hammers came at them, all attached to clockwork booms or springs. Tagen and Sveta fled, running a gantlet in a serial killer's cavalcade. Several jack-in-the-boxes flew around them, biting or laughing.

Steel teeth gnashed Tagen's elbow. A hammer thudded into his back. Sveta wheezed as a pincer slammed into her leg but she ducked a vicious saw swiping over her head. The Clown faces retracted for another sadistic bout.

Dark shapes whirled at the edge of Tagen's sight. Everything blurred. His palm glyphs warmed as he waved the shapes away.

His hand touched the Styx's black surface through a windowscape of Tarot cards.

Tagen surrendered to the darkness, to the colored lights swirling overhead. Clinging to Sveta, confidence filled him. They jumped over a super-heated floor vent, then dodged a hammer. It shattered a Clown face. A jack-in-the-box dive-bombed them but exploded in a scalding steam vent when they rolled aside. Sensing a space of calm and safety nearby, Tagen pulled her along with him.

None of the traps reached them in the small area.

Catching his breath, Tagen studied their prison. The glowing lights and faces peppered the Funhouse's shadows with jittery radiance. Broken mechanis animals littered the floor. Several corpses lay in the corners, bludgeoned and burned beyond recognition.

"Are you all right?" Tagen raised his hands to Sveta's shoulders.

"By Charon, she was right. You do have the glyphs." The flashing lights illuminated Sveta's shocked expression. "No wonder you saw how to avoid these traps."

Tagen coughed. "What? These things on my hands? Why did the High Priestess call me a 'cartomancer'?"

A spinning saw blade passed a few inches above their heads.

Sveta stood close, avoiding the traps still in operation. "Cartomancy. You know, card magic, used by cartomancers. The High Priestess is the most powerful one in Meridian. She lets a few serve her as Clown Seers but they lack real affinity with the Clown Tarot. All can be identified by a palm glyph, like a Sun, Moon, or Star. I've never seen any like yours."

"So what is she, a witch?" Tagen asked. "How did she make those cards float in the air like that?"

A hammer slammed into the floor nearby.

Crowding against him, Sveta shouted over the Funhouse's din. "The more attuned a cartomancer is with the Tarot and its imagery, the greater their power. Perception, divination, emotion. She is so skilled at interpretation, she doesn't need a physical deck. No one else can read the Clown Tarot like she can and she outlaws any other deck."

Tagen caught his breath again but the blow on his back still throbbed. "So that's why you wore gloves, and why the High Priestess was so pissed that you drew that card."

"Yes. The Sky Nomads kept me hidden. Until now." She looked away.

"I said I was sorry."

She looked back at him and sighed. "Doesn't matter now. She'll kill us and put our heads on display. I'd heard rumors she did that with all cartomancers, but actually seeing the truth…"

"To hell with that. We need to escape." He raised his palms. "Maybe if you tell me more about this 'magic' I can do something with it."

Sveta rolled her eyes. "You don't have a Tarot deck. Besides, cartomancy isn't taught. It's gained or lost, based on one's state of mind, or so I've heard."

"Well, this city has certainly screwed with my state of mind." He considered telling her of the crazy phenomena that'd saved him from Gutter Knights and cannibals, but she probably thought he was weird enough already. "So how do magic cards work?"

"The cards themselves aren't special," Sveta said with scorn. "Those who have studied the Tarot's images discover universal archetypes behind the art, or so Georgio told me. Truths about ourselves waiting to be unlocked. After a lot of meditation and memorization of these images, a cartomancer uses the characteristics within the art to change things around them. The Lovers card might let you seduce someone or a Knight card might aid you in a fight. But you have to be attuned with the Tarot's power. Those that are have these glyphs on their palms."

"So you stare at cards all day…" Tagen tried to breathe. Cards. Alexis had hidden them after one of their arguments. The fright in her eyes whenever he asked about them. Memories of searching her closets while she was away. Had she been protecting him from Meridian?

"It's more than that." Sveta shook her head. "There's no way you're a cartomancer. You don't even know the basics. What abilities do you get with the Six of Pentacles? What's it mean if the Ace of Swords is drawn, reversed?"

"Hell, I don't...hey, the High Priestess thinks otherwise. Look at where I am!"

They stared at each other. She broke eye contact first.

"You said you came to Meridian because you saw it in the cards," Sveta said. "Do you claim to be from one of the legendary cities out in the Styx? Georgio says people flew to them in airships before the High Priestess forbade it and destroyed all the aircraft. I think that's just a myth, like Charon's Barge."

"I'm a suicide, Sveta. I took my own life to enter this city. Everyone here is dead, just like me." A Clown face floated above them, laughing with robotic coarseness.

She snorted. "I don't believe that any more than the High Priestess did."

"Remember that scar around Darwick's neck, how he reacted to my questions? Someone hung him in his past life. I saw a city of happiness in the cards. Now I barely remember who I was, or why my wife...I hoped in Meridian, I'd regain both."

"No here one remembers," Sveta muttered, and he strained to hear her over the Funhouse's devices. "Why else do you think people join the Clowns? They receive food, entertainment, sex. The High Priestess tells them there is nothing else. They believe it."

"What do you think?" There was so much he needed to learn but they lacked the time. He worried their conversation would be interrupted any moment.

"I don't care," Sveta said. "Georgio wants to rebuild airships and find the other cities. I just want...I don't know. Stability. People should deal with their problems, not run from them. Deal with all this pain."

"Am I the Magician?" Tagen asked.

Sveta didn't answer.

"Hey, about this cartomancy…well…I think I've already used it, somehow." He took a deep breath, then finally described the incident with the Gutter Knights.

"I don't know how you're doing such things. Cartomancers need a Tarot deck to use their magic." She stared at him with an unreadable expression.

"What about the High Priestess? Her cards…floated."

Sveta sighed. "She's ruled Meridian for a long time. After so long…listen, I don't know, okay?"

"So maybe I can do things without the cards. How else can you explain it?"

Sveta's silence annoyed Tagen but he maintained his composure. The racket of the Funhouse continued, yet so far, the space they stood in hadn't been endangered. Even the flying jack-in-the-boxes ignored them. Orange light passed over them, highlighting Sveta's lithe form.

"What's up with all your tattoos?"

Shifting on her feet, Sveta crossed her arms. "I've always had them."

"Before Meridian?" Tagen wouldn't let go of the idea.

For a moment Sveta appeared as a frightened young woman instead of the steely eyed, resolute one he'd seen thus far. Before he realized it his hand rested on her wrist.

"I woke up in an alley, naked. My tattoos still stung. Like someone had put them on me, then dumped me in the trash." Sveta didn't brush his hand away. A calmness flowed between them. He didn't understand how he knew, but she had tremendous strength inside, just waiting to burst forth. Nine of Pentacles indeed.

"What about before?" he asked. *In his mind Sveta stepped onto a different path in a majestic forest. A dark path.* His palms itched and the vision faded.

The Funhouse's racket droned in the background. Sveta squeezed his hand.

"The ambulance couldn't do anything. It hurt so much to breathe…" She lifted the left side of her blue leather vest. For modesty, she covered her left breast with her right forearm. Tagen's cheeks warmed with embarrassment though not for nudity's sake. This was far more than a physical reveal: she was showing him how she'd died.

There, just below her left breast, was a bullet hole. Tagen squinted as a red light passed over them. The tattoo around the hole reminded him of the Death Tarot card: a lone cloaked figure on Meridian's dock with a Mecho, a Clown, and a nude woman lying dead nearby.

"I don't know who shot me, or why." Sveta lowered her vest back into place. "But I remember how much it hurt. Not just the wound but…"

"Leaving others behind." Tagen envied her recalling so much. Even painful memories were golden currency for one's soul when all else had gone.

"Yes. But that's enough, Tagen." She gently removed his hand from her wrist.

"Enough what?" he asked.

"Showing me. I didn't want to know—"

Steam vented near Sveta's head and Tagen pulled her down with him. He thought he'd seen past all this hellhole's traps. As the steam jetted closer, Tagen sought another safe place in the Funhouse.

His senses told him there wasn't any.

Something floated over them and clicked.

He and Sveta glanced up. Another jack-in-the-box hovered over them, green eyes glowing. Tagen's brow furrowed.

"Khyran?" he asked.

"What?" Sveta asked.

Helping her up, he gazed around the Funhouse. "Where's Andromeda?"

The Funhouse shut down. The door creaked open.

"Right here," Andromeda called from the entrance.

Heart thumping in his chest, Tagen took Sveta's hand and ran to the doorway. Whether or not he could trust Andromeda, he knew an opportunity when he saw one.

"How?"

"No time, Jackpot. We're leaving." Andromeda inserted two daggers into her skirt and stepped back. Two Clowns lay at her feet, their throats slit.

Andromeda led them from the Funhouse into a tent filled with sleeping Clowns, where they tip-toed past. Many snored where they'd fallen, some with hookahs still in their mouths. Outside, the partying within the Circus had died down.

"Here." Andromeda handed them both a wig. Next she took a handful of white grease paint from a baptismal pool and rubbed it all over their faces. She gestured for Tagen to remove his shirt, then covered his torso in purple paint. When Andromeda turned to Sveta, the Sky Nomad wouldn't relinquish her vest.

"Fine." She smeared yellow paint down from Sveta's neck, between her breasts, and all over her stomach. "You can whine about it later. Come, before that piece of shit Darwick finds us."

"Where are we going?" Tagen asked but Andromeda waved his question away as she led them past more tents.

Armless and legless Clowns hung from sideshow cages, laughing. Two women giggled and cut strips from a drugged man's backside. Tagen wondered if he even needed a disguise. These people were inured to everything around them, save for the pursuit of perverted pleasures.

One Clown on the ground tugged at Tagen's ankle. "Get down here and fuck me, honey." Tagen tried kicking her away but the woman wouldn't let go. "Get down here!" she yelled. Several Clowns stirred nearby.

Andromeda grabbed the Clown's head and jerked. The woman's neck snapped. Sveta pushed Tagen on as a mellow tone rung twice throughout Meridian.

"The Alueryic Clock has started another cycle," Andromeda whispered. "You two troupers keep up."

Tagen almost reprimanded her for murdering the woman but two Clowns of Staves walked from behind the tent ahead of them. The entrance to the Circus waited behind the two warriors.

"This place is dead. Wanna have a grind show with us in the Row?" Andromeda juggled five copper shards with ease. The sensual change in her stance and tone surprised Tagen. This woman was a chameleon. He'd be wary of her.

"Are these new converts? Looks like they need another baptismal." One Clown patted his stave and regarded Tagen with suspicion.

Trying to remember a Tarot card that might help him, Tagen laughed as if they'd told a joke. He'd saved himself from other attackers, hadn't he?

Knight of Pentacles, Ace of Swords, Two of Staves. Each card image passed in his thoughts as he concentrated. The Clowns stepped closer, frowns deepening.

Nothing happened. Tagen thought harder until his face flushed. Still nothing.

Andromeda glanced back at him, urging him with her eyes.

"Uh, I'm baptized, all right." Tagen stepped forward and slapped Andromeda's bottom. Her tight, warm skin almost made him slap it again.

One of the Clowns spat and glowered at them.

"Damn right he is." Andromeda leaned into Tagen and kissed his lips. He couldn't deny the elation her touch brought or the gliding enthusiasm of her tongue. She smelled better than a bed of gardenias. His hands brushed her thighs.

"The High Priestess tells us to share our back yard with everyone." Andromeda pushed Tagen away with some reluctance. "Right?"

Tagen tugged Sveta close, then patted her thigh. "Sure. Going have a great time in the Row. You should come." Focusing on the two Clowns, he imagined their mindset. Strict, bloody, sadistic. No way they'd let them pass, but...he thought of the Five of Swords. A figure holding three swords—Andromeda, Sveta, and himself—while two others departed, their swords on the ground. Hell, this wouldn't work either, he was no cartomancer…

"Huh. Get your asses out of here, then." The warrior spat again, and both of them walked on.

Had it really worked? He'd seen no vision like the other times.

After a few moments Tagen released Sveta. She glared at him. At least she'd the good sense not to struggle in front of them. Once they slipped from the Circus, Andromeda led them past a city block before pausing near a Bone Guild kiosk. Rain slid off Tagen's grease paint in slimy rivulets.

"Nice acting, Jackpot, but that's the only time you can touch my ass. We were lucky back there. Hungry?" Andromeda pulled copper shards from her skirt pocket. She didn't look at him.

Tagen wanted to say no but his stomach stirred. Soon he gulped down bits of kelp but this time, he cast aside the pink chunks. Sveta watched in surprise, then did the same.

"I'll teach you pickled punks yet. Anyway, let's catch itchy feet and go." Finishing her own meal, Andromeda didn't eat the meat cubes, either.

"Hurry where?" Sveta tried cleaning the yellow paint from her body with water from a nearby gutter. "I need to get back to Nomad Way." She shot Tagen a look as if he should go with her.

Looking up and down the street, Andromeda's cap points bounced. "I wouldn't. Once they find you gone, that's the first place they'll look, Nomad Girl. Even Georgio knows that or he would have gotten to you first."

"My name is Sveta."

"Wonderful. Anyway, we don't have many joints in Meridian where we can hide. I know a trouper who can help." Andromeda walked away from the kiosk, and Tagen and Sveta trailed after her. Khyran hovered above them.

"Like who?" Sveta asked, sounding irritated. Tagen himself found it hard trusting a Clown after what they'd been through but Andromeda had rescued them, after all.

"The Mechos. Shit, who else?" Andromeda glided past other Clowns and hapless beggars with ease as if she'd planned in advance. Walking along the fringes of Vagrant's Row, Tagen and Sveta hurried to keep up.

"I don't like this," Sveta whispered to Tagen. "My people can hide us."

"I can hear you back there," Andromeda said. "You don't know the take and we're short on time. It was my kinkers that died trying to rescue you."

"You're a Blade of Charon?" Sveta grabbed Andromeda's arm. "Does Georgio know about this rescue?"

"He will. Quit grandstanding." Andromeda pulled free and quickened her pace. Ahead, the steam-enshrouded buildings of the Mecho District appeared over the ramshackle venues of Vagrant's Row.

Tagen wanted to trust Andromeda but he also wanted Sveta's help. What did the Sky Nomads know? Sveta's story about airships leaving the city intrigued him. Maybe he could find Alexis easier that way. She had to be here somewhere.

"So what's your plan?" Tagen asked. "You said you knew someone who could help me."

"Now that the High Priestess knows about you, you'll be hunted," Andromeda said. "I know of a few safe havens, but even those will be discovered. That slut sees everything that happens in Meridian. Only cartomancy will help us."

"He knows nothing of the Tarot." Sveta indicated Tagen with her eyes.

Andromeda's expression hardened. "Then someone should teach him. He's got all three glyphs."

"So I can leave Meridian with these?" Tagen held up his palms, showing the glyphs. "Yeah, right. I didn't come here to fight some rebellion."

"Too late for that." Andromeda gripped his arm. "Get it through your noggin, Jackpot. If you keep remembering things, you have no choice but to fight against the High Priestess or leave Meridian. There's no other pitch."

Tagen yanked away from her. "I don't like ultimatums."

Staring skyward, Andromeda loosed a breath. "Fine. But either way, you need help. I'm offering."

Sveta rolled her eyes but Tagen finally nodded.

As they exited the Row Andromeda approached a large pile of doll parts in the ruins of an older building. Filthy torsos, limbs, and heads spilled over the walls into the gutter. Some lacked eyes or had puncture holes in their plastic skin.

Andromeda picked up a doll head and kissed it. Tagen thought of all the people trapped in Meridian, resembling these cast-off dolls. Forgotten lives, broken pasts.

"What is that? What's she doing?"

"Doll House," Sveta replied. "An important shrine in Meridian. People either cast a doll part into it for luck or kiss one's lips if they lack a piece. Some believe the shrine contains souls who didn't get off Charon's Barge and sailed further into the Styx. More silly legends, really."

"Charon?" Tagen asked.

"Just a Meridian superstition," Sveta replied. "Some believe he ruled the city long ago. The Clowns leave Doll House alone as long as they don't think it's a threat to the High Priestess."

Tagen nodded at the yellow paint on her body and smirked. "Suits you."

"Piss off." Sveta grinned. "You should see yourself."

Andromeda waved them toward her. "Let's go. The Mecho District is another block down." She tossed the doll head back into the pile. Its mouth bore a slight purple smear from her lips.

Around the next corner, gouts of steam rose into the air. The steamlamps made it look like a cloud of golden dust. The Circus was still too near for his taste, though. He never wanted to enter that hellhole again.

"What are these Mechos, anyway?" Tagen asked.

"You'll see," Andromeda said. "That's where all the mechanis comes from. Runs all the steam power in the city." Khyran hovered above, keeping watch.

"Yes, from Azibar's command," Sveta said in a cold tone.

The two women stared at each other for a long moment. Neither looked afraid of the other. Tagen finally stood between them.

"Hey, what is it with you two?"

Andromeda played with her cap points. "The Nomads had a run-in with Azibar and his Mechos a while back. Nasty little blood opera. I understand how you feel, Nomad Girl, but once the painted freaks start their search, no other joint will be safe."

"Like hell. Azibar serves the High Priestess." Sveta glanced at Tagen with worry. "You shouldn't take him in there, that's all."

Andromeda stepped past Tagen and shook her head. "Think I'd save you from Her Ivory Highness if I thought Azibar would send you right back to her?"

"Then why help us? You're a Clown." Tagen raised his brows.

Though Andromeda smirked, her eyes glinted with fury. "Because I'm not a fucking Clown, Jackpot. And because I know how you can escape Meridian."

2: Reconnection

Radomir picked up the doll head the Harlequin had discarded. Her purple lipstick was still smeared over the plastic mouth but he examined it for other clues. Clues that would lead him to the new-comer, yes. He'd done the same with Mecho heads before melting them down for Gutter Knight armor. Always something extra, yes.

Turning the doll head over, he found a scrap of paper inside. He pulled it out then gaped and dropped the doll head. It clattered in the street. Paper was a rarity in Meridian—paper Tarot cards even more so. The card's material meant nothing compared to the image on it.

Radomir held the upper half of a card, depicting a man raising his right hand into the air with the left hand pointing at the ground.

Though no Tarot devotee, he'd never seen this picture before—but he would have remembered it. It evoked awe and yearning in him. His armor felt lighter. The gutter stench stunk less.

Doll House and Vagrant's Row faded from his sight while Radomir's head swam with bright colors and high-pitched sounds. *People sat around a table, wearing small pointed hats, while he cut slices from a cake. A single candle smoked in the cake's center.*

"Brian," he said as his son's face entered his thoughts.

Slobber dribbled from Brian's mouth and Radomir removed the pacifier. The people at the table laughed and sang a song about a happy birthday.

Radomir chuckled even after the images faded.

Meridian's rain-soaked streets once again dominated his vision…but not his mind. He studied the ripped card again.

"Know you," he whispered, ignoring the odd stares from passerby. "Know you, Magician."

The figure had Tagen's face: clean-shaven, with blue eyes and long black hair.

After looking around Radomir picked up the doll head and stuffed the paper back inside it. He placed it exactly where it had lain before. The Harlequin had left it there to be found, yes. Maybe she had seen, too. Seen what lay beyond Meridian.

IV.

THE EMPEROR

1: He Who Seeks to Remove the Veil

The Mecho District hummed and throbbed with latent activity. Unlike the surrounding city, it shone beneath brighter steamlamps and even more lighted signs. No Clowns ambled about, no Bone Guild kiosks dominated the street corners. The buildings looked cleaner and newer, with riveted beams supporting a mini-cityscape of geometric high-rises. Tagen marveled at gutters pooling rainwater in useable vats and was amazed at the lack of trash on the curbs. So much for eternal torment.

For a moment his heart fluttered. The district resembled the place he'd seen before dying: the city on the Ten of Cups.

Could Alexis be here?

Andromeda elbowed him. "It looks great, but don't get too hung up on it. It's still a doniker I wouldn't piss in." Khyran landed in her hands and folded into a rusty box.

"How can the dead build all this?" He slumped in wonder. "For what reason?"

"Not this again," Sveta muttered.

"Keep your voice down," Andromeda said. "Legends say Meridian offered a second chance, when Charon ruled it. When everyone remembered who they were."

"A second chance at what?" he asked. "Getting murdered and eaten?"

Andromeda sighed. "I'll tell you later. Come on."

Sveta pulled off her ragged Clown wig. "Everybody knows Clowns don't frequent this place. We'll attract too much attention."

"Is this 'Azibar' expecting us?" Tagen removed his own wig. It stank of urine.

"Yes. Here, wash yourselves off in that trough nearby." Andromeda pointed at a water-wheel turning in a gutter trough. Steam jetted from a bronze clockwork motor in the wheel's centrifuge. Its rotation powered a large turbine atop a nearby building, which in turn fed electricity into copper conduits along its walls.

"What about you?" Sveta cupped water in her hands and wiped off grease paint. Tagen did the same, cleaning his face first. The nasty paint smothered him. He wondered how the Clowns tolerated it.

"I'll be fine, Nomad Girl. The Clowns aren't outlawed here— they simply don't come 'round." Andromeda's frequent glances at each alley said otherwise.

While Sveta cleansed herself of yellow paint, Tagen squinted at her tattoos. Images formed there he didn't recall from before. Pictograms of books and obelisks, along with vague characters shrouded in black.

"Enjoying the show?" Sveta cinched her vest tighter around her breasts.

Tagen cleared his throat. "I was looking at your tattoos."

"That's what they all say, Jackpot," Andromeda said, though she also took a special interest in Sveta's body art.

"What?" Sveta combed fingers through her braids, eyes narrowed at Andromeda.

"Nothing. Ready?" Andromeda left without waiting for their answer.

Contrasting the rest of Meridian, residents in the Mecho District walked in ordered fashion on the sidewalks. No one argued, gnawed bones, or copulated in dark alleys. Everyone possessed some form of mechanis enhancement: people with steam vents in their backs and sides, metal filament hair, or wheels instead of feet. Many had clockwork limbs. Gears spun within joints so well-oiled, they made little sound.

Tagen tasted lubricant and tinny metal in the air. "These Mechos…their bodies don't glisten from the drizzle. Like they're not even in the rain."

"Their flesh absorbs the water to power their steam novelties." Andromeda winked at him. "You're a quick trouper. That's good."

Small vehicles rolled past in the street, their large steel pistons belching steam. They reminded Tagen of a streetcar. Some transported spare parts, vats of thick black fluid, or tin-skinned technicians. No wonder everyone in the district looked trim, fit, and cheerful. Compared to the Circus's horrors, this was paradise.

A few individuals had their entire body sheathed in a metallic coating. It clung to their limbs, muscles, and face like a second skin, similar to the Mechos he'd glimpsed in the Bazaar. Their hair consisted of stiff metal shavings, or even a perpetual vent of steam trailing over their head. Each of these people had green, glowing eyes like Khyran. Other denizens gave these particular Mechos a respectful berth. All of them were perfect specimens of physicality.

"What are those people?" Tagen asked.

"The true Mechos," Andromeda said. "They have reached the pinnacle of the mechanis art, though I hear they need lots of maintenance. Just look at all those streetcars."

Tagen caught Sveta's distasteful glances and didn't blame her. It was too perfect in the Mecho District. Few passersby talked to one another, or even acknowledged their presence—but everyone smiled. The voices he heard contained steady, artificial modulation. He got the impression they only cared about others like themselves.

After traveling two blocks, the scent of oil and steam moisture grew heavier. Towering steamlamps dominated the street corners. Boilers thrummed between structures, powering massive turbines inset into the exteriors of skyscrapers. The buildings took on a sleeker quality, their walls formed of beaten, shaped metal. Beneath them, snaking conduits carried electricity to the entire city, vibrating the streets. The hiss of steam ejection and the whine of clockwork gears created an incessant hum.

They passed the huge Alueryic Clock, sitting astride large bronze and silver pylons. A long, golden arm formed the only hand on the clock, which Tagen assumed represented hours. Gears turned, locked, and whirred as the device tolled three times. It rung throughout the district, and perhaps all Meridian, with a mellow, bell-like quality. Despite their proximity to it, the tolling didn't hurt Tagen's ears.

"That novelty was here before the Sky Nomads," Andromeda whispered. "The last vestige of Alueryic mechanis. Not even Azibar can replicate that thing's precision."

"Alueryic?" Tagen frowned in confusion.

"From Alueryeum, a joint out in the Styx," Andromeda said. "Very ancient."

Sveta rolled her eyes again.

Tagen brushed off some of the mildew still clinging to his jeans. "How long have I been here?"

"Does it matter?" Andromeda's question was tinged with annoyance.

He glared at her. "It matters."

"A year or a hundred, it's all a mud show." Andromeda's eyes softened. "You'll need my help to find what you're looking for."

Tagen flung wet bangs from his face. "I won't wait much—"

"Looks like Azibar found what he was looking for," Sveta said. "Georgio said someone betrayed the Sky Nomads, selling their mechanis knowledge to the Mechos."

Andromeda cleared her throat but said nothing.

They neared the tallest building: a tower-like structure with elevators going up and down its sides. Backlit signs dominated one entire side, displaying the profile of a proud Mecho face. A constant steam cloud billowed from its summit, reminding Tagen of a volcano or smokestack.

Why could he remember such trifling details from his past life but not the most important ones? The sight of every woman reminded him that Alexis could be anyone in this awful city. Irritation filled him and he wheeled on Andromeda.

"Why can't we search here—?"

"Soon," Andromeda said, her eyes on the tower's summit. Near its foundation, a copper podium sparkled with electrical terminals. Dozens of Mechos listened to a copper-skinned female who stood atop it. Many applauded her words.

"The Rostrum, where the Mechos listen to mechanis pitches," Andromeda said. "One of Azibar's sycophants will let us see him."

A dozen bronze guards encircled them. Their features looked flatter than other Mechos and they carried pistols fitted with clockwork gears and steam injector coils.

"They will?" Tagen frowned at Andromeda but she whistled two loud notes.

The copper female left the Rostrum and approached. Her eyes glowed blue instead of green. She wore no clothing, showing all her metallic perfection. Tagen stared at her luscious curves, full breasts, lithe limbs. High cheekbones and generous lips completed her face. Instead of hair, a halo of steam coursed from her cranium. She looked familiar…

No, this wasn't Alexis. These Mecho types were too damn creepy.

"What a pleasure to greet visitors to the Mecho District. I am Mannequin, Consort of Azibar. I see that none of you have been augmented. Would you like to upgrade yourself from the filthy, decayed state that plagues Meridian?" Her accent didn't have the modulation other Mechos possessed. It sounded as smooth and delicate as fine glass.

Tagen appreciated Mannequin's beauty but she resembled a little girl's doll: lovely, beyond perfect, with impossible physical attributes. Her waist was too thin and her smile too easy. A sheen of oil covered her body.

"We're here to see your ringmaster." Andromeda seemed not the least bit intimidated by Mannequin's glistening presence, though Tagen could reach out and touch Sveta's revulsion.

Mannequin's blue eyes widened and emitted mechanical clicks. "Oh? Azibar doesn't just see anyone, I'm afraid. Perhaps I can interest you in a copper heart, or a nicer set of oil jelly breasts—"

"Azibar's expecting us." Andromeda rapped the rusty box in her hands and a thin tin sheet slid out from the bottom. She handed it to Mannequin.

After a quick perusal, the too-beautiful Mecho smiled through copper lips, showing silver teeth. "Right this way, into the Spire."

The bronze guards formed ranks on either side of them.

"Are you sure about this?" Tagen whispered to Andromeda.

"You're the cartomancer, Jackpot," Andromeda whispered back. "You can see more than I."

"I see us in deep shit," Sveta said. "I don't need cards for that."

2: Willing Slave

Darwick knelt before the High Priestess as her fingernails scratched a web of pain over his chest. The tent's shaft of light wreathed her in a circle of holiness above and beyond the wreckage of Meridian. So beautiful, so perfect—and he had failed her. Her ruby eyes stabbed into his.

"How did they escape? They had no Tarot deck on them. No friends among my Clowns. How, Darwick?" She cupped his chin and leaned close.

His lips trembled. "The Funhouse was locked like always, High Priestess. I came back into your tent—"

"So none guarded the Funhouse door?" she asked.

"Yes, High Priestess. Somebody killed 'em." His words came out in a whine.

"Then how do you think they escaped?" Her lips brushed his cheek, though her fingernails broke the skin around his throat scar.

The Circus tent faded into a sunlit vista of wide-open prairie. *A red shape lay sprawled in the fresh grass. Someone laughed and thumbed through a deck of cards. He tried blinking the sun from his eyes as he waited atop the horse, below the tree branch affixed with a noose. Waiting for the sheriff to slap the horse and leave him dangling.*

"How, Darwick?" the High Priestess asked, dispelling the vision.

"Maybe Tagen is the Magician. Maybe that's how he did it." He'd say whatever she wanted, needed to hear. Anything to remove the blame from himself and soften the rage in those vermilion eyes.

The High Priestess slapped him. "No he isn't! I control this city, I am the only interpreter of the Tarot!"

Red cape swishing on the tent floor, she paced around him. Her eyes darted over the tent like a frightened steer in a lightning storm. Darwick had branded many of them, he now remembered.

No! He remembered nothing but Meridian!

Seeing the woman he loved so afraid burned Darwick's heart into vengeful ashes. He knelt before her, face level with her navel. Darwick gripped her legs above the knee and gazed up at her. Such boldness might bring his death, but he needed to help her.

"Darwick?" she asked, a confused expression on her peerless face. Something slid from the corner of her eye and coursed down her cheek. It dripped off her chin and splashed onto his mouth. A tear. His goddess had shed a tear in her fright. He licked it from his lips. It tasted oh so fucking sweet.

Darwick kissed her stomach and met her gaze. "I swear I'll find 'em and make 'em pay. I'll fucking tear Meridian down until I get my hands around Tagen's throat!"

She smiled and held his head against her loins. The glyphs on her palms glowed red. "I know you will…my Knight of Swords."

His need to serve her, protect her, intensified so much he thought it would burst from his chest. The strange memories fragmented as the High Priestess hovered over his existence. Only she mattered.

3: Lordship of Flesh

Tagen studied the Spire's interior while Mannequin led them inside. Gears turned and steam jets activated at regular intervals. The aroma of oil, hydraulics, and stale water vapor hung in the air. Soft light steamlamps lit an expansive lobby. Four elevators led to a penthouse far above.

Several Mechos in golden body shells stood at attention. They held long brass cylinders as thick as Tagen's thumb. Their musculature dwarfed any Mecho he'd seen.

A legless, four-armed Mecho played a floating harpsichord above them. The instrument mixed delicate tones with sharp steam bursts. Though it sounded better than Clown rhapsodies, Tagen still preferred Georgio's violin.

Mannequin sighed a gust of steam. "Oh, aren't our Mecho nocturnes delightful? They blend the ambience of progress with the melodies of intelligence."

Tagen and Andromeda shared a skeptical look.

In the lobby's center were several counters coated in various metals. Each held objects out of place in the Mechos' neo-industrial world. Some contained mildewed books and scrolls, with titles like 'Lineage of the House of Acheron', or 'Aetheric Quatrains'. Other counters displayed palm casts, in silver, of glyphs similar to those on Tagen's hands. One had small ship models equipped with dirigibles or wings. He thought of Sveta's airship story. At least Azibar respected knowledge, unlike the Clowns.

While Andromeda and Sveta followed Mannequin to an elevator, Tagen examined a counter where a tarnished metal mask rested on a black velvet cushion. A plaque read 'Gorgon acolyte, pre-Nomad migration'.

An intuition tickled his consciousness. Now he remembered! Alexis's cards had featured a golden mask on their reverse. Had she come this way? Was this a clue she'd left between the gulfs of life and death?

"Please, I need to..." He reached for the mask.

Mannequin caught his wrist.

"Apologies, but Azibar has declared this exhibit off-limits," Mannequin said.

Tagen's hand pulsated and she released his wrist, her blue eyes dimming for an instant. A brief burst of steam jetted from her ankle, knee, and elbow joints. Some of her internal gears faltered.

"Sorry." Tagen joined the rest on the elevator. Sveta chided him with a glance.

"Wonderful, you pissed her off," Andromeda whispered.

Mannequin finally left the counter and stepped onto the elevator. Gears turned on either side of them. Bronze bars slid into place before them for protection. A metal wire hoist pulled the elevator up at a smooth clip, while vents gushed steam below. The lobby shrunk beneath them.

For the first time, Tagen realized no Tarot symbology marked any building or person in the Mecho District. The entire place lacked décor of any kind, as if the persistent metallic sheen and vapor clouds sufficed as ornamentation.

When the elevator stopped, the bronze bars slid back. Mannequin led them into the penthouse on the Spire's top floor. The chamber had a rounded ceiling, where a hole released a perpetual steam cloud into Meridian's sky. Tagen wiped fresh sweat from his brow due to the heated air.

Vats of black liquid, racks with spare limbs sheathed in copper, and cots of metallic organs lined the room. A clockwork telescope stood on a tripod. Everything had a clinical placement Tagen found disturbing. It stifled life.

A copper sarcophagus stood upright in the chamber's center. Small vents along it hissed steam every few seconds. It bore the visage of a handsome man with a kind smile, holding a thin brass rod. A mosaic of golden Mechos walking over the Styx covered the floor around it. Copper conduits and coils lay at the sarcophagus's base, leading to larger conduits along the walls.

"Do you feel it?" Sveta whispered in Tagen's ear.

"I feel power. Not in the machines, but something else."

"Yes, that's it." Sveta looked around. "I don't like it."

"Quiet," Andromeda whispered. Tagen wondered why she had brought them here, but he still wanted to trust her: she'd been the first in Meridian to help him, she'd been right about the Clowns—and she'd promised to tell him how to escape the city.

Mannequin curtsied before the sarcophagus and placed her feet into the mosaic's ring. Vapor jetted from tiny holes in the ring. The sarcophagus whirred and clicked. Gears along the sides turned and it opened in a rush of super-heated air. Two glowing green eyes peeked through the cloud. The smell of scorched metal stung Tagen's nose.

"Azibar, you have visitors," Mannequin said as if seducing some-one. Maybe, with that mechanical voice, she couldn't speak any other way.

"Excellent," the figure in the opened sarcophagus said in a rich, timbered voice. "I trust you have been cordial to them?"

"Yes, Azibar. I even offered improvements, but they declined." She placed both hands behind her back.

"Soon, all in Meridian will see the way." Azibar exited the steam cloud. The sarcophagus snapped closed behind him.

He looked the perfect man, with exacting symmetry and pro-portions. Instead of the hulking forms of his guards below, Azibar possessed a sleek body rippling with sculpted muscles. A square, sensuous jaw and noble nose marked his face. Unlike Mannequin, golden-wire mesh clothing stretched over his copper flesh, resem-bling a toga. Copper filament hair swept past his brows like a wreath crown.

"Ah, Andromeda. I received your message, and must say that I am delighted to see you." Azibar looked her up and down. "Though you really should dispense with those archaic Harlequin trappings. You would look so lovely in mechanis gold."

"Perhaps." Andromeda curtsied and doffed her cap.

Tagen and Sveta exchanged a frown.

Smiling, Azibar walked toward the sarcophagus. As his feet touched the mosaic around it, the sarcophagus reshaped itself into a copper throne. A flaring neon sun shone atop it. He sat in the chair. Small tubes extended from the armrests and inserted them-selves into his forearms. The throne vented steam.

"So you have brought me something wonderful?" Azibar looked at Tagen.

"This kinker is Tagen, newly arrived in Meridian. He is a car-tomancer." Andromeda flicked her gaze from Tagen to Sveta. No mention of Sveta's own cartomantic skills? Odd. What game was Andromeda playing?

Azibar leaned forward on his throne. "And you rescued him from the High Priestess? Were you followed?"

Andromeda shook her head. "I don't think so, but she'll be searching every flea bag and garbage joint for him. Show Azibar your palms, Jackpot."

Stepping up, Tagen raised his hands. Azibar gasped a small steam cloud.

"Yes, he has the glyphs," Andromeda said. "I think—"

"I think it's time you tell me what the hell's going on," Tagen said. "Yes, I am new here. I already know the Clowns are bad news. What's so special about these markings, or this Magician prophecy I keep hearing about?"

Azibar sat back and sighed. "I am glad you were captured, Tagen. You have seen firsthand what the High Priestess does to Meridian. She enslaves people with her Clown Tarot and her sickening displays of lust and addiction. She offers little solace from the decay and depression strangling this city."

"But you serve her with all your machinery." Sveta crossed her arms. "You keep the city running for her. My people know what you're about."

Azibar nodded. "The Sky Nomads are in thrall of her as well. Do you deny it? Telling people's fortunes with her approved decks on street corners? No, you don't understand. I want to stop the High Priestess and bathe Meridian in light and hope."

"What's that got to do with me?" Instinct told Tagen to say nothing about Alexis. People who wanted things couldn't be trusted.

"Nomad Girl here drew the Magician card for him in a reading," Andromeda said.

Azibar stood and the metal tubes retracted inside the throne. "Truly? Then you can help me even more, Tagen. Look out the window at my district. Is it dirty, falling down? Is it filled with rampaging murderers, or vendors selling human meat? No. I would make Meridian a sanctuary of perfection, order, and method. Everyone would have the body they wanted. And, once you showed me the city you came from, I could spread what I have to offer."

"I didn't come from a city in the Styx. I'm dead, like the rest of you. I took my own life." Tagen tensed as the Mecho leader laughed.

"Not that fantasy again, please. First the Clowns with their ridiculous Tarot religion, then the Sky Nomads claiming to have flown airships over the Styx. Don't be like them. The proof is all around you. I can give these people a new life."

"Don't you remember anything, then?" Tagen asked. "Who you were, before all this? You really believe you've always been coated in copper?"

Azibar's eyes flared. "Spare me your quaint beliefs about a past life. There isn't one. I can guarantee your future. Show me the path to the other cities, just as you found the path to this one. Help me end the High Priestess's tyranny and show everyone the glory of steam, biofluid, and copper skin."

"Wait," Andromeda said. "First we must overthrow the High Priestess. We need the Stygian Tarot, the deck created by Charon. If Jackpot here really is the Magician, then he's our only pitch. But I want what you promised me."

Smiling, Azibar spread his arms. "I am nothing if not gracious, Andromeda." He pointed at the rusty box she held. "However, I can't guarantee it will work. And we'll need more than a deck of cards."

A Tarot card appeared in Tagen's mind: Two of Swords. *A woman held a sword in each hand while blindfolded. Andromeda's painted face reflected on one blade, while Azibar's glowing eyes reflected off the other. The blindfold slipped from the woman's face—Sveta's. Behind her, a group of people drowned in the Styx.* Either way he went, people would suffer.

"I don't serve anyone," Tagen said. "I want to find someone and leave Meridian."

"Of course you don't serve me." Azibar smiled as wide as a shark. "Yet I am your only chance. Think on that."

Andromeda clasped Tagen's arm. "We'll find the Stygian Tarot first, Azibar. Shit, you know the High Priestess's powers, what she can do. We can all enjoy this haul, but the hasty hand gets severed."

"Very well. Yet, Tagen needs a disguise…and I require a guarantee." Azibar stepped onto the mosaic around the throne. Gears churned beneath the floor. Frowning, Tagen stepped back. The edges of Azibar's copper lips turned up in self-satisfaction.

A motorized arm shot from the floor. Tagen pushed Andromeda from its path. It struck his chest, piercing the skin.

"You bastard!" Sveta screamed.

Tagen winced and fell to his knees. Something thick and cool worked its way through his body. Andromeda rushed to his side but Mannequin blocked her. Azibar chuckled in metallic tones.

"You won't waste your talents, like Khyran. This time, I'll achieve my goal."

"Asshole. What did you do?" Sveta's gaze could have cut iron.

"Injected him with biofluid. It will spread through your body, Tagen. You'll feel stronger and you'll be harder to injure or even kill. Meridian's base urges will plague you less. Yet, without a copper heart to process it, the biofluid will clog together. I can remove it with my machines, if you find this silly deck Andromeda mentioned. If you help me crush the High Priestess and show me a path from Meridian."

"Or what?" Tagen managed through gritted teeth.

"You'll die." Azibar laughed. "I suppose, in your case, it will be a second death."

Andromeda glowered at Azibar. "This wasn't part of our deal, goddammit!"

Fidgeting with his gold-mesh toga, Azibar sniffed. "If you still desire what I have, you'll do as I say. This is Meridian. Unless it's the Mecho way, your only alternatives are being a slave in that Circus, drowning in the Styx, or ending up in a Bone Guild kiosk as pink giblets." He glanced at Tagen and smiled. "I suggest you all get going and find that deck, hmm? I'm surmising you have until the Alueryic Clock tolls twelve times."

"That's not long enough and you damn well know it," Andromeda said.

"You've performed wonders for me in the past, my lovely Harlequin. Don't disappoint me, as you have others." Azibar pointed at Khyran's box in her hands.

While Sveta helped Tagen to his feet, his body coursed with pent-up energy. His heart beat faster and his lungs worked harder to pump air. Dark shapes whirled in his peripheral vision as he stared at Azibar.

For a moment, instead of the copper magnificence standing before him, Tagen visualized a hunched man with boils on his face, whipped by men in medieval armor.

"A hunchback?" Tagen asked. "You were a hunchback?"

Azibar's copper brow creased in anger. Golden teeth bit into a copper lip. Steam blew from multiple vents across his body.

"How many times did they whip you?" Tagen whispered between labored breaths.

"Show them out, Mannequin." Azibar's timbered voice broke into rough modulation.

More questions came to Tagen's lips but chest spasms made him scream instead.

V.

The Hierophant

1: Channel of Grace

As they left the Mecho District, Tagen clutched his chest. Even though his stride had more strength and his limbs flexed with empowered muscles, it felt like he was having a heart attack. Though angry with Azibar, his emotions leveled off. He didn't ogle Andromeda as much, nor get frustrated with his situation. Hunger was nonexistent.

The biofluid inhibited Meridian's urges, just like Azibar claimed.

Sveta held onto his arm but he pulled away.

"Thanks, I'll make it," he said in a tight voice.

Sveta whirled on Andromeda. "And no thanks to you. What agreement did you have with that copper-plated asshole?"

Andromeda didn't back down. "Damn it, I didn't want this garbage show, either. But now we have no choice, do we?"

"We're near the Mecho District." Sveta gestured around them. "Why not get him a copper heart or something?"

"Azibar's no floss head," Andromeda said. "Only his surgeons can fix Jackpot. Mechanis organs are usually implanted before biofluid is pumped into the body."

"I bet you know all about that, don't you? Georgio told me how you turned over Nomad secrets to Azibar." Sveta balled her fists.

"Where to now?" Tagen asked, as much to find out as to stop their bickering. They'd argued since exiting the Spire and he tired of it. Vagrant's Row lay two streets away. No Clowns in sight—yet.

Andromeda righted the cap on her head. "Beneath the city. We don't have much time to find that deck."

"No," Sveta said. "Tagen needs to see my people. They might be able to help him. Besides, after he did this to Tagen, why would you trust Azibar?"

Andromeda's hand neared her skirt. "That copper turd is our only chance—"

"To hell with that," Sveta said. "I'm taking him to Nomad Way."

"Wait a damn minute. I'm not going anywhere yet." Tagen gasped, clutched his side, and straightened himself. "Andromeda, you said you could find the person I'm looking for. That you knew how to leave Meridian."

Andromeda broke eye contact. "We'll need that deck first. We're wasting—"

"You never planned on helping me, did you?" Tagen shook his head.

She gripped him by the shoulders. "This kinker you want might be anywhere or anyone in Meridian. Shit, they might already be dead, or languishing in Clown Alley."

"But if we're all dead, why would that matter?" Tagen pushed her away.

"I told you. If you die here, the city absorbs who you were." Andromeda bore down on him. "Now stop fucking around and listen—"

"I didn't come here for this!" he yelled, then coughed.

Alexis wept on the bed as the television replayed coverage of the congressman's death. He'd been found, shot in the back of the head, in an elevator. A child patient had found the body and now sobbed before the news cameras. Tagen downed another vodka shot and hurried out the door. Alexis called after him. He walked faster.

The child sobbed louder and Tagen realized he knelt on the curb, clutching a grimy boy to his chest. He smoothed the boy's filth-caked hair, wishing he could help.

"Tagen," a voice called, but he ignored it, focused on the boy's sorrowful eyes.

"Tagen!" Andromeda cried.

He blinked, then released the boy as he tried to bite Tagen's face. Andromeda kicked trash at the child, who spat at them and fled into an alley.

"I only wanted to help…" Tagen wiped the boy's saliva off his cheek.

"There's nothing you can do for them." Andromeda helped him up.

"But I—"

"I know." The empathy in Andromeda's eyes hinted at a lifetime of such episodes. Tagen was drawn to it; another person who recalled kindness in this hell.

"Why did you pick him up in the first place?" Sveta's voice broke his reverie.

"Hell, I don't…" Tagen rubbed his forehead. "I thought I remembered…"

"The Stygian Tarot could help you remember everything," Andromeda said. "It could show a way from Meridian."

He regarded her evenly. "Why do you care if I remember or not?"

Sveta gave Andromeda a questioning look.

"Because remembering is the only way Meridian will let you go." Andromeda nodded at people in the alleys, the gutters. "Those troupers forgot who they were. Meridian's urges fill that space, Jackpot. They're no better than slaves to the city's will."

"And the Stygian Tarot will prevent that?" Sveta asked. "Why's it so special?"

Steadying himself against a steamlamp post, Tagen studied Andromeda's face. "You know where it is, don't you? Or you wouldn't have made a deal with Azibar."

"It's a legendary Tarot deck, long thought lost," Andromeda said. "One the High Priestess can't decipher. I have a pitch where it is."

"Then why did we go to Azibar at all?" Sveta nodded toward the Mecho District.

"I have my reasons." Andromeda said. "But we need to hustle. Standing around bitching at me isn't going to make it cherry pie."

Tagen flinched from the biofluid snaking in the veins along his arms. "Damn, this feels…this stuff is mellowing me out, but how do you two deal with Meridian's urges?"

"Interpreting the Tarot strengthens the will," Andromeda said. "It's harder to blow off a cartomancer. Another reason why the High Priestess executes them."

"And another reason why we aren't following you. Come on, Tagen." Sveta offered him her arm.

"Thought you were pissed at me for getting you into this?" he asked Sveta.

"Georgio needs to know," she said. "Azibar is far crueler than you realize."

"If your people can help me…then let's go. All of us." He looked at Andromeda.

"Fuck the gilley wagon, then." Scowling, Andromeda followed them.

He didn't enjoy depending on others in Meridian. He barely knew anyone, didn't know who to trust—but the biofluid was spreading faster.

2: Conformity

Trying to vent his anger, Azibar paced around his laboratory. Tagen's audacious insinuation, of Azibar having a different life before Meridian, mortified him. He had crafted the perfect world for himself here. Had not that fool seen the district outside, all its splendor? Azibar wouldn't entertain the possibility of anything else, past or future.

One of the tramps his guards had brought in groaned on his cot. His ugly organic flesh pressed against the cot's bronze restraints.

"Fear not." Azibar neared the man. "My merger of mechanis, with biological tissue, has alleviated the urges plaguing you and all this city's residents. Hunger, libido, aggression—each weeded out through my experiments."

"No...no!" The man's body stiffened. Pliant copper tubes inserted themselves into his neck and cranium. They drained out his spinal and brain fluid with wet, belching noises. A blank expression stole over the man's repulsive features.

Azibar stepped back as three Mecho surgeons flanked the cot. Using a compressor, they replaced the spinal fluid with hydraulic oil. Substituted his veins with copper mesh tubing. Replaced all that nasty red blood with biofluid.

Other surgeons separated subject bodies into pieces and kept them alive via electrical current. One surgeon tossed a flailing teenage girl down a bronze chute, leading to the undercity. Not everyone's body accepted his gifts. He'd disposed of the cast-offs and replicated the successes.

"Excellent. Carry on." Azibar left the laboratory for his throne room.

The biofluid mixture, containing water from the Styx, disrupted the chemical reactions necessary for emotions. Thus, a Mecho had full control of his or her body. That the High Priestess used Meridian's urges to control the Clowns sickened him.

He gazed out the window at the Styx. Its black waters turned one's flesh gray and emaciated its imbiber. The Bone Guild drank it so their vendors would have no appetite to pilfer their own kiosks. Gutter Knights sampled it to aid with their composite bodies.

But none of them had beaten Meridian's urges, like he had. He knew how cruel the city was. Azibar closed his eyes and squeezed the windowsill.

The first time he'd tasted the Styx, he'd lost the hatred for those who'd eaten his original legs. The Clown women had no power over his desires and he never again salivated upon seeing a Bone Guild vendor. From the refuse piles, he constructed a body shell to protect himself. Improving it over time, he'd required only one thing: the secret of Nomad mechanis.

Andromeda had given it to him, for her own selfish agenda. He had not betrayed her, so much as spared Meridian from her impulsive rule. Now she had brought him a second gift, in hopes he would support her. He'd never seen someone so desperate.

They were all slaves to Meridian and its alabaster potentate. Azibar glanced at the polished golden disc affixed to the wall. When he finally freed Meridian, his kingdom would have a sun…with him providing the light.

"I trust your studies have been productive?" Mannequin entered and lay a hand on his shoulder.

"Quite, my dear, quite." He smiled at her. "We are almost ready."

"It is becoming more challenging to convince everyone that your rationing of materials is in their best interest. My last speech received quaint accolades."

"Come and I shall explain." Azibar headed for the nearest elevator.

Mannequin joined him and they descended to the lobby below. His guards stood straight as always: never tiring, never eating.

Walking between the counters, he scanned each collection of artifacts, hinting at other places besides Meridian.

"There are more cities out there." Using a single finger, he flipped through an ancient tome inscribed with Charonic script. "Alueryeum, the Elysian Gardens, the Donjon of Tartarus. Even the Aether Stairs. I will find all the places mentioned in these tomes. I will set all their people free."

"Like me?" Mannequin asked.

"Of course, my dear." Azibar caressed her chin. "How many Legionnaires are ready?"

"Fifty, Azibar."

He smiled at her exquisite body, her peerless face. Sheathed in the pinnacle of his mechanis art, Mannequin was the spokesperson for the Mecho philosophy.

Then why did her blue eyes flicker and lazy steam emit from her head vent?

"Do you require servicing, my dear? You are due for another speech to the latest group of adherents in two more tolls."

"No, Azibar," Mannequin said, but her speech contained coarse elements.

"What is the matter?" A single steam jet ejected from his side. "You cannot hide things from me…my dear."

"I feel strange in this body," Mannequin said. "I feel…ugly."

"Impossible! You are the most beautiful being in all Meridian. You are the jewel in my crown, my copper queen. Why do you say such a thing?" He took her hand.

"When I touched Tagen's wrist, I just…I remembered who I was." Her eyes closed. "I liked what I saw. Curly brown hair, real flesh. Maybe new adherents shouldn't cover that up with a body shell?"

She opened her eyes and smiled at him, though he sensed she wanted to express other emotions. Emotions he hadn't made allowances for when he'd crafted her face. It should always be smiling. Sadness had no place in the Mecho world.

Azibar lowered his voice. "Have you so easily forgotten what those savages did to you? How I discovered your broken form in a pool of your own blood, how they violated you until—"

"No!" Mannequin leaned into him. "Please, I am eternally grateful. But…weren't there others besides me? Did you save them?"

"Only you could be saved, my dear." He stood back and frowned. "Yet, if you think Tagen knows what is best for you…?"

"Forgive me." Mannequin hung her head. "Perhaps I simply need a refit."

"Now you sound reasonable." He escorted Mannequin to a Mecho guard. "See her to the lab."

As they departed, Azibar leaned on one of the counters. What had Tagen done to her? His copper fingers brushed one of the airship models and he removed it from its stand. So small and fragile in his grasp. The more he stared at it, the tighter he clutched it.

Tagen had enacted some cartomancer trick on her, nothing more.

The airship cracked in his grip. Vapor gushed from his exhaust vents.

Just a paltry ruse meant to throw him off, but he'd make Andromeda pay…

He imagined he crushed those men in plate armor, making them pay.

"No," he whispered, voice modulating in and out. The scene in his mind wouldn't go away. *Armored men. Whips. Lacerations across his body. Bleeding red blood.*

"No!" His voice filled the lobby. The vision faded from his mind. As his fist unclenched, fragments of the airship model slid from between his fingers.

He had worked too long, too hard, to tolerate any obstacle. As he gently placed the fragments back onto the counter, Azibar wondered what had made him lose control.

Azibar paced in circles. Tagen was trying to confuse him, like he'd done to Mannequin. The addled fool would have to be reined in. Azibar only required a cartomancer to navigate those cursed black waters. None of his instruments could penetrate such abysmal doldrums.

And even if Tagen did fail him, Azibar harbored a contingency. He pressed a button on the counter's underside. An alcove opened in the wall. It contained a headless body hanging from a compressor rack. Clockwork motors and biofluid kept the body in stable condition.

"Andromeda has been so easy to manipulate." Azibar lifted the corpse's right hand. It bore the Sun and Moon glyphs. "With your death, Khyran, I gained a kingdom."

3: Gutter Savior

Though Sveta steadied him, Tagen stopped walking.

"You okay?" She touched his chest.

Andromeda took his right arm. "We should keep going, Jackpot."

Doll House stood across the street from them. Most people had let them be, since Clowns and Sky Nomads were both respected— but Andromeda acted extra anxious. She'd asked Khyran to patrol the air above them three times already.

Though the biofluid hammered in his body, Tagen experienced Meridian's sights, smells, and sounds with greater clarity than before. Closing his eyes, he felt part of it.

In Tagen's mind, a lonely mounted knight held up a pentacle coin, as if looking for where it belonged, or waiting for someone to accept it. The Knight of Pentacles.

He touched Andromeda's hand. Her unease percolated through his skin.

"Who are you waiting for?" he asked.

Andromeda jerked her hand away. "Some trouper who can help."

Before he could ask more, a short figure crept from behind Doll House and approached them. The person clanked with each step.

"A Gutter Knight," Sveta whispered. "Let's go. There's always more than one."

The figure came closer. As it passed under a steamlamp, Tagen recognized Radomir's stitched-together face and metallic smile.

"Come on!" Tagen tried pulling the two women along but Radomir raised a hand.

"Almost cut you up, yes? But not now." Radomir hurried over, his armor jangling. Andromeda and Sveta both frowned. Tagen stiffened. This man had already tried to kill him once. Even admitted to it. As Radomir came closer, though, a difference shone in the man's pig-like eyes.

"Why?" Tagen winced, his heart fighting against the biofluid.

Making no threatening moves, Radomir waited a few paces away.

"What do you want?" Sveta asked in a no-bullshit tone.

"Wanted to see him. Magician." Radomir pointed at Tagen. "Knew to find you. Let me see Brian again, yes."

"So you've seen him. Wonderful. Now hitch your freak show ass somewhere else." Andromeda dropped a hand to her skirt.

Quicker than he looked, Radomir rushed forth and took Tagen's hand.

"How you let see? How you help remember him?" Radomir glanced at Sveta and Andromeda, then raised a hand to his face, as if trying to hide the stitch marks.

Something stirred in Tagen. A deeper emotion. Not pity, or sympathy. He recalled their scuffle in the alley when he'd first entered

Meridian. The Tarot visions, his itching palm. Radomir's about-face and flight. Without knowing why, he reached out and gripped the Gutter Knight's shoulder.

"I wish I knew, Radomir. But thank you for telling me." His smile became a grimace as the biofluid burrowed further into his body.

"Not look so good, Magician." Radomir glanced at Andromeda. "Maybe help?"

"Not unless you can pump out biofluid," Andromeda said. "We have to be going."

"Could help him. What's the matter, no copper heart?" Radomir touched Tagen's chest and neck, then shook his head. "No injector pulse or heat trap vent."

Sveta tapped Radomir's shoulder. "You can help him, then? If so, come with us. My people can pay you."

Shaking her head, Andromeda sighed. "Damn it. Oh well, Nomad Girl, he's your bally boy, not mine. Khyran, keep an eye out."

"Can fix him, too," Radomir said as the jack-in-the-box flew past.

Andromeda's glare could have snapped steel. Radomir scurried to help Tagen.

The group shuffled away from Doll House and toward Vagrant's Row. While the others talked—or argued—back and forth, Tagen considered Radomir's words. How had he helped the man remember anything? Why couldn't he do the same for himself? He tried focusing on the images in his mind: driver ID, The Ten of Cups in Alexis's hand. That shoulder holster. The golden mask.

The water was cold as he washed blood off his hands. From the corner of his eye he spied Alexis, hiding those cards in the closet again. She looked worried. His phone rang and they both stared it with dread. He reached for the shoulder holster.

Try as he might, Tagen couldn't recall anything else, save for one thing. On the Ten of Cups, Clowns danced before a glittering city in the background.

This time, a figure waited at the city's edge for him. One of the Clowns had Andromeda's face.

4: Intended Mercy

"No, fix him before meeting Sky People," Radomir said.

"Sky Nomads," Sveta corrected him and glanced down at Tagen. "Listen, if we piddle around, the Clowns will find us sooner or later."

Tagen sat on a curb outside the Row, while Andromeda bought sweet kelp wine from a Dionysiac kiosk. The biofluid inside him made it harder to breath or walk. Azibar must have thought they'd return to him in no time.

The Alueryic Clock tolled four times in the distance.

"Longer we wait, harder to stop. Find something with this, yes?" Radomir produced a copper coil from his armor and scuttled into a nearby alley.

Pacing the curb, Sveta kicked trash into a gutter. Why did she want to help him?

Andromeda returned and offered Tagen a wine bladder. A brown, syrupy liquid glistened inside.

"What vintage?" he asked, then coughed.

"Just drink it, smartass," Andromeda said. "If Ratty Boy works on you, you'll wish I'd hauled more." Khyran landed on her shoulder, watching him.

Tagen sipped the wine and spat it back out. It tasted worse than beer ran through a rusty tap, then mixed with rotten pears. Of course he'd remember something useless like that and not better things.

Andromeda leaned one hand on a curvy thigh. "Drink."

They locked stares.

"Careful. I might use this card magic, cartomancy—whatever it is—on you."

"Go for it." Andromeda's brows raised.

Finally, he grinned. She smirked and relaxed her stance. He emptied the bottle, forcing himself not to puke it back up. It warmed his gut, at least.

"How did I make Radomir remember?" Tagen asked.

Andromeda cleared her throat. Sveta avoided his face.

"So neither of you know. Is this what the Magician's supposed to do?"

"That's just a legend," Sveta said. "I'm not sure what you are, but it's not that."

"Look at Radomir," Tagen said. "Whatever I'm doing, it's real."

"I've been in this joint longer than either of you. I've never seen such a thing." Andromeda rubbed the hand Tagen had touched earlier.

Radomir hurried back from the alley, clutching something. "Traded copper coil for biofluid filter. Hard to find good barter in Row."

Grunting in pain, Tagen squeezed the curb. The concrete crumbled in his strengthened grasp. No broken skin, no bruises. He lifted his hand and gaped.

"Don't scratch your nuts too hard, Jackpot." Andromeda took the empty wine bladder from him. "Start tinkering, Ratty Boy."

Sveta sat before Tagen and held his hands. "Stay still. He says this will hurt. Just don't mash my fingers."

"Course will hurt, yes?" Radomir shoved something sharp into Tagen's back.

He bit back a cry as Sveta held his eyes in hers. Such an unusual stare. It grounded him in another place, another time. Another life. He must have been a cop in his previous one. Damn, that would've been hard on Alexis. Had that torn them apart?

Maybe he'd not given her heartache enough attention and she turned to those weird cards for answers. Whatever the reason, she'd trusted in them. And so he would.

"Teach me how to meditate," Tagen said. "If I'm a cartomancer… then tell me how it works."

"You don't have a deck of cards." Sveta's flat tone didn't dissuade him.

"Just tell me." He recalled the imagery from Alexis's Tarot deck. Swords, cups, pentacles, coins…

"Concentrate on a Tarot image. Imagine yourself as the person on that card. What do you see, how do you feel?" Sveta seemed afraid of his answer.

Rain pattered on Tagen's shoulders. Radomir dug into his back, making him cringe. Andromeda's brow furrowed with worried curiosity.

Envisioning a card in his mind, Tagen relaxed. *The Hierophant. An older man sat on a throne, gesturing at two acolytes. Teaching. Relaying information, a blessing of future wisdom. Reversed, the image denoted… rebellion. Denying Sveta's doubts, casting aside Andromeda's secrets…*

Shadows crept at the edges of his vision. Vagrant's Row faded from sight.

"What's happening?" he asked.

Ambulance lights blinded him while someone tried to dig a bullet from below his left breast. Blood covered his left side, which rose up and down with racking breaths. Tagen lifted his hand from the blood pooling underneath him. It belonged to a woman.

Sveta.

Gasping, his sight flipped back to Meridian. Radomir continued digging into his back. Though Sveta's jaw quivered, she didn't break her stare. His eyes closed as the dream-like images kept coming.

Careful hands pored over Sveta's nude body in an alley, marking the places for her future tattoos. One of the hands had glyphs on its palm. The ambulance lights flared in Tagen's eyes again.

Did he visualize her past, and her arrival in Meridian? He concentrated on his own history. Where were his memories of Alexis?

He thought of the Hierophant again and tried to teach himself.

"Hold him, Nomad Girl." Andromeda's voice echoed as if she were in a tunnel.

Tagen's sight blurred. *Sveta lay on a gurney outside the ambulance. Blood oozed from the bullet hole in her torso. Two people watched paramedics put her into the emergency vehicle: an older man and woman, both of them crying. Sveta's parents.*

"I can't hold him," Sveta whispered.

"Almost done, yes?" Radomir said.

Tagen tried to release the vision, tried keeping it from Sveta as he sensed her anguish and pain. He realized she didn't want to see, hadn't wanted to know that people grieved for her outside Meridian.

In his mind, the Hierophant stumbled from the throne.

Shadows convulsed in his peripheral vision. Her hands slipped from his. Something popped and whirred in Tagen's back. The biofluid now crawled instead of raced through his veins.

The vision in his mind morphed from the ambulance to a car. He drove it through a gated driveway. Outside the car, trimmed bushes and a mowed lawn stretched around a three-story mansion. Windows reflected sunlight across the lawn and driveway, where marble statues ringed a stone fountain. A woman waved at him from the doorway. Something gleamed on her finger.

"Why did you leave?" Tagen whispered.

The mansion faded. Her face shimmered like a mirage. The green vastness between them grew larger and larger. He pounded on the car windows.

"I came here to find you!"

Shadows and rain lashed his consciousness. Tagen's palms burned white-hot. Everything morphed back into the trash-filled curb. Squeezing his eyes shut, he hoped to reclaim some of what he'd just seen. Hoping to see her again.

Nothing came.

In the darkness around him, Sveta sobbed.

5: Apostle

Radomir finished capping the biofluid filter in Tagen's back. Sveta withdrew and wiped her eyes, her shoulders trembling.

"Ratty Boy, is he okay?" Andromeda glanced at Sveta with alarm. "Who was he talking to? You?"

Sveta crushed her damp eyes shut.

"Filter is pumping, yes," Radomir said. "Won't cure him. Needs steam heart, or Mecho surgeon."

As a Gutter Knight, he'd performed many such tinkerings with mechanis. His own body contained trace amounts of biofluid, which bled off into a filter implanted in his stomach. It helped him resist the urges to eat, kill, or screw—such emotions hampered business. His old business.

Andromeda knelt beside Sveta, who sobbed and held her head against her knees.

"Listen, Nomad Girl. Jackpot's fixed for the moment. Let's leave the Row." She nudged her gently. "Okay?"

"She remembers." Radomir put his steam torch and scalpel back under his armor. "Maybe let her think, yes?"

"We don't have time, Nomad Girl—"

"Fuck off for a minute, all right?" Sveta wiped her eyes and rose in a huff. Her angry gaze focused on Tagen's unconscious form, demanding answers.

Andromeda sighed and stood. "Fine. But get yourself together."

Radomir knew what Sveta had undergone. But he didn't know what he'd do with himself now. Brian, all those pleasant recollections of the life he'd had before Meridian…

He stared at Tagen's still form. Maybe if he followed this man, he would know.

VI.

The Lovers

1: Between Vice and Virtue

After opening his eyes, Tagen lurched to his feet and knocked Radomir over. The Gutter Knight's armor jingled like some fat, red holiday persona on a street corner, ringing a bell. What had that guy's name been? Something about claws? Tagen grunted and stood straight. He kept recalling useless tidbits from his former life and not the important ones.

"Easy." Andromeda grabbed his arm and steadied him. "How do you feel?"

Something vibrated at regular intervals in Tagen's back. He frowned. Though the biofluid didn't cause any pain at the moment, the fact he bore Azibar's technology inside his body riled him.

"Okay, I think." Tagen relaxed. "I can breathe normally again."

Sveta stared at him from the street, eyes filled with uncertainty. With her braids dangling from her head in sad droops, she looked so vulnerable. How old had she been, upon dying? Younger than he, but still an adult.

"Filter won't last long." Radomir avoided Andromeda on the curb. "Without steam heart, biofluid always seeps out, yes."

"Then let's go to the undercity," Andromeda said.

Sveta shook her head. "Tagen still needs to see Georgio in Nomad Way."

"The painted freaks will find us that close to the Circus," Andromeda said.

"Enough, you two. I've had it with the arguing." Tagen flexed his hands, feeling the biofluid move in him.

Andromeda whistled a few sarcastic notes. "Then which way?"

A fresh drizzle fell. Trash stirred in swamped gutters. Steam fog filled the avenues, as if the city breathed and stirred. Inhaling, Tagen closed his eyes.

Every memory reminded him that he needed to recall his past life, before it was too late. Andromeda, Azibar, and the High Priestess all wanted something from him. If Alexis had believed that it was here in Meridian…then he had to believe it himself.

On the curb, Radomir stood between Sveta and Andromeda like a mediator. He held the empty wine bladder Tagen had drained. Sveta's silver braid clasps gleamed for a moment and the lamp light glistened off Andromeda's body paint. Tagen knew he must make a choice. Maybe with the biofluid curtailing his urges, he could think clearer.

"I think we should…" Rain trickled down his brow into his eyes, as if Meridian obscured his decision.

Card after card slipped from cold fingers. The paper images plummeted like dead birds into an ocean of red. Tarot characters teased him with possibilities, insinuations. One card in particular flipped over and over, showing the golden mask reverse, then an obverse of naked figures. He reached for it.

Tagen stepped left. When he opened his eyes, Sveta stood closer to him than Andromeda. Yes, this was right. He owed her for making her see those painful memories.

"Nomad Way, then. Can your people really help me?"

"We'll see." Sveta walked down the street.

Eyes downcast, Andromeda fidgeted with her cap points. Her disappointment chafed his conscious. She might be secretive, but at least she understood how he felt.

Nodding and mumbling, Radomir seemed happy just traveling with him.

As they departed Vagrant's Row, Tagen regarded the city with renewed suspicion. Meridian lacked certainties in its swirling, trash-filled gutters. Here, only his interpretations defined his reality—a prospect he found disturbing.

2: Infidelity

Darwick gazed over the Sky Nomad section of the Bazaar, where he'd captured Tagen earlier. Nothing hinted at that asshole's whereabouts. Accompanied by a dozen warrior Clowns, he'd backtracked from the Circus. Still no fucking sign of them. He'd heard that skilled cartomancers could hide themselves, or use people's perceptions against them. Bullshit. Only the High Priestess possessed that kind of power.

"Nobody see anything?" he asked his fellow warriors. All shook their heads.

Tramping through the empty Bazaar, Darwick stepped on something other than paved stone. He bent and picked up a scrap of paper. Turning it over, he froze.

He held the bottom half of the Magician card he'd ripped, before seizing Tagen and Sveta. The drizzling rain ceased while he stared at the image, now nothing but the lower half of a man's body, standing over a table. Below it, in stark black letters, read 'The Magician'.

A tremor throttled his heart as his thoughts shifted.

He remembered dangling from the tree. Strangling to death, since the initial jerk hadn't broken his neck. Darwick tried to speak, but only the hiss of his last breath came out. Blurred figures watched him die under a hot sun. Locks of red hair, lifeless eyes. The scarlet dress he'd bought in town, with money from his steer sales. Blood-stained lips.

Darwick blinked and the vision faded. Trembling in rage, he almost crumpled the half-card. His fingers halted. After examining it a long moment, he shoved it into his pants pocket.

"They ain't here. We'll search the docks." He would find Tagen. Find him and end these stupid hallucinations.

3: Dilemma I

The filter allowed Tagen some of the biofluid's benefits. His steps gained strength. The insistent hunger faded. He could focus. After overtaking Sveta several times, though, he eased his pace. She knew the way. He didn't.

Andromeda kept quiet and Khyran remained a rusty box in her hands. The inner strength he'd first seen in her eyes now mingled with…turmoil? A lump of guilt crept into his throat. She had saved him from the Circus, and the way she looked at him now…

"Does this mechanis offer limitless energy? I feel like I could walk forever." Tagen pointed at Khyran's head. "He never tires, either."

"Of course not." Andromeda frowned. "We'll need sleep, but not 'round here."

"Where?" Tagen frowned. "Listen, I'm sick of nobody telling me—"

"Meridian is different." Andromeda's brow creased. "Troupers here don't age, or have children. Once there were more plants, but now every trouper wants meat. And for every kinker the painted freaks kill, three more wake up in Vagrant's Row, just like you. Any more fucking questions?"

"Hey, I didn't mean…this isn't the afterlife I expected, okay?"

"It's not you," Andromeda muttered. "It's what I let Azibar do to you."

"I'm sure you had your…reasons." He gave her a questioning look.

Andromeda pinched his arm. "I'll let you in on the take later. Too many ears in these streets, and…"

Her touch summoned images in his mind. *Andromeda danced across a tightrope over a hundred feet in the air, without a net. The crowd watched in terrified admiration. With angelic grace, she twirled to the center of the rope and curtsied. As the audience applauded and blew whistles, a figure in the shadows fired a gun. The bullet sheared through one end of the rope. Andromeda plummeted. Tarot cards spilled from her costume. The Magician card flipped end over end before her face, until she struck—*

"That's enough," Andromeda breathed, though she didn't remove her hand.

Years of her life filled his thoughts. Her emotional highs and lows. He had to catch his breath at the onslaught of recollections not his own. It was as if he'd known her for years. It was similar to the intimate familiarity he'd felt upon viewing Sveta and Radomir's past. Unlike them, however, Andromeda's eyes revealed that she now saw him the same way.

"How do I keep doing that?" he asked.

"Wish I knew." She exhaled with deep satisfaction, avoiding his eyes.

"Sorry." Tagen cleared his throat. "You were magnificent. Dazzling, even."

"What do you mean, 'were'?" She tried smiling but grief shadowed her features.

Though Tagen let her be, his mind still reeled with questions.

What was Meridian's purpose? Did Azibar have the right idea for surviving it?

And the pain in Andromeda's face…he couldn't imagine how long she'd been here. All the horrors she'd seen. She was strong, though. But after what he'd done to Sveta, he feared what he might awaken in others. He could offer no comfort.

They walked down damp streets strewn with refuse. Steamlamps flickered above them, never emitting enough light. A Clown juggled skulls and femurs on a corner while others sat and watched. In the gutter, a man slurped gray scum from a small skull.

Tagen stopped. "Andromeda, give him money for food."

Sveta pulled his hand. "Don't waste your time."

"Sorry, nothing left to barter," Radomir said.

"He'll go to the candy butchers and you know what they sell," Andromeda said.

"Please." He spread his hands.

Andromeda studied Tagen for a long moment, then tossed the man a copper shard. As the beggar ran off, squealing in delight, they continued on.

"How can you all live like this?" Tagen asked. "Doesn't it bother you?"

Sveta's mouth tightened. Radomir hung his head down.

"Haven't you seen enough to know these troupers have nothing?" Andromeda asked in an exasperated voice. "No licorice opera to look forward to, no expectations. Only what the High Priestess or Azibar offers."

"Then why are we here?" Tagen asked.

"Charon knows," Andromeda said.

"Maybe help them, show what was shown me, yes?" Radomir's pig eyes held thanks but he touched his stitched cheek and glanced down. Tagen reached out to him, but Sveta tugged his hand again.

"No. Not everyone needs to see. Not everyone wants a past." Sveta avoided Tagen's eyes but she didn't need to say more. The vision of her parents, watching her die in the ambulance, seemed as real to Tagen as his own memory.

"I didn't mean—"

"I know," Sveta said. "Just come on."

4: Ardor

Andromeda recognized Tagen's effect on them all: a cartomancer showing someone their inner self. The way Khyran had shown her, before his fall.

The way she'd trained him, when she still possessed an inkling of cartomancy.

One could become drunk with it, swimming in a sea of emotions released by simple images on a deck of cards. The Tarot depicted a journey, a story. One of growth and realization. Like so many others before him, Khyran had reached too far. Reached for what lay beyond the decayed city they now walked through.

Could she convince Tagen to reach for it?

Andromeda wanted to believe something else existed in the Styx's black waters. Once, the Tarot had showed her a dream. One of an ivory-walled city, with Sky Nomad airships flying over it. Beautiful Harlequins and shining Mechos had walked along its pristine streets. Georgio claimed she was the last Harlequin he'd seen in Meridian; a mystical caste that once served the House of Acheron. It was just a dream.

"But some people die several times for their dreams," she whispered to Khyran.

Tagen was correct about life before Meridian but she'd never seen any cartomancer awaken it in people. She didn't need her own past weighing her down right now. As a performer, she'd amused people with her juggling, acrobatics, singing, or Tarot readings. As a dissident, she'd tried to bring down the monarchy.

After her death, she'd plied all of those skills in Meridian.

Khyran's eyes slid open and looked up at her. Reflected in them was her old self. Reminiscence trickled through her mind like water down a dry throat.

For her, the Tarot's journey had been a stairway spiraling down into despair. A hurtful lie, like the Aether Stairs that Georgio claimed was out there, beyond Meridian. Most hurtful were the lies she kept telling herself.

After the High Priestess took over the Circus, Andromeda's cartomancy had become dormant. She'd loved more than one Magician, in effort to win back her position, though Khyran's loss still left her empty. With every toll of the Alueryic Clock, it became harder resisting Meridian. More and more she enjoyed killing Clowns. If she didn't escape soon, she'd be just like Darwick, or worse.

The city hadn't taken her yet. There was still time.

She'd given Khyran the Stygian Tarot to defeat the High Priestess, but Andromeda herself couldn't read the deck. Tagen might. Then there was Sveta's tattoos. Georgio had always been crafty. That copper prick Azibar thought she'd turn Meridian over to him after the High Priestess fell? Hardly. All she wanted was to dethrone that bitch and make Khyran whole again.

She needed Tagen for these things. Maybe more.

Khyran transformed into a Mecho head and blinked at her. Even in his condition, she knew he still sensed her feelings. Smiling, she clutched the head close. Khyran's love had saved her from the alleys, had given the Blades of Charon hope.

A hope she still believed in as she examined Tagen's walking form. Her breathing quickened, though she'd long mastered Meridian's cravings. A nagging doubt still gnawed at her, though: did she hold the Magician in her hands, or did he walk before her?

Fresh rain chilled Andromeda's skin. Meridian had never offered answers. Neither could she.

5: Loathing Temptress

"Show me."

The High Priestess leaned over her card table. She'd sent away all the usual spectators and sycophants. Now alone, she removed her cape and crown. Laid them in her wooden chair. Kneeling before the table, she hugged herself close.

The Tarot cards on the table stared back at her. Myriad images of promise and doom. Whenever she had privacy, she performed readings for herself. Ruling a slavering mob rarely gave her the opportunity. Always they required demonstration of her wisdom. She had little sympathy for her victims, or for the unpainted masses throughout Meridian. Fools, all of them. If only she could escape them more often.

This city might be hers, but the price…

"Why can't you show me?" the High Priestess asked the cards. Never had the images failed her in discerning other's futures. She alone mastered the Tarot, she alone predicted the life and death of all. It was her city, because…she had nothing else.

She couldn't leave. Couldn't remember when she hadn't strolled its filthy streets.

The cards on the table were the same as every time before: The High Priestess card, representing herself. The Magician card and then the Tower. It showed a lightning bolt striking a clockwork turbine tower. Two Clowns fell from it into the Styx.

Destruction, a fall from grace. The end of all she knew.

The High Priestess didn't know her real name. She had taken her current title after drawing the selfsame card. Before she'd taken

Andromeda's Circus and created her Clown cult. Andromeda had only entertained, while she'd given these miserable people a goddess, a semblance of joy.

To think someone would take it from her.

She grabbed the Magician card but it melted in her palm. Another floated from the deck to her hand. Trembling, she stared at the reverse face of a smiling Clown.

"You obey me." She laid the card face up on the table.

The Magician.

Backing away, she hid her nakedness with her hands. While she loved displaying her vibrant sexuality, this simple image made her ashamed. She couldn't see Tagen in her mind's eye. No other person had avoided her cartomantic sight. Not Emrys, or Khyran.

Not Andromeda.

The High Priestess's cape and crown rose from the chair and returned to her body. She strode from the center ring into the aisle containing the impaled heads. So many she had condemned and none of them the Magician. Glazed eyes stared at her much as the cards had. Bereft of life, yet containing immeasurable depths she couldn't penetrate any longer. Preserved through Meridian's power, they had given her their magic, their memories. Now they offered nothing.

"Show me," the High Priestess said into one's eyes. Her white-painted visage looked back at her in the dead orb's reflection.

"Show me!" she screamed.

6: Dilemma II

They all followed Sveta along an abandoned dock. Rotten sailcloth and burnt wood littered the quay. Rusted iron posts, once used to hold boats fast to the pier, now hung with painted skulls. For the first time since peering from that building in Vagrant's Row, Tagen gazed out over the black, endless Styx. Its placid waters contained no ripples or foam. No waves lapped against the misshapen docks. No current ran through the foreboding water.

"Why hasn't anyone either scavenged this stuff or made a home here? It's quiet, compared to the rest of the city." The pump in Tagen's back clicked and he grunted.

"The High Priestess forbids anyone living near the Styx," Sveta said. "Though few ever enter the waters. Whenever someone dives in, they never return. Anything the water touches usually turns black, anyway."

"Then where does the kelp come from that the Bone Guild sells?" Tagen asked.

"It's harvested beneath the city, in sewers leading to half-submerged chambers," Sveta said. "My people harvest it too."

"But all this wreckage…" Tagen shook his head.

Sveta pointed at the flotsam on the quay. "The Clowns make sure no building materials exist for a boat, though I've heard some people keep small rowboats and the like hidden. Anyone caught concealing one is executed."

"You ever ride in one?" Sarcasm tinged Andromeda's question.

Sveta's jaw tightened. "Why would I? There's nothing out there."

The Styx held Tagen's gaze the longer he looked at it. It could have been a mirror. A reflection of shadows and desire. His eyes closed to slits. Silent, unknown words moved his lips.

"Jackpot?" Andromeda asked.

Tagen concentrated on the Stygian expanse. Images filled his mind: *Darwick on a street corner, inquiring after them. Clown warriors terrorizing others for information. Bare, grease-painted feet stomping down mildewed cobblestones.*

Eyes fully open, Tagen looked around. "The Clowns. We have to hide."

"Shit. You're sure?" Andromeda's hands neared her skirt.

"I feel them, too." Sveta met his eyes, some of her resentment gone. "They are coming this way."

"Can't be taken. Want to see more." Radomir reached for Tagen, then shrank back. "But can't. Can't face the High Priestess. Too many I've sent to her tent, yes."

A cold chill swept over Tagen as he looked at Radomir.

"Who have you hauled to her, you little rat-bastard?" Andromeda loomed over the Gutter Knight, despite the fact he wore armor and no doubt hid several weapons within it.

"Card readers, Blades, prophets." Radomir produced the curved black dagger Tagen recalled from the ambush. "Sorry. Give back, yes?"

Andromeda grabbed Radomir's throat as Khyran hovered over her. The curved dagger clattered onto the street.

"Stop!" Touching the crazed Harlequin made Tagen reel backward.

Tagen envisioned himself beside Andromeda, while the High Priestess ordered a man's head lopped off right before her. Biting into her fist, Andromeda gagged herself to avoid screaming. The scene faded into one of Andromeda staring at herself in a cracked mirror, applying paint over her nude body. She spent extra time on her face paint. Tears made it run every time.

"You piece of shit!" Andromeda's voice degraded into heaves as Tagen finally pried her off Radomir. Sveta caught the Gutter Knight before he toppled off the quay.

"What the hell is wrong with you?" Tagen cried.

"He's a pitchman for the Clowns!" Andromeda drew a curved black dagger from beneath her skirt.

"Sorry, sorry—" Radomir fled, disappearing in the shadows between steamlamps.

"He meant cartomancers? You must have known one." Pity crossed Sveta's face.

"He'll betray us, Jackpot. Fuck! You should never have trusted him." Utter hatred ruled Andromeda's eyes. "How else do you think he got this sharp novelty? He must have alerted the Clowns to my kinkers' ambush!"

Voices and sadistic laughter echoed down the quay. Tagen beckoned his friends and moved down the dock, the biofluid pumping energy into him.

"Rat bastard must have led them here." Andromeda sheathed her dagger and the one Radomir had dropped.

"There's nowhere to go," Sveta said.

Tagen knew she was right. Their footsteps would creak over the wooden dock if they ran. Maybe if he tried some of this card magic…

Tagen concentrated on a card he remembered, the Page of Cups. *A young man stood beside the sea, holding a cup aloft.* Like Sveta had instructed, he imagined himself as this person. Tried to think of how it could help them escape.

And here he was, standing beside the Styx, the cup of his heart empty for Alexis.

Shadows moved at the edges of his vision and his palms itched. Heart racing, he spotted a sewer grate casting runoff into the Styx.

"What about that grate? If we hurry, we can reach it before the Clowns find us."

They crouched along the quay. The voices grew louder.

"It's on a timer," Andromeda whispered. "It flushes excess water from the gutters. In a few moments the current will increase and we'd drown."

"We have to try," Tagen said.

Sveta took his hand. "Come on."

Together they rushed over snapped paddles, splintered masts, shattered helm wheels—a desolate graveyard of mariner's implements. The High Priestess wanted no escape from Meridian, even if it meant destroying things to her detriment.

"This will stop that timer." Andromeda paused at a bronze valve set into the dock.

Tagen turned but Sveta pushed him past a rusted capstan. "Hurry!"

With a swift kick, Andromeda struck the valve. The grate stopped spewing water.

"Come on!" Tagen whispered, beckoning Andromeda.

"Wait, you're going to—" Andromeda fell silent as footsteps rattled over the dock.

Reaching the grate, Tagen stilled himself against the stench and putrid forms pouring from it. Biofluid swelled his muscles and he thrust up the grate hatch. Its solid mass still made his limbs shudder.

Sveta hesitated, then hurried into the grate. The hatch's weight stole Tagen's breath. He glanced at Andromeda, who had gone rigid.

Silhouettes of lanky, armed figures appeared on the quay between the steamlamps. Worry spread over Andromeda's face as the shapes came closer. He started to go back. He couldn't let her face them alone.

"It's too late, we have to go," Sveta said into his ear.

Cool resolve filled Andromeda's eyes. Her painted jaw set into an admirable line.

Tagen backed into the grate with Sveta just as nasty water sloshed around his chest. The dark torrent raced into the Styx. With one hand around Sveta's waist and the other clasping a wall groove, Tagen barely held his head up above the runoff.

Darwick appeared behind Andromeda as the hatch snapped over the grate.

"Andromeda!" Tagen said in a fierce whisper. The water flow continued, tugging them toward the hatch.

"Hold on to me," Tagen managed without getting the foulness in his mouth. As Sveta's arms encircled his neck, he used both hands to climb away from the hatch using the wall grooves. After a short eternity, he pulled them both from the muck and onto a higher sewer level. Without the biofluid's strength boost, they'd have drowned.

"She's still back there." Tagen tried to focus on a Tarot image, hoping one could show what was happening to Andromeda. Nothing but murky shadows filled his mind.

His palms glowed in the darkened sewer tunnel. Violet light bathed them both as the glyphs twinkled.

"Your cartomancy…you found us an escape path." Her eyes widened.

"Not all of us," he said.

Tagen listened for any sound of Andromeda's fate. A shout, a scream, anything. Only the running water, emptying through slots at the tunnel's end, broke the silence.

"We have to help Andromeda. That Clown asshole might—"

"She's a Clown too, remember? No matter what she says, she's painted like one."

"You never did like her." He brushed past her and studied the tunnel. It went on for a distance before branching off.

Sveta followed. "I don't deny it, but there's nothing we can do now. Look, I don't want her to be caught by Darwick, either. It's us they want, not her."

She tripped on a loose stone in the tunnel and caught herself on his back. Tagen wheezed, the implanted filter still tender.

"Sorry," she said, righting herself.

Turning, he regarded her with bewilderment. Faint light shone through small cracks overhead, but his eyes adjusted quickly.

"What do you mean, 'us'? I'm supposed to be this damn Magician, remember? Darwick hunts me." He trudged on until Sveta grabbed his arm.

"I've had about enough of people grabbing me—"

"They know I'm a cartomancer now, thanks to you," Sveta said. "I didn't want to draw that damn card. I'm a wanted woman in this city, don't you see? And the High Priestess, she won't give it up, either."

Tagen met her stare while Meridian's cold, slimy runoff swirled past their ankles. "I didn't want you to see your parents. You think I wanted you to relive your own death? That I wanted to change Radomir? I still can't remember my whole name!"

Though Sveta's grip on his arm eased, she didn't let go. "I know you didn't. I know. But that doesn't make it hurt any less. Maybe it helps some people, like that Gutter Knight. I don't know. The rest of us must shoulder our pain. People here, we forget, or don't even know, who we were. If there even was a 'before', like you say. It scares me, Tagen. You scare me." She released him and walked past.

"Thanks. Maybe you should have left me to the Clowns, then."

"Don't be an ass," she said. "Look, just be quiet for now, okay? I'm trying to find our way out of here. Besides, you saw those heads in the High Priestess's tent. I wouldn't wish that on anyone and that's what will happen if Darwick catches us."

They passed a fork in the tunnel. Brown, frilly kelp fronds crowded the passages ahead, rising to their knees. He had no urge to eat any of it. How could anything grow in these reeking passages? In one tunnel, though, the kelp had been cut down.

"Who harvests these spaces beneath the city?" Tagen asked. Sveta had hesitated at the last two turnoffs. Maybe she'd lost her bearings. For him, the path remained plain.

She stopped and shot him a glance, her hair clasps striking each other.

"You can see it, can't you? The way out of here."

"I think so." Tagen took her left hand and her Moon glyph glowed green.

"How did you do that?" she asked. Tagen didn't answer as he traced the lines in her palm. Concentrating, Tarot imagery filled his head: *the Fool waded through the sea as a Knight of Cups offered him a hand across the water.* He glimpsed the same Tarot images on her right shoulder.

"There." He traced the outline of the cards in her tattoos. Sveta stepped back.

"What are you doing?" she asked.

His hands glowed violet as he touched her skin. Strange, how everyone's flesh in Meridian remained warm and vibrant. His fingers lingered on her shoulder. As the images faded, Tagen sensed that the right tunnel should be taken.

"Thought I saw something. In your tattoos."

Sveta swallowed. "Let's go, huh? It stinks down here."

"We stink." He picked at his sodden shirt.

As they went along, Tagen's Star glyph thrummed. Whenever they neared a wrong tunnel, the glyph numbed. When they entered the correct one, the glyph thrummed again. He didn't know why, but instinct told him to trust the sensations.

Farther down the next tunnel, an emaciated, gray-skinned man reaped kelp with a rusty sickle. He wore leather breeches and bone jewelry.

They both ducked back around the corner. Sveta mouthed the words 'Bone Guild'. He nodded and entered a different passage, then halted.

Dozens of signs lay piled in a corner. The same ones the shackled people had worn around their neck in the Bazaar.

The Star glyph thrummed anew, urging him on.

"Tagen?" Sveta's voice shook.

"This is the way."

Bloodstained cleavers and saws hung from a rack around the next corner. Human cadavers dangled from hooks in the ceiling, of every age and gender. A little girl's chest had been slit open. An elderly man lacked arms and legs. Faces, breasts, limbs, and rumps lacked hunks of flesh. Blood dripped into the sewer water.

The sight and stench churned Tagen's stomach. A boiling rage seared into his heart. He forged past the bodies. Cold, blood-slicked limbs slapped against his shoulders.

Tagen reached under his left arm but he had no gun in this life.

He could still serve justice.

"Wait," Sveta whispered, but he ignored her. The tunnel stretched on, filled with scores of bodies. Something shredded through moist objects. A mechanism ejected steam.

Tagen turned a corner just as a man cut a child's body in half with a steam-powered saw blade.

Biofluid surged in him as Tagen flung the saw blade aside and slammed the gray-skinned man into the wall. The child's body slid from a hook and splashed into the water.

"Why do you do this?" His fingers tightened around the gray neck. The Guild member just stared at him with dull eyes. "Why?"

"Tagen, stop," Sveta said.

"Who are you? What are you?" Tagen's limbs shook with fury.

"All who feast shall rule the Styx with Charon," the man uttered, his voice like dry paper sliding over sand. "The path from Meridian is through the flesh."

"You son of a bitch," Tagen said through clenched teeth. "Why?"

The man smiled with yellowed teeth. "All who feast shall rule—"

Tagen snapped the man's neck.

Bloody water splashed him as he let the body fall. Sveta stood nearby, not looking at him. It had been so easy, had felt so goddamn good—

"Tagen?" Sveta asked. He hated the fear in her voice.

He stumbled back into the hanging bodies. Some of them were still warm.

"Why, you motherfuckers?" Tagen ripped hooks from the wall, the ceiling. More bodies slipped into the water. He continued until he couldn't see any more of them.

"Why...?" Quivering, he leaned against the wall and wept.

"Please," Sveta said. "We must go."

Tagen yanked her arm and fled through the tunnels until he couldn't smell the bodies. All the while, the Star glyph thrummed.

"Calm down," Sveta breathed, her face pale.

Grunting, Tagen quelled his fury. Though the biofluid eased, the filter hurt like a knife in his spine. He waited a few seconds before moving again.

"This city is nothing but shit. Nothing but..." He frowned at her. "Why did you want me to stop? That bastard deserved it."

"Because I could tell you enjoyed it," she muttered.

Slumping against the wall, Tagen clasped his head in both hands. "I wanted him to stop...I want all this to fucking stop."

"How?" She wiped her eyes. "I hate it too, but what else is there?"

"We need that deck Andromeda talked about," he said.

Sveta flung up her hands. "You think the High Priestess will let you leave, just because you have some ancient cards? She commands the city's power. She'll stop you."

"Then I'll beat her with...with whatever the hell magic I can do."

"But you can't," Sveta said in a soft voice.

"Then why are you even helping me?" He glared at her.

"Because I'm afraid of what will happen if Meridian claims you." She offered her hand and he finally took it. "We're almost there."

They entered another passage. The water stank less and the sounds of the city amplified above them. More light shone down through the street's cracks. Soon, they approached another grate, one without a hatch. Water spilled into a lichen-covered gutter.

Tagen paused. A single red flower lay atop the lichen. Its petals budded in organic splendor as he picked it up.

Sveta leaned close. "What is that?"

"It looks like a rose…no, wait, there's a yellow center inside."

In his mind, a red flower brushed a woman's face. Blood lay around her. Steam hissed from something nearby.

The vision ended and Tagen cupped the svelte blossom close.

"I've never seen anything like it," Sveta said.

He handed it to her. The flower became a brilliant red.

Sniffing it, Sveta smiled. As she handed it back to Tagen, it wilted and turned black. The petals fell off and washed down the sewer.

"Huh? What just happened?"

For a long moment she stared at him. "You must see Georgio. He will find a place for you among my people."

While she exited the grate, a tattoo on her back resembled another Tarot card: the Ten of Cups. No Clowns danced in her version, but two other people he didn't recognize faced each other.

"Tagen? Hurry."

"He followed her up into Meridian's steam-lit cityscape.

7: Painted Obstacle

Andromeda remained aloof while Darwick approached her. Twelve other warriors followed him over the quay. Holding Khyran's box under her left arm, she leaned her right hand on an outthrust hip. Best to play the role for now. How in the name of Charon had Jackpot and Nomad Girl survived that gutter purge? If cartomancy had been the reason…the city was strengthening its hold on him.

"You there, with that Mecho shit in your hand." Darwick regarded her as prey.

"What you want, floss brain?" With a flick of her head, she tossed a cap point from her face. She'd never quaver before these assholes. So many had died on the edge of her daggers, she'd long lost count.

"We're looking for a man with long black hair, blue eyes. Got black cartomancer glyphs on his palms. Goes by the name of Tagen. Travels with some Sky Nomad bitch, with brown braids and tattoos all over. Green eyes." Darwick stopped right beside her, his leg brushing her thigh.

Shrugging, Andromeda didn't recoil from his closeness. She dared not show any repugnance. She'd never killed more than eight Clowns at once.

"Haven't seen the fuckers, but I saw some sellouts building a row boat earlier. Looked like Gutter Knights." Maybe they'd find Radomir and gut that little rat shit. If she'd known he had been a Clown informer, she'd have killed him after he'd helped Tagen. His seeming redemption was nonsense.

Darwick slapped her bottom. Her skin burned from the contact.

"What are you doing down here? Shit, there's much better fun to be had at the Circus." His tone bore suspicion rather than sexual intent. Andromeda knew Darwick's reputation as the High Priestess's pet butcher.

"You're right, this joint is boring. Hey, why are you looking for those two? They piss the High Priestess off or something? Or are you looking for fun?" She made eyes at him and pouted her lips. Clown warriors only got off by shedding blood, anyway.

As his dark eyes ogled her body, though, she regretted her flirting. He had the gaze of a killer on crusade.

Darwick patted her bare stomach with the flat of his blade. Dried blood on it scratched her painted skin. Her muscles tensed and her chest throbbed.

The blade's tip hovered over the clasp keeping her torsolette on. Andromeda slid her right hand down her thigh to her skirt.

"I…" Veins bulging on his temples, Darwick touched a scar on his neck. The sword wavered away from her body.

"You okay? Maybe you should visit the grind wagons at the Circus, or I could—"

"Fuck off," Darwick said. "Get back to the Circus if you want something between your legs. You see those two, spread the word.

They're cartomancers that escaped the Circus. I'll kill 'em on sight." He looked her over again, then motioned for his comrades. While they tramped across the quay, Andromeda maintained her inviting smile.

As soon as they left earshot, she fled across the rotted dock toward Nomad Way. She cradled Khyran's box closer. "Let's hope that old fool has forgiven me."

VII.

The Chariot

1: Tests of Initiation

Nomad Way was covered in swaths of grubby white canvas. Painted designs embellished the tattered surfaces: Tarot characters outlined in subdued blues, reds, and yellows, as well as faded sketches of suns, moons, stars, and airships. Incessant rainfall had blended the colors into tangential rainbows. The entire district overlooked an abandoned pier that might have housed something as large as a cruise liner.

"Here it is. Once inside, we should be safe." Sveta readjusted her vest. Rain glistened off her tattooed flesh in cryptic swirls.

With so much weighing Tagen's mind, he was tense about entering yet another nightmarish tableau. He'd not found the slightest clue about Alexis, the biofluid scraped through his veins, plus Andromeda might've been captured. Or even killed.

"You okay?" Sveta tugged his hand.

"Sorry. Still getting used to this place."

They passed under the canvas sheets and into Nomad Way. Tagen stared.

Clean streets wound past shelters fashioned from canvas, wood, and rusted parts. Colored lanterns flickered from poles attached to steamlamps, illuminating the steam fog in chromatic eddies. Wind chimes hung from gutters that led into water filters. Rainwater churned in brass fountains, only to be boiled off in compressors that warmed homes.

Residents peered at him from their makeshift dwellings, dressed like the Nomads he'd seen in the Bazaar—blue clothing and silver jewelry. Many sported tattoos but none compared with the artistry of Sveta's. Children tossed a painted ball around. Graceful men and women danced to the same music Georgio had played in the Bazaar. They flipped their hair or shook their garments in mirth.

"This place is beautiful." Tagen gazed around. "No wonder you hid here."

People stopped dancing and the children ended their play. All gaped at Sveta, then cheered and mobbed her. Comforting hands patted her cheeks and shoulders. Voices rose in jubilation. The musicians performed a frenetic mazurka and people frolicked anew.

"You must hurry to Georgio," a Nomad man said to Sveta. "He just returned from the Circus. We all heard about your escape."

The man's words ruined any celebration for Tagen. Now the Clowns would come.

After hugging many in the crowd, Sveta led him down several streets. Residents stopped talking or working and watched them pass. Did these people ever receive visitors? No Bone Guild kiosks or vulgar displays lined the thoroughfares, no Clown Tarot graffiti. Mothers baked kelp-meal bread on outdoor grills while shooing off hungry teenagers. The district's quiet wholesomeness made Tagen wistful for his previous life.

Surely, if Alexis had come to Meridian, she'd be here.

They stopped before a tent where an antiquated ship's wheel stood near the door, beside piles of ragged netting. Wind chimes with cartomancer's glyphs drooped from a pole, as if waiting for a breeze to help them sing. A violin played a forlorn tune inside.

"Georgio?" Sveta asked. The violin ceased. "Is there any Clown paint still on me?" she whispered.

He touched her cheek. "Got it."

She nodded, but he'd lied—Tagen had just wanted to touch her. Sveta's tattoos morphed in his vision, then looked normal again. Rubbing his eyes, he said nothing.

"Come in, Sveta," Georgio called from inside.

Motioning Tagen along, Sveta ducked into the dwelling. He trailed after, his hand brushing the tough, ancient canvas.

Rain pattered on the tent's roof. A few stools sat around a steam lantern, offering both light and heat. Dried kelp, mushrooms, lichen, and moss hung from the tent's beams. Tapestries formed of intricate knots covered the walls, depicting Nomad heroes and airships. Georgio sat behind a solid wooden table, where several charts and scrolls lay. He set aside his violin.

"Ah, the man from the Bazaar." Georgio stood. Tattoos of suns, moons, and mapped globes lined his chest and arms. A silver medallion, similar to Sveta's, hung from his neck.

"Georgio, this is Tagen." Sveta hesitated. "He's a cartomancer. We both escaped from the Circus."

Glowering, Georgio stepped from behind the table. "Damn those Clowns. First I couldn't get into the Circus, and then word spread of your escape. I came back here to await you, though other Nomads still search. Are you hurt? What happened?"

Sveta described their exploits since their capture in the Bazaar, though she omitted Tagen's abilities and their companions. While she spoke, the steam lantern flared in Tagen's vision. It flooded out the tent interior, piercing his mind.

Within himself, Tagen saw Georgio standing over a dock, holding a lantern with his head bowed.

"What did you just see?" Georgio stepped closer. Sveta frowned and circled around Tagen.

"What do you mean?" Tagen asked, but Georgio's eyes penetrated his soul.

"I can tell you had a vision, because your palms flashed violet. What was it?"

Tagen told him. Both Georgio and Sveta listened attentively. When he finished, Georgio's demeanor calmed.

"What about your reading in the Bazaar? Sveta, what did you see?"

Sveta fidgeted with her vest and tossed her braids behind her shoulders.

"Sveta?" Georgio asked.

"I drew the Magician card. A paper card, unlike those in my tin sheet deck." She then described the other cards in the reading.

The rain outside ceased. Silence ruled the tent. Even the steam lantern stopped venting. Georgio's eyes ticked with nervous energy and he gripped the table for support.

"The High Priestess did a reading for us both," Sveta said. "She drew the Magician for Tagen, like I did."

Tagen shook his head. "Hey, I just want to find someone in this city, then leave. Andromeda said Azibar—"

"What? Sveta, you didn't mention them." Georgio's brow furrowed more in concern than anger. "Tell me everything."

Tagen told all: Andromeda's Blades of Charon, Azibar's treachery. Georgio glanced at Sveta with disappointment.

"You should have known better than to visit the Mechos," Georgio said. "Azibar uses Nomad mechanis in foolish, sick ways. Knowledge that Andromeda gave him. Beware that Harlequin. She reaches for something that is no longer there."

Tagen leaned forward. "She told me how I can leave this city."

"She thinks it is so simple?" Georgio scolded him with a look.

"She mentioned the Stygian Tarot," Tagen said.

"Though sorrow come with parting pain, he shall come back to Meridian again," Georgio mumbled, staring into space.

"Please, no riddles," Sveta said.

"Well?" Tagen asked. "Did she tell me the truth?"

"Not entirely," Georgio said.

Tagen gripped a stool in frustration. The wooden seat shattered in his grip. He stared at his splinter-covered hand as the filter burned his back.

"Control yourself!" Georgio cried.

"Azibar injected him with biofluid." Sveta touched Tagen's arm. "Careful. The biofluid won't be slowed by that filter forever."

"Well, can the Nomads take this stuff out of my body?"

"It might have been possible, if you'd reached us right after your injection." Georgio shook his head. "It has spread too far in your body, now."

Sweat slid down Tagen's face. "Sveta says you can hide me here. I wouldn't get in the way, or stay long. I just need time to—"

Georgio grunted. "They will hunt you down. Clowns, Mechos, others. The Sky Nomads cannot protect you."

Blanching, Sveta grabbed Georgio's hands. "We must! The High Priestess would never know."

"We pay lip service to the High Priestess, just like Azibar and his Mechos," Georgio said. "I won't risk her wrath if they track you here—and they will. Darwick doesn't give up until his blade is wet. Azibar expects Tagen's return, for he'll die without Mecho aid. Soon the Mechos will begin searching, too."

Sveta shook her head. "No, we can—"

"I won't have the High Priestess harm Nomad Way because of me," Tagen said.

Sveta crossed her arms, looking more helpless than strengthened.

"Threaten?" Georgio scowled. "She would have us butchered."

"Then to hell with the High Priestess!" Tagen cried. "Why don't you fight back?"

Georgio sat back down at the table. Anxiety weighed down his tired, wrinkled features. "Because we can't. Long have the Sky Nomads waited to sail over the Styx again. Long has the way been lost to us."

The filter in Tagen's back gave a slight pop. He winced. "Yes, but—"

"The High Priestess rules the minds of most," Georgio said. "Her crude pleasures make an easy lure to those who cannot recall their past. All we can do is keep our traditions alive in stories and tattoos. Keep our paper maps and charts locked away in metal chests from the rain. That keeps my people's minds free of her distractions."

"Then why hide Sveta?" Tagen's skin grew hot. "Did you put those tattoos on her? They aren't like yours, or the other Nomads I've seen."

Georgio snorted and looked away. "I took her in to save her from the Clowns. If you met the High Priestess, then you saw the heads in her tent. A whisper of love, a whisper of hate…tie a silk thread to the Circus gate."

"So you serve her, while hating her." Tagen flung splinters from his hand.

"I do what I must. My people have survived. They have a better life than most in Meridian." Fierce pride rose in Georgio's eyes.

"Life?" Tagen whispered. "Why doesn't anyone remember their past life? I came here to remember, to find out who I was. To find my wife, who died before me. I thought Meridian would be a place of peace, free of pain. That's what I saw in the cards before coming here. Before I killed myself."

"No." Sveta shook her head. "You can't expect the same results as Radomir. You don't know what you're doing."

"Radomir, the Gutter Knight?" Georgio asked. "He'd turn on his own for a copper pin. Why were you dealing with him?"

"It was his doing." Sveta pointed at Tagen.

Tagen recounted Radomir's behavior and his effects on the Gutter Knight. Georgio paled, while his hands rustled over the charts.

"Never in all the tales of my people, have I heard of such an influence on another person. The old stories of Charon, the cartomancer who once ruled this city, suggest wondrous powers and deeds, but nothing like this."

Tagen rubbed his face. "I keep hearing of this 'Charon'. Did the High Priestess take his place?"

"No. Legend says Charon traveled the Styx in his barge, guiding the dead to other cities. Some say he tired of the task and sailed into unknown lands, while the more popular story is that his lover, the masked Gorgon, stabbed him with a dagger she'd dipped in the Styx. The waters darkened the metal and blinded Charon to its dangers. The invisible blade, so to speak. Either way, Meridian fell into darkness. Its purpose remains corrupted, until Charon and the Gorgon return."

"What purpose?" Sveta asked.

"My old Acheron atlas, passed down generations, says that Meridian is not the dead's final destination," Georgio said. "We are trapped here."

"Then one can sail over the Styx? Do you know of a way?" Tagen half-stood.

Georgio scratched his beard and stared off into space again. Hope and despair mingled in his blue eyes.

Sveta glared at Tagen. "No. Don't you tempt him. Can't you see the danger?"

"Sveta…" Georgio's eyes refocused on them. "Do a reading for him."

"No." Sveta rose. "I don't want to see."

Tagen sensed she already saw something about him. Something she didn't want Georgio to know.

"If he is the Magician…" Georgio extended his hand.

"That prophecy won't help us." Her resentment of him filled the tent.

"Sometimes, prophecy is all an old man has," Georgio said. "Please, Sveta. I'm no cartomancer. The cards are silent for me. Through you, they can speak."

After rummaging through a wooden box in the corner, Sveta returned with a tin sheet Tarot deck. Rather than shuffle them with her hands, the images moved and exchanged places themselves. She hadn't displayed such abilities in the Bazaar where others could see. What else could she do?

And could he do it?

"Lay your hands out, palms up." Sveta still avoided Tagen's eyes. It bothered him that he'd angered her, even hurt her with recollections from her past. How could he control these powers? It rankled him that he couldn't unravel more of his own memories.

Tagen did as she asked while Georgio watched. In the faint lantern light, he compared the tattoos on Georgio's body with Sveta's. No two looked alike. Whereas Georgio's resembled sailor's decorations from Tagen's former world, Sveta's were ambiguous and dark.

Sveta drew the first card. Tagen's heart shriveled with trepidation.

The tin card struck the table. He gasped as if cut. The Knight of Swords seemed to ride across the table, sword raised.

"Injustice," Tagen said. *In his mind, scenes played of Clowns killing people in the streets, or the Bone Guild carving corpses for meat sales. Children played with mechanis dolls with Mannequin's likeness, imposing Azibar's idea of perfection on bodies remaining forever young in the stasis of Meridian.*

"Tagen?" Sveta asked, but she no longer sat before him. *Someone else sat at the table, reaching for him. A candle burned, lighting fine dinner plates and wine glasses.*

The second card landed: Ten of Staves.

Swimming in the pool behind their mansion. Sleek skin breaking the water in summer sunshine. Cuddling before the fireplace during a winter power outage, warmed by blankets, flame, and passion. Marriage arrangements, talk of children, adding a nursery to the mansion. Making love to her in the fountain on the lawn, bodies clasped tight in swirls of crystal blue.

"Alexis…" he murmured.

Traveling the world, shaking hands with men in suits, funneling money into hedge funds, backing charities. Making people smile with jokes, small talk. Making the world a better place, wearing that hidden gun. But always, Alexis was absent.

"Why?" Tagen asked the woman opposite him. *His blurred vision obscured her face. A small ring passed from her hand to his over the gourmet dishes. Nervous, he grabbed the ring and knocked over a wine glass. The shards cut his flesh. Blood mingled with the red wine, bathing the ring. A wedding ring.*

"Why, Alexis?" Tagen struggled to remain seated.

The dinner table dissolved and Georgio's charts reappeared. Wavy lines tossed and flowed over the parchment, carrying the ring with it. Tagen reached for it, but his blood-stained hand smeared the chart.

"Leave him be, Georgio," Sveta said.

A hand snatched the chart. He looked up as a woman in a golden mask stabbed him in the heart.

Tagen's eyes flared open.

Fog saturated the tent. The third card struck the table. It burned an imprint into the wooden surface, then melted into slag. In the ashes lay a paper Magician card.

Georgio and Sveta scooted back from him. Blinking, he realized tears dribbled down his cheeks. He raised his shaking hands. Though he held no ring, dried blood stained both palms. On one of Georgio's charts, a crimson smear formed an arrow pointing at Tagen.

"This was the exact same reading the High Priestess gave you," Sveta murmured. "You didn't act like this in her tent."

Tagen's palms glowed violet as he picked up the Magician card. As soon as he touched it, the character's face morphed into his.

Georgio lurched back. "You are he. The prophecy, as told by the High Priestess." He pointed at the smeared blood arrow on his chart. "You are the way, Tagen. It points to you. You can lead us from Meridian."

Shaking her head, Sveta slammed her deck down. "No! The prophecy says that the Magician will change Meridian. It doesn't say anything else. Nothing about leaving!"

"It's time, Sveta. I remember how to build one. An airship." Georgio's eyes twinkled like a child's upon learning the universe is open to him.

Sveta stood. "Don't you dare! The Clowns will kill everyone in Nomad Way if they so much as suspect a craft being built."

"Tagen has changed my mind," Georgio said. "Emrys and Khyran weren't the Magician. Neither were any of the others before them. Fighting avails us nothing. Someone has come to show us another way."

Leaning on the table, Tagen controlled his breathing. His wish to see more of his past had been granted at last. He wanted to know Alexis's full name and why she'd left him. The reason for her suicide teased the edges of his consciousness. Something had been wrong with him, destroying his life.

"Look at him, Georgio," Sveta said. "You saw him did during my reading. With memory comes pain. Meridian is terrible, but don't let false hope drive us to destruction."

"We also cannot let fear control us. You two get some rest. I need to think and decide." Rising, Georgio met Tagen's eyes. "You have shown me something I shall not forget." He rolled up the smeared chart and left the tent with it.

Tagen continued staring at the Magician card while Sveta stormed out, head in her hands. Red flowers bloomed at the Magician's feet, just like the one he'd picked in the sewers. On one of Sveta's tattoos, a woman sat among similar blossoms. As he lay on the floor, he wanted to know if she had seen the woman's face in his vision.

Not Alexis's. The one wearing the golden mask.

2: Triumph in the Mind

Ducking into a rubbish-filled alley, Radomir caught his breath. He'd ran several streets from the dock where Andromeda had threatened him. Why should he care what that uptight Harlequin thought? Before meeting Tagen, he'd have shoved a knife into her pretty body, yes.

Then why let shame and remorse suffocate him?

True, he'd informed on cartomancers in the past. Even led Clowns to their location, knowing what the High Priestess would do to them. Only profit had mattered then, yes. A few copper slivers, or a Clown woman he could fuck in the sewers. Few things had been beneath Radomir before Tagen's coming. Now, he sunk down in the trash and tried to calm his guilty heartbeat.

"Sorry, so sorry, yes?" Reaching for the darkness above the city, Radomir paused. *Memories of twinkling pinpoints of light, in the skies of his former life, came to mind.*

Stars. They had been called stars.

It was the same shape he'd seen on Tagen's palms, along with a sun and moon. A light from faraway, come to banish Radomir's darkness?

He touched his face and hung his head.

Who had he been before Meridian? When he'd held his infant son Brian, or worked every day in that office. The well-dressed, clean man from his memories wouldn't have tolerated such a person like Radomir. Brian didn't deserve a father who sold people and junk as a peddler of dead dreams on a steam-lit curb.

Radomir thrust himself up from the garbage. Energized, he righted his armor. Readjusted his bronze helmet and tightened his gauntlets. He'd make amends, prove Andromeda wrong. He'd tell others about the Magician and the wonderful memories Tagen awakened. Yes.

He'd do it to honor Brian and the man who used to hold him with loving arms.

3: Confidence

Azibar sighed with steam-vented relief as Mannequin sauntered from the elevator into his throne room. Three disembodied heads sang an aria from a floating pedestal. Gears whirred as their mechanical voices performed in perfect timbre and pitch. They sung so much better than they had in their original, grotesque bodies.

Once again Mannequin's face and form shone with Mecho perfection. How silly of her, allowing a cartomancer to disturb her. Now he knew why the High Priestess brooked no competitors: if one card-shuffling charlatan could annoy a Mecho, what might they do to all Meridian?

"My dear Mannequin, it is so good to see you." Azibar ogled the fine heat sink vents along her torso, the copper-plated skin glistening with fresh oil. Anything could be repaired with the correct application of gears, injectors, and biofluid.

"And you as well, Azibar." There was still something odd about her.

"You still think yourself ugly, repulsive?" He gripped the throne's armrest.

Above them, the singing heads clamped shut.

"No, Azibar. I am ready to give the next lecture at the Rostrum." She bowed.

"Good. Now that is settled, we can start the weapon testing. Soon my Legionnaires will clean up Meridian's streets. Shall we begin?"

"Of course." She pulled a lever on the wall and an alcove opened.

A large Mecho exited it, seven feet in height. Contrasting the tight metallic shell worn by Azibar and Mannequin, the Legionnaire had angular armor and bulging musculature. Veins popped out along bronze-sheathed arms, pumping copious amounts of biofluid. A horizontal, glowing red slit sufficed as eyes. No mouth, no nose. Only two aural cavities, on either side of its head, marked it as anything resembling a human.

Azibar rose from his throne and paced the circular chamber. "The only way to defeat the High Priestess will be to destroy her armed zealots, piecemeal. With each loss, she will doubt the power of her hegemony. Then, her willpower will lessen, and Meridian will abandon her. We'll slaughter her painted fools and frame the carnage on someone else. Have you any ideas?"

"Perhaps the mercenary gangs," Mannequin said. "The Knaves, or the Orphans?"

"No," Azibar said after a few moments. "They often work for the Clowns. I have funds set aside to pay them for the final push on the Circus."

"What of the Blades of Charon?" Mannequin asked.

He laughed. "Their numbers are too small for that ivory lamia to believe Andromeda could manage such a coup again. It nearly succeeded, when she attempted that with Khyran. Hundreds of rebels, perishing for naught."

"I…did not know." She bowed her head.

"Be thankful you did not witness it," Azibar said. "Please, continue."

Mannequin pulled a second lever. Another alcove opened and three Clown warriors tumbled from it. Each wielded a sword. Their eyes bulged with rage.

"What the fuck is this?" one of them asked.

He nodded and the Mecho solider clanked toward the Clowns. A razor-sharp steel blade, three feet in length, extended from its right arm. The Clowns had no illusions about the Mecho's intent and backed away, brandishing their own pitiful weapons.

"The High Priestess will piss on your face for this!" one Clown shouted. The Mecho soldier swiped him in half with the steel blade. Hot blood splashed over the floor.

Azibar nodded in appreciation. "Nice. Let them attack you this time."

The Clowns slashed and stabbed the Legionnaire, but their weapons didn't pierce the thick metal skin. Azibar couldn't deny the crazed bravery of the High Priestess's fanatical followers. Once he showed the city how weak she truly was and exposed her Tarot lies, such fanaticism would be at his command.

"What would you suggest, my dear?" He smiled at Mannequin.

"The…the arc rod?" She turned away from the spectacle.

"Yes, try the arc rod," Azibar said.

A slim rod extended from the Legionnaire's left arm. The Clowns tried fleeing past the solider but it kept them corralled near the wall with its steel blade. As the Clowns yelled and cursed, the metal rod glowed with electrical current. Blue sparks arced from it and struck one of the Clowns, burning his flesh off in patches.

Shrieking, the Clown collapsed to his knees.

Azibar clapped. "Very good! Now, increase the voltage."

More sparks shot from the rod. The Clown's body sizzled with current until a large hole burned through his chest. The blackened, smoking corpse slumped onto the floor. Azibar's nasal filters closed. He hated such stench, just like he did the rest of Meridian's smells. The comforting aroma of oil and burnished metal was far better.

"See, my dear?" He turned Mannequin around to watch.

The final Clown, a female painted in red swirls, licked her blade.

"Such indefatigable resolve. I will ensconce it in copper-sheathed glory, enforcing laws in the people's name." Azibar waved a hand. "Give her a pistol."

One of his guards tossed a clockwork pistol to the Clown. She snatched it and fired three shots at the Legionnaire. Every shot pinged off the thick armor.

"Hold," Azibar said. "You have witnessed the power of the Mechos. You know your High Priestess won't save you. Join me and

I can make you like her." He gestured at Mannequin, who watched the proceedings with her typical, radiant smile.

"Fuck you!" The Clown lunged at him but Azibar motioned for the Legionnaire to stand still.

As her sword rose above her head, Azibar's hand shot out and clasped her throat. The Clown's blade bounced off his copper skin. He held her a moment, staring into her wide, angry eyes. Only now did fear enter them.

"I will cleanse Meridian of you vermin," Azibar said through gritted teeth. "My sun will light the darkened minds clouded by your ivory whore's lies."

The Clown spat at him, but a steam vent on Azibar's chest evaporated the saliva before it reached him. He loved displaying the utter control he'd mastered over his body. Only though order, method, and perfection could people be happy. Still smiling, Azibar snapped the Clown's neck and tossed her to the Legionnaire.

"Take her to the lab and have my technicians put her into a guard shell, as well as that one you dismembered. I want the High Priestess to see her own followers at my back when I face her."

Though the Clowns lacked discipline, Azibar recognized their ferocity. They displayed no care for their own welfare and possessed high pain thresholds. Clown warriors preferred the hand-to-hand, personal kill, which also intimidated enemies. Even his Legionnaires could still be mobbed, their biofluid lines cut. This would have to be a cautious rebellion, despite his superior soldiers.

The only possible allies to be had were the Gutter Knights. Those tinkering scavengers would jump at his offer. As for those ignorant Sky Nomads…well, he supposed the Bone Guild would need a bribe to enter his service. Cartloads of Nomad cadavers should do it.

"If you have these soldiers, Azibar, why the ruse with Tagen?" Mannequin asked.

"Tagen will supply the diversion," Azibar said. "The High Priestess will be so desperate to remove a cartomantic rival, that she will not realize my plan. When she does, I will already be in my new form. She will beg me…the way others have begged her."

Mannequin gently took his hand. "Why do you hate her so?"

He glanced at their joined hands, then pulled free. "She is a tyrant, a succubus drawing the life from this city. I want her deposed and Meridian filled alight with glory."

"Azibar…?"

"You may leave me, my dear." He stared at the wall until her elevator descended.

The disembodied heads started a new aria as he neared the clockwork telescope. A wall panel opened, granting a view of the Circus. Looking through the instrument's eyepiece, he wondered if the High Priestess copulated with her dogs even now.

Perhaps he'd feed her someone's legs, the way his had been hacked off and eaten by her followers. Eaten, even as he'd begged her for mercy. He still recalled that laugh…

The armored men raised their whips once again.

"You do not deserve this city," he whispered.

4: Promised Victory

Khyran hovered over Andromeda's head as she descended the steps from Meridian's street into Lotus Station. Railcar tracks crisscrossed the length of the undercity, though few vehicles remained in service. Most had been appropriated by Azibar for his own use, leaving the rest of the Station dank and desolate.

She entered an area filled with rusted gears and clogged turbines. Two boys and a girl slurped muck from a sewer grate. An old blind man hobbled by on piston-driven legs. Garbage clogged the railcar tracks. Most metal rails had been salvaged by the Mechos. In the cracks between the rails, the Styx awaited any daring to brave the wet darkness.

During all her time in Meridian, she'd never liked coming down here. As if the city might draw her into its bowels and never let go.

Though few steamlamps shone in Lotus Station, fissures in the street and sewer grates allowed in dim light. Enough for Andromeda to see those hurrying toward her.

One emitted a low whistle. Khyran vented steam and blinked.

"Think they'll trust my pitch now?" Even though Khyran couldn't reply, she often answered his motorized workings as if they were words. She had to believe they would speak again.

Andromeda pursed her lips and returned the whistle. Long ago, she'd whistled tunes to smiling crowds in the old Circus. The High Priestess had hated the sound; thus, it served as the Blades' signal.

Saissa and five others stopped a few rails from Andromeda. They all wore black leather outfits, though personal trappings negated them as uniforms. Each had the curved, engraved dagger all Blades of Charon carried. Charonic sigils marked each hilt, blessing the weapon for accuracy and sharpness. Every steel blade had been dipped in the Styx.

"Aye, is you. Found ye message in Doll House, that is. Nice lip marks." Saissa drew a hand across her mouth. "But that Devil Clown searches the city."

"Yeah, Darwick is looking everywhere for two cartomancers," Jaabir said. "We lost four trying to rescue them. You think that paper scrap you left in Doll House is gonna convince us?" A clockwork mask covered half his face and a leather skullcap hid his hair. Steam vented from his right side. His left hand ended in a pincer.

"Jackpot's the Magician, I tell you. Shit, Jaabir, we must troupe together now more than ever." She told them about Azibar injecting Tagen and their separation near the docks.

"That's bad, that is. But we thought Khyran was the Magician, too. The reason why ye took his head to Azibar?" Saissa raised her brows. Jaabir and the others nodded.

Her question chilled Andromeda. All this time, she had never told the Blades of her love for Khyran. Instead, she'd lauded him as the Magician they'd been seeking. Her deal with Azibar also remained secret—he'd keep Khyran's body until Andromeda gave him what he wanted: the path from Meridian. Not that she ever intended to give it to him.

"Maybe there's more than one Magician." Andromeda disliked withholding things from them, especially since no other Blades remained. The ones who'd kept the Stygian Tarot from the High Priestess since her takeover of Meridian, the ones who had fought for the people. Amidst their rebellion, Andromeda had found love in Khyran.

Now it was all a fairy tale that Tagen had dispelled with his arrival.

"Can't be." Jaabir's mask clicked with each word. "That's why we gave Khyran the Stygian deck. Now it's lost."

Andromeda cleared her throat. "Yes, but he failed. The prophecy didn't come true—because Jackpot is our ace note. He must be. As for that deck…I know where it is."

"Aye, then, how's about telling?" Saissa asked. The others waited as the typical screams echoed through Lotus Station. Even Jaabir leaned closer with interest.

"A Sky Nomad produced that paper card in a reading. She has the deck." In truth, Andromeda wasn't certain, but Sveta's tattoos were too familiar and Georgio sheltered her for a reason.

"One who read this?" Saissa held up the card fragment. "Old Georgio don't like ye. Nomads know ye betrayed 'em."

Damn, Saissa could always read her. The longer Andromeda went without the Tarot's embrace, the more naked she felt.

"I'm not fucking perfect. I've lost kinkers, too. You don't want in on this, fine. The fact the High Priestess wants Jackpot dead is enough reason for me to help him. To believe in him." Her fingers tightened on Khyran's box.

Saissa looked from Andromeda to the card fragment, then handed it over. "Aye, I'm with ya. Right, Jaabir?"

"Hell, not gonna let you fight alone, Andromeda. I don't mind dying. Just not for nothing." Jaabir grinned and squeezed her shoulder. The others nodded.

"Nomad Way?" Saissa readjusted her dagger bandoleer.

"Yes…and thanks, everyone." Andromeda hesitated, taking in Lotus Station once more. Wondering if she could hide in a dark corner like all these others. Hiding from Meridian, or from themselves.

Saissa waited while the others departed.

"I'm sorry." Andromeda pinched her shoulder. "Didn't mean to blow you off."

"No apology for love in Meridian." Saissa glanced at Khyran, then kissed Andromeda's cheek. "C'mon."

Love in this city? Only those who still remembered their past could claim to know it. Everyone else had their obsessions and lusts, fed by Meridian's power. Not love.

It had taken her lifetimes to learn the difference.

The way Tagen always tried helping people, his unshakable conviction that he'd find what he was looking for—no one had inspired her like that in a very long time. Not even Khyran had tried to help children in the gutters, or feed the hungry. Andromeda knew that instinct, the pressure on heart and conscious, to aid others. She'd ran the Circus that way. Tagen holding that child reminded her of the person she used to be.

The one she still could be.

And the way he'd kissed her—she'd not wanted to let him go. She craved that contact, that sharing, that need to touch another human being with emotional intimacy.

But the more Andromeda thought of Tagen, the more guilt she felt concerning her former lover. And the heavier the guilt...the more she hated using Tagen for vengeance.

Trailing behind Saissa, Andromeda avoided looking down at the Styx's black depths. Khyran once mentioned a vision he'd seen, of her dancing over the Styx itself.

Those dark waters had long swallowed her dreams.

VIII.

Strength

1: Closing the Jaws of the Lion

Tagen looked up from where he lay on the floor. Leaning against the tent's central pole, Sveta watched him. She wore clean clothes, a darker blue than her previous set.

"How long did I sleep?" He rose and sat at Georgio's table.

"Six tolls of the Clock." Every few moments, her gaze flicked to his wrists.

"Is that where…?" She took up a stool beside him. "I can't imagine how you—"

"What did you see?" He sat up straight.

"You ate dinner with a woman. She gave you a ring. You were angry and hurt. I saw you weeping over her body…then you sliced…" Sveta paused and stared upward. "I saw you die."

"How did you see that, when I didn't?" He half rose from his stool, staring at her. "Why you, and not me? How are we both seeing these visions?"

He tried to concentrate on a Tarot image. Anything to help him understand. The Strength card came to mind. Yes, he'd make them tell him what this was all about, force them to the ground just like the woman on the card, use this damn magic to find her…

Different images crashed through his mind instead: *swords slicing through rotten staves, coins plunking into dirty cups. Falling from a tower.*

His hands spread out as Sveta's Tarot deck floated before him. The cards flipped and shuffled themselves, then landed onto the table in a neat pile. Biofluid stung his veins. The filter in his back sputtered.

Sveta jerked back. "How did you do that? Those are my cards."

Tagen shook his head. "I don't...I tried to use cartomancy again."

"You're still a novice. Your raw talent might harm us both." She edged away from him, rubbing her tattooed arms.

"No, I can do this..." He focused on what he thought he saw in her body art.

Dark tendrils writhed at the edges of his vision as Sveta's tattoos jumped out at him. They contained more Tarot characters and images, more uncertainty.

His mind's eye displayed dark streets, Mecho eyes, and a black flower strangling him with its roots. As he touched the images, symbols burned into his mind.

Obelisks. Tomes. Masks. Pathways. The suits of a different Tarot.

"Tagen?" Sveta asked in a worried voice.

The symbols faded from sight. He now stood beside Sveta, hands coursing down her arms and over her flat stomach. Touching her cleared his mind, replaced his depression with determination. Each tattoo promised to reveal something different.

"What the hell are you doing?" Sveta shivered beneath his touch.

His hands kept traveling along her flesh. Seeking. Demanding. One more tattoo might reveal Alexis, might show him all those precious memories. Only when he reached her thighs, did Sveta slap his hands away.

"Take your damn hands off me! Asshole." She drew back, face flushed.

Tagen looked down at his hands, then her face. His cheeks burned. "I didn't mean...just so many pictures. I saw paths, Sveta. In your tattoos."

"Hell, you should have, as much as you kept pawing me. I'm not like Andromeda, I don't let just anyone touch me. Asshole. Those biofluid hands of yours didn't know when to quit."

He held up his still glowing hands. "No, I saw them. Really saw them. I think your tattoos are, I don't know—cartomantic or something."

Indignation drained from Sveta's face. He risked nearing her again and pointed at the tattoo beneath her wound.

"When you showed me…that, I saw a card there. The Death card. It wasn't until then that I could see the ambulance and—"

"Bullshit. Meridian's urges influence you after all." Sveta stormed from the tent.

"Damn it." Rubbing his face, Tagen sat back down. He knew what he'd seen. Somehow, he sensed Sveta had seen it, too. Her fear seemed more about her tattoos than him touching her. In the sewer she hadn't minded his closeness…so why now?

The wedding ring entered his mind and Tagen wondered if some past sin plagued him in this afterlife he'd entered by mistake—or by fate. Was it his fault, then? The blood rushed to his temples.

"What I am supposed to—"

Sveta's cards shuffled themselves on the table.

Energy vibrated through his body. Shadows fluttered in his peripheral vision.

If he was a cartomancer…this so-called Magician…then what would the cards show him, through his own reading? He took a deep breath. Emotion welled in his heart.

"Will I find Alexis in Meridian?" Tagen drew the top card and laid it facedown.

The Strength card again.

What the hell did it mean? That the chance of finding her here remained strong? That she was strong enough to survive Meridian?

Turning the card over, its metallic finish reflected his own face back at him in the lantern light.

"I will find you."

2: Messenger

Pushing aside the leather flap, Radomir entered the Gutter Knight den. Many such lairs existed throughout Meridian. The Knights obeyed an unspoken code of mutual protection and hiding. Members could stay in any den, provided they didn't steal or over-crowd the rest. He usually enjoyed socializing with his fellows, but now his metal teeth clinked together with anxiety.

Inside, two steam lanterns revealed garbage mounds, spare parts, bones, and six other Knights. All wore the usual black-stained, filth-encrusted armor. They reached for pistols or daggers until Radomir spoke the cant.

"Nodule coil double screw. Empty kelp vat?"

Lezzek snickered and put away his pistol. "We have room for you. Hurry and close the flap."

Radomir sat on a cushion stapled together from Clown wigs and gnarled leather. "Good trading, yes?"

"That aperture netted me this piece." Lezzek drew the pistol again. Its injector coils and bronze sight gleamed in the lantern light. A bronze wheel was attached to the hammer and a wooden grip wrapped around a silver trigger.

"Pretty nice, huh? I always haggle for the best stuff. Might trade it to a Mecho for some bitching new eyes. I hear they can see in the dark with those glowing green ones."

"Find loot better in alleys, yes," Radomir said, but neither the pistol, nor Lezzek's plans, excited him. It was all so petty and empty, just scavenging, stealing, and bartering.

One Knight opened a damp leather sack. Within its dark folds, a young woman's head caught the light. The Knight chuckled and twirled the woman's hair. The others discussed visiting the Bone Guild later. Another Knight, new to the group, stitched bloodied squares of flesh over his own cheeks.

"Need new life, yes." Radomir sucked in though his teeth.

"You okay, Radomir? Acting awful damn strange lately. Ever since we ran from that bastard in the Row." Lezzek peeled back his cheeks and gnawed a gristle-caked bone. Mismatched ingots and stones served as teeth and his gums squirted biofluid.

His comrades' appearance and activities had never bothered Radomir before. Now he wanted to shout at them. There was so much more than this horrid existence, yes.

"Magician," Radomir whispered.

"Huh?" Lezzek chuckled. The other Knights sniffed or spat.

"Magician!" Radomir stood and kicked the cushion away. "Showed me memories. Can show everybody memories, yes. Before Meridian. Can change you."

Lezzek cast the bone aside and pulled his cheeks back in place. "So? You believe that prophecy shit? Maybe you should take us on a good hunt, if you're still pack leader. How about Boulevard? Might find some nice stuff this time."

"No more hunt, no more Gutter Knight, yes? Hunt for truth now. Help Magician."

"Truth's not worth anything on the street." Lezzek belched and spat a bit of gristle on Radomir's boot. Once, Radomir had slashed off Lezzek's lower jaw for such an insult. The other Knights measured him with their eyes.

"Magician helps remember…" Radomir spread his hands, imploring. "Life before this place. Life full of friends, full of…full of beauty."

The other Knights laughed.

Radomir grabbed the sack and poured out heads, limbs, organs. "See life, see beauty? Beauty you killed, for Meridian. Life, you took…for Meridian."

Their tense silence annoyed Radomir even further.

Lezzek leaned forward. "Don't you remember your Gutter oath? That everything is ours for the taking—but Meridian will never take us?"

Raising his voice, Radomir thrust his hands into the air. "Barter truth? Barter dignity? Pack leader paid in shame, yes. Shame and loneliness."

"Maybe you should find another den—before we barter you." Lezzek caressed the pistol's handle. The other Knights leered.

Radomir met their stares, then left the den. Coarse laughter echoed behind him.

3: Liberation

Georgio entered the tent with a bundle of clothes. A curved sword now hung from the old Nomad's side. "Sveta appeared upset. What did you do to her?"

"I…well, I touched some of her tattoos. Tried to tell her I saw things in them, but she got pissed off and left." Tagen spread his hands. "It's not what you think."

"And it's not what you think, either. When I found Sveta, she was lying naked in an alley. I saw the glyphs on her palms, so I brought her here and gave her some Nomad clothes." He thrust the bundle at Tagen. "Now I do the same for you."

"Thanks." Tagen grimaced as biofluid crept further into his system. The filter clicked louder than before.

"If you had a copper heart, I could fix you," Georgio said.

Tagen clenched his fists at the growing pain in his body. "Why did Andromeda give Azibar your secrets?"

Loosing a heavy sigh, Georgio sat down. "Desperation."

"Did he gain knowledge of airships or something?" Tagen asked. "I saw scale models of them in his lobby."

"Andromeda used to run the Circus. By the Styx, she was lovelier then than she is now. Like the legendary Harlequins of the Elysian Gardens. Her acrobatic and musical shows delighted people." A wistful smile stole over Georgio's face.

Thinking of Andromeda's willful eyes and supple grace, Tagen wiped sweat from his brow. He still felt guilty, leaving her. "And then the High Priestess came."

"The High Priestess redefined the Tarot with her powerful cartomancy and took the Circus for her own. Soon after, she claimed all Meridian. Or did Meridian claim her?"

"So the city can still seduce those it grants its magic to?" Tagen asked.

"Those most of all," Georgio said.

The one boon he'd found in this afterlife was the magic and it posed the most risk to him. Tagen frowned. "What happened to Andromeda then?"

Georgio turned a ring on his finger. "Andromeda has fought the Clowns ever since. She thought Azibar could help, with his mechanis genius. Even I'll admit he can do wonders with it—and horrors. Yet, he's no better than the High Priestess. That's why the Mecho District has most of the city's metal and mechanis engineers: Azibar hoards it. That copper tyrant lacks the secret of airship construction. Otherwise, he'd have one."

"Can you really escape that way? Sveta doesn't think much of your plan."

"Sveta doesn't believe in the Magician Prophecy," Georgio said. "Maybe I shouldn't myself. Too many others believe it, however. Enough to kill. That is the paradox of Meridian. We are all dead, yet we can die again here. Why, no one knows."

Tagen leaned forward. "Has the city always been like this? The violence, the grime…people eating each other. You said it became corrupted."

"If Charon's heart you fix, it is your luck to go over the Styx— that's an old Sky Nomad proverb." Georgio stopped turning the ring and looked at him.

"His heart?" Tagen asked. "Does that have something to do with the legend of him getting stabbed? If you fix his heart, you escape over the Styx?"

"Someone must take Charon and the Gorgon's place, for Meridian to resume its role: that of redemption."

Tagen's mouth went dry. "What do you mean?"

"Andromeda told you half the truth—that only those who recall their past can escape. Your past informs who you are, your decisions. Without it, you are an empty shell, filled by the city's compulsions. Yet, Meridian must be ruled by one not corrupted by its power—else we are all trapped here, even those who remember, like you and me."

"And what happens to those who find 'redemption'?" Tagen asked.

"No one truly knows." Georgio glanced at his charts and books. "I believe we could leave the city, like the Sky Nomads of old. Like Andromeda told you."

"I left her on the dock, while escaping the Clowns." Tagen looked at his feet.

Georgio smiled sadly. "If anyone can survive out there, it is that Harlequin."

"She believes in a past life, too." Tagen gripped the table's edge. "Most other people—the High Priestess, Darwick, Azibar—they called me a heretic, or a fool. Radomir thanked me for showing him pieces of his. Sveta hates me for unlocking hers."

"That girl doesn't hate you. Yet she hurts. People often deny their pain, or unpleasant things about themselves. Some of us face it anyway." He held Tagen's eyes for a long moment.

"You're sure?"

"Clean up using that water trough over there and eat this. Then go talk to her." Georgio left a covered bowl on the table and departed.

Tagen rubbed the glyphs on his hands. Maybe he'd come to Meridian, because he'd been afraid. Because the woman at the table had rejected him.

Alexis? Or the masked woman? Did they seek redemption?

After stripping, Tagen washed the sewer filth from his limbs, using the trough water. The water gave off a slight spice scent, similar to what he'd smelled on Sveta in the Bazaar. The Sky Nomads possessed excellent manners, for none had commented or let on that he and Sveta smelled like a latrine.

Next, he put on a blue leather vest, black leggings, and black leather boots. They fastened with tight clasps. He examined his thicker biceps and veiny forearms. Not bad, maybe he could at least fight now. He glanced down at his muscular, engorged chest, the spidery black lines just under the skin. The filter vibrated in his back harder than usual.

By now, the covered bowl's spicy aromas drew his attention. Though the biofluid kept hunger in check, he was curious. He removed the earthenware cover. A cloud of scented vapors bathed his face. Fried moss, spiced mushrooms, lichen mush, and kelp bread made him smile. The pile of pomegranate seeds, though, gave him pause. Where did Georgio find such a delicacy? Tagen ate it all with relish. It was the first sensation in Meridian to make him feel human again.

Human. Could he call himself that now? He studied his graying hands, tainted with biofluid. The same hands that had broken that Guild member's neck.

A place to find redemption…Georgio's words sobered him. He had to control himself. He'd not return to Alexis as a murdering psychopath.

Tagen exited the flap where Sveta had left. Several open pens lay behind Georgio's tent, each filled with old navigational equipment. Everything from simple paddles, to complicated objects like sextants or telescopes. The Sky Nomads hid much the Clowns hadn't destroyed.

Leaving the pens, he entered an atrium. An extensive dock waited below, swathed in shadow. Three small pomegranate trees made him smile. Their red blossoms were the exact same flower from the sewer—and his visions.

Several steam lanterns burned in an enclosure housing a large globe-like object. Notched markings ran along a metal band encircling the globe. Tagen tried to remember if the globe's continents matched those of his former world. A secondary metal band displayed what he assumed were stars, possibly even planets.

"It's an astrolabe." Sveta walked out from behind it and looked him up and down. "I see Georgio finally gave you some clothes."

"He also wanted us to talk."

Sveta ambled around the astrolabe, not looking at him. The lanterns lit up her tattoos with tranquil luminescence while she traced a hand over the globe's surface. At her touch, each star lit for a moment, shining dull yellow, fierce blue, or harsh red.

"Georgio wants many things," Sveta said. "Things he can't possibly have. Things you have tempted him with."

"Why blame me?" Tagen asked.

Sveta whirled on him. "Because you might take from me the only family I've ever known! Then you show me the family I once had? I'll never see them, hold them—even know them as people. All I have is the memory of them weeping, while I died in that stupid ambulance."

"Not because I wanted to—"

Sveta strode toward him. "Georgio had given up on leaving Meridian, given up on the Magician ever coming here to save us. How dare you prey on the lost dreams of an old man! You will build up his hopes, and the hopes of others. I wonder where you'll be when those hopes are crushed in this cesspit of a city."

"You act like I chose to affect these people, or that I chose to make Radomir remember. I didn't, no more than I chose for you to see. Besides, what the hell is wrong with hope? Why do you keep going on, if all you have is anger?"

"This place helped me deal with my anger," Sveta said in a terse whisper.

"What are you afraid of?"

"I'm not afraid." She inched away.

Tagen grasped her shoulders. "You think this is all you'll ever have, and you fear these images on your skin."

As his fingers brushed her tattoos, his Sun glyph flashed. Sveta gasped.

In his mind, the atrium morphed into a dining room. Sveta sat with her family at a table, eating and laughing. A younger man and older woman sat beside Sveta—her siblings? Clinking glasses, warm stares. Smiling faces, hearty laughter.

"No," Sveta mumbled.

Glyphs burning hot, Tagen tried to stop the vision, but the room became a restaurant. *A waiter brought more wine to a table where Tagen and a woman sat. She turned away from him, beckoning the waiter. A wedding ring twinkled on her finger. Lifting a wineglass for a toast, his heart beat with happiness.*

Gathering his will, Tagen concentrated on that moment. Tarot images flipped through his mind. Which could he use to open the memory further? Burst through the gulf separating him from all he'd been, and—

The atrium reappeared around them. Tagen held the masked woman close.

"Tagen, let go."

He stood over Alexis's body again. The wedding ring mocked him with a gleam as he swiped the knife over his left wrist.

On the Ten of Cups, the High Priestess beckoned him to Meridian.

"Please, let me go."

The masked woman became Sveta in his arms. Meridian rose above them in towering monoliths of decay and despair. The city's collective suffering flowed through a huge gutter into his heart. Dragging him down.

Tagen pressed Sveta closer, his fingers seeking more tattoos.

Obelisks. Tomes. Masks. Pathways. The path from Meridian, charting through darkest water. Tarot suits filled with ambiguous images, tinted sepia green and dark violet. Naked women in masks, winged fiends perched on obelisks. Grimoires with damask pages, or torn signposts along a footpath. The same block-like script he'd spied on the black dagger marked each card.

"Tagen?" The astrolabe's faint light reflected off Sveta's silver hair clasps as the visions finally left his thoughts. Though the atrium appeared normal again, Tagen quivered. Now he leaned on her more for support, than to examine her tattoos.

Releasing her, Tagen staggered back. He had glimpsed a thousand doorways, a thousand faces unmasked. A veil had lifted—with him behind it. Could he handle further exposure to the mysteries imprinted on her skin? *Once again, his mind displayed the flower falling on a woman's cheek, in pools of blood.*

Sveta helped him to a bench nearby. "Are you all right?"

"Haven't you seen these things?" Tagen asked. "Your tattoos?"

Sveta looked into his eyes. "I have. That is why I fear them."

"But why?"

"Each is a mirror, reflecting a person I don't want to become," Sveta said. "Each is a door I don't want to open."

"What if we open them together?" Tagen gripped her hand. "She might be beyond those doors, those mirrors…"

"I have seen greater misery in Meridian. That's why I'd hoped we could both hide here…but you will only bring more pain, more death."

He released her hand and slumped on the bench.

"Did you love her? The woman with the ring?" Sveta studied him.

"Of course. She was my wife."

Light rain misted over them. It beaded on his skin, reflecting the astrolabe's light.

"I still don't believe you're the Magician," she said.

"I don't care what I am. But I can't help what I do."

4: Missionary

Radomir withdrew the steampainter from beneath his armor. In the past, he'd scrawled insulting graffiti over Clown Tarot images, or advertised spare parts for sale in Vagrant's Row with sprayed letters. Now he put the device to different use.

After making sure none saw him on the street leading toward Nomad Way, Radomir painted his fourth such sign, comprising one single word.

What would it do to people, or would they even notice it?

Mere mention of the Magician would awaken others, yes. Everyone should recall their past, their true identities. Every letter he painted was an ode to Brian. The memories of his infant son were proof something better existed past the Styx, past the darkness.

He would seek Tagen out again, once he'd proven to Andromeda that he wasn't a Gutter Knight anymore. But first, Radomir wanted all Meridian to open its eyes.

5: Fortitude

After leaving the atrium, Tagen and Sveta passed through Georgio's tent and entered the street. Neither spoke. Outside, several Nomads huddled in groups, laughing or dancing to mazurka tunes. Georgio leaned against a lamp post nearby.

"I can't believe I'm in the same city." Tagen smiled as a girl danced, waving a silk streamer. The blue, translucent fabric tinted their reality into azure shades.

Sveta gestured at the scene. "This is what I will lose, if I release what's in my tattoos. How can you expect me to do that?"

Moments passed as they continued watching the revelry. Tagen finally faced her.

"I don't," he said. "But I not giving up on finding my wife."

Sveta slowly nodded.

"Glad to see you two worked out your differences." Georgio walked over to them. "How do you like your new clothes, Tagen?"

"Much better, thanks." Tagen ran a hand over the finely tooled vest, replete with navigational etchings. "What's the meaning of this color, or the symbols?"

"Our oral traditions relate a time when the skies were blue over certain cities in the Styx," Georgio said. "We wear blue to honor that. I don't know why those symbols appear on cartomancer's palms, but Sky Nomads used them to navigate the air above the Styx. Of course, that is only legend now. Few of my own people believe this."

"Then why believe in the Magician?" Pain traveled along Tagen's back and up his arms. The filter spurted.

Staring faraway, Georgio sighed. "Emrys, an old Tarot seer, once told me that the Magician is 'a prince from another world, on his travels through this one'. Emrys is dead now, killed by the High Priestess's agents. He lived in Meridian long before my arrival, even before Andromeda came. That man never told a bad fortune."

"And that's good enough for you?" Tagen shook his head.

"Look around you," Sveta said. "People need to believe in something. There is nothing here but unfulfilled desire and pain. The Magician is supposed to change all that. Without those things, the High Priestess will lose control."

"And you, Georgio?" Tagen asked. "You think I can chart a course from Meridian? Azibar wants the same thing. What makes you any different?"

Sveta punched Tagen's shoulder. "You know better than that. Asshole."

"He's right to ask," Georgio said. "It's true, people need to believe in something, whether it's the Clown Tarot, Charon, or the supposed perfection offered by Azibar."

"But what do the Sky Nomads offer?" Tagen asked.

"Nomads find happiness in each other, or in our tales of heroism and exploration," Georgio said. "We take care of our own."

"Then why leave?" Tagen asked.

The same question appeared in Sveta's eyes. The mazurka picked up in tempo. Now he knew why the area was bordered in canvas: it was a visual and auditory barrier obscuring the city outside.

"We are in Meridian's stasis," Georgio said. "Charon, for whatever reason, forsake his duty. Stranding us here. We've all died once. We shouldn't have to again."

"But if Charon abandoned this city—what would it matter if the High Priestess loses control?" Tagen asked.

"Meridian needs strong rulers to reverse its decay," Georgio said. "I fear what would happen, should no one command its power. Where the dead would go."

Hesitating, Tagen glanced from Sveta to Georgio. "What do you remember?"

Sveta glared but Georgio smiled. "I was an explorer for a king and queen, traveling in waterborne vessels. I don't recall much besides that."

Concentrating on Georgio, Tagen saw himself on a wooden a ship, plowing through sapphire waters. *A sandy shore with lush tropical foliage awaited him. The vision blurred, then refocused on Georgio. The old Nomad stood on the shore with men in steel armor and baggy pants. Georgio planted a banner in the sand and raised a sword. Dusky, half-naked people watched from behind palm trees.*

"What is it?" Sveta asked.

"No, it's okay." He described his vision.

"How can you do that without a deck of cards?" Sveta asked.

Georgio shrugged. "He is the Magician."

Before she could reply, Tagen waved a hand. "Wait. You said something about the city controlling the High Priestess. If I keep doing these…things, I'll be, what? As cruel as she is?"

Georgio shook his head. "Only if you give in to it. Emrys once said that if a cartomancer abuses his or her talent, then Meridian claims them. They are no longer themselves, but instruments of the city's darkness. Andromeda told me, long ago, that dark shadows always hung at the edge of her sight, as the city constantly fed her magic, while tempting her with it."

Tagen drew in a long breath and shuddered. Those same shadows had plagued him ever since waking up in that alley.

"What would she know?" Sveta asked. "She's just using Tagen."

"I know what he put on my chart," Georgio said. "The line pointed to him."

A Nomad man rushed up to Georgio and whispered in his ear. Georgio paled.

"Clowns are coming this way, about twenty warriors. No doubt searching for you two. Sveta, take him beneath the city. Along the old railcar system."

"Oh shit," Sveta said. "I'm sorry, Georgio. I shouldn't—"

"No, you needed to come here. We'll be fine. But get him somewhere other than here. Boulevard, perhaps." He hugged her, then stared at Tagen. "Don't get caught, either of you. I'm not ready to act yet, so don't force my hand."

Tagen nodded as Sveta tugged him toward an alley behind Georgio's tent. After pushing aside a pile of rubbish, she revealed a hatch with a ring set in it. They pulled it open. Darkened steps awaited them.

Shouts echoed over Nomad Way.

"I swear, if anything happens to Georgio—"

"It won't." Tagen pulled her along. Hot biofluid dripped down his back.

IX.

The Hermit

1: In Search of Truth

Nomad Way's canvas edifices and tranquil streets made Darwick itch all over. No Tarot imagery, no Clowns screwing each other, not even a fucking Bone Guild kiosk to feed him. Did these people think they were above the High Priestess, then? Why did she tolerate their bullshit?

Several Nomads standing near a steamlamp stopped their conversation and watched him. Darwick strutted over, patting his sword blade.

"Pay attention, shitheads, or you'll give us an excuse to burn the rest of what you got. I'm looking for a newcomer to Meridian. Name's Tagen. Long black hair, blue eyes. Stupid fucker escaped the Circus with some Sky Nomad tramp. She has braided hair and crazy body tattoos." He circled around the group while other Nomads peered from their tents. Their silent, knowing stares made him spit.

An older man stepped from the group. "We haven't seen anyone like that. Yet the Nomad woman, you say—what did she do?"

Darwick flattened his lips. "Both are cartomancers. The High Priestess wants 'em for questioning."

A lie. He had permission to kill the pair on sight. These assholes didn't need to know everything, even if they claimed allegiance to the High Priestess.

"We don't have any cartomancers among us, just a few simple fortune tellers loyal to the Clown Tarot." The old man stared back, calm as a Mecho guard. Darwick recognized him as the violin player from the Bazaar.

"What's your name?" Darwick asked. "I've seen you too much here lately."

"Georgio," the old man said. "If we see anyone like those two, we'll bring them to the High Priestess ourselves. We don't pander to heretics here."

"My ass. We'll keep searching, but I'm leaving some Clowns here to catch 'em. You know, in case they drop in sometime." This Georgio prick was too confident. The district's colored lanterns, all these unpainted faces…his grip tightened on the sword and he sucked in air through his nose.

"Though it wouldn't hurt to peek while we're here, right?" Darwick grunted low in his throat. "Search their fucking tents!"

Georgio didn't flinch while the Clowns shredded a few tents with their swords. Others smashed steam lanterns with their clubs. Rather than the usual pleasure, though, an emptiness gnawed at Darwick's guts. Seeing the cozy homes and relaxed atmosphere ruined by his Clowns made his heart ache more.

They had peace, some measure of contentment. A naïve satisfaction with their isolated culture, free of noise, obscenity, and strife. He hated them for it.

He held her as the men galloped to the ranch. Trembling, she squeezed his hand.

Deep, yearning pain overcame Darwick and he hunched over. Who was she?

"I'm scared," she whispered.

"Me too." He stiffened as the horses cantered to a stop. "But I ain't leaving you."

The love in her eyes helped him ignore the guns now aimed at them.

Darwick broke a lantern, forcing the emotion away.

2: The Light of the World

The sounds of Clowns haranguing Nomads filtered down the staircase where Tagen and Sveta had fled. The stone steps were slippery with mildew and ended abruptly in a wall of garbage. They dug through the trash-filled enclosure, then stumbled onto a spacious landing.

A great curved tunnel, hundreds of feet wide, greeted them. Other platforms and landings were spaced along the sides. A few steamlamps kept the darkness at bay. In the tunnel's center, a rusted rail track meandered into the unlit distance. Between the platform and track lurked a black void, bridged with disintegrating concrete walks. Cloying moisture hung in the air, its ancient rot filling Tagen's nostrils.

"Where are we?" he asked.

"Lotus Station. The Clowns know about it too, so hurry."

They left the landing for the track, which lacked several rails. Tagen had to jump over empty spaces, where far below, utter darkness awaited. Occasionally it reflected the steamlamp light back at him.

It was the surface of the Styx.

Though less people occupied the undercity, their numbers still surprised him. Naked waifs leaned against each other, children with clockwork torsos ran around in private games and a man dragged a dead woman into an alley. Blackened, mildewed trash lay in scattered clumps. Frescoes of a masked woman could be seen on the walls behind an epoch of grime.

"Where are we going?" Tagen asked, breathing hard. The biofluid inside him conferred strength but each step sent the substance deeper into his body. His toes and fingers hurt, while his whole back burned as if he stood beside an open flame.

"Not sure yet. Maybe Boulevard, I don't know. Just keep up." Sveta's slim body displayed its raw athleticism: firm leg muscles contracted, then released. No wonder she dressed sparingly—Sveta moved like a leopard in a jungle.

Stubbing his foot on a bent rail, Tagen lurched toward the Styx.

She grabbed his hand as part of the track slipped into the waters below. The splash echoed throughout Lotus Station.

Tagen caught his balance on another rail. "Thanks."

As he released her hand, Tagen focused on the rails ahead, the path it created over the Styx and through Lotus Station. Though shadows hedged his eyesight, Tagen concentrated. He barely avoided another hole in the rail. A chill numbed his limbs.

Trying to ignore the depths below, Tagen imagined a Tarot card in his mind. One with some kind of illumination.

The Hermit. Holding a lantern aloft against the darkness of fear and ignorance.

A path appeared, superimposed over the track. Ethereal shadows in his peripheral vision revealed more holes and cracks. The Star glyph on his palm thrummed.

He followed, and this time he knew the correct places to step, the pitfalls to avoid. Soon he ran alongside Sveta. She gave a grudging smile.

They passed through a section where no steamlamps shone. Stepping with confidence, they maintained their pace in total darkness. Tagen suspected he could close his eyes and find his way anywhere he wanted. Anywhere, to anyone, to anytime…

A door opened in his mind.

Georgio stood on a dock, holding a lantern. Below the dock, a man drowned in the Styx. Images of masks floating in water flowed into Tagen's consciousness. Tarot cards spread before him, each showing his face in some strange pose or situation, as if he were every character in the deck. One card flipped over. It showed Andromeda, walking a track similar to what he and Sveta now traveled.

She clutched a Magician card to her chest. Searching for him.

Tagen ran faster.

She cared about him. No one else in Meridian had displayed it as much as she.

Had Alexis cared about him? Did she, still?

He floundered in the water near the dock, until a hand pulled him up.

The vision faded as they entered another part of Lotus Station. Flickering lamps dispelled the darkness once again. Sveta jumped off the track to a platform. Tagen followed, heart pumping too fast.

"Andromeda is down here, too." Tagen gulped air and coughed. Black flecks struck his hand. The bitter tang of metal filled his mouth.

"How do you know?" Sveta looked around with a grimace.

"I guess it's this magic again," he breathed, wiping his brow.

"She's still—" Sveta hushed as a clockwork woman with two heads argued with herself on the platform.

"Bitch, I need that arm!"

"It's on my side, hussy!" The women's voices echoed down the Station. Others stared at them with either hungry or fearful eyes.

"So?" Sveta said. "Andromeda knew we were going to Nomad Way—probably led Darwick right to us."

A group of slobbering children and the two headed woman approached them.

Tagen shook his head. "I trust her. She wouldn't have rescued us and then told Darwick. Come on, this place is getting to me."

A child with piston legs and an oversized bronze mouth neared them.

"Me too," Sveta whispered, backing up with him to the platform's edge.

"Food," the child said, its voice creaking with damaged modulation.

With so much augmentation, Tagen couldn't ascertain the child's gender. Who would do such a thing? More cyborgs came from alleys and darkened corners, gaping in total madness.

"The Wretched." Sveta gripped Tagen's hand. Heat from her palm glyphs radiated up his arm. "We should go. Now."

"No, stay," moaned an armless, naked woman with clockwork legs. She rushed Tagen, vents in her legs and back hissing like snakes. Black saliva dripped from her mouth onto her bulbous, copper breasts. Her hair had been ripped away, leaving raw scalp. One eye glimmered faint green.

As Tagen gazed into the woman's single eye, his mind shifted.

From mental shadows the Emperor card appeared in his thoughts, his copper throne sitting atop a pile of crushed, maligned humanity.

"Azibar did this." He jerked as something hot and moist swiped his right cheek.

Blinking away the vision, Tagen edged away from the armless woman as she tried to lick him again. Sveta clutched at him while the children edged closer.

"Love me." The woman pouted her lips. "Love me, Magician."

"Why'd you call me that?" Tagen asked.

"Down here, we see who you are," the woman said. "Love me!"

Sveta's hands dug into his sides. "She's crazy, can we just go?"

"Wait a—"

The misshapen children rushed them. Clockwork jaws clanged open, emitting shrill cries. His foot slipped from the platform but he cast out his right arm while holding Sveta's hand in his left. As they both tumbled over, he grabbed the adjacent track's edge. Fingers dug through rust and grime, clasping the metal. Sveta grunted and held on.

On the platform, the armless woman pined after Tagen. In her damaged Mecho eye, he caught his reflection: right arm extended upward, holding the rail. Left arm extended downward, holding Sveta. The Magician pose: as above, so below.

The Styx yawned beneath them—an unknown temptation, the ultimate mystery.

A hand rose from the black waters, offering him red, bulbous pomegranate seeds. The woman across the dining table passed him a bowl filled with them.

Tagen's grip weakened. What was the city offering him?

Each of the chalices on the Ten of Cups overflowed with the crimson seeds. The woman at the table beckoned for him to drink from one.

He'd killed himself once…maybe he could do it again and escape Meridian.

"No," Sveta said below him. "Don't you dare."

"It worked before." A chill permeated him.

"Damn it, don't drag me down with you!" Sveta cried.

Somewhere in the distance, the Alueryic Clock tolled eleven times.

The children swarmed over the armless woman on the platform. With rusted iron teeth they bit hunks from her still-firm, curvaceous body. She didn't scream or resist, but continued staring at Tagen.

"Remember me, Magician," she said before a small girl chomped her throat in a geyser of red. Her single Mecho eye dimmed to black.

The hand dropped the seeds into the Styx.

"I'm sorry, Alexis," Tagen mumbled. "I couldn't find you here—"

"Tagen!" a voice further down Lotus Station shouted. The echo filled the subterranean passages like a million voices calling his name. The chill evaporated from his body, replaced with a stinging, desperate heat.

Tagen's right hand slipped an inch. Sveta gasped below him.

"Don't give up," she said. "Don't flee your pain."

"I'm not, I just can't hold on—"

A shape with glowing green eyes hovered near Tagen's face.

"Khyran!" Tagen grinned. "Where's Andromeda?"

Khyran landed on the railing and inserted his lower half into a slimy socket.

"Look out!" Sveta screamed.

The clockwork children, finished with the woman, had linked themselves together into a human bridge. Impatient hands, some dripping blood, clawed after them. In another moment they'd snatch Tagen from the rail.

Something loud clicked above them as Khyran's head turned in the socket. Tagen turned away as a bloodied child's hand neared his cheek. He gritted his teeth and summoned the biofluid inside him.

"Grab the railing, Sveta!" His corded muscles bunched with power, then flung her up to the rail as the children reached Tagen. Pincer hands dug into his vest. Saw-blade fingers nipped his pants. He met their eyes and concentrated.

"Tell me," he said. "Tell me who you are."

The metal rail melted beneath his right palm glyphs as his mind's eye opened.

Lives ripped asunder. Cast down into filth pens. Used to perfect Azibar's Mechos. No longer children, but cyborgs enslaved to lower instincts.

A pang stung his heart. These children had never wanted such burdens or horrors. *In his mind, a child rode a horse through a lush garden. The sun blazed overhead.*

Bronze-claw hands grazed his neck.

In his previous life, he'd aided children's charities. Fed them, clothed them. As a cop, protected them. He concentrated harder, so they'd see and feel the hope within him.

The railing clicked again. Khyran hovered away. Sveta said something but Tagen maintained his focus. Using the power of Meridian, he blinded the children's consciousness with the garden's sun.

The children cried out with mechanical whines and warbling squeals. Lotus Station rung with their macabre chorus.

Tagen's grip slipped from the railing.

Two hands yanked Tagen onto the rail. The track shuddered, then moved from the platform with grinding noises. A railcar glided down the track. It had a flat surface with short, crenellated sides and a piloting console. Steam billowed from vents underneath it.

Andromeda hauled him into the railcar, then collapsed onto it herself. Sveta knelt beside Tagen, shaking her head. Six people in black leather boarded next. Khyran hovered above them while the vehicle slid along the track, leaving the platform behind. The children withdrew from the edge and clattered into piles of quivering limbs.

Had he enlightened the Wretched, or burned away their remaining sanity? The dank, lightless tunnels offered no answer.

3: Denial I

"This had better be good, shitface. Those two could be getting farther from us every second." Darwick walked outside Nomad Way with the warrior he'd posted to keep watch while they searched Georgio's hovels.

The warrior pointed at a section of canvas across from where they'd entered the district. The word painted in large, blue letters forced Darwick's hands into fists.

"Tear it down! Right fucking now!" He rushed back into Nomad Way and glared at Georgio. The other Clowns ceased their searching and gathered, weapons ready.

"What's that shit out there? You tell me no one has come here, but you paint 'Magician' outside your district?" He leveled his sword at Georgio's face.

"It wasn't our doing." Georgio was as calm as the Styx.

Darwick bared his teeth. Everyone should fear a representative of Meridian's only goddess. He'd murder the city's entire population just to make her smile.

Georgio he'd murder for himself.

"I'll burn this fucking district down," Darwick said. "I'll—"

A noise echoed beneath the street. Maybe a scream, or a mechanis machine bursting a vent. No…it had to be them. The High Priestess was guiding him. He wouldn't disappoint.

"That came from Lotus Station. Fuckers ain't here. We'll search below."

Darwick turned back to Georgio. "I want that fucking word ripped down and the canvas burned. I want icons of the High Priestess put in its place. I want her face tattooed on your body, Georgio. When I return, these things had better be done."

He led his warriors to the nearest access hatch outside Nomad Way.

4: Inner Light

Tagen leaned against the railcar's side as it ran on automatic. Though the vehicle traveled at a slow pace, it kept them from the platforms they passed, where more of the Wretched waited. Hundreds of people skulked in Lotus Station, many cast off by Azibar as failed experiments. All these cyborgs made Tagen consider the biofluid inside of him.

It made him stronger, but did that matter in this darkest of afterlifes?

"How'd you find us?" Tagen nudged Andromeda's leg.

"A 'thank you' would be nice, bally boy." Andromeda's brows rose.

They locked stares until he finally chuckled. "Thank you."

She winked at him, then smiled.

"Well, how did you find us?" Sveta's accusatory tone made them frown.

"I was headed to Nomad Way, after you two blew me off near the docks," Andromeda said. "I bluffed past Darwick and his freaks. How the hell did you survive that sewer, anyway?"

"Magic," Tagen said.

"Stop joking." Andromeda stood.

"I'm not."

A tense silence stole over the railcar. Everyone flicked their gazes to him. Fingering the holes the Wretched had ripped in his vest, Tagen glanced up at Andromeda. Her cap points bounced as she looked elsewhere.

The railcar turned a corner where two men clawed at each other, either in hunger or carnal desire, Tagen didn't know. The more he saw of Meridian, the more it carved his heart into sickened morsels. There had to be a way to change it all.

"Georgio told me how the city really works," Tagen said.

"I didn't lie to you." Andromeda's jaw firmed.

Tagen savored that look for a moment, then smiled. "No. But leaving will be harder than you made out."

She gave a sarcastic whistle. "Welcome to the shit show."

"Thanks," Tagen said. She finally grinned.

"Andromeda says ya are the Magician," a dusky woman in a black cap asked. "Aye, maybe the Tarot showed ye how to escape?" He recognized her dagger bandoleer, also worn by the others: Blades of Charon.

"I sure hope so—gonna be a wasted trip if he's not," a dark-skinned man with a clockwork half-mask said. He had a pincer for a left hand.

"This is Saissa and Jaabir," Andromeda said. "Kinkers of mine. These others—"

More Wretched wailed from the next platform they passed.

"Why did Azibar do all this? Is this all that's beneath the city? Discarded people?" Tagen coughed and wiped away black spittle. His legs spasmed visibly.

"Aye, and a shame it is." Saissa looked at Andromeda.

"Leftovers from his quest for perfection," Jaabir said.

"The Nomads never used mechanis this way." Sveta shot Andromeda a dark look.

"Let's see how you're doing." Andromeda sat beside Tagen and patted his cheek, then examined his arms. She rubbed his chest and pressed his stomach. Though the biofluid had lessened certain cravings, Tagen still tingled at her soft touch.

"What are you doing?" Sveta asked in a defensive tone.

Saissa smiled at Sveta. "Hold, lass. Our Magician here has biofluid poisoning. His lips are safe."

Sveta blushed.

"Very funny," Andromeda muttered, then squeezed his legs. Her hands lingered on his thighs. "It's spread through him quickly."

"A filter change won't help him now," Jaabir said. "Black veins are showing through his skin."

A heavy frown weighed down Andromeda's face. Sveta crossed her arms and squared her jaw.

"So where do we go?" Tagen asked, trying not to think of his deteriorating condition. His back numbed.

Andromeda stood, her frown melting into eager determination. "Boatman's Corner. The painted freaks won't mob us there. We get you a new filter, then we get the Stygian Tarot."

"I'm not going back to Azibar," Tagen said.

"Just listen to me, Jackpot," Andromeda said. "He has something of mine."

Khyran vented steam and flashed his eyes. Familiar with the jack-in-box's warning style, Tagen stood up. Sveta joined him while the others gripped their daggers.

Down the track, a whooshing sound reverberated, then came closer. A maniacal laugh echoed down the tunnel.

"It's Darwick," Sveta said.

"Motherfucker." Andromeda drew a black dagger in each hand from her skirt.

"Remind me to kick your painted ass later," Sveta told Andromeda.

"Kiss mine, Nomad Girl. I didn't haul them here."

"Can't you two ever get along?" Tagen asked as the whooshing became louder.

"Doubt it," Andromeda said. "But she needs to be pissed right now."

A second railcar filled with whooping Clowns followed them. Darwick kicked the lever on the console, urging the vehicle faster. Twelve other Clown warriors shouted challenges. As his railcar neared theirs, Darwick pointed his sword at Andromeda.

"You're mine, bitch!"

Andromeda smirked and crossed the daggers over her chest. "My dreams are dead, my mercy is slack, slay all those whose heart is black."

Tagen tensed. The filter whirred faster in his back. What could he do? No weapons, no—

Three howling Clowns leapt from their railcar onto his. He punched the first one. Blood squirted from a rubber nose piece. Strong hands forced him back as grease-painted bodies crushed into them. A blade swiped his left arm. Teeth grazed his cheek. He backhanded another Clown, mashing lips. Knuckles wrapped in bronze rings crunched into his stomach, sending him to his knees.

"Fight, Nomad Girl!" With cool skill, Andromeda stabbed and thrust. She sliced a Clown throat, then dodged two swords at once.

Tagen tried to stand until a Clown of Staves whacked his head with a thick wooden staff.

"Tagen!" Sveta yelled.

Hot blood coursed down his temple but Tagen staggered to his feet. Khyran struck the Clowns with electrical current from his mouth. Painted flesh burned and wigs ignited. Screams and shouts boomed in the tunnels as the two railcars sped along.

Saissa gutted a red-painted woman, while Jaabir clipped a man's nose off with his pincer. Sveta elbowed, punched, and kneed her enemies amid the crack of bones. Two Blades already lay dead and Darwick shoved a third into the Styx below. Knives and swords arced through the air.

Tagen yanked Saissa from the path of a Clown club and met the warrior's crazed eyes. The battle's noise faded. *He opened cartomantic doors in his own mind, then shoved the Clown's consciousness through them.*

Thinking he had more surface to move on, the Clown stepped off the railcar's edge and plummeted into the Styx.

A sword pierced Tagen's right arm. Instead of bleeding, his arm wound sealed with black liquid. He grabbed the Clown's wrist and snapped it like a twig. The fanatical warrior head-butted Tagen, then bit his shoulder.

"Bastard!" Andromeda eviscerated the Clown and yanked him off Tagen.

Sveta kicked a Clown off the railcar, then punched another's face, crushing fake and real nose. She moved like she had on the steam rail earlier, quick and confident.

"Fucking kill them!" Darwick knocked Andromeda aside and grazed Sveta's arm with a slash. Andromeda lunged; Darwick busted her mouth with a backhand strike.

Bodies moved so fast in the shadows, it became hard to discern friend from foe. Maddened strikes created murderous silhouettes along the tunnel walls. Wrathful screams reverberated into the darkness.

Darwick slapped Sveta down after feinting with his sword, then stomped on her. Tagen slammed aside two Clowns and gripped Darwick's throat.

"Come get it, shitface!" Darwick slashed Tagen's chest.

Tagen's mind exploded with a hot sun overhead and a horse beneath him. Several men in filthy dusters watched him with harsh stares. Two gambled on his fate with a poker deck. One drew the Joker and chuckled. A noose tightened around Tagen's throat.

"Aw, horse shit," the man with the Joker said. "Hang him anyway. I ain't gonna be held responsible for stealing them steers. Luck of the draw, huh?" A silver star shone on his shirt.

"Glad you see things our way and all, sheriff," one man said. "Hurry, so my boys can start putting my brand on this here herd." He sneered and handed the sheriff a fat roll of bills.

"I love you, darlin'."

The whisper took Tagen's breath, sundered his heart.

A body in scarlet clothing lay in a crimson, broken mass nearby. Locks of red hair contrasted with the green clovers on the ground. A lump rose in Tagen's throat and he glowered at his murderous captors. He tried to proclaim his innocence but one of the men slapped the horse. He plunged into agony.

The vision ended. The lump in his throat remained.

Screaming, Darwick slashed again. Tagen grunted as the edge ripped his stomach open. Biofluid kept him going, powering his muscles further, but he couldn't break the damn Clown's neck. Something prevented him, stayed his hand.

"You won't fucking hang me again!" Darwick drew his sword back for another strike. "Ain't nobody going to take her from me!"

"You were innocent?" Tagen managed as Darwick yowled and thrust.

Metal slid through Tagen's abdomen.

"Tagen!" Sveta and Andromeda shouted together.

For a moment, the only sound was the railcar sliding along the tracks.

Tagen winced and released Darwick, who stumbled backward. Sveta knocked a Clown off the railcar and stared at the sword protruding from Tagen's stomach.

Andromeda slashed Darwick's face and kicked him back onto the other vehicle. "Khyran, now!"

Khyran fired a green bolt at the other railcar's console, melting the controls. As Darwick shouted after them, his transport puttered to a crawl.

Tagen's eyes closed.

5: Denial II

Darwick stood as the other railcar hovered away. On it, Tagen collapsed with Darwick's sword in his gut. Those other stupid assholes just stared.

He had saved the High Priestess; the heretic Magician was slain! He'd hunt the Harlequin and her friends soon, but the main threat to his ivory goddess was eliminated.

But the pain in his chest might tore him apart.

His executioners had been wrong—Darwick hadn't stolen those steers, nor committed any crime. They had taken all he'd possessed. Everything he'd loved. The red hair in the grass stung his heart. All his hate boiled forth and he shoved one of his surviving warriors off the railcar.

Darwick kicked the blackened console but the transport didn't speed up. He glanced at the remaining three Clowns. Eight—well, nine now—had died or fallen into the Styx. Big fucking deal. He'd regroup, report to the High Priestess, and then he'd find that Harlequin bitch. He leapt from the stuttering railcar onto the nearest platform. The rest followed suit.

Though his body smarted from cuts and bruises, Tagen's question wounded him. Innocent? He studied his blood-smeared palm. The sword grew heavy in his other hand.

What would she think, if she could see the things he'd done?

Cold water splashed over him and he jumped out of bed. She dropped the wash basin and fled. Darwick tried to chase her, but tripped—she'd laced his boots together. She tossed her head back and laughed. It was the most beautiful sound in the world.

No. The Magician was dead. So were all those bullshit images in his head.

6: Premonition Light

As Darwick's vehicle faded from view, Tagen sagged to his knees. It was odd that the sword, embedded in his stomach, with its tip exiting his back, didn't hurt him much. His skin acquired a slight gray tint, along with more spidery black lines.

"Fuck those freaks." Andromeda gripped Tagen's shoulder. Her mouth and shoulder were bleeding.

"You okay?" he asked.

Andromeda nodded. "Takes more than Darwick to send me to Charon, Jackpot."

"Tagen? Hang on. Okay?" With blood and sweat matting them, Sveta's braids resembled vines.

"Your arm," Tagen said.

"Stop worrying about the rest of us." Sveta tied a tourniquet above her right elbow where Darwick cut her. Fresh bruises covered her stomach, forearms, and cheek.

Anger electrified his being. They all suffered because of him.

"The biofluid has congealed his wounds. Shit. Jackpot, we have to pull the sword out." Andromeda sheathed her daggers and wiped her mouth.

"Did the others make it?" Tagen looked around.

"We lost four Blades." Jaabir tossed aside his ruined bandoleer and stared at Andromeda. Saissa cleared her throat and worked the piloting console.

They'd died fighting for him and he'd never learned their names.

"We're all fine." Sveta cupped his chin, her features scrunched in concern.

"Hold him, Nomad Girl." Andromeda bent before Tagen and wrapped her hands around the sword handle. What were those shapes on her palms? He leaned forward.

"Stay still." Andromeda's fingers closed around the handle, eyes locked with his.

"Not like that." Sveta half-rose. "He needs proper care."

"I took him to Azibar once," Andromeda said. "Sure as hell not doing it twice. Though it saved your life, Jackpot."

"But it might—" Sveta said, but Jaabir patted her shoulder.

"Meridian's full of 'mights', pretty thing. We gotta take it out, or the biofluid will congeal around it. We'd have to use a steam torch to cut it outta him."

"But if he's the Magician…" Sveta's eyes met Tagen's.

"Thought you didn't believe that? I don't blame you. Now I'm just a pin cushion." Biofluid rippled beneath Tagen's skin. The filter in his back had blown loose.

"Doesn't matter what I believe," Sveta said. "Just…I don't know."

"You two finished?" Andromeda pulled on the sword. The muscles on her arms contorted. With hands below his stomach and behind his neck, Sveta held Tagen steady.

As the blade exited him, Tagen's mind's eye opened. *A hand rose from the Styx, holding aloft a steam lantern. A beacon to further destinations…but nothing appeared on the endless horizon. Nothing but himself walking over the waters, all his palm glyphs glowing. Behind him, the one holding the lantern bobbed to the surface. It was Georgio.*

His mind's eye closed. Sensation slammed into him: nerves erupted, hands numbed, eyes rolled and blinked. His mouth opened so far his jaw popped. Awful tingling sensations filled his stomach as, with a suctioning noise, the wound sealed itself.

If he could puke, he would have.

"What the fuck am I? I can't die, I can't live…" The words crawled from his mouth in a rasp. He glanced around, hoping the nightmare had ended.

Masked frescoes along the walls of Lotus Station peered at him once again. The railcar passed a platform where a nude man danced for a group of decapitated heads. No new memories, then. No redemption. And he still hadn't found Alexis.

He rubbed his finger where his wedding band should be. Maybe he'd stopped wearing it, before coming here. Before dying.

"Feel better?" Andromeda flung the sword overboard.

Tagen looked down at his stomach while Sveta pored over it. She tugged off his vest, squinting at every little cut.

Andromeda tsked. "Easy, Nomad Girl. People are watching."

Sveta cast her an angry glance.

"Coming round Boatman's Corner," Saissa called over her shoulder.

"Next two platforms, if I remember correctly." Andromeda examined herself and tried wiping the Clown blood off. "I look like shit."

"First intelligent thing I've heard you say," Sveta said. The two women shared a brief laugh.

"Azibar's goop seal the entrance and exit wounds?" Andromeda asked, cradling Khyran close to her chest. What was her connection to that floating head? Maybe that was her path to redemption.

"They've sealed, thank Charon." Sveta rubbed some of the bruises on her body.

Grunting, Tagen shifted his body weight. Nothing spilled from the sealed-over gut wound. "You both really know how to fight. Sorry I didn't help more."

"You held your own," Sveta said. "Me, I've always taken care of myself."

Andromeda nodded. "I learned long ago not to become cherry pie for the Guild."

"That lettering on your daggers…it looks familiar." Tagen glanced at Sveta. He'd glimpsed some of the same letters on her tattoos.

"Charonic sigils," Andromeda said. "Old city legends claim that words written in them have power."

"Don't need clockwork pistols when we got these." Jaabir donned an extra dagger bandoleer he'd taken from a fallen Blade.

Coughing, Tagen stood. Sveta helped but he patted her hand. "Thanks, I got it."

He drooled black, metallic-tasting liquid and coughed with racking heaves.

"No, you don't," Andromeda said. "You need another valve, or worse."

"The Corner coming up," Saissa said.

"Charon go with you." Jaabir pushed three Blade corpses into the Styx. Andromeda turned her head and closed her eyes.

Tagen gripped Andromeda's shoulder. "I'm tired of people dying for me."

She gave him a hard look, yet as the railcar whooshed through the tunnels, her anger lessened. They faced each other, him still touching her painted skin.

"You never get used to it," Andromeda said.

"At least they died with some of their memories," Tagen said. "Does that mean that Meridian didn't absorb—"

"I don't know." Andromeda turned around. He sensed her grief, her guilt. Brought on by him. Redemption, indeed.

"Do you have a place to hide in Boatman's Corner?" Sveta finally asked.

"We'll be safe. Georgio pitched it to me once." Andromeda snorted at Sveta's confusion. "Lots of history between him and me, Nomad Girl."

"I think Georgio's in trouble," Tagen said. "I had a vision of him holding—"

Andromeda whistled low. "We're almost there. Get ready to jump off this gilley wagon. We'll sort out this sideshow in the Corner. Especially you, Jackpot."

The railcar passed another platform. Andromeda nodded to Saissa and released Khyran. The jack-in-the-box latched onto the console and slowed the vehicle. Saissa and Jaabir stood with daggers ready. Since no Wretched barred their path, the pair jumped off, followed by Sveta. Tagen hesitated beside Andromeda.

"What about your promise to help me?" he whispered in her ear.

She looked away and smoothed her skirt.

"I want to believe you," he said. "I want to—"

She kissed his cheek. Nothing but a slight peck, but it took his breath.

"Aye, ye two coming?" Saissa called from the stairway above.

Tagen started to speak—wanted to speak—but Andromeda hurried off the railcar.

X.
WHEEL OF FORTUNE

1: Divine Intention

Radomir tossed aside the empty steampainter and gazed up at his ninth 'Magician' graffiti. He'd painted it across an eighty-story bridge in the Terraces, climbing along the iron railing. With patient care, he'd inscribed each letter between bouts of rain and attached steam lanterns to highlight the inscription. Meridian's largest skyscrapers were in the Terraces, with nothing higher but Azibar's Spire.

Everyone would see his work.

He waited on a nearby curb while people walked under the bridge.

Clowns halted and shouted curses. A few Mechos stopped and regarded the word quizzically, but continued on. A man paused and read the word over and over. Several others joined him before the Alueryic Clock tolled again. Soon a large crowd gathered, pointing and whispering among themselves.

"Get back, assholes!" Warrior Clowns beat the crowd with their staves, but nothing could break the word's grip on them. The people pushed forward. Staves crushed cheeks and snapped elbows. Desperate, flailing limbs shoved the Clown warriors.

Radomir straightened and wrung his gauntleted hands. "No."

"Break up or we'll execute you all!" A Clown smashed a man's stomach with his stave. Several bloodied forms crawled away from the fight. Voices in the crowd rose.

"He can help, yes?" Heart pounding, Radomir raised his hands. No more death, no more suffering, couldn't they see?

One Clown bludgeoned a small girl to the street. Her head bled into a sewer grate.

Sharp metal slid into Radomir's hand. One instant he stood on the curb; the next, right beside the Clowns. The girl's head kept bleeding.

She was so small, not much older than Brian.

Light glinted off the metal in his hand. Red drops dusted his armor. An anguished grunt escaped his throat.

Two Clowns lay on the curb, crimson pooling around their copses. His shiv, now in hand, dripped with blood. It had been so easy, with their backs turned. So easy to kill, to avenge. Yes.

The crowd stared at Radomir, then mobbed the remaining Clowns.

"Not a murderer," Radomir whispered, more to Brian than himself. He wanted to run but hands grabbed him. Excited faces appeared inches from his.

"Who painted that sign?" someone called out.

"Have you seen the Magician?" one man asked, steam venting from his shoulders.

A woman with Tarot cards tattooed on her cheeks shook him. "I saw this same word, painted near the Mecho District. What does it mean? Has the Magician come to Meridian? Like the prophecy?"

"Fuck no, it's a prank!" someone cried.

"The High Priestess has lied to us!" another called.

Several people around Radomir nodded. Their eyes desired something the Clowns or Mechos couldn't give them. Something Meridian forbade them with its inky black borders. Radomir knew where they could find it.

"Seen the Magician, yes? Showed what lies past Meridian. Memories from before."

Those around Radomir fell silent.

"Blasphemy!" a man shouted, but others raised their fists and yelled otherwise.

A cacophony of voices filled his ears. The crowd swelled in size. Some took paint from the Clown corpses and scrawled 'Magician' on their bodies.

Radomir put away his shiv as fear strangled him. He didn't know what to do, he couldn't help these people!

But the Magician could.

2: Tempting Fate

Azibar tried to ignore the Wretched while riding his railcar through Lotus Station. Though most of the undercity's tunnels and rail tracks sat in disrepair, his servants maintained those near the Mecho District. If only he didn't have to see these past disappointments every time. Hideous things. Perhaps he should have terminated each failed experiment.

He glanced at Mannequin and smiled. Ah, a reminder that such activities had been worthwhile.

The railcar stopped and he stepped onto a platform with Mannequin. A private elevator awaited them, protected by four Mecho guards. They saluted and stepped aside. The device hissed steam, then lifted him and Mannequin into a small orange tent within the Circus, off-limits to all Clowns. It was empty, save for a bronze lever. Azibar pulled it. He knew a pulse had been sent along a wire buried in the Circus. A pulse sent to a certain tent.

He patted Mannequin's hand while they waited. "You have spoken little since we left the Spire. Are you well, my dear?"

"Yes, Azibar." Steam exited a vent below her copper-coated navel.

Leaning close, he cupped her perfect chin. "I am sorry you had to witness the plight of those who cannot be like us. It is a great burden, inspiring others to our way of life. Not all can handle such responsibility."

Her internal pumps stuttered. "I do not understand. You want this for everyone."

Handing out wind-up toys to the children before her armored thugs caught him.

Sadness overcame him. "Not all can accept greatness…even within themselves."

The tent flap opened.

Azibar bowed as the High Priestess entered. Her red cape hung over one shoulder, revealing her firm breasts, curved thighs, and incomparable face. She wanted to be a Mecho. Why else imitate their metallic flesh with her false ivory coating? She was nothing but a whore pretending to be a virgin.

"Why have you come here?" she asked, not even acknowledging Mannequin.

"You haven't heard, my dear alabaster beauty? Perhaps there is legitimacy to all this gossip, then." He savored her anger, running his tongue over golden teeth.

"Heard what? You interrupted my ministrations to tease me with useless information? There are far better tasks for you, Azibar."

"My first duty is to you, my dear."

"Why don't you repair the steamlamps in Vagrant's Row? The Bone Guild needs more boilers and turbines for a new branch of kiosks in Paradise Lane. The Clowns of Pentacles need a fresh mint of copper shards to pay the faithful. You have your duties. I have better things to attend."

In maintaining the city's mechanis, he'd gained the High Priestess's graces. Andromeda assumed he'd help her rebellion. Silly Harlequin tramp. Instead, he'd made himself indispensable. None knew how to keep the city's machines running but him.

"I hear the Magician has come to Meridian. It is as you prophesied, High Priestess." He did his best to keep mockery from his half-bow.

She flinched in a reaction he'd never seen in her before. The High Priestess had watched children be executed for having even one palm glyph, without exhibiting the slightest pity or revulsion. Nevertheless, Azibar relished her fear. Craved, it even.

"Darwick is taking care of that problem. It is not your affair. You are my engineer, nothing more." The High Priestess placed hands on luscious hips.

"Oh? Your rabid dog hasn't contained the unrest building in the streets. Per the prophecy, however, since you can't detect the Magician like you can everything else in Meridian, I'm not surprised you didn't know."

Her brow furrowed. People had died for saying less. Azibar didn't fear her...but her cartomancy couldn't be underestimated. He would play her servant a little longer.

"Unrest? Impossible. My Tarot has the loyalty of all."

"I have seen at least three instances of the word 'Magician' painted on buildings in large letters. Even on one of those superstructures in the Terraces. My technicians mentioned that crowds are gathering. Several people have been killed. If you can imagine that, in Meridian." He didn't bother hiding his smirk.

"I told you, Darwick is seeing to it." How beautiful her frustration was.

"Is he?" Azibar moved forward. Mannequin stepped to his left, blocking the exit.

"Careful, you copper turd. I am not so easily taken." The High Priestess withdrew a golden Tarot deck from behind her back.

Steam squealed from a vent in Azibar's neck as he stepped back. Both her hands had been on her hips and she wore no clothes. The deck couldn't have been hidden within her cape.

"Shall I show you?" Her red fingernails flicked through the cards.

Mannequin's inner gears whirred as she retreated behind Azibar.

A voice outside spoke. "High Priestess, forgive me, but Darwick has returned."

The High Priestess narrowed her eyes, then departed the tent. The flap closed behind her. What was this? No Clown knew about their secret meetings. Azibar activated a filter over his eyes and peeked through a crease in the flap. Nothing would give him away more than his glowing stare.

Outside the tent, a red-painted Clown—Darwick—knelt before the High Priestess. Azibar sneered at the man's adoration. The ivory bitch knew how to seduce others, either with her body or Tarot propaganda. He envied her for it, though. If only she would join him, he wouldn't need another cartomancer to cross the Styx.

That meant there were limits to her power…she couldn't leave Meridian either, or she already would have.

"Where are the two cartomancers? Did you kill them?" Her tone bore sensual command, like a silken garrote strangling someone.

"Tagen still has my sword in his guts," Darwick said. "The other one will be easy to find, but I think the Sky Nomads helped 'em."

"Are you sure Tagen is dead? I have word of 'Magician' graffiti painted on walls, of crowds gathering. And the Sky Nomad, Sveta. She must be caught. Fool, any cartomancer might try to challenge me!"

Azibar waited, hoping she'd send Darwick after Georgio. He still hated that idealistic old man for keeping mechanis secrets that not even Andromeda had been able to pilfer. And now Georgio harbored a cartomancer? How interesting.

"I will find her, High Priestess." Darwick lowered himself further to the ground. What a weak-willed cretin. She could squat down and piss on him and Darwick would still worship her.

"First, I want you to break those crowds up, kill any who resist. Arm the warriors with pistols and crossbows. Remind these heretics who rules Meridian." She held out her hand and Darwick made love to it with his clumsy mouth. Surely she had better lovers? It deflated the rumors of a Clown harem fucking her whenever she wanted.

After Darwick left, she reentered the tent. Her ruby eyes pierced him.

"I did not lie, High Priestess," Azibar said. "If an uprising is underway, are your warriors able to contain it?"

She opened her mouth but he continued.

"Let my guards help. You know how I detest any disruption of the city's order."

"Perhaps," she said. The card deck shuffled itself in her left hand. She hesitated and pursed her lips. While Mannequin monitored the tent flap, he stepped closer.

"Why do you humor these fools?" Azibar whispered. "You deserve so much more, my dear. Someone loyal to you, who is above Darwick's bestial displays. You are a queen. Shouldn't you have refinement?"

He stood so close that her breath fogged up his copper cheeks.

"They worship me," she said. "That is all I need."

"I know you suffer," Azibar said. "I have removed suffering from my Mechos. The same could be done for you, my dear."

Her red-painted lips opened in a wide smile. "Truly."

"Master the flesh, dominate the emotions." His fingers slid down her chin, glided along her neck. Massaged the cleft between her breasts. "Then we'd truly rule Meridian."

"Yes…" She pursed her lips and he closed his eyes.

Something metallic touched Azibar's hands: a golden Tarot card lay in each palm. Her deck drifted through the air, then flurried back into her grasp.

"I am the seducer," the High Priestess said. "You have nothing I want, or need."

He glanced at the cards in his grasp. The right hand clasped the High Priestess card. The left, the Emperor.

"There we are." She drummed her fingers on his metallic chest. "Normally, the Emperor trumps the High Priestess. But, sometimes, even Emperors bow."

She held up the Wheel of Fortune card. On it, a Clown and Mecho rode a clockwork wheel along Meridian's docks. As he peered closer, the image morphed right before his mechanical eyes.

The wheel rolled, crushing the Mecho underneath. Steam ruptured. Biofluid stained the dock. Atop the wheel rode a paragon of alabaster loveliness. As the wheel continued rolling, the destroyed Mecho reassembled itself into a carriage atop the wheel. The Clown—the High Priestess herself—sat in the carriage.

Azibar recoiled, steam hissing from every vent. The cards in his hands melted into golden slag, which he flung away. She lifted the deck and blew as if blowing him a kiss. The same cards fluttered about him and faded from view.

"Never forget what you saw." She ran a fingernail over his copper lips. Rubbed her painted breasts up against his chest.

"I fashion the wheels that turn Meridian." He glared at her. "I can have—"

"Nothing, without my blessing." She looked at Mannequin and laughed. "Pretty. But she isn't me. Perhaps, if your guards find Sveta…I shall indulge you."

The High Priestess left the tent.

Azibar activated his internal oil reserves. Fine, clean lubricant poured from his hands, lips, and chest. He didn't want her taint on him. Despite her reading, he would defeat her. The overconfident hussy had given him exactly what he wanted—sanction to march his soldiers through Meridian's streets.

3: Stygian Destiny

Groaning in pain, Tagen exited Lotus Station with Sveta's help. They ascended a chipped stone stairway. Ancient etchings of oars and sails decorated its steps, worn down over untold centuries. The scent of tar and smoke filtered from the city above. Tagen coughed and leaned more on Sveta's shoulder. Though his limbs surged with strength, his body spasmed and shivered.

"You're leaving a biofluid trail," Jaabir said.

"Hurry," Andromeda said. "There's no Circus freaks 'round here, but still plenty who will rat us out for an ace note."

They all left the hatch, which led into an alley built of human skulls. Names and pictograms had been scrawled on many. Which of these came to Meridian in search of someone, only to die a second time? Tagen tried not to look at them.

While Andromeda sent Khyran around the corner, Saissa and Jaabir stripped off sections of their clothing. Tagen appreciated how they could discard a detachable sleeve, vest, or a hat and appear different. Afterward, Saissa applied yellow lipstick and finger bone earrings. Jaabir's mask reformed around his neck as a choker. He covered his pincer with a glove.

"Why all these skulls?" The biofluid taste in his mouth made him grimace.

"Kinkers used to leave them for the Boatman," Andromeda said without turning. "Now, we build with them. It's the closest thing to a graveyard here."

"The Boatman?" His palm glyphs itched.

"Charon. Legend says he used to haul dead souls on his barge to another city, while his wife, the Gorgon, gathered them here. But he never came back. Blame him?" She motioned them on when Khyran returned.

Rusty steamlamps provided sparse light over Boatman's Corner, though many lanterns hung from balconies. Gutted skyscrapers existed alongside towers constructed from bones. Several statues, similar to those ringing the Bazaar, stood in cracked, forlorn repose along cobblestone streets.

The Styx waited nearby, though no dock or quay allowed easy access. Instead, a long precipice, hundreds of feet long, led to the dark waters. Balconies and walkways snaked over the Styx like suspended piers. A block of taverns clumped together near the city's edge buzzed with conversation and music. People smoked hookahs, drank gutter beer, or listened to Mecho nocturnes on the sidewalks in a relaxed air. Most gave Andromeda a wide berth.

"People know you here?" Tagen asked.

"They know I'll send them pitching to Charon." There was no pride in Andromeda's statement.

Though Boatman's Corner looked safer than other parts of the city, Tagen sensed a morose anxiety underlying everything. Like waiting for something they had forgotten.

"See what you can scrounge for Jackpot," Andromeda told Jaabir. "Saissa, buy sweet kelp and salted mushrooms from Ingratio's tavern. Stay clear of Hexla's joint, since the Guild cooks for her now. We'll meet at the Femur Tower."

"Charming place," Sveta muttered.

"At least the Clowns avoid it." Tagen sagged on her shoulder and she grunted to keep him up.

"Easy, Nomad Girl. Now we both have him." Andromeda took Tagen's other arm and led them past an avenue of burnt lighthouses along the precipice. People stared from windows and doorways, wearing an odd assortment of clothing: ragged Harlequin outfits, blue Nomad cloth, brown trench coats, or long black robes. No one wore grease paint.

Ahead, a fourteen-story tower, fashioned from femur bones, dominated a cul-de-sac. Tarot graffiti covered it and a long pier stretched from the summit. Light rain dribbled down the ossified masonry.

Khyran inserted himself into a square depression on the Tower's bronze door. He turned the lock and the two women helped Tagen inside.

Sveta grew quiet but Andromeda's face relaxed. After hovering to a pedestal, Khyran transformed into a rusty box.

"What is this place?" Tagen asked.

"The Blade's joint." Andromeda activated a steam lantern. "Georgio claims it was a watchtower, back when troupers kept an eye out for Charon's Barge."

Rain dripped from ceiling cracks. Ragged carpets covered the stone floor. Paintings cluttered the walls but rain had made the colors run, leaving amorphous shapes in warped frames. A worn privacy screen stood before a spattering interior gutter. The runoff emptied through a floor drain. In one corner, wide steps led upstairs. A silver Tarot deck with melted edges lay on a wooden table.

"Careful." Sveta helped Tagen as he eased onto a wire frame stool. "Why did you bring us here?"

"Because I live here, Nomad Girl. Sit down, we're safe for a few tolls of the Clock." Andromeda removed her cap and deposited her daggers on the table. Stepping out of her shoes, she ran fingers through her wavy blonde locks.

"How long?" Sveta's voice was full of distrust.

"Long enough." Andromeda stepped behind the privacy screen. "There's plenty of spare rooms on the upper floors, so we all can get some sleep."

Tagen eyed her silhouette as she stripped off her torsolette, skirt, and stockings. She stretched and grunted, then stood beneath the gutter and washed herself. Her clean skin shone through a few holes in the screen.

"Enjoying the show?" Sveta whispered with a scornful look.

"Do I look like I'm enjoying anything right now?" He held up a hand. Veins trembled just beneath his skin.

Blushing, Sveta walked away.

Saissa bustled in and lay a box of packaged vegetables on the table. From a cask in the corner, she poured hot, yellow-brown liquid into ceramic cups.

"Lichen tea." Saissa distributed the cups and Tagen sipped the creamy, sweet-smelling draught. Sveta tasted hers and nodded.

"So why are we safer here?" Tagen asked. "Why no Clowns?"

"The Corner is among a few joints that retain some of Charon's power," Andromeda called over the screen. "The High Priestess's magic is weaker here."

Because no one was supposed to rule the city alone, Tagen realized. It needed two—Charon and the Gorgon; a king and queen. Georgio had said as much. But who would share such power? No wonder there hadn't been two rulers at once for so long.

Andromeda left the draining runoff and dried herself with a threadbare blue cape. Next, she lathered white grease paint over her body. The privacy screen hid little. Though Tagen tried not to stare, her nonchalant lack of modesty enticed him.

Dressing behind the screen, Andromeda mumbled a tune in sensitive tones. She donned another torsolette, short skirt, fishnet leggings—all black this time. Silver skulls hung from the points of her matching cap.

"Still a Clown?" Sveta's question lacked any curiosity.

"I'm a Harlequin, you floss head. It doubles as a disguise." Still behind the screen, Andromeda pulled a cracked mirror off the wall and turned her back to them.

Tagen wanted to see her face. What did she hide behind the paint?

Saissa nudged Sveta. "Bathe, afore Jaabir comes round."

Sveta blanched. "Not now. Thanks."

"Please, Nomad Girl, you stink," Andromeda called from behind the screen. "But really, we need you to. I recognize your tattoos."

Tagen sat up straight. Saissa spilled her tea.

Stalking over to the screen, Sveta raised her voice. "How? You never said anything before."

The images he'd seen in Sveta's body art came back to Tagen: *Obelisks. Masks. Tomes. Pathways.* Shadows lurked at the edges of his vision, with block-like letters haunting his eyesight.

"There's a reason Georgio took a bally girl like you in," Andromeda said. "I hope your tattoos are what I think they are."

"The Stygian Tarot?" Tagen stood beside Sveta.

Andromeda stomped from behind the screen. "How the fuck do you know that?" The diamonds beneath her eyes were now painted black, complimenting her lips. The rest of her face was silky ivory.

"I've looked at it. While Sveta and I were in Nomad Way…I saw things in her tattoos." Each breath made awful sucking noises and every heartbeat hurt.

Saissa tugged Sveta's arm. "Aye, bathe, so we see 'em."

Sveta pulled away. "Did you put these on me, Andromeda? Tell me right now!"

"No, but I think I know who did." Andromeda glanced at Khyran on the pedestal.

"Who was Khyran?" Tagen asked.

Andromeda cleared her throat and didn't answer.

"We've trusted you," Tagen said. "Now trust us."

Moments ticked by as they stared at each other.

"My former lover," Andromeda finally said. "The High Priestess beheaded him, like all the other cartomancers. Like she would have done to both of you."

"Then why…why is he like that?" Tagen asked.

She hesitated, then walked toward the pedestal. As Khyran became a jack-in-the-box and hovered to her shoulder, Andromeda faced Tagen. "I thought he was the Magician. I thought he could red light that ivory witch. Armed with the Stygian Tarot, against her Clown deck."

Tagen's heart swelled for her. Sveta put a hand to her mouth.

"I formed the Blades of Charon after the High Priestess took the Circus from me," Andromeda said. "I amused kinkers to take their minds off this blood opera. She wanted them to worship her, so I hid the Stygian Tarot, since I couldn't interpret it. Yes, I was a cartomancer, but the city chose her. All other Tarot decks lost their magic."

"Aye," Saissa said. "Fools thought Charon would save 'em."

"Save them?" Sveta asked. "How? Charon's just a legend."

"Charon isn't the godlike ringmaster some troupers imagine." Andromeda paced the room. "He was Meridian's original ruler. The ferryman who can lead us to the proper joint where we belong. Meridian always chooses a powerful cartomancer to manage it, even if that trouper resists. The High Priestess filched my spot, but abuses her control. Her and her freaks."

"You used Khyran to win back your city, with the Stygian Tarot?" Tagen asked.

"I never said this was my city." Andromeda looked stung by his comment.

"What the hell's so special about this deck of cards?" The bio-fluid engorged Tagen's chest, adding force to his words. "How can it defeat the High Priestess?"

Andromeda gave him a bemused look. "Are you fucking with me? You've felt its power and don't think it's special?"

"Tell us the rest." Sveta was rigid with tension.

"Charon is supposed to have crafted the deck with his magic," Andromeda said. "None have ever been able to read it. Troupers used to fight over it, turn Meridian into a garbage joint while looking for it, even before the High Priestess came. Supposedly each card is a doorway, a mirror of infinite possibilities. But only the strong-willed can survive gazing into it."

"Enough about cards!" Sveta cried. "Who put these tattoos on me?"

Andromeda stopped pacing. "Maybe Khyran did, to hide it. He never told me, before challenging her in Clown Alley. I've not seen the Stygian deck since—until we met, Nomad Girl."

"Sounds risky, hiding it on a new arrival," Tagen said. "So that's why…you took Khyran's head from the High Priestess's tent and made a deal with Azibar, didn't you?"

Shoulders sagging, Andromeda lowered her gaze. "Azibar couldn't revive him fully. So he kept Khyran's body safe."

"And bargaining Tagen for Khyran's body would get it back?" Sveta asked. "How could you? After the way your lover died—how could you do that to us?"

Andromeda's lip quivered but her eyes hardened. "Because Khyran still lives. He might be just a fucking toy to you, but he's alive. I have to believe he can come back. I have to believe he put those tattoos on you for a reason, preparing for his return."

Saissa stepped between them. "Enough, lassies. Bath time."

"No." Sveta stepped back.

Tagen gently squeezed Sveta's shoulder. "We must see them."

"I don't want to see, damn it," Sveta whispered. "The things I've envisioned…it's all shadow and death. You all think the Magician will save us. The prophecy doesn't say that. Look what happened to Khyran, Andromeda. You want that for Tagen?"

"I don't need you fucking reminding—" Andromeda took a deep breath. "You have the most important skin in all Meridian, Nomad Girl. We must see."

"Think of Georgio, your people," Tagen said.

Sveta finally nodded. While she removed her clothes, Tagen turned around. Saissa and Andromeda whispered to each other.

A vision stole over his mind. Churning shadows obscured his sight. From the darkness, a single object flipped end over end toward him. A Tarot card, depicting a spinning wheel. A masked woman sat atop it, while a muscular man with a steam-vent chest rose beneath it. Clouds parted around the wheel as an airship sailed over the Styx.

"The Wheel of Fortune," Tagen murmured as the vision faded. The Moon glyph on his palm glowed.

"Damn cartomancers," Saissa muttered. "Aye, if ya see what we do, then ye might as well turn around."

Tagen did. Sveta stood beneath the gutter, water coursing over her damp braids. Exquisite, nebulous images ran the length of her body. Sometimes the images shifted before his eyes, which they hadn't done before. It was like a pathway snaking over her flesh, connecting each image.

Minor Arcana of Obelisks, Tomes, Masks, Pathways. Major Arcana of shimmering faces. Some were mirror images of himself. Sometimes Sveta or Andromeda. Sometimes a woman at the dinner table, giving back the wedding ring. The golden mask gleamed in one of the mirrors.

Were these his memories? He stepped closer and ran a hand down Sveta's back. Both of them flinched as images filled his thoughts.

Weight training. Kickboxing. Testing marksmanship at a firing range. Sveta had been training to protect herself. That explained her martial skills and athletic build. Explained the bullet hole beneath her left breast, and her fearless demeanor.

Maybe they'd both been cops, or security guards.

The Tarot cards rose from her flesh and floated around him, each branding his consciousness, tossing him into mirror reflections of himself...

Sobbing, Sveta withdrew from him. "Enough! I can't look at her any longer!"

Physical and mental paths led away from Meridian. Away from the Self. The Wheel of Fortune turned and the woman atop it removed her mask. The man under it escaped the Styx and the wheel became the sun.

Tagen's vision ended and he staggered back. No cards floated in the air. The images along her sensuous physique didn't morph or writhe…but he knew.

A path existed there, one over black water, or a dining room where wine spilled on tablecloth. A path through a blade, into the veins of a city where people lay trapped in awe of others. Tagen could show them all where they might go.

He could make everyone remember.

"I saw how to…how we might leave this city." Every word hurt Tagen's chest.

Andromeda faced Sveta. "We need to see the tattoos on the front of your body. Jackpot needs the whole picture, or it'll do him no good against the High Priestess."

"Give me some time, all right?" Sveta cried. "Shit, I can't get her out of my mind."

Tagen's chest throbbed with pain. His neck veins jumped. "Who, Sveta?"

Saissa stared at him. "No cards? How ye do a reading with no cards?"

"Even Khyran needed a deck for his cartomancy to work," Andromeda said.

"I don't—" The ache in his chest pounded Tagen to his knees. The pain in his mind gleamed in a thousand mental mirrors. It was too much, looking into the Stygian Tarot's mysteries.

"Shit, the biofluid," Andromeda said. "Saissa, see what's keeping Jaabir."

Tagen closed his eyes against the agony. *The Wheel in his mind turned again, crushing him along a neon-lit thoroughfare.* "Tell me, Sveta!"

Sveta stared down at him. "She rejected you…she came here to leave you!"

"What?" A terminal chill encased Tagen's heart.

Andromeda embraced him. "Hang on, Jackpot. Jackpot? Look at me!"

As he opened his eyes Andromeda gasped. The veins along Tagen's face popped. The biofluid dominated his system.

"I saw her, Tagen," Sveta breathed. "Alexis hated you. She wanted a divorce."

Passing the ring to him across the table. No wedding ring on his own finger.

His mind sputtered into a dark abyss. The Stygian Tarot's mirrors crashed into his consciousness and he flopped onto the floor.

"By Charon, no…please, no." Andromeda knelt over him, her eyes misting over.

Tagen sobbed, whether from physical pain or emotional anguish, it didn't matter anymore. White hotness burned into his back as he met Andromeda's eyes.

"She died to escape me…and I died for nothing."

In Tagen's mind, the Wheel of Fortune sank into the Styx, taking him with it.

4: Merciless Fortune

Hair-tingling chills overtook Andromeda as Tagen lost consciousness. She felt his neck, his wrist, lay an ear against his chest. Cradled his face in her hands.

It had been twelve tolls, but Azibar was wrong. Meridian was keeping him alive.

The city nearly possessed him now.

Sveta, naked and dripping, clung to the screen, crying. Andromeda had shared visions with Khyran—she knew how it felt. The ultimate meeting of thoughts and emotions. One's joys and agonies became the other person's.

Had Khyran tattooed the Stygian images on Sveta's body? She'd given him the deck after his first display of cartomancy in Paradise Lane. What a wonderful moment that had been. He'd challenged the High Priestess's rule in the very streets. The Blades of Charon had rallied around him in the hundreds. Most died in the assault on the Circus, but not Andromeda. Khyran had asked her to sit out that final battle.

Maybe she should have fought and died with him.

After gathering her clothes, Sveta ran upstairs. It'd be hell, convincing her to let them see the rest of her body. Andromeda loathed to ask, after seeing Nomad Girl's pain.

Khyran hovered above Tagen and flashed his eyes.

"What?" Andromeda asked.

He floated over to the table. Directly above the silver Tarot deck.

"I can't read them anymore," Andromeda murmured. "They're just cards now."

Cards she had watched Khyran shuffle and draw, cards he'd placed over her naked body during their lovemaking on the Corner's balconies.

Cards she's wept over and nearly thrown into the Styx.

Andromeda brushed a hand through Tagen's damp hair. Even in repose, his right arm pointed above his head, while his left pointed to his feet. As above, so below. The mantra of the Magician. Mirrored lifetimes, reflected experiences. The same as Khyran had once told her.

Squeezing her eyes shut, she accepted that Khyran had never been the Magician. He must have known that another was coming to Meridian, to fulfill the prophecy. And Tagen would suffer even worse if he followed Khyran's path.

But the way he wanted to help others…the way he always looked at her…

"I can't love you both," she whispered.

It had felt so good, kissing him on the railcar. His proximity while she bathed had thrilled her. Calling him that silly nickname, since it frightened her to say his real one. Giving in to these feelings would make her forget the horrid city outside…

It wouldn't let her forget she'd planned on using him.

Andromeda sobbed, breathing hard. Meridian still held her in its cursed grip. Regardless, she kissed Tagen's lips as the tears finally fell. Beading on his face like rain.

"If I love you…you'll die." She crept up the staircase.

XI.

JUSTICE

1: Dedication to the Highest Things

Tagen sat up on the musty carpet. His heart didn't throb as much, nor did he taste biofluid. Along his arms, the black lines had receded from his veins. He was alone in the Femur Tower's main room.

Holding his head in both hands, Tagen tried to fathom what Sveta had told him. Alexis had hated him and sought a divorce… which meant she'd committed suicide…just to get away from him. He touched the scars on his wrists. Remembered the charities he'd helped, the people he'd made happy or protected.

"I'm not a bad person," he whispered. "I'm not like them out there."

On the television, the congressman's family wept during the state funeral.

He stood, clenching his fists. Sveta and the others had every right not to believe in him. Alexis had lost faith in him, for some reason.

But here in Meridian…he had to believe in himself now.

The Alueryic Clock tolled seven. They'd let him sleep so long?

Or they had abandoned him. Tagen unclenched his fists and headed up the stairs. On the second floor, he ran into Sveta as she exited a bedroom.

A look of pain passed between them. Pain he had revealed and shared with her. Alexis, committing suicide, coming to this terrible city…but Meridian's suffering topped his a million fold.

"Where are the others?" Tagen tried not to look at her tattoos.

"Saissa and Jaabir went on errands. Andromeda's on a higher floor, I think." Sveta shied away from him and walked downstairs.

If every new memory brought him closer to redemption…what would be left of him in the end? How could he escape this city when he couldn't escape the past?

Tagen slowly climbed the stone steps, passing the Tower's other floors. Some housed rusty parts, or empty cots. Another had a box of colored balls, juggling pins, and a corroded unicycle. One entire floor held training rooms, with wall targets, gymnast bars, and stuffed punching dummies. The next contained paper books, wrapped in oiled leather. There was even a Sky Nomad tapestry, showing airships hovering above a city of silver spires, but age had rotted its beauty.

Going up the final flight of steps, Tagen had to lean against the wall. Alexis must have really despised him. Damn, he couldn't get that out of his mind. He could still be alive, if she'd simply told him how she felt. He'd died for nothing!

What a selfish fuck he was. She was dead. That was all that mattered.

He wiped his eyes and glared out a window.

It was done. He couldn't change it. But he could do something about Meridian.

The uppermost level contained expansive windows and a blackened firepit. Dented sheet metal posters hung on the walls, advertising an older Circus. Each featured Andromeda, juggling pins and knives. Her joyful smile belonged to another person.

He touched the poster, fingertips fogging up the cool metal. If only his cartomancy could make her smile like this again.

A balcony with a rickety handrail stretched from the doorway. It extended over the Styx for at least a hundred feet, supported by rusted struts attached to the Tower at an angle. Parts of it sagged or had missing planks. He stepped out onto it.

The Styx devoured the horizon as far as the eye could see. With less steamlamps in this district, Tagen detected a grayness near the edge of his vision, like a sea just before dawn. He wondered if cartomancy showed him this, or if others saw it, too.

Standing there, he enjoyed the sweet sting of solitude. Each lighted building, with all its tenets, was a reminder of how alone he was now.

A tender, soulful voice sang a few wordless notes. Tagen's breath caught.

The notes danced up and down a melodious scale. Tagen closed his eyes and loosed a deep breath. So lovely and soothing. Nothing in Meridian compared to it.

The song stopped and his heart sank.

Balanced atop the balcony's rail, Andromeda hummed a few more notes.

Tagen studied her slender form. Free of the torsolette and skirt, she wore a two-piece ensemble that revealed most of her painted body. She'd never looked so helpless; not even Khyran hovered nearby. She stared across the Styx, locks of blonde hair catching the glow of distant skyscrapers. Curved blades and a crumpled cap lay nearby. A telescope was anchored to the railing beside her.

Though Tagen didn't want to disturb her, he needed answers. Her answers.

Ignoring the missing or cracked planks, he walked on. Like the race over Lotus Station's railcar track, his feet fell true as his Star glyph pulsed. His steps made no sound on the tar-coated, metal planks. Rain drizzle fell by the time he reached the end.

"Hey."

Andromeda jumped and turned. "Shit, you forget how to knock?"

"Sorry."

Hopping down from the rail, her eyes softened. "You okay?"

"I guess." Tagen looked around as the rain fell harder. "We should go inside."

"Give me a break. It's not like we'll catch a cold." The downpour washed away some of her body paint. "Especially you."

"I'm the Magician, remember?" Tagen rolled his eyes.

Her eyes lingered on his face "I've never seen shit like that. Cartomancers read and interpret cards. Manipulate kinkers' minds. You're another sideshow entirely."

He leaned over the rail beside her. She gripped the railing. Heat rose in his face. She licked her lips several times before speaking.

"I used to watch the Styx with this telescope. Even Azibar, before he became a Mecho sellout, looked through it. I thought surely, a ship would come. That we weren't the only city, that Georgio's silly legends were true. I might even see Charon on his barge. But I never saw anything."

"Until you met Khyran."

Seconds dragged by before she spoke.

"I gave him the Stygian deck, after finding it in Boulevard. Cards plated on thick, palm-sized sheets of steel, dipped in the Styx. Some troupers say that Charon made them from his own sword and armor. I thought Khyran could beat that ivory witch with them." Andromeda punched the railing.

"Why did you play Azibar against her? He doesn't seem like your sort."

Glaring at him, Andromeda stepped close. "He isn't. He wanted to end her reign too, pitched that he wanted Meridian to be one big shining opera. But Azibar is like her."

"Who would take her place if you won?" Tagen stood closer so his voice would carry over the rain. "You said Meridian must have a cartomancer, no matter what."

Andromeda stared over the railing.

"What if I can't find a path from Meridian? What if I can't decipher the rest of the Stygian deck?" Tagen turned from her and gazed over the city.

Even from here, the bulging sore of the Circus shone through the other quarters. A perpetual exhaust cloud floated over the Mecho District like a disembodied spirit. The canvas of Nomad Way, the gutted hulks in Vagrant's Row—dozens of other districts he hadn't visited extended out into the Styx, as if held together by some force of will.

"Then you'll be claimed by the city. Just like her." Andromeda's jaw clenched.

"What if I face the High Priestess?" he asked, more to himself than her. "What if I can help these people, this city?"

Andromeda whirled on him. "You're not a fucking messiah. That's what got Khyran red lighted."

"Then why'd you give him the Stygian Tarot?" He stepped closer, not backing down from her.

"Because I loved him," Andromeda said. "I believed in him."

The rain washed away most of her face paint and Tagen's skin chilled. The diamond designs under her eyes weren't simply painted on—they had been notched into her skin.

She met his stare with defiance. "That witch carved them there, before taking my Circus. So that I would always have to paint my face to hide them."

He grasped her hands. "Then help me stop all this misery—"

"You can't!" she cried. "The city is too powerful!"

Tagen's nostrils flared. "Then why was that deck tattooed on Sveta? Why fight the High Priestess this long? Why care if I remember?"

"I don't know!" Her nose almost touched his.

"Stop avoiding my questions!" He snatched her hand. His palm glyphs glowed violet as the vision began.

One swipe, a gush of blood, and Khyran's head came free. It bounded around the stage until the High Priestess lifted it by the hair for all to see.

"Behold, the head of the Magician, the head of a heretic! Behold, the justice of the High Priestess!"

Tears flowed down Andromeda's face yet no sobs came. Her heart hardened into dark fruit, feeding off the vines of hatred budding within her. For a long moment, she stared at Khyran's headless body, then walked back through the cheering, hooting mob.

"Aye, what happened? Ye had a chance...Jaabir, Georgio, even Azibar waited for ye to act. Damn it, Lassie, look at me!" Saissa grabbed Andromeda by the arm and yanked her around.

"What should I have done?" Andromeda shoved Saissa into the Circus wall as they exited the grounds. "Huh? Kill that bitch, or end Khyran's suffering? Know what that would have done? That would have ended any fucking chance of us saving Meridian. Of beating the High Priestess."

Saissa's eyes widened and she pushed Andromeda into a nearby gutter. "Ye were afraid. Aye, fearing that ye'd not get what ye think is owed to ya. Afraid ye'd not get this city back. That it?"

Andromeda splashed across a clogged gutter puddle. "I…I don't know."

Saissa grabbed Andromeda's chin. "Aye, that it?"

"Fuck off!" She slapped Saissa, who punched her jaw. Trying to rise, Andromeda coughed as Saissa landed atop her, knees pressed into Andromeda's stomach. The will to fight drained from her.

"Damn ye, that it?" Saissa yelled in Andromeda's face.

"I don't know!" Andromeda's voice trailed off into a great sob and she went limp in the gutter. The remainder of her body paint tainted the puddle with whites, greens, pinks. Reds, from the spray of Khyran's blood.

"Are ye so selfish?" Saissa's face scrunched up. "Ye let him die for it?"

"There's…there's still the Stygian deck. If I find it, maybe I have a chance," Andromeda whispered. "I mean, we would have a chance…"

Saissa gripped Andromeda's throat and raised a fist.

"Do it," Andromeda mumbled, tasting her own tears.

Weeping, Saissa rolled off Andromeda. They both lay in the filthy puddle. Waves of sound from the cheering mobs bounced off the walls, disturbing the gutter water around them.

As the vision ended, Andromeda shook, her eyes drowning in shame.

"You created the Clowns," Tagen said. "You've used Khyran, and others before him, to take Meridian back. But you fell in love with your last puppet, didn't you? Now you hope, by defeating her, you can erase your guilt. Don't you?"

She turned away.

"Look at me, damn it. Don't you?"

Andromeda yanked her hands back. "Goddamn you. What do you know? You look at those cards, see my life, and think you know the take? My Circus was only one tent, a refuge for new kinkers. A place to forget this pain opera for a while. The High Priestess has turned it into a freak show of suffering."

"Then help me." He touched one of the diamond scars. She shivered.

"You'll die. I'm not a cartomancer anymore, but I know the take. I did fall for my instrument of vengeance. That's why I can't watch this anymore." She caressed his chin.

"I've died before." His fingers traced from the diamond scar down to her neck.

"But not for me," she said. "I won't let you."

Hands cupping his face, Andromeda leaned into him. Her lips brushed his, then their mouths melded together in hot, covetous play. The rain gushed over them but he was already drowning from the need to touch her. To be touched.

Again, it was as if they'd shared years together. Each knew the other's erogenous zones, how they wanted to be caressed—with the emotional desires burning far hotter.

Both had seen their lovers die. In this afterlife, each was the other's salvation.

Embracing her, Tagen sucked her tongue into his mouth. Moaning, Andromeda rubbed his crotch with her knee. He squeezed her firm rump with both hands. Whether or not the city of the dead fed their lust, Tagen cared not. He'd never felt more alive.

She tasted like life, felt like pure joy. Each gasp filled his nose with her gardenia scent. Andromeda climbed into his arms, tongue still fused with his own. Wet, trembling limbs slid against each other. He supped water off her breasts Whispered her name.

As she raised her leg and lay it against his shoulder, Tagen ran his fingers up her inner thigh. The warmth awaiting him there promised everything he wanted…

On the apartment floor, Alexis's blood engulfed the Ten of Cups.

"I'm sorry," he said, catching his breath. "I can't…"

Andromeda held onto him, shaking. "I…I know." The rain slacked off.

Tagen steadied her against the railing and gently set her on her feet. His body tingled, wanting more from her…but guilt welled up in him. Alexis still might need him. Even though she'd rejected him.

"It's not you," he breathed. "I swear, it's not—"

She lay a finger to his lips. "I know, Tagen."

"You said my name." He took her hand.

She faced the railing. Cleared her throat. Didn't let go of him. They gazed out over Meridian for some time. Occasionally, she squeezed his hand.

"Tell me what I need to know," he finally said.

"The Stygian deck is all cherry pie because it might show a path from Meridian."

"How? I don't understand why you, Azibar, or anyone else expects me to see such a path. So far, I've seen emotional paths, but—"

"They're the same." Andromeda faced him. "You saw a path in the cards, in your past life. It's by grasping an emotional path that one can chart a new destination. That's how you arrived in this joint. You were looking for someone. She was very important to you. That emotion, combined with your willpower, drew you here. Even I saw Meridian on a card, the night I died."

His mind's eye showed what Andromeda had fought against: the agents of a king, intent on her not stirring unrest with her demands. Spying on her home. Sabotaging her horse carriage. Thugs beating before her next show. Rebellion was in her soul.

"I can feel it when you do that," she mumbled.

"Sorry." Tagen rubbed her glyph. "Dazzling, remember?"

They shared a brief grin.

"So why didn't Khyran find a way?" he asked.

"Khyran might have, but he wouldn't leave Meridian. Like you, he wanted to change this shit show. That's why Georgio can't fly away in an airship, even if he had one, or some kinker have luck with a rowboat. They travel blind in the Styx, unless they see the way in their heart and mind. The Stygian Tarot offers mastery over both."

"No wonder the Clowns don't guard the docks—they don't have to," Tagen said. "But what of Radomir and Sveta? Could Khyran bring out other's memories—?"

"No. Your ability to bring out a kinker's memories, as well as other things, I've never seen." She frowned but held his hand against her side. Sensing the emotions inside of her, Tagen waited for her to finish.

"I don't know if Khyran put the tattoos on Nomad Girl. We split up so I could get the Blades ready, while he prepared to face the High Priestess. He had the time. But I really don't know."

"Then I need to talk with Khyran. I need a deck of cards." He wanted to see what he could do with them. Wanted to prove to Andromeda that his convictions were right.

Her eyes widened. "No. He's suffered enough."

Tagen placed her hand against his cheek. She swallowed.

"We all have." He released her and left the balcony.

2: Injustice

Darwick lifted his new sword, shinier and straighter than his previous one. To hell with those clockwork pistols. Killing should be up close. Let the fucker know who cut him down. He stalked down the street, flexing every muscle in his body. A hundred Clown warriors followed him.

The crowds in the Terraces backed up but didn't disperse. Some waved hand-painted Magician banners, while others bore similar designs on their bodies. They stared at him with questioning eyes. The accusing eyes of his murderers, hanging him for something he hadn't done. Like those assholes, the crowd wished to steal his happiness.

He hated Tagen even more for showing him those memories. Nauseous guilt flared inside him. If the High Priestess ever discovered his heretical visions, she would kill him. Though he would die for her, he didn't want to die a traitor. He'd been loyal to her, ever since she first came to him in Gibbet Avenue…

While eating the cooked human flesh, Darwick glanced at the curbs, the alleys. People steered clear of him. His name was painted on the buildings across the street, marking his territory. No gimmicks. Just his blade up their fucking asses if they crossed him. There had to be some sort of order in this crazy city.

"I told you I would return," a familiar female voice said behind him.

He kept eating, slurping on the broiled flesh, chewing tiny pieces of fried gristle.

"You have restored order here. But your followers have accused you of doing these things for yourself, haven't they?" Her voice was close to his ear, her warm breath on his neck. The scar tingled and he flung away the empty tray.

"I catch you spying on me again, I'll—"

As he turned, hands balled into fists, the High Priestess shuffled a golden Tarot deck. Though fresh rain beaded her nakedness, her body paint still hadn't worn off.

"You ain't afraid, without all those painted shitfaces protecting you?"

"What are you afraid of that others will see? You are not a man that cares about opinions. What is in your heart, that Meridian hasn't taken away?"

Darwick smacked the cards from her hands. The golden rectangles flipped end over end through the air, then rattled down on the cobblestones. Her eyes narrowed.

"Ain't nothing in there. You hear me? Ain't nothing in there for you to see with those dumb cards."

She slid her wrist from his iron-hard grip with ease. "Then why didn't you murder those children from the other gang? You are no coward."

"You saying I should have?" Where the fuck had she been, watching him to know all this? Had she seen him mounting that Knave bitch, fucking her so hard she cried? Cleaning his teeth with the garrote, tasting little slivers of flesh left over from his victims? Or had she seen him—"

"It is because I have seen those things, that I know you made the right decision," she said. "Meridian is lawless. It needs order."

"I could take whatever I fucking want from you." Darwick crushed her against him. No grease paint sloughed off in his grasp. Like she really was that pure and white. Not dirty, like everything else in Meridian. "What do you want from me?

"I want justice." She caressed his cheek. "I need you."

Her touch sapped his strength, emasculated his rage. Teased his heart.

He faced away, then glanced at his feet. There, all the golden Tarot cards were face-up. Each one depicted the Hanged Man.

Each one had his face.

He gasped and choked as he fell to his knees. "No...I was..."

She gripped his head in both hands, fingernails poking his cheeks. "That is how you see yourself. Now, see how I want you to be."

Darwick looked at the cards. They'd all become the Knight of Swords, depicting him wielding a crimson blade—standing on a mound of his friends and enemies.

"What is your answer?" Her moist red lips brushed his cheek.

He laughed long and hard.

The memory faded as he raised his voice so all in the street could hear.

"The High Priestess has declared believers in the Magician to be heretics! She has already given you the answers you want, from the Clown Tarot. She welcomes you to her Circus, to receive baptismal for your transgression."

His prepared words didn't calm the crowd. Curses and rocks flew. Someone tossed a bloody Clown wig onto the street before him. Darwick stepped closer.

"Break this shit up, or you'll be slaughtered for the Guild's kiosks!"

In reply, one woman threw a defaced banner of the High Priestess into a gutter. Several Clown heads rolled from between the crowd's legs, stopping at Darwick's feet.

"You're fucked, Darwick! The Magician's coming!"

"To the Styx with you, and that painted whore!"

"What are you afraid of, Clown? The Magician has been prophesied!"

Sinews flowing with pent-up rage, Darwick rushed forward. With a shout, he slashed with his sword. A head came free, then an arm, sliced away at the shoulder. Blood splashed him, the street, and other heretics. His fellow warriors joined in. They crushed and gutted any who didn't run. Limbs floated in the gutter. A child's head rolled past Darwick's feet. A woman wept over a man while holding in his entrails.

"So you shitheads like dying? You think this stupid Magician cares about you? Only the High Priestess cares!" He flung dripping viscera off his blade.

Clowns behind him discharged their pistols. Dozens more fell dead or dying.

Darwick strode forward. The crowd screamed and fled. A few diehards struggled but he swiped them down without mercy. Man, woman, child—it didn't fucking matter. Soon his new sword became his favorite color: red. His naked toes squished through crimson pools, his heels quashed lifeless faces. He picked up a piece of canvas, painted with a man pointing up with one hand, the other pointing down.

"I already killed you." Darwick cut the canvas in two.

Bone Guild members hurried behind him with hover gurneys. Gray hands plunked people onto them, live or dead. Vents hissed under the gurneys, keeping the floating coffins aloft. Other Guild members scalded the occupants with hand-held stewers, enfilading them with steam exhaust. The screams were beautiful.

Darwick himself didn't wait—he cut off a man's ear and gnawed on it. His goddess was safe. Now he could enjoy a victory feast.

A Clown of Staves strangled a man with his hands, laughing. Darwick spat out the ear and back-handed the Clown. The victim collapsed on the cub, coughing.

"I don't want to see that shit! Hear me?" Darwick kicked the Clown, then rubbed his own neck. The other warriors raised their eyebrows or cocked their heads.

He stalked away, simmering like he had in the hot sun, astride that stinking horse. A terrible weight fell on his heart. The killing, the blood, the screams—none of it gave him the same orgasmic, electrifying pleasure as before. Even the ear tasted like shit.

The bloodied streets made him think of the crimson-splattered clover beneath her red tresses. Her screams had been anything but beautiful.

Darwick walked away faster. When he'd sworn himself to the High Priestess, his only memories were of blood, survival. These new memories were different.

After he'd finished thrusting into her, the last man rose and pulled his pants up. She wasn't moving. Blood no longer bubbled from her shattered nose, or busted lips. Darwick tried to call her name…but the rope was too tight around his neck.

"I was…"

He was no better than the sheriff and those ranchers. He was worse.

Earlier that morning, they'd held each other under the creaking windmill.

"I love you so much, honey." She smiled up at him. "Forever and ever."

Darwick knelt behind a Bone Guild kiosk and wiped his eyes.

3: Copper Scales

Flipping the cape over his shoulder, Azibar smiled. He had saved it for this event, when he could strut through Meridian with his unstoppable soldiers. His engineers had fashioned it from tiny copper strands, burned purplish-blue with steam torches. Fifty Mecho Legionnaires marched behind him, venting steam in unison. Mannequin held the end of his luxurious cape.

As they neared Doll House, a pack of Clowns finished slaughtering several Magician heretics. This group was isolated from the other painted mobs the High Priestess had sent out. Excellent.

The Clowns looked up from the mutilated bodies. He enjoyed their shocked expressions. None outside his labs had seen the Legionnaires.

"What the hell do you want?" one warrior Clown asked.

Azibar grinned and raised his hand—the signal for his engineers to shut off the steamlamps along the street. The lights dimmed and winked out.

Capable of seeing in any light, Azibar's enhanced eyes showed all. He held Mannequin close while his soldiers eviscerated torsos, burned away faces, and swiped Clowns in half. Their swords didn't even scratch Legionnaire armor. Pistol shots bounced off his hulking troops. Clown blood pooled alongside those they had just murdered.

A few Clowns ran, then collapsed in smoldering heaps when the Legionnaires fired their arc rods. Ah, the scent of burnt flesh mixed with ozone.

He rubbed his copper hands together while the Legionnaires reformed ranks. "See, my dear? More imperfections eliminated. Soon I will report this to the High Priestess. She will go into a rage and try to tear the city down, hunting for Tagen. Are you listening, my dear?"

Kneeling over a young girl's body, Mannequin smoothed the corpse's dark hair. Her blue eyes blinked on and off, and her back vent released a continuous vapor cloud.

Azibar cleared his throat in an old habit. No phlegm would ever coat his bronze esophagus and palate. "Mannequin, come along. There will be much better candidates for the Mechos I'll model on you, my dear."

"I like this one," Mannequin said. "She's lovely."

Azibar's teeth ground against each other and he raised his hand. The steamlamps reactivated and Mannequin jumped back. Even though Mecho vision offered substantial clarity and depth, it still didn't match the effects of light.

"She's even lovelier." Strained modulation crept into Mannequin's silky voice. "Why not her? Why can't you revive her? Without biofluid. Without a copper heart."

He yanked Mannequin to her feet. "That is nothing more than an animal. A mistake. Why would I preserve something so ugly, so base?"

"I'm sorry," Mannequin said. "I guess it was a trick of the light."

His fingers tightened on her forearm. Tiny cracks appeared in her copper flesh. "You have not been the same since Tagen's visit. You were absent from the mechanis exhibition after your last

Rostrum speech. The surgeons said you failed the latest stimulus tests. Shall I send you back for an overhaul?"

"There is no need. This is all so…new…to me." She curtsied.

Smiling, he released her. "Of course. I've kept you in our district too long. You're not accustomed to these gruesome sights. Only by facing this city's decay, will you understand what it is that we must abolish."

She continued staring at the corpse. He whispered in her ear.

"Meridian rules the flesh. As it ruled this poor child. It cannot control those who reshape themselves with metal and purpose. As long as we can bleed, lust, and starve, we shall always be the city's victims. Help me change that, my dear."

"I understand…Azibar." She bowed her head.

Azibar motioned the soldiers on. "March to the nearest access hatch to Lotus Station. Make forays throughout the city and eradicate any Clown packs you encounter. Be prudent."

The Legionnaire captain nodded once. "Yes, Azibar. We will leave no witnesses."

The High Priestess would beg for his help, once her warrior zealots met slaughter after slaughter in Meridian's streets.

Unlike her, her would listen…and deliver.

4: Believers

After leaping over a gutter, Radomir ran around another corner. The screams of Magician faithful echoed off the Terraces behind him, as the Clowns showed no mercy. Good thing Radomir knew most access locations to Lotus Station, or the sewer tunnels where the Bone Guild congregated. Even knew of a Gutter Knight den a street away, yes. Would the High Priestess find him wherever he went? He kept running.

Finally out of breath, Radomir halted behind an old steam pulley. Once used to haul cargo from Meridian's docks, now kelp and wine bladders hung from it overtop a teal neon bulb, advertising a Dionysiac hub. He caught his breath and peered down the neon-lit avenue. The Clowns' laughter faded but many in the street slunk into alleys.

Radomir had seen people die before—had even slit a few necks himself. But the butchery visited on the crowd he'd led toward the Circus had been terrible. People lacerated into warm chunks, children dashed against walls. The pleading wounded, crushed by grease-painted feet.

All because they'd followed him.

He wept. All his hopes, all feelings of responsibility and change, now floated through bloody gutters. Rain drenched him, as if the city itself cried for the perished. Had he abandoned Brian the same as he'd ran while Clowns killed the Magician faithful?

Maybe he belonged in the gutter, after all.

Down the street, a small boy with filth-caked hair caught his attention. The child didn't cry or look afraid. He clasped a canvas banner someone had made, advertising their hope in the Magician's coming. It dragged behind him across the wet pavement. Several people peeked from alleys and doorways.

Radomir trembled with shame. A child showed no fear to walk in the open, bearing news of the Magician? He rose from behind the steam pulley and stepped into the street. As the child approached him, Radomir held out his hand for the canvas banner. The little boy hesitated, then handed it over.

"Why didn't that Magician stop them Clowns? You said you knew where he was." Since none aged here, the boy's voice sounded young—but his eyes held centuries.

A woman dressed in pink rags stepped from a doorway. A man with clockwork arms and legs crawled from an alley. Several others entered the street, staring at Radomir. At the banner in his hands.

"Find him, yes?" Radomir turned to the steam pulley and pushed on a stuck lever. It didn't move. He poured his anguish and determination into it. Muscles he should have used to fight the Clowns, yes. Energy others could have used to flee their pistols and swords. Radomir grunted and closed his eyes.

Laughing, Brian pushed a floating balloon at the birthday party.

The lever moved. He worked another one before the bundle hit the street. He lowered it down and motioned to the boy. The child removed the bundle and affixed the banner to the hook.

A man tattooed with images of women copulating with wine bottles exited the adjacent building. "Hey, cut that shit out. I've a business to run, wine to sell."

Radomir pushed the lever. The pulley lifted the banner into the air. Rain soaked it, making it hang straight down. Backlit by the neon bulb, the Magician stood over them in painted starkness.

"Maybe reconsider what you sell, yes? Find the Magician this time." Meeting the wine merchant's eyes, Radomir took the little boy's hand.

They walked down the street, away from the Terraces. Some of those watching followed, first with tentative glances, then with firm stares.

Moments later the wine merchant, the woman in pink, and others walked alongside Radomir.

5: Cracked Pillars

"Tell me!"

The High Priestess slammed the next Tarot card onto the table. On it, a Clown leaned on a staff, while behind him loomed a wall built from other staves. A bandaged cut bled from his temple and the Clown glanced over his shoulder, as if danger lurked beyond his improvised fortification. The Nine of Staves.

The trapeze lantern passed behind her and returned. In the transition from dark to light, the image on the card changed. Now she leaned on the staff and the wall of staves bore the heads of executed cartomancers.

She flung the deck from her. Golden cards clattered on the tent floor. She threw off her cape and walked into the aisle. Hundreds of decapitated heads stared at her. She snapped a finger and the Tarot deck reassembled itself and landed in her outstretched palm. The glyphs on both her hands glowed red.

Her followers believed she kept all these heads as trophies. A reminder that only she was Meridian's true prophet. While correct, her main reason remained her inability to either leave the city, or recall her past. None could ever know this.

Long ago, the heads had once revealed information to her mind's eye. A library of dead, dormant thoughts she could access via a card reading. Some of them remembered other places, other people.

Things she wished she could remember.

"Why can't any of you tell me?" the High Priestess whispered.

Once, she had considered ordering Azibar to reanimate them with his genius. She yearned to ask them again, relearn what they knew. None responded to her anymore.

"Why?" she screamed.

The cards flew from her hand and formed a doorway. Trembling with anger, she rushed through it. Tarot images passed through her mind, attuning her with the cards and their meanings. Like each time before, the cards showed her nothing about herself. Just hinting at enemies, like the Nine of Staves card. Or the Magician, showing her arrival so long ago, when the Circus had been but one tent.

She deserved love, needed compassion. Fanatical worship and adoring stares from drooling fools was better than nothing. Besides, she'd given these people something. A distraction from the horrible prison called Meridian. A belief that she held all the answers for them.

She had none for herself.

When Andromeda saved her on the streets, eons ago, the High Priestess had enjoyed the Harlequin's sympathy and attention. She became the beloved fortuneteller in the Circus and the attention she received increased a thousand fold.

Once she realized power came from that attention…her need for it increased a million fold. It was all she had to fill the void in her heart. Andromeda never understood.

As the High Priestess spread her palms, the glyphs continued glowing. The cards formed a mirror. She hesitated. She'd heard the

Stygian Tarot might be a mirror, showing the other side of Meridian, revealing a person's true self.

"My Tarot can do the same." She focused on the image before her.

She gasped at the woman staring back at her. Completely nude, her body painted in white grease paint. Beautiful, sensual, and proud. Admiring her contours, she sucked on a finger. Yes, she deserved to be worshipped.

Her lips left no impression on her body paint. Why? She wondered what lay beneath the greasy covering.

She tried rubbing some off her arm—but beneath the paint, her flesh remained perfect alabaster. The High Priestess tried wiping her face. The more she rubbed off, the more her cheeks and forehead shone ivory.

"What is my name?" she asked herself in the Tarot mirror.

The image morphed into the High Priestess card. It showed her sitting nude between a black pillar and a white pillar, both venting steam. A veil decorated with red flowers hung from the pillars behind her. The Styx yawned at the veil's edges.

"Who are you?" she asked.

In the image, she turned on the throne and thrust side the veil.

The High Priestess fell to the floor. Golden cards rained down around her.

Someone other than herself waited beyond the veil. A different cartomancer.

"No!" Darwick shouted as he ran into the center ring where she lay. He lifted her, his eyes aflame with hurt and rage.

She touched his cheek. "The Magician is not dead."

Darwick shook his head, his beating heart vibrating through her own body. "I killed him, High Priestess. But his followers...the Nomad, and a Harlequin..."

Spiteful resolve filled her. "Andromeda? That selfish bitch never wanted me to find myself in the Tarot. She gave people nothing. I give them everything."

"That ain't all, High Priestess," Darwick muttered.

Catching the hesitation in his eyes, she lifted herself up. She would not lose Meridian. Damn the Tarot. She commanded the cards, she made the future hers.

"What has happened?" She burned inside, remembering Azibar's slur about her inability to see the Magician's whereabouts.

"Three packs of warriors have been massacred." Darwick's voice shook with fury. "At each scene, we found dozens of dead heretics. They're rising against us!"

The High Priestess pounced on Darwick and gripped his throat. "They dare not! I am their goddess! I am Meridian! There is nothing without me."

Darwick's eyes glazed over as if he suffered deep pain. She released his throat.

"What is wrong with you? Will you not defend my honor?" She rubbed her thigh against his shoulder. The glaze slowly left his eyes.

"I will fucking kill all of 'em," Darwick breathed. "I was innocent."

"Innocent of losing so many warriors?" She sniffed. "I want you to find Tagen and Sveta. Find Andromeda, the Harlequin. Do you see what they're doing to me?"

Rubbing his neck, he still looked addled. Meridian was feeding her less power, then. The city was already abandoning her. She would not waste any more time.

She knelt on the floor beside him. "You love me, don't you?"

"Yes, High Priestess. Ain't nobody more faithful than me."

She kissed him, while he groaned like a man in sweet pain. She liked the taste of his desperate sweat, the dried blood on his lips where he'd feasted on a defeated heretic.

She ran a finger from between her breasts, down to her crotch, and wetted her finger in hot moistness. She put the finger into his mouth.

"Find them and I shall reward you with whatever you desire."

Darwick slobbered on her finger, lapping up her wetness. The High Priestess laughed, rallying her dog to sniff out her prey.

6: Ultimatum

Tagen sat at the wooden table with Sveta. Neither spoke but they shared an occasional glance. The return of Saissa, Jaabir and Khyran gave a welcome respite from their silence.

A frown weighed down Saissa's brows. "Clowns are killing people in the Terraces, and the Row. Aye, hundreds dead, that is."

"Word here in the Corner says there's a revolt against the High Priestess." Jaabir set down a copper valve and coil on the table. "You look better, Tagen."

Andromeda descended the stairway, wearing the black torsolette again. She'd repainted her face and body. "What's with the lot lice out there?"

"Magician heretics, marching round Meridian," Saissa said.

Sveta stood. "Who did they kill? Which district?"

"Fuck. How did this start?" Andromeda glanced at Tagen, but he shrugged.

"Hey, I've been here all this time. I haven't even talked to anyone—"

"Radomir," Sveta said. "Or Azibar. No one else knows about Tagen."

"Gorgon's tits, people," Jaabir said. "I tell you, word has gotten out. Someone has rallied resistance to the Clowns."

"They'll all die. I've seen this pitch before." Andromeda plopped onto a stool and rested her chin on her hand. Khyran landed on her shoulder

Tagen stood. "You're just going to sit here? They're dying because of me, don't you get it?"

"I get it." Andromeda glared. "I told you, it's a hopeless blood opera."

Saissa snorted. "Hold there. We Blades have scrapped 'em Clowns good all this time, and you telling us it's no good?"

Jaabir nodded. "Yeah, that's bullshit talk, Andromeda. It's just us now. We got the Magician, and Saissa told me pretty thing here has the Stygian deck on her skin. Your palm glyphs don't read the cards anymore."

"That's right, Andromeda, you can't see the future." Tagen's anger rose. "If I can do something about this, I will. I've seen enough of Meridian's suffering."

"You've also been mistaken before." Sveta glanced at his wrists.

Tagen glared at her. "Not everyone gets to be hero when they want to be."

"You don't need to be a martyr, either," Andromeda said. "What will you do? Give them floss on a stick, try to pitch to the High Priestess? Fight them?"

"I'll show them the pathways I saw in Sveta's tattoos," Tagen said.

Sveta wouldn't meet his eyes.

Andromeda rose and jabbed a finger into his chest. "You need to train your magical talents. You're not strong enough to comprehend the entire Stygian deck!"

"Sveta, will you let me see the rest of your tattoos?" Tagen asked.

Sveta hugged herself. "No. I told you, you're not the Magician."

Shaking his head, Tagen turned away. "Maybe Khyran knows."

Before Andromeda could react, he touched the jack-in-the-box and concentrated. She shouted for him to stop but his mind's eye opened wide.

Khyran, a whole man, lay on a cutting block in the Circus. The High Priestess licked her lips, while a busty Clown executioner sharpened her axe. Wearing pink and green Harlequin colors, Andromeda stood in the crowd. Tears ran grease paint furrows down her cheeks.

"Show me," Tagen whispered.

Khyran had believed in himself and his love for Andromeda. Tagen understood his desire to end Meridian's pain, to remove the yoke of the High Priestess. Yet, in a darkened alley, Khyran handed the Stygian deck to a figure in the shadows. Someone else had tattooed the images on Sveta. Over these visions and sensations came the pain Khyran now felt. He hated his Mecho existence and wanted Andromeda to forget him and move on. He wanted to be shut off and allowed to die.

Tagen's vision ended as Andromeda ripped Khyran's head from his grasp.

A steel Tarot deck spilled from Tagen's hands over the carpet. All the cards lay face down, save for one: a Mecho sitting on a clockwork throne, holding a sword and a set of scales. Half his face was smeared with grease paint. A curtain concealed a hidden vista behind him.

"Justice," Tagen murmured. The steel cards faded. The others gasped.

Sveta stumbled backward. "You no longer require a physical deck…"

"But you can't control it, either," Andromeda muttered.

"Jaabir, get a message to Georgio," Tagen said. "I will be the path. He'll know."

"You haven't deciphered the whole Stygian deck," Andromeda said. "You don't have all your memories."

"I protected people in my former life," Tagen said. "Maybe that's why I'm here."

"Goddammit, Jackpot, listen to me! This won't defeat the High Priestess!"

Tagen concentrated. A black mirror hung in the shadows of his peripheral vision.

Meridian's power.

As he focused on them, the copper valve and coil flew from the table and attached themselves to his upper back. The coil connected with the valve and filter. Biofluid gushed in his veins. His palm glyphs flashed.

They all gaped at him and backed a step.

"That's just meant to keep you going until I found more stuff," Jaabir said. "Gonna kill you, you ain't careful."

"I've died once already. Maybe it'll mean something this time." Using what he'd learned from Andromeda and Sveta, Tagen focused on the Justice card in his mind. He poured all his emotional need into it: justice for his friends, this city's people.

Justice for his broken heart, still seeking Alexis.

The room and his friends faded from sight as Tagen entered the mirror at the edges of his vision. A damp street materialized under his feet and the Terrace's high-rises glowed above him.

7: Affirmation

"Shit!" Andromeda knelt in the space Tagen had just occupied. He was more powerful than she'd realized. And she'd let him go.

"Georgio doesn't have an airship from a children's story," Sveta said. "Tagen might as well be asking him to prepare a funeral barge. I have to warn the Nomads."

Andromeda rose and blocked the doorway.

"Don't." Sveta glared.

Saissa and Jaabir tensed but Andromeda shook her head at them.

"You're a cartomancer, so that means you're on Meridian's take," Andromeda said. "Shouldn't we follow Jackpot and try to help him?"

Sveta blushed. "He doesn't even know where he's—"

"We know exactly where he's going." Andromeda maintained her stare.

"He thinks he's helping people, but he's not," Sveta said. "He's making their suffering worse. We have to master our pain."

Andromeda didn't move from the doorway. "We're not abandoning him."

"You just want him for your own selfish goals," Sveta said. "I don't want him to turn me into…"

Confused, Andromeda cocked her head. "Nomad Girl?"

"Never mind," Sveta whispered.

Khyran hovered to the table and took up the silver Tarot deck in his mouth.

"I used this before the High Priestess came to Meridian," Andromeda said. "You once drew the Magician for Jackpot. If you don't think he's the Magician, try again."

Rolling her eyes, Sveta drew the top card. She jerked back and frowned.

"Come on Nomad Girl, stop playing 'round." Even though Andromeda didn't think much of Tagen's plan, he had to be the Magician. Knew it in her heart.

Sveta's hand shook as it turned the card over. The Lovers. On it, a Harlequin woman held a white flower, while a winged man held a red one. Andromeda admired the old artwork. Her friend Pixie had painted the deck's images in wonderful blues, reds, and yellows. They depicted Harlequins, winged Pages, and glittering kings and queens.

"The Lovers," Andromeda said. "Time to make a choice."

"Tagen will bring ruin to this city," Sveta said.

"Then what's the deal with you following him around everywhere?" Jaabir asked.

Andromeda stared at her. "She thinks she has to stop him."

"I've seen who he is," Sveta said. "What this city becomes."

"And now that he's looked into your bally tattoos…" Andromeda sighed.

"Yes, our memories are linked, now," Sveta said. "Every time he remembers something new…so do I. It's driving me crazy. What am I supposed to do?"

Andromeda scowled. "Meridian is feeding him power. If he gets more, before regaining all those memories—then the city will fill the gaps with its darkness."

Saissa and Jaabir waited. Andromeda tried to control her breathing.

"I'm still going to Georgio." Sveta placed the card back into the deck.

"If you've got itchy feet, then we're coming, too." Andromeda let her pass. She couldn't force Sveta to do anything; the city's very magic was imprinted on her flesh. And Tagen needed that magic, if she…if she…

She thought of the memory Tagen had shown her on the balcony. Her selfishness, her refusal to save Khyran. All because Andromeda had wanted to survive and continue her war of vengeance.

Tagen needed that magic…if they all expected to survive.

While Saissa and Jaabir gathered their things, Andromeda donned her original Blades of Charon outfit: corset, knee-high stockings, gloves, skirt, and shoulder pads. All of it was black leather, reinforced with fine steel mesh underneath. Heavier than her usual disguise, but necessary. She topped it off with a matching, three-pointed hat, with an onyx diamond at each end.

Lastly, she sheathed her daggers under the skirt. For countless time, she had dipped each blade in the Styx to blacken the metal. An old Meridian myth claimed such weapons slipped through an enemy's defenses. It represented her own cartomantic blindness, since the waters darkened the dagger's engraved glyphs.

Was her heart blind as well?

Tagen thought he knew what the city needed. Just like she had, once.

Venting steam, Khyran led them out. As a crowd gathered near the Corner's taverns, someone held up a crude Magician banner. Andromeda whispered to herself.

"Though sorrow come with parting pain, he shall come back to Meridian again."

XII.

THE HANGED MAN

1: The Great Work

Walking from the Terraces, Tagen kept the Circus in sight. He grew angrier with each footstep. The copper valve meant to stem biofluid thrummed in his back and his muscles bulged anew. He wouldn't believe Andromeda's despairing view, despite Khyran's demise. Abiding Meridian's cruelty equaled abetting it.

Maybe if he ended this misery…he could find Alexis.

Ahead, a building with the word 'Magician' painted on it in large blue letters caught his eye. Some of the paint had run but the word remained legible. A group of battered, bloodied people stood beneath it, whispering among themselves. Downtrodden faces turned and gazed at him.

Tagen raised his right hand in greeting, while his left pointed down to the street. Concentrating on his emotions, his Sun glyph glowed violet. A steamlamp flared behind him. The crowd gasped and cowered.

"It doesn't have to be like this." Tagen scanned the frightened faces, the seeping wounds. The marks of the High Priestess's terror.

An old woman hobbled toward him. "Are you the Magician?"

"I'm Tagen." He took her hand and his mind's eye opened to a log house on a riverbank. *Pomegranate trees thrived beside a garden filled with squash and beans. Three grandchildren ran around a kitchen table, while the old woman stirred cake mix in a wooden bowl. He picked a red pomegranate blossom, remembering the one he'd given Sveta in the sewer. He handed it to the old woman.*

Harsh steamlamps flooded out Tagen's vision. The old woman knelt before him, gigging like a small girl. She held a red bloom the size of her fist. Dew dripped from its petals. The crowd circled around Tagen, gaping and pointing.

He could make his visions a reality. Was it his intent, or Meridian's?

"I can see them," the old woman whispered. "I can see my grandchildren."

Her happiness proved infectious as others leaned closer, hands outstretched. Instead of grasping them, Tagen closed his eyes. The Tarot cards he'd seen on Sveta's back flooded his consciousness. *Obelisks, tomes, masks, pathways.* Even without knowing the whole deck, confidence burst in him. He opened his eyes.

Those who'd reached to him now held a paper Tarot card, personalized to their memories. Some squealed with delight. Others sobbed in grief. All regarded him as something other than human.

"Where are you going?" The old woman clasped the blossom to her chest.

"The Circus," he said.

"You'll be killed!" a skinny man with bronze hands cried. "The Clowns are murdering any who ask questions about you."

"The prophecy cannot be denied," a boy said.

"They won't kill you, if you show them what you've shown us." The old woman smiled. Years lifted from her face.

"I'm not afraid anymore." The crowd parted for Tagen. As he continued toward the Circus, many, including the old woman, followed him.

2: Revelation I

With Khyran hovering after her, Andromeda hurried from the railcar in Lotus Station. Sveta ran over the platform with dour fatalism, the faint steamlamps lighting her tattoos in a rippling picture book of mystery. Andromeda wished she could read it. Then she would take on the burden Tagen thought he could handle.

Khyran had hid a lot from her, even in their last moments before he'd confronted the High Priestess. Like Tagen was doing now. Too much had been left unsaid between them. Those moments with him on the balcony…

Several Wretched watched them from an opposite platform. Andromeda had to look away. She'd found Khyran down here when he'd first arrived in Meridian and saved him from the Wretched. It tore her heart that she had made him like them, a Mecho cripple, just to cling to her feelings. Selfish feelings.

Sveta led them across a catwalk. Each step sent masonry dust into the Styx below.

"So what's the plan?" Jaabir asked.

"We find Jackpot and let him see the rest of Nomad Girl's tattoos." Andromeda twirled a dagger on her fingertip. "You got a better pitch?"

Sveta's face flushed. "I'm not showing him—"

"Aye, look," Saissa said.

On the next platform, several Nomads carried copper and bronze parts down the stairs from the hatch above. Sveta's expression changed from denial to shock.

"Seems Georgio's already heard about Jackpot," Andromeda said.

They followed Sveta into Nomad Way through a hatch. The multi-colored steam lanterns and mazurka music made her realize how much she missed Georgio and other friends. Juggling, dancing, or singing now seemed someone else's pursuits. In her war against the High Priestess, Andromeda had abandoned so much.

Would she have to make sacrifices for Tagen, too? Was he worth it?

Activity buzzed around the district. Men and women gathered machine parts, while others packed food and personal items into canvas bags. Everyone looked ready to go on a long journey.

Georgio stood outside his tent, rolling paper charts in oiled sheets. Sveta's brow wrinkled in worry.

This was something rehearsed, then: an exodus. Barging in on Georgio now might deepen his distrust of her. Andromeda shooed Khyran and Saissa to remain with her behind the corner, but Jaabir ignored her. Shit, what was he doing?

Georgio set aside the charts and hugged Sveta, his face alight with relief. "I knew you'd make it back."

Andromeda caught his gaze poring over Sveta's tattoos. Maybe he'd been worried about more than just Sveta's welfare.

"Why are supplies being taken into Lotus Station?" Sveta asked.

"Meridian is revolting against the Clowns. Darwick and his fiends have killed many people. The time has come to leave. Where's Tagen?" Georgio's gaze hardened. "Who's this man? He looks like a Blade of Charon."

Six armed Nomads set aside their boxes and waited behind Georgio. Steam jetted from Jaabir's side vent.

"Tagen went to the Circus to challenge the High Priestess. He thinks he's the Magician." Sveta rubbed her arms. "This is Jaabir."

Jaabir stepped forward. "She's right, Georgio. But Tagen is the Magician. He asked me to tell you to get ready to leave Meridian. Seems you heard already."

"Where's your traitorous leader?" Georgio asked. "I know she didn't follow Tagen. Like she didn't stand with Khyran."

Ignoring the armed Nomads, Andromeda walked right up to Georgio. "You never bled with Khyran either, and you believed in him. What makes Jackpot any different?"

Georgio grunted and looked away.

"You can't just leave the city. This is all we have. You don't really believe that mark Tagen made on your chart? He's not the Magician!" Sveta's words held little conviction and she avoided Andromeda's stare. "How will you do it? Walk on water behind him across the Styx?"

"If that is what it takes!" Georgio cried, then his face softened. "A change of view, a sense of waste, a change of residence in haste."

The Nomad proverb reminded Andromeda again of how much she'd missed in her bloodless feud with Georgio. "I'm ready for that pitch, you old trouper."

"Why should I believe you?" Georgio asked. Several tense seconds passed.

"The Blades of Charon are just us three, Georgio. You could have a revenge opera right now. I've not always done the best thing. But I'm going to do the right thing."

Georgio glanced from Khyran to Andromeda. "He always wanted to see you juggle, like you once did for Emrys, Pixie, and me. When Khyran came here, your Circus had been taken. The only Harlequin he knew was the one before me now: angry, hurt, and armed with Charon's steel. He wanted to see the happy one you used to be."

"Aye, I would see that too," Saissa whispered.

"Khyran will see me again if I get my take." Andromeda flicked her cap points. "You helping me or not? I won't leave Jackpot to fight alone."

Sveta pleaded them with her eyes, her fists balled in frustration.

"Yes," Georgio final said.

Andromeda half-smiled. "Got any grease paint? You're not going to this freak show dressed like that."

3: Stygian Nimbus

Two blocks from the Circus, Tagen halted as another crowd gathered in the street ahead. They carried canvas Magician banners. Many were bruised and cut from fighting Clown warriors. What would he tell these people? The scope of what he'd entered gave Tagen a headache. Sweat ran down his back. With a heavy heart, he studied everyone in the crowd, searching for Alexis's face…or even the golden mask.

At their forefront stood a short figure with a stitched-together visage: Radomir.

The Gutter Knight regarded Tagen with reverence, while the crowd hushed. Clown whoops reverberated down an opposite street. For once, the rain ceased altogether.

Radomir grinned and pointed at Tagen. "Magician, yes?"

Those behind Tagen shouted in agreement, while those behind Radomir clambered forward. Hopeful faces and sorrowful words assaulted Tagen. Dozens touched him. A few kissed his fingers, his boots. One woman with half a clockwork face kissed his cheek before Radomir pushed them back.

"Listen, yes?" Radomir glanced toward the Circus, then at Tagen. Fear and hope lighted the man's porcine eyes.

"Save us!" the woman with the clockwork face yelled.

"The Clowns are coming, what will you do?" someone asked.

"Can you show us the way?" a woman in pink rags asked.

"Give us meaning, Magician! Give us life!"

Rising voices filled his ears. Tagen tried to look everyone in the eye, tried listening to all their entreaties. It was impossible.

Shutting his eyes, he focused on the Ace of Cups in his mind. *From it, he poured nourishment and epiphany into the thoughts of those around him. He opened their minds, cracking the barrier Meridian had placed there.*

An overwhelming emotional wave rippled through the crowd. Some staggered. Others fell to their knees. The effect produced scores of reactions: anger, grief, acceptance, happiness, regret.

The shadows appeared at the edge of his sight. Churning, darkening. Hinting at what else he could do with these people. All of Meridian lay at his feet, if he simply…

Tagen rubbed Alexis's back until she fell asleep. She always enjoyed that, after they made love. Entwined in the sheets, her breathing fell into a rhythm. He watched her for a time, wondering if their lifestyles would ever match, if she would ever understand the things he did to keep her happy.

The last two months had been hard. He'd worked extra, trying to pay the mortgage, financing a new car—maintaining appearances was expensive. Maybe he'd ask for even more work. Lay off the alcohol this time.

But his work was never easy, either.

He rose from the bed and glanced out the window. Rather than the lawn and fountain he was accustomed to, a steam-lit city filled the view outside. Monolithic skyscrapers, pulsing neon signs…

That couldn't be right.

"Alexis?" He ran to the bed and shook her, but his fingers stuck in the grease paint covering her shoulder.

"No," he mumbled, heart squeezing into an icy ball of fear.

Laughter made him hurry outside. Naked Clowns played in the fountain. Gutter Knight disassembled his car. He turned to run back into the house but it was gone. Instead, he stood in Meridian. The rain was colder than he remembered.

Wait, he had no memories of cold rain in Meridian!

The vision faded and once again Tagen stood at the forefront of a crazed mob.

He drew a deep breath. Andromeda had warned that the city would take him, if he couldn't remember it all soon.

The shouts increased to a roar. The mob swelled. Shadows ruled his sight.

"Wait!" he cried. "We must—"

The crowd pushed Tagen toward the Circus on an unstoppable flood of souls who demanded everything Meridian—and the High Priestess—had denied them.

Chanting his name, the number of Magician faithful grew larger with each street it passed. Many denizens retreated into their homes or alleys. Some cringed in damp gutters. Not everyone wanted to challenge the Clowns. Meridian contained the only life they had ever known.

His followers now knew different. Those with pleasant memories adored him, while those with the opposite sought revenge on anyone they could mete it on. How would he control them?

Tagen didn't want more bloodshed, he wanted truth and an end to suffering. Such simple things often cost more than anyone wanted to pay—even himself. He tried to calm the crowd but Radomir nudged him and shouted to all about the Magician prophecy.

"Gave back my Brian," Radomir said. "Giving back all our lives, yes?"

The question made Tagen's throat dry. "We'll...we'll see."

As the crowd neared the Circus, his heart pounded a ferocious beat.

What if Sveta had been right about him all along? Andromeda believed in him—but not in hope for Meridian.

Did he believe?

Radomir tugged his vest. Tagen took a deep breath and tried to clear his mind.

The crowd hushed.

Hundreds of Clowns barred their path. Darwick, coated in fresh red paint, shot Tagen a hellish glare. The Clowns wielded clockwork pistols, steam-powered crossbows, swords, staves, chains, clubs, and even jagged bones. Their lank, semi-nude bodies were lathered in an anarchic kaleidoscope. Frayed wigs lent them a maniacal air.

"All you shitfaces, put those fucking banners down and listen!" Darwick called. "The High Priestess has said the Magician cult is a heresy. Disobey her and die."

"Fuck off, Clown asshole!" the woman in pink rags shouted back.

"We won't obey that whore!" a man behind Tagen cried.

Tagen tried to remain calm as his followers taunted the Clowns. Radomir looked up at him, waiting. Now, here where he'd planned to be, Tagen didn't know what to do. His cartomancy hadn't revealed any outcome here, no hint of what would happen.

"You don't have to serve her, Darwick," Tagen said. "You were an innocent man once. Would you be the villain now?" He tried summoning the Stygian images in his mind, but none came.

Darwick laughed, though his gaze held much pain. "So you survived. You still ain't fooling me, shitface. You ain't taking her, or Meridian, away from me."

"She's already taken it from you," Tagen said.

The crowd behind him cheered and tossed rocks at the Clowns. Radomir rubbed his gauntleted hands and nodded.

"Cut these fuckers down!" Darwick pointed his sword at Tagen.

Tagen raised his hands. "No, you don't have to—!"

Twenty Clowns fired pistols. Bullets whizzed past, smacking into flesh. People around Tagen screamed. A dozen fell dead. Two vapor grenades landed in their midst, scalding people with super-heated steam. Howling like demons, the Clowns charged.

Concentrating, Tagen tried to summon the Stygian deck into his mind. Tried to use its mirrors to reflect pain back at the Clowns. Again, nothing happened.

Tagen reached under his left arm. No gun holster was there.

Radomir drew a steel shiv. Others in the crowd produced clubs, stones, or bone knives. A scant few drew their own pistols. Many turned to run. Shouts from behind added to the chaos and Tagen wheeled around. Clowns charged into the mob's rear.

He'd led them into a trap.

Since he couldn't summon cartomancy, Tagen let the biofluid surge through his body. The copper valve and tin filter throbbed in complaint. Enhanced muscles gifted him brutal striking power. He shoved aside Clown warriors so they wouldn't hurt the people behind him. As he punched out a Clown's teeth, he envisioned him as a normal man, with a fine daughter and beautiful wife. A Clown woman he bashed to the street had once been a princess in a desert kingdom of silk-clad riders.

Every time he struck a Clown, pieces of their past life entered his mind. Like Darwick, they'd been people once, and could be again. Each Clown he killed reminded him of the life he'd ended. His drive to reach the High Priestess exploded in his heart.

He'd been a cop, a good person protecting the innocent. He was still that man.

Yelling, he pressed through a barrage of sword thrusts, fists, and club strikes. Pistol shots grazed his shoulders. Blood welled and then sealed over dozens of wounds on his body. The biofluid kept him going, but his heart and lungs burned. The copper coil on his back flailed like a live snake.

Radomir kept pace with him, stabbing and slicing, though Clowns ripped hunks from his armor. The other Magician faithful fought for their lives. Slashing, punching, shooting, even biting if necessary. Others surrendered, begging the Magician to save them as the Clowns massacred them. People slipped in the blood-slick street. Bodies clogged the gutters.

Anguish sapped Tagen's strength. Please, this wasn't what he wanted—

Darwick closed with Tagen and swung; Tagen ducked and punched him in the stomach. Engorged with biofluid power, he elbowed a few teeth from the Clown's mouth. Darwick shouted and thrust his sword into Tagen's left side. Another Clown wrapped his chain around Tagen's head and pulled, bloodying his temples.

"Fucker." Darwick laughed. "Hold him down! She'll have her prize."

Grunting, Tagen yanked a Clown's arm out of socket. Radomir slashed like a madman at his side but three more Clowns forced Tagen to the pavement. Darwick kicked Radomir away.

A Clown woman shoved her dagger through Tagen's right palm, pinioning it to the street. He busted her jaw with an upthrust knee. All around him, Clowns crushed those who had dared challenge their white-painted goddess. He had achieved nothing.

A group of thin, gray-skinned Bone Guild members waited for the combat to end, their hover gurneys ready.

Tagen tried focusing on the Clowns around him so they'd see the path he'd intended. The mirrors in his mind could show them. "You're not animals! You're not murderers! Listen to me. Don't be her slaves any longer!"

Darwick shoved his sword into a wounded figure lying nearby: the old woman with the red flower. Her eyes turned glassy, staring at Tagen with an eternal question.

The red blossom rotted. Blackened pomegranate seeds slipped from his hand.

"Goddamn you Darwick!" Tagen punched a Clown's nose in a shower of red. Urging the biofluid into his legs, he tried to rise, tried to reach the old woman—

A spiked club struck his stomach. The chain tightened around his head. The copper coil snapped loose on his back and the valve and filter spurted. His physical demands broke what Jaabir had intended as a temporary fix.

A Clown woman dry humped him. "Hey, I just fucked the Magician!"

Darwick slapped her off and stepped on Tagen's neck. Biofluid pumped strength through him but too many held him down. His heart hammered, his muscles strained. The chain pulled taunt around his head. Another sword stabbed into his leg. The tip exited his calf and screeched on the pavement.

A sickening silence fell over the street.

"Nobody touch him! We're taking him back to the Circus." Darwick's eyes filled with glee.

Two Clowns dragged Tagen through the bloody street, over corpses and severed limbs. People who had believed in him, or wanted a glimpse beyond Meridian's darkness. His friends' warnings haunted him as biofluid squirted from his nose.

6: Disciple

Radomir rolled into a gutter and crawled through crimson-stained water. Clowns were still slaughtering the remaining faithful in the street. The corpses numbered in the hundreds. Though he hurt from several wounds, Radomir drug himself to a sewer grate. He kicked aside the rusted bars and slid inside, like the slug he now regarded himself.

Inside the grate, Radomir studied the battle's aftermath. Darwick and his cruel comrades dragged Tagen down the street toward the Circus. The moaning wounded didn't dissuade the Bone Guild from tossing them onto hover gurneys.

The Magician had failed them. In the one moment Radomir had truly believed, Tagen had been beaten down like a thug in the street. So sure he could defeat the Clowns and their High Priestess. So confident, yes.

Now, believers lined the pavement in broken heaps. Neon signs lit it all in grotesque, hyper-reality. So many people had been gifted a glimpse of their memories by Tagen, only to be butchered before they could ponder such revelations.

Gutter water splashed over Radomir. Maybe it would wash it all away, yes.

The water ran red.

He forced himself from the sewer grate. He couldn't handle being washed in the blood of those who had tried and failed. Perhaps he should've killed Tagen when they'd first met, yes? None of this would have happened. These people wouldn't have died.

Radomir sheathed his shiv and walked away. Stepping over the corpses, a victim's bronze choker caught his eye. What could he bargain for it in the Bazaar?

No. He left the choker alone. With the veil pulled aside, Radomir couldn't go back. He turned and made for the Circus, stepping on a Magician banner as he went.

Maybe if Tagen died, he could be a Gutter Knight again.

Brian laughed and reached up to him with simple, innocent love.

Radomir raised a hand, as if wiping spittle from his infant son's mouth.

Stumbling, he looked down. An old woman with lifeless eyes lay in his path. She held a red bloom. Moisture beaded its petals. Radomir took it and stared. The Magician card scrap at Doll House had depicted such flowers…

He tucked the blossom inside his battered armor and quickened his step.

7: Revelation II

"The High Priestess will parade Jackpot around before she red lights him," Andromeda said. "That buys us a little time. But we must go."

With Nomad Way only a few blocks from the Circus, they'd just heard of Tagen's capture and the street massacre. Eager to move, Saissa and Jaabir already wore Clown wigs and green face paint. Nomads talked among themselves in small groups. Most were unsure of this new Magician, or if they'd support him.

Georgio turned a ring on his finger. White and orange paint covered his face. He looked her up and down with his sharp, blue eyes. "Nothing can bring Khyran back. I'll help you rescue Tagen, but that's it. Azibar has nothing I want."

Andromeda stared at her palms. Each bore the Sun, Moon, and Star glyphs. Like Tagen's. Their shapes reminded her of Sveta's body art. She looked into Georgio's eyes. "Khyran gave you the Stygian deck. You tattooed Nomad Girl."

"Nothing gets past a cartomancer for long, even a dormant one." Georgio's smile faded as he stared into space. "We found her in an alley in Boulevard. An odd place for a new arrival. She had the glyphs to boot. With each tattoo, one of the cards disappeared until none were left. Sveta has the entire deck on her skin. I didn't know any other way to preserve them for the Magician, whoever he turned out to be."

Andromeda touched his shoulder. "Why haven't you told her?"

Closing his eyes, Georgio scratched his beard. "She's become like a daughter to me. No one would think to look at the tattoos of a Sky Nomad fortuneteller. When Tagen saw things in them, I knew he was the one."

She didn't reply as Sveta exited Georgio's tent, her entire body covered in white and pink paint. None of her tattoos shown. A pink corset and skirt concealed little of her figure. A drooping pink cap sat atop her braided head.

"Well?" Sveta asked.

"Well, now that you're all prettied up, we can go," Andromeda said. "Ready?"

"Ready as an oiled Mecho, that is. Aye, but are ye ready?" She and Jaabir measured Andromeda with their eyes.

"Always." Andromeda had watched Khyran's execution because she couldn't reveal herself. Because her war against the High Priestess had to go on, instead of Khyran's life.

But Tagen...

Blood covered Andromeda's body, though not all of it was hers. Grimacing against the pain, she limped from the alley. Rain fell heavily on her quivering shoulders. The urge to vomit burned her throat.

With bare knuckles, she'd killed three of them in that alley. The others stopped attacking her and ate their fallen comrades. Right in front of her.

She remembered falling from the tightrope after the gunshot, then waking up here. It wasn't Hell. It was the city the fortuneteller had shown her on that Tarot card.

Andromeda unclasped her hand. She held the same card the fortuneteller drew for her. The Magician's face was hard to make out in the downpour.

"Help me," she managed through bloody lips.

Ever since her arrival in Meridian, the Magician had been linked to her destiny.

But Andromeda didn't give a damn about prophecy any more. Tagen needed her.

8: Martyrdom

A pair of bare, white-painted feet stopped inches from Tagen's face. Clowns in the tent around him cheered and whistled. He craned his neck upward while the High Priestess lowered her hand. The Clowns fell silent. A cruel smile parted her face.

"So this is the Magician. Quaint. All too quaint." She gestured. Darwick and another Clown hauled Tagen to his feet.

The dagger remained stuck in his hand and the chain still hung from his head. The biofluid had congealed his wounds, but it bubbled from his lips with each heartbeat.

"Carry him behind me to the stage," the High Priestess said. "Has the Carousel been readied? Are the stands full?"

Darwick grinned. "All's ready, High Priestess. Everybody wants to see you."

"It doesn't have to be this way," Tagen said. "Listen—"

Darwick punched him in the mouth.

"I am the only way," the High Priestess said.

After she exited the tent, Darwick hauled Tagen behind her onto a wooden stage. Harsh steamlamps blinded him. A wave of voices battered his ears. Blinking his sight back into focus, the scene came alive like a waking nightmare.

Thousands of Clowns howled from bleachers in a semicircle around the stage. Several fired pistols into the air. Thousands more citizens stood outside, gawking at him. Skull-shaped confetti floated down from Mecho jack-in-the-boxes. Giggling Clown women danced around a nicked tent pole offstage. A dark-stained wooden block sat center stage, with a notch to accommodate a human neck. A large-breasted Clown woman waited nearby, wearing a black mask and holding an axe.

Behind the stage, a clockwork carousel whirred into action. Instead of horses, Mecho torsos gyrated up and down. Steam jetted from their exaggerated brass heads. Cheering Clowns sat astride each one, painted like Tarot characters. With handheld steampainters, they drenched the audience with sticky liquid candy. A Clown band performed a frenzied rhapsody offstage.

Why had he ever thought he could change these people?

The High Priestess swept her arm over the gathering. All quieted, and the rhapsody musicians ceased playing. With red cape thrust over both shoulders, her wondrous nudity glistened like nothing else in Meridian.

"Behold the true faithful, Tagen," she whispered, then raised her voice. "The infidel has been defeated!"

The Clowns roared in eager approval. Faces accused Tagen as if he'd slain those people in the streets, not them. Their ivory goddess held them in a thrall so strong, he nearly cheered along with them.

The High Priestess leaned close to him. "You could have had this, Tagen. I would have made you happy and content. Yet you took my gifts and sought to usurp me!"

She slapped his cheek and the Clowns applauded. His suffering would placate what she couldn't offer them. He was the enemy to be publicly demonized, humiliated, and executed. The crowd's righteous fervor made him sick.

"Am I not the only path in Meridian?" The High Priestess spread her arms. "Have I not given you happiness and escape? Have I not given you meaning?"

The audience cheered and the stage shook from their stamping feet. Some fired their pistols again. Tagen scanned the expanse of painted bodies. The presence of Azibar, with several bulky Mecho guards, surprised him. Gutter Knights, Sky Nomads, Bone Guild members, and others rubbed shoulders in the congregation.

A white-painted Clown in black leather stared at him. She held a rusty metal box.

Hope sprouted in Tagen's heart.

Several painted individuals stood beside Andromeda: Sveta, Georgio, Saissa, and Jaabir. Shaking with excitement, he concentrated on the Stygian images. *Masks, tomes, obelisks, pathways…*

The High Priestess once again addressed the crowd, ruining his focus.

"See how all Meridian pays homage to the Clown Tarot? Let everyone know how we reject the Magician, who would lead us into the Styx with his lies!"

The crowd chanted 'death to the Magician'. The High Priestess smiled.

"You won't control them forever," Tagen said, then coughed up a gob of biofluid. Despite the raw noise of her bellowing fools, his words carried to her ear. She flitted him a glance laced with hatred and contempt.

"What shall we do with him?" she asked the crowd.

Calls for beheading, castration, dismemberment, and even rape bombarded him. Darwick rubbed his neck scar and smirked.

Tagen's throat tightened.

"Hang him!" Darwick shouted.

The High Priestess's face lit with glee. "Yes! On that tent pole nearby."

Clowns removed the chain around Tagen's head, wrapped it around his left ankle, and placed his hands behind his back. Darwick re-pinioned them together with the dagger in Tagen's right hand. The blade slid through both palms.

They trussed him upside down by the chain on a length of rope. With vicious tugs through a pulley, they hauled him thirty feet above the crowd. The chain links hooked onto a large spike at the pole's top. Tagen's right leg dangled and he tried to keep it upright. The weight on his left ankle threatened to rip it from its socket. The pain shortened his breaths.

"Behold the Magician, become the Hanged Man!" the High Priestess called, and the Clowns lauded her with whistles and laughter. Stones, mud, and even rubber noses filled with shit pelted Tagen in a hateful shower. Rain fell, steady and cold. His body shook as biofluid filled the veins near his heart.

Tagen closed his eyes. Their taunts and missiles meant nothing to him. He had failed everyone, starting with himself. The Ten of Cups mocked him with its joyful scene. Dancing Clowns, with Sveta looking on. Opening his eyes, he scanned the crowd. He met her eyes in an instant, seeing through her painted disguise.

His temples throbbed. Metallic-tasting bile poured from his mouth. Blood rushed to his head.

"Alexis…"

The crowd surged beneath him, shaking the pole. He swayed back and forth from his ankle. It popped out of place and his leg muscles tore. A ragged cry burst from his lips. The movement turned him toward the stage. He locked eyes with the High Priestess.

Ruby depths invaded the window in his mind. Tagen screamed.

Loneliness, pain, fear. A new identity in white, covering up the one she couldn't remember. Her eyes widened and golden cards floated around her. Her Tarot characters tried confusing his thoughts, or deflect him from what lay inside her mind. A sepia-toned green and violet mirror pierced her deceptions.

In his mind, he tried to make her look into one of the mirrors.

The High Priestess shrieked, shattering his vision.

"Kill him! Kill the Magician!" She held her deck in both hands, insecure in her nakedness instead of confident in it.

The pole swayed further, lowering Tagen toward the crowd. His eyes fluttered in a painful haze. A Clown jabbed him with a sword. Another smashed his cheek with a club. As Tagen swayed back, Darwick threw a sharpened stave from the stage.

The stave impaled Tagen's right side. Biofluid spilled out. The valve and filter on his back exploded. Bloody shrapnel enfiladed the audience. The chain around his ankle snapped and he fell into a morass of painted limbs and sharp blades.

"Alexis!"

His vision went as black as the Styx.

XIII.

DEATH

1: The Veil of Life

Radomir pushed through the Clowns to Tagen's body. They stomped, spat, even urinated on it. Shoving them aside, he shielded Tagen with outstretched arms. Fists and staves smashed him, denting his armor. Blades punctured it, their tips scraping his flesh. Enraged visages and ragged shouts filled his reality. He bent under the pain. The strikes intensified. Blood and biofluid leaked through cracks in his armor.

Staggering, he shoved two Clowns back. "Can't kill him, no, can't—"

A stave hammered Radomir's chin. He collapsed alongside Tagen.

Inches away, Tagen's eyes stared into nothingness. Hadn't they been blue? *Blue as the backyard swimming pool he'd taught Brian to swim in. Blue like the sky outside his office window.*

Now Tagen's eyes were solid black.

"Not dead, yes?" Radomir uttered through busted lips.

Feet slammed into Radomir's side. Three staves struck his back. Jeers and curses filled his ears. Closing his eyes, Radomir waited for his own end. The noise and activity around him became a dull rumble.

In Radomir's mind, Brian's stroller escaped his grasp as someone bumped into him on the sidewalk. An oncoming bus slowed, its brakes screeching.

Leaping onto the pavement, his hands bumped the stroller from the street. Brian wailed. The stroller cleared the pavement as relief flooded Radomir's heart. His son would live.

Someone grabbed his hand. His eyes flew open amid bright violet light.

A chrome bumper crushed Radomir's body, ending the memory.

Pain faded from his limbs. Strength trickled into his muscles. If his death had served a purpose, so would his second life.

Radomir gripped the hand and rose.

2: Realization

"Tagen!" Andromeda screamed.

Daggers slashing through painted flesh, Andromeda battled her way to Tagen. Behind her, Sveta elbowed and kicked past Clowns to reach him. The mob churned with frenetic energy. Cold terror sliced into Andromeda's heart. Old memories tore at her consciousness, reminders of past failures.

She wiped her bloody nose and reapplied her face paint. "I'm still going on."

The old fortuneteller, who'd been with the circus for years, shook her head. "The king wants you dead. You barely escaped his ruffians and you saw the card I just drew. If you perform tonight, you'll—"

Andromeda snatched the Magician card from the table. The man's handsome face was framed by a city lit with strange lights, overlooking an onyx-black sea.

"Who is he? The Trickster, the Bateleur, the Artisan? Spare me your Tarot novelties. I don't need a ruse to win over the people."

"No, but you need to pierce the veil that shadows their minds," the fortuneteller said. "What do you see there, on that card?"

Andromeda's body tingled. The longer she stared, the more she felt the Magician's stare. The more she liked it.

"Keep it," the fortuneteller said. "Remember it, when you're on that rope."

Grinning, Andromeda stuffed the card into her costume and left.

A great weight seemed to hamper her movements. Lips trembling, she couldn't breathe. The Clowns kept striking Tagen's body.

Khyran showed her the card. "I told you, the prophecy cannot be undone."

Standing atop Femur Tower, Andromeda laughed. "If you're my bally boy, then I'm up for that skin opera."

He smiled sadly. "The Magician will own your heart…but the price…"

"I'll pay it." She kissed him.

Tagen couldn't be dead. The cards had said she'd fall in love with the Magician, who would change Meridian. But Meridian hadn't changed yet.

As Khyran fired electrical bolts at the maddened Clowns, she remembered when he'd been done this way. The High Priestess had positioned Khyran like the Ten of Swords, with as many blades in his back before the executioner decapitated him.

Grunting, she cut down another Clown. The High Priestess wouldn't have the man she loved. Not this time. The image of the Magician hovered in her thoughts. Focusing on it, Andromeda sliced a painted neck and pushed forward.

Sveta got ahead of her, disappearing into the forest of painted nakedness. Cheers for the High Priestess filled the air. Andromeda blinked as dark shadows filled her sight.

A pistol shot blew past her head, then a stave thumped her back. Andromeda leapt over the Clowns. As she raised her daggers, enraged fingers tore her back from Tagen.

The press of bodies proved too great. The Clown mob hungered for any scrap of the Magician, any chance to deface his body. Just like they had Khyran.

With a sob clogging her throat, Andromeda flung a dagger at the High Priestess. A golden Tarot card deflected it. The High Priestess stepped back.

"Infidels are in the crowd!" the High Priestess called.

Dozens of grease-slicked hands tugged Andromeda into the mud.

3: Stygian Phoenix

"Don't you know what the hell a restraining order means, Justin? Stay away from me. I mean it."

Alexis slid her wedding band across the table.

Tagen straightened himself in the chair at the dinner table. Though the Circus and the Clowns were gone, the same ache welled in his heart. Each cut and bruise still marred his body. Blood and biofluid slid down the chair's legs under him.

He ignored the waiter walking past with his tray, discounted the other patrons' light conversations and smiles. All he could focus on was Alexis's face, returned to his memories at last.

"Sveta?" Saying her name hurt his throat.

"I know what you do," she said in a harsh whisper. "I'm not living that lie."

Tagen shook his head. "Listen, I'm sorry, I don't know what you're—"

She scooted her chair back and rose. "I rented a different apartment and I started that self-defense course. Don't even think about following me this time."

He started to rise, then his hand knocked over a wine glass. It broke on the table and cut his palm. Blood and wine flowed around the wedding ring.

When he looked back up, Sveta…Alexis…was gone.

In his mind, a mirror shattered over the Styx. The shards sliced away the curtain draped over his memories.

"I don't give a goddamn what you think of me." Tagen stalked closer to Alexis but she hurried behind the coffee table in her apartment, Tarot cards spilling from her trembling hands. "I don't give a goddamn what those stupid cards say. You're my wife. You belong to me."

He couldn't believe he'd just spoken such words. Across from him, Alexis wept, mascara running down her face. Her left eye was swelled shut and blood dripped from her fattened lip. Her blouse was ripped open.

Blood leaked from his nose where she'd landed a hit.

"You never loved me." Her voice was strong. "I was your cover while you killed people for that son of a bitch you work for. Like you killed that congressman. I was your pretty wife at all those parties, those bullshit fundraisers where they laundered money—"

Tagen yanked out his gun from under his left arm and flicked the safety off. It was a move he'd performed many times. It had earned him everything. Even Alexis.

She sobbed and laughed at the same time. "Go ahead. I know where you're going. Where you belong." She held up a card with Clowns and cups on it.

"Come home." Tagen aimed the gun point-blank. "That's where you belong."

Alexis shook her head. "No. I'm free. You can't—"

Tagen fired.

The bullet plowed under her left breast and exited her back. The wall behind her was splattered with crimson. Alexis wheezed, then fell over the coffee table. More cards littered the floor, along with her blood.

Gun still smoking in his hand, Tagen shook with anguish. "Look what you made me do...look at what you made me fucking do!"

As she slumped off the table and lay on her back, Tagen knelt beside her. The gun slipped from his grasp. Blood continued to spread. She stared up at him, defiant.

"The cards..." Her wet cough dominated the room.

Tagen raced to the kitchen and grabbed a butcher knife. If he made it look like he'd defended himself from her...he lay the blade over his right arm.

"It's calling...for you..." The light left Alexis's right eye. Her fingers relaxed around the card in her hand.

"I'll tell them you attacked me, you goddamn bitch." Tagen sliced once, then again on his other arm. "I'll tell them I had to shoot, that I had to—"

His eyes were drawn to the card. The Ten of Cups, or some crazy shit like that. Alexis had turned to the occult after their split. Hanging with all those pagan whackos. As he kept staring at it, his flesh chilled. Something wet slid past both his wrists.

Looking down, Tagen moaned and dropped the knife. With his attention on that card, he'd carved designs into his palms...and sliced both of his wrists wide open.

He tried to call for help but he collapsed beside Alexis. Their blood mingled and washed over the Tarot cards as his body shivered with terminal cold…

He'd murdered Alexis. He'd never been a good person. Everything he'd come to Meridian for was a lie.

Dark waters swallowed him. Weeping, Tagen barely kept his head above the surface, hands scrabbling to gain purchase on anything. Anyone.

A grease-painted foot stomped his chest, ending the vision.

Tagen felt around him with his left hand. It touched another's and he gripped it. Clown faces leered down at him as his eyesight fully cleared.

A sword neared his throat. A dangling penis squirted urine on him. Tagen concentrated. Shadows in his peripheral sight gave way to black, depthless mirrors. It was the city's power.

He'd murdered Alexis. He'd never been a good person. Everything he'd come to Meridian for was—

"To set it right." Tagen focused on a Tarot card in his mind: the Seven of Swords.

Using the city's magic, he passed from the Clowns' perceptions, their very sight. They stomped and stabbed the ground beside him. Just like those people he'd fled in Vagrant's Row, after first coming to Meridian.

Rising, Tagen pulled on the hand. Radomir stood up with him. Though haggard and bleeding, something different lit the Gutter Knight's eyes. The Clowns still ignored him, even as Sveta thrust through them and halted. Their eyes met for an instant, then Tagen lifted his right hand into the air.

The mirror in his mind showed himself with black instead of blue eyes. As Meridian's power flowed into him, the shadows in his peripheral sight darkened.

Every tent flap blew open in the Circus. Doors and windows in the streets outside opened. Trash tumbled past clogged gutters.

Tagen no longer perceived himself standing on the ground. He imagined himself before the High Priestess. Like the Knight of Swords, he galloped on the air itself.

In the next instant, he looked into her eyes a pace away on the stage. Radomir and Sveta still stood where he'd fallen.

The High Priestess wavered. Some of her cards fluttered to the stage. A few Clowns saw him and shouted. Darwick raised his sword.

"Now they will see. Now they can choose." Tagen closed his right hand and opened his left. A steel Tarot deck appeared there. Cards fell from it into the crowd below, each one bearing a mask instead of a Clown's face.

In his mind, Tagen yanked off the masks obscuring the Clowns from themselves. He shoved their psyches before the black mirror so they could truly see. The black mirror of the Styx itself, one of the trump cards in the Stygian Tarot. It reflected nothing back but their own fears, doubts, and pain.

A swell of sensation, akin to waking from a dream, passed over the Circus audience. The shouting faded and the Clowns calmed. The rain stopped. Surprised voices rang out over the mob: anguished cries, shouts of fury. Others ran from the Circus. The rest either turned on each other, or stared at their painted bodies in surprise.

Tagen concentrated, trying to show them a better path…but Meridian's dark forces channeled through him into the Clowns. He groaned as the shadows crept into his consciousness…reminding him of who he'd been…

"Stop!" Tagen cried, his knees slamming into the stage.

"They belong to me." The High Priestess drew card after card. Each one struck his psyche in a torrent of hateful imagery. "As you soon will."

Kings of Swords and Staves tried to batter down Tagen's mind, but the Magician's calm eyes rendered them lame. Images of shattered towers and drowning men weighed him down until Tagen summoned gargoyles from black waters to protect him. The High Priestess thrust them aside, her golden cards encircling him. One flipped over and faced him, ending the vision.

The Death card. On it, the dead, nude woman had Alexis's face.

"No…" Tagen collapsed on the stage.

"You wish to find her here?" the High Priestess's voice purred in his ear. "Then let me show you."

The High Priestess's cruel laughter heralded new images: Alexis drowning in the Styx. Alexis sexually violated by a Clown gang. A Bone Guild vendor slicing off Alexis's stiff fingers while boiling her head in a brass vat. Alexis in white grease paint, fucking Darwick and giggling. The wedding ring closed around his neck, while Andromeda carved out his heart and suckled it. Alexis cutting the golden mask off another's woman's face with a razor blade.

Alexis…Sveta…putting his gun to her head.

"No!" he screamed.

Laughing, the High Priestess cast more cards at him. "You're too weak to rule."

Sobbing, Tagen tried once more. Despite the High Priestess's mental assault, he managed to focus on the background of the Death card. Two clockwork towers, with a small orange tent between them. A Clown tent…

While fighting the Stygian blackness, Tagen glimpsed a path through the horror in his mind. The tent led to Lotus Station.

Across the Circus, the same tent stood, its flap open. Tagen forced himself to roll off the stage and he flopped down into the mud.

The High Priestess tossed the Eight of Swords at him. Now Tagen stood, bound and blindfolded, surrounded by swords thrust into the ground around him—just like the figure on the card. Eight Clown warriors rushed at him.

After ripping off the blindfold, Tagen cut his bonds on the swords around him. Muscles quivering, he knew he wouldn't last much longer.

The High Priestess laughed while golden cards fluttered before his face. Each bore an image of him shoving a knife into Alexis's heart. Tagen tried to run but swords and staves blocked him. The Clown warriors leered, their sinews tighter than a spring.

A curved sword sliced off a Clown wrist. A black dagger slit a painted throat.

"Run!" Andromeda shouted.

Tagen fled as Andromeda and Georgio defended him. Hovering overhead, Khyran spat green charges on the Clowns. Sveta and

Radomir both pulled him into the crowd away from the warriors, where many Clowns still stumbled in confusion. Saissa and Jaabir covered their escape, flinging steel with deadly accuracy.

With Stygian mirrors floating in his mind, Tagen rushed toward the tent flap. Everyone he touched cried out as their mind snapped open. He gagged as the awful shadows again stained his sight.

The mob panicked, then a stampede erupted. People screamed while others trampled them. Carousel riders toppled off their seats. The bleachers collapsed as Clowns fought to escape.

Darwick and other warrior Clowns charged after them.

"Head for the orange tent," he breathed.

They all pushed through the crazed multitude. Gutter Knights wrestled Bone Guild members for fallen bodies. Mechos shouted for their old limbs or organs back. Instead of showing them an alternative to Meridian, Tagen had released their primal instincts. The High Priestess had merely contained them.

"What the hell's in that tent?" Andromeda asked.

Tagen tugged her through the tent flap. The rest followed just as Darwick slashed the fabric.

Khyran bumped into a clockwork lever and the ground opened up beneath them. All plummeted down a small passage. In a tumble of limbs, Tagen found himself trying to crawl out from under Andromeda. Georgio grunted as Saissa and Jaabir fell on him.

The dark tunnels of Lotus Station awaited them. Prying himself from the press of bodies, Tagen's hands clasped the crenelated edge of a railcar.

He'd murdered Alexis.

Sveta's brow furrowed. "Are you okay?"

He swallowed, waiting for her to scream at him, strike him. Kill him. But there was no sudden recognition in her eyes.

He'd never been a good person.

She didn't know who she really was. What he'd done. How could she not know?

It only made his guilt worse.

Murdered Alexis. Never a good person.

As four Mecho guards turned and lowered their arc rods, Khyran activated the railcar's controls. The vehicle zipped into the darkness. Tagen slumped over the edge.

Andromeda grabbed him. "I've got you, Jackpot. I've got you."

He'd murdered Alexis. He'd never been a good person. Everything he'd come to Meridian for was—

Tagen pushed Andromeda away and wept.

4: Transition

Azibar couldn't believe what he had just witnessed. No cartomancer had ever escaped the High Priestess, and her Clowns now ran about like maddened animals. At least his Mechos remained levelheaded. While she screamed at her followers, he led his Legionnaires to the stage, buffeting aside any in his path.

"Shall I restore order, my dear? Or do you have it under control?" He allowed some modulation into his voice to cover any mockery.

"I'll show you order." Eyes narrowed, the High Priestess scattered her cards into the air. Many fleeing Clowns halted and looked back at her. Her palms glowed red, matching her fierce gaze. The cards floated back into her hand, as, one by one, Clowns returned to the stage.

Azibar hesitated. He still had no way to combat her cartomancy. At least, not in his current body.

"How dare you flee while the infidel escapes! Do you think his power is greater than mine?" Her words stirred debris on the ground and transformed it into Tarot cards. The objects floated around the Circus like angry flies.

Though Clowns replied in the negative, Azibar caught their subdued tone. He smiled until the High Priestess dropped off from the stage and sauntered among them. Baffled faces scrunched back into visages of pure enslavement.

A sword tapped Azibar's arm. Darwick stood beside him, crazed eyes bulging.

"You ain't bowing, Azibar. Or do you support that shitfaced Magician?"

Azibar vented steam right in Darwick's face. "Careful. She has many favorite dogs to service her. Don't make her search for a new one so soon."

Darwick's body quivered with murderous need. "You don't show the proper fucking respect, copper man. One day, you will."

"I'm sure. Now run along, before she finds your replacement in one of those larger Clowns." He smiled as Darwick stalked off.

There was no need to fear any of her cretins—especially now. Though not helpless, her prestige had suffered. While most Clowns returned, a significant number did not. Those crowds of simpletons outside the Circus had evaporated. Even the Bone Guild gathered bodies with reluctance. The High Priestess would need to strike hard and quick to win back Meridian's respect. A service he could provide.

And what of this new Magician? Azibar rubbed his copper chin.

Tagen's cartomantic abilities had been evident, and yet...he should be dead. If not from Darwick's stave, then from biofluid poisoning. Perhaps Tagen had absorbed or ejected the biofluid. That was something none had ever managed.

At this point, though, he needed something else to force Tagen's cooperation. Bending over, he plucked a black dagger from a Clown corpse. The signature weapon of the Blades of Charon.

"Oh, my lovely Andromeda," Azibar whispered. "I do so enjoy when you deliver what I want."

5: Transfiguration

As the railcar screeched to a halt, Tagen stumbled onto a different platform in Lotus Station. The others slowly followed him.

"Jackpot?" Andromeda whispered. "Jackpot...here, lean on me."

He allowed her to touch him, though he didn't deserve it.

"By Charon and the Gorgon," Georgio said. "You should be—"

"Dead. But this city wants me alive." Tagen steadied himself against Andromeda.

"Anybody says he's not the Magician now?" Jaabir asked.

Andromeda straightened. "Did you see the shadows again? Do you remember—?"

"All of it." He took a deep breath and stared at the Styx below. There was no redemption here. Only reminders of what a fucking bastard he was. Tagen recalled everything now; his first job as a hitman, his first date with Alexis. The crime syndicate he'd served. The face of every person he'd ever murdered.

"I'm sorry I doubted you." Sveta clasped Tagen's hand so tight, her nails bit into his skin. The genuine apology in her eyes made him nauseous.

He'd murdered Alexis. He'd never been a good—

"Where the hell are we?" Tagen pulled away from Sveta. Though he didn't taste biofluid anymore, the dark liquid's power still flowed in him. He flexed his fingers, biceps. All his wounds had sealed. How, since he had no copper organs?

"I'd say we're below Boulevard," Saissa said. "Judging from the graffiti, that is."

Andromeda removed her cap and shook dried mud off it. "Jackpot here needs to see those tattoos, Nomad Girl. The High Priestess has been shaken, but she'll—"

"I failed," Tagen said. "I'm not the…I won't lead you all to your deaths."

They all gaped at him.

Gripping his tattered vest, Andromeda shook her head. "You're not red lighting us now. What happened in that blood opera?"

He gently removed her hands. "I remember now. Who I was. What I was."

"You're not that trouper anymore," Andromeda said. "No matter what you saw."

"But I can't forget," Tagen said.

The look in her eyes told him that she wanted to help him forget.

"The city is still feeding you its magic," Andromeda said. "That means it is still choosing. You, or the High Priestess. If you learn the rest of the Stygian Tarot, you can defeat her. You could haul us all from this joint."

The hope on the others' faces—even Sveta's—churned his guts.

"I'm not your goddamn hero!"

Andromeda slapped him.

Tagen glowered at her. Biofluid popped in his veins. Shadows taunted his vision.

"I don't give a shit who you were before," Andromeda breathed. "But the kinker I care about is a good person. The Tagen I know would never hurt me."

"Stop it, you two!" Sveta cried.

Fists squeezed so tight his knuckles cracked, Tagen faced Andromeda nose to nose. "But you don't know me."

"Then stop grandstanding and do your worst." Andromeda closed her eyes.

Tagen touched her neck.

Jaabir and Saissa aimed daggers at him. Scowling, Georgio drew his sword. Khyran jetted steam and waited, while Radomir cringed. Sveta regarded him with scorn.

One flick of his wrist and Andromeda's neck would be broken. Like he'd killed that Bone Guild asshole. The man he used to be wouldn't hesitate. The old Tagen might have even enjoyed it.

Her pulse thrummed beneath his fingers. He licked his lips.

She still believed in him.

Shaking with a sob, he caressed her neck, then drew her close in an embrace. Andromeda exhaled and moaned into his chest, hugging him tight. The others came over and patted their shoulders. Though she hung back, Sveta gave him a nod of respect.

"You always this stubborn?" he whispered in Andromeda's ear.

"Only with you." She kissed his neck and stepped back.

"Now that's settled…?" Jaabir gave them both questioning looks.

After studying Tagen for a moment, Georgio grunted. "Follow me."

They all trailed after the old Sky Nomad. With sure steps, Georgio led them across a decrepit concrete bridge and over the railcar tracks to an opposite platform. A few Wretched squeaked inside an alcove nearby as Georgio led the group up a pitted stairway to an exit hatch. A moon, star, and sun were carved into it.

"Seems you've been vacationing here," Jaabir said.

Glancing at Radomir, Andromeda grimaced. "Shit. I guess we can trust you now, Ratty Boy?"

"Make things right, yes." Radomir rubbed his gauntlets together.

Georgio stared at the Gutter Knight. "I've never seen one of your kind act so selflessly. Maybe you can help us further."

"Georgio—?" Sveta started but the old man shook his head.

"Later. Now keep up." Georgio opened the hatch. Light drifted over his painted face as he ascended a set of stairs. Tagen hurried after him, with Sveta right behind. After the rest came up, Jaabir shut the hatch. The sound echoed off the structures above.

They entered an avenue of dressed stone buildings aligned in neat rows. Some stood in good repair, while others were little more than rubble piles. Steepled roofs and conical towers climbed into the black sky. The scent of chalk, mixed with mold and dust, stifled Tagen. A steamlamp flickered on and off, jetting exhaust in noisy spurts.

A chill seeped into Tagen's body. His palm glyphs warmed. Turning round in a circle, he took in every building, every street. The entire district throbbed with a latent force he couldn't identify. A vibration in his heart, a tickle in his muscles.

There were also more shadows in his peripheral vision.

Boulevard was a faded dream from a fairy tale. Columns carved with masked faces held up roofed porticos. Elegant fences curled in floral designs, caked with moss. Every street corner was marked with plaques etched with Charonic sigils. Kelp clogged murky pools in the street. Defaced statues stood guard over forgotten homes.

Few people traveled the sidewalks and no gutters hung along the buildings. Rain stood in rancid puddles. Little mechanis was evident, save for an abandoned Bone Guild kiosk on a curb, its neon sign broken.

"This place was old when the Sky Nomads found Meridian," Georgio said. "Its Alueryic architecture predates Charon's departure.

None knows who lived in these buildings. The Clowns avoid it. Something about it upsets them."

Andromeda maneuvered past a brackish puddle with effortless grace. "The pitch goes that Charon lived here. Meridian's first cartomancer needed a palace, I suppose."

"Yes, and a Harlequin cartomancer came here, seeking a miracle," Georgio said.

"She didn't find it." Andromeda kicked at the puddle.

"Do you deny finding the Stygian deck in the Temple?" Georgio asked.

Flicking her cap points, Andromeda looked away. Khyran entered her grasp and became a rusty box.

"Where are you taking us?" Tagen asked.

"There." Georgio pointed at a cathedral-like structure ahead. "The entrance is in the Temple."

"Can't go in, can't go in," Radomir muttered. "Charon protects, yes?"

Tagen nudged him and the Gutter Knight fell silent.

A single steamlamp stood over the building, lighting stained glass windows. They traveled up the Temple's stone steps. Georgio rapped the wooden door once, hesitated, then gave three quick raps.

The portal slid open. A Nomad man peeked out.

"Hurry, let us in," Georgio said, and the other Nomad nodded. Sveta tensed at Tagen's side. The door opened wide enough for them to pass. Once everyone entered, the Nomad shut it back.

An altar with a black obelisk dominated the initial chamber. A sun, star, and moon had been carved on it—exact matches to the glyphs on his palms. Further in, the Temple's interior shone from the backlit stained windows in greens and violets. They depicted a figure paddling a barge over the Styx, a masked woman holding Tarot cards, a winged fiend reading a tome, and obelisks jutting from black waters. Charonic sigils covered every window frame.

"The Stygian deck," Tagen breathed. "Those are its suits. Charon on his barge, the Gorgon in her mask...but the other two..."

Andromeda's eyebrows rose. "Good, you're learning. No one knows who the winged trouper is, or what the obelisk represents. Maybe through you, we'll find out."

"Purple is Charon's color?" He looked at his palms. "And green is the Gorgon's?"

Was the city selecting him for Charon…and Sveta as the Gorgon?

Sveta fidgeted with her corset and looked elsewhere. He loathed being near her now. Ruling this city, with the woman he'd murdered, would be a nightmare.

"Did the supplies reach you from Nomad Way?" Georgio asked the man.

The Nomad nodded. "Yes, but word is the Clowns are in an uproar. The Bazaar's been closed, and even the Gutter Knights are lying low."

While the others talked in low voices, Tagen remained focused on the stained glass. The figures seemed to move whenever he examined them from a different angle. When the woman's mask turned gold, he paused. The next second, it was normal again.

Sveta drew close and looked ready to speak, but he walked on.

"I have something to show all of you." Georgio walked down the Temple's center aisle and entered a shadowed alcove. Inside, he pushed a loose brick in the wall. Stone grinded on metal and a passage slid open on the stone floor.

"I've never seen that before," Andromeda said.

"Hurry. The Clowns don't know about this, and we dare not give them time to find it." Georgio descended into the secret passage.

Tagen led the rest down narrow steps as Georgio guided them into a winding tunnel. Black-stained stone hemmed them in and Andromeda clutched Tagen's shoulders the whole way. An earthy scent hung in the air. His boots clomped over ancient, packed dirt. After taking three right turns, they entered a large stone chamber lit by dozens of steam lanterns.

Radomir hesitated. "Many parts."

"Charon's eyes," Jaabir muttered.

"Aye, and his nose, too," Saissa whispered.

A dozen Sky Nomads worked around an object at least seventy feet long and twenty feet wide. Copper coils hung along its riveted, metal sides. Three steam compressors rose and fell, feeding electrical current through a router into copper conduits and capacitors. A deflated mass of canvas hung suspended from scaffolding above them. Thick metal cables dangled from it to the object's top.

Georgio grinned. "We should have the airship ready soon. I named her *Persephone*. Legend says she was a princess who escaped some dark underworld."

The Nomad mechanics tugged a fully assembled steam engine through a hatch on the hull. Sturdy railing protected the deck and graceful metal etchings marked every inch of the airship: stars, suns, moons, and various other Sky Nomad emblems. The metal hull had a hand-beaten look, with light catching numerous tones and textures across its surface. Bronze rudders, stabilizing fins, and rain collection sluices had all been handcrafted, granting *Persephone* an organic aspect.

Andromeda frowned. "What, are you leaving the city? Now?"

"That is my intention. The Magician will show the path. " Georgio exuded more confidence than Tagen felt on the matter.

"Wait...I still don't understand what happened to me inside the Circus. Whenever I use this magic, I feel part of this city. If I fail—"

"You won't," Andromeda said. "If you learn the rest of that deck."

"I don't know." Tagen sighed. "The knave's tongue, the sting of lies...beyond dark waters are blue, blue skies?"

"Yes. Bluer than anything in Meridian." Georgio beamed. "All you need do is pierce the darkness out there with your magic, so we can see the horizon. After that, I should be able to navigate *Persephone* to one of the old cities on my charts."

Yes, this was the path. Leave this terrible city, leave Alexis behind...

Tears filled Sveta's eyes. "No, Georgio. You can't! Those charts are based on childish stories. You don't know what's out there. Just because Tagen tried to take on the High Priestess—"

Waving her words aside, Georgio approached the airship. "No one has ever done that before and lived, Sveta! If the time isn't now, then when?"

The group stopped before the bronze hull. Georgio patted it like some old companion. Gazing all around, Radomir grinned. Khyran popped from his box form and hovered about. The very sight of the ship raised their spirits. Tagen didn't share their elation. How was he supposed to 'pierce the darkness'?

"So many parts," Radomir said. "Get all these yourself, yes?"

"Only after much time and patience," Georgio said. "I've been working on this for countless tolls of the Clock, using ancient blueprints. After what I saw in the Circus, I know you believe in the Magician. Can you help us get this ship together faster?"

Radomir's armor jingled with his excited movements. "Find help in Boulevard. Return, yes?"

Georgio nodded and Radomir hurried back into the tunnel.

"Lemme help too," Jaabir said. "Pretty good with copper conductors."

Saissa joined in, carting equipment and tools for the mechanics. A light mood permeated the Sky Nomads.

Loosing a breath, Tagen shook his head. They all must think he would lead them to some shining city in their imagination. If they knew he'd been a murderer, what would they think then?

"Sveta might be right, Georgio," Tagen said. Andromeda regarded him with neutral eyes, while Sveta nodded and came to his side.

"I see many things. I see this ship in flight over Meridian. I see a sun shining over its buildings." He closed his eyes and visualized it. *A round, blinding disc, like a lighthouse beacon, but a sun nonetheless. Georgio's airship flew above it, with him and Sveta aboard. Something was wrong, though...*

"Don't doubt yourself," Georgio said. "Surely you are the one. We have to try."

Sveta crossed her arms. "Will you use him, then, like you've used me? I heard what you told Andromeda. You put these tattoos on me. Why did you lie?"

"To protect you," Georgio said. "Khyran saw his own death in the cards. He said the true Magician was coming. Those were his last words to me."

Andromeda went very still.

"Tagen is the Magician," Georgio said. "Look at his eyes. Instead of blue, they resemble the Styx itself. Like Charon in the old stories."

Tagen touched his eyes in self-conscious curiosity. Murky energy swirled in his palm glyphs. *His mind's eye saw through the mask Sveta wore, viewing the unsure, injured woman beneath. Trying to hold Khyran's head, Andromeda barely stood atop an obelisk. Georgio browsed through a molded tome, never finding the page he wanted. Tagen himself stood in a path of black water, leading nowhere.*

Shaking his head, he cast away the vision.

"What did you see?" Sveta asked. "It's not your fault Alexis left. Stop running from that pain."

Tagen flinched and looked away. In studying her tattoos, he'd unlocked something inside them both. He needed to unlock more. Meridian remained a prison he lacked the key to.

"Ready?" Jaabir asked the mechanics after snapping a coil into place.

"Aye, ye already have steam," Saissa said.

They all turned and watched a compressor pump hot air into the dirigible. Vents hissed for the first time. The Nomads cheered and patted each other on the back. Tagen tried shouldering the extra pressure their happiness brought. He didn't want to lead these people to their death—or a place worse than Meridian.

Andromeda squeezed Tagen's hand. "The city might not let you go."

"Can you let me go?" he whispered in her ear.

Hanging her head, Andromeda released his hand. He wanted to hold her, to give her the affection she asked for with her eyes—but he'd been an evil man. The city might turn him back into one.

Sveta frowned. "Don't indulge an old man's hopes. Don't feed false dreams."

"I've no dreams left," Tagen said. "They won't cloud my view of the path."

"You'll do it?" Georgio asked.

Everyone paused and waited.

"Yes," Tagen said.

Georgio patted his shoulder. "We should get ourselves ready. The Clowns won't wait long, nor Azibar. I saw him there at your…hanging. If he knew I had this ship, he would do everything in his power to get it."

"I'm not leaving without Khyran's body," Andromeda said in a dry voice.

"No one asked you to come," Sveta said.

"It's not up to you, Nomad Girl," Andromeda said. They glared at one another.

Georgio sighed. "You must let Khyran go. Once this ship is ready, we sail. I'm sorry, Andromeda."

"Goddammit, Georgio—"

He cut Andromeda off with a gesture. "I won't risk my people's lives for your obsession. Khyran was my friend, but I know Azibar. It is time I see to my own people."

Andromeda's brow lowered, but before she said more, Tagen made her face him. "We'll get his body. I swear it."

In her eyes he glimpsed his own, reflected in dark orbs. Who was he now?

Georgio shook his head and pointed at the Nomads working nonstop. "Too dangerous. Everyone will be aboard. The whole city will see us. Are you both mad?"

Tagen didn't look away from Andromeda. Her chest rose and fell with anxious breaths.

"That's my price, Georgio. Consider this the first step on the path."

6: New Enterprise

Just as he suspected, Radomir found Lezzek and three other Gutter Knights prying parts from the ruined Bone Guild kiosk. He'd remembered his former comrade's plans of looting in Boulevard and contained his joy at finding them so easily.

His armor clanked. Lezzek drew his pistol.

"Who the fuck is that?" Lezzek cocked the pistol's hammer.

"Nodule coil triple bolt. Peeking for shine?"

Lezzek uncocked the pistol but didn't put it away. "Yeah, we're looking for loot. That you, Radomir? Thought you'd found some lame ass religion."

Radomir scanned the streets. Boulevard made him uneasy. Maybe Charon himself watched from the alleys, or waited atop the Temple, yes. Every carved mask on the buildings might hold the eyes of the Gorgon, so deep red they were brown.

"Need mechanis help. Nomads pay in silver, maybe gold, yes?" Georgio had made no such promise but a chance to escape Meridian outweighed such concerns.

"So?" Lezzek asked. "The Sky Nomads have never asked for help before. What the hell are they building, then? You in good with them now, is that it?"

"Help Magician. Help Meridian. Want gold or not?"

Lezzek's companions gathered beside Radomir, but he himself snorted. "Go and be saddle bitches for the Nomads, then. Plenty loot to be had the easy way. Gutter Knights don't work for anybody."

Shaking his head, Radomir led the others to the Temple. He'd help with the airship, show Tagen and Andromeda that he was the same man who'd saved Brian. No one would ever suspect or doubt him again.

7: Ivory Corruption

"Look to me! Do I cower before the Magician's heresy?"

The High Priestess walked around to each and every Clown, reassuring them of her power, their righteous cause. Darwick followed, admiring her milk-white form. Though she strolled through the Circus mud, she always appeared so much cleaner than everyone else. Only someone pure and holy could have such qualities.

"You are the chosen of Meridian. Will you allow the Magician to take from you what I have given? I have made you smile, laugh. I have given you color in place of the Styx's blackness. I ask you, will you let him take all that away, just because you showed a moment of weakness?"

"No!" Painted fists rose into the air.

"Gather all my warriors," she whispered in Darwick's ear. "Then wait."

The High Priestess departed the Circus grounds for her tent. For the first time in uncounted centuries, she felt tired. Her limbs ached. The cards weighed down her hand.

The powers Tagen displayed…no cartomancer had ever contested her and escaped. Perhaps the Stygian Tarot had been found. When she'd defeated Khyran, elements in his mind had been unreadable: mirrors and characters from the Styx. Tagen's thoughts had contained the same.

Scowling, the High Priestess leaned on her high-backed chair. The Tarot heightened a cartomancer's perceptions. The card faces could be anyone, or anything. The most powerful cartomancers could appear in any time, any place.

Meridian enveloped all her time and space.

The High Priestess glanced at the trapeze. Before she had taken over the Circus, Andromeda had performed many exotic tricks on it. How the crowd had adored her.

With clenched teeth, the High Priestess raked her nails across the chair. Andromeda had lost her cartomancy when she lost the Circus. Meridian always favored the strongest with its blessings. Closing her eyes, she gritted her teeth to hold back a sob.

When one could no longer remember, all that mattered was affection. She'd craved it, creating raucous displays in Andromeda's Circus. Reveling in her nakedness, while her admirers multiplied. But Meridian had fooled her with such love and adoration.

One would do anything to maintain such an illusion. Lies, murder, betraying Andromeda…no price was too steep to ensure the illusion abided. Now she herself was becoming that illusion, a phantom powered by the city's darkness.

But it was all she possessed. She would fight for it.

Her Tarot deck spread itself in the air before her. Golden emblems of possibilities awaiting her divination.

The three cards she had drawn for Tagen—Knight of Swords, Ten of Staves, and the Magician—lined up for her, along those she had drawn for Sveta: Nine of Pentacles, Four of Cups, and The Star. The High Priestess smiled as Meridian's energy entered her body once again.

The cards formed new images in her mind: *a red flower, its petals falling onto a woman's cheek. Tagen sinking in the Styx, trying to reach a lantern in the dark waters. Azibar powering a blazing sun. A handful of pomegranate seeds. Doors of light flung open, blinding Tagen. Black, thorny vines.*

"I will not be replaced," she whispered.

XIV.

TEMPERANCE

1: Verge of the Horizon

While Georgio joined the rest in assembling *Persephone*, Tagen went back up the stairs into the Temple. Shadows continued appearing at the edges of his sight as the district's power throbbed in him. Was this the heart of Meridian?

Pacing back and forth, he gazed up at the stained glass images again. There was a story there, like that illustrated in the Tarot—yet the characters kept changing. One recurring element was violet palm glyphs. Yet, every bend of the light showed them on a different person. None of them looked like him.

Since his hanging, hunger and anger had remained in check. Now only emotional needs fired his desires. By gazing into the Stygian Tarot's mirrors, he had conquered the biofluid inside him. The Styx itself ran in his veins.

Perhaps this was an opportunity to right the wrongs of his past life. Here, he could let Sveta—Alexis—go her own way, without ever revealing her complete past. He would bear the burden, not her. She'd suffered enough for multiple lifetimes already.

That left him free. Like the Knight of Pentacles, waiting by the shore.

Damn, he was such a bastard.

A splotch of white paint remained on his hands, from where he'd touched Andromeda. Would she always need him, as much as he wanted her? For though guilt tainted his conscious, the only desire in his heart was for her. She deserved better.

But the vagaries of this place, of the Styx itself, still cast doubt on his emotions. Tagen wanted—needed—to care for someone after discovering what a monster he'd been. He wanted to believe that he still could.

He rubbed his temples. Perhaps Alexis had been right...he'd never loved her. By whatever powers ruled the Styx, he hoped she never remembered Justin Tagen. That might be his one true redemption.

"Why are you avoiding me?"

Though her voice chilled his skin, he turned and regarded Sveta with a neutral expression. "I'm not."

Sveta leaned against a column carved with obelisks. Still covered in grease paint and wearing the pink Harlequin outfit, she was a facsimile of Andromeda.

"You've acted differently since we escaped the Circus."

Tagen frowned. "I was more or less executed. What do you expect?"

"You act the same toward Andromeda." Sveta's lips flattened.

"Hell, are you jealous?" He laughed at the irony.

"What if I am?"

Her question was like a punch in the gut.

A hurt look crossed her face when he didn't answer. "Even if I don't like what you're doing, or who you might be...I still have feelings."

"I'm sorry." That simple declaration spanned epochs.

She came near him. "Those people down there, working on that silly airship, they have feelings, too. How many will die before you accept that?"

"Damn it, those people believe in me!" As Tagen paced back and forth, the glass panes cast green and violet shadows over the stone floor.

Sveta circled him like a bird of prey. "I told you what I saw. The people who would die. The suffering. Is this the path you'll lead

Georgio and my people on? The way you'll lead Andromeda, so she can live forever in anguish?"

Clenching his fists, he stopped pacing. "At least I tried. If we leave Meridian, the other cities—"

"I don't believe in them," Sveta said. "Georgio has his childish hope and the mythology of Meridian. Andromeda has Khyran and her revenge. All you have is a hungry heart. What comes after? Can you see it in your cards?"

"Then why help me at all?" Tagen asked.

She gripped his torn vest and kissed his lips.

Light flared from a stained glass panel depicting Charon and the Gorgon, holding hands. Her tattoos crawled over her flesh. Meridian had finally given him what he'd sought but now it ripped his heart apart. Even if he still wanted her, Tagen couldn't savor her attention. It reminded him of pulling that trigger, of kneeling in her blood…

Their lips parted awkwardly. He backed away.

"Why?" The genuine sadness in her voice robbed him of strength.

"I can't stay in Meridian," he said. "I survived that execution only because the city wanted me to. It's taking me, Sveta."

"We could do this," Sveta breathed. "The city wants us to be—"

"Then show me the rest of the Stygian cards," Tagen said.

She closed her eyes. "You don't know what you ask. What I might want in return." The stained window's colors tinted her skin like a character straight from the Stygian Tarot. His mind opened to it.

A lovely winged woman poured steam from a metallic red chalice into a stone white chalice. The woman had one foot on Meridian's dock and one foot in the Styx.

"Temperance," Tagen breathed.

"Our painful pasts can be put to good deeds," Sveta said. "As we drain poison from ourselves, we pour sustenance into others."

He stiffened. "You've no idea what you are asking for."

"Did Andromeda?" Her eyes glistened.

"Leave her out of this."

"I would like to." She reached for his hand. He backed away.

"Let me examine the rest of your tattoos. Let me help these people."

She glanced down at her body, then glowered at him. "I...I can't."

As she hurried down the steps, Tagen stared up at the colored glass panes.

One figure was shrouded in black vines...while another wore a golden mask.

2: Equilibrium

Andromeda sat on the curb outside the Temple, holding Khyran. Boulevard's desolate avenues had always chilled her, but she needed solitude. Shit, she'd just be in the others' way while they labored on the airship.

The look in Tagen's changed eyes was burned into her mind. Remembering his past had hurt him deeply. Even worse, she sensed he didn't want it to cause her pain.

Which made her want him even more.

Khyran's glowing eyes flickered.

Holding a breath, she touched his face. None of his original flesh remained. All of it had been sheathed in bronze. Even the lips doubled as an exhaust, which he used on enemies. Andromeda kissed them anyway, wincing as the warm metal stung her nerves.

"I owe it to you to least try, damn it," she whispered, trying not to think of Tagen's lips, his hands on her. Their moment on the balcony, her feelings during his hanging. Once again the iconic Tarot image of the Magician teased her thoughts.

"I want him, Khyran." Guilt squeezed her heart. "Dammit, I'm sorry."

She set Khyran down beside her and studied her palms. Long ago, they'd glowed green, interpreting the Tarot. People had been content with her simple readings. With a heavy heart Andromeda recalled the nameless woman she'd found in the gutter outside the Circus. The wondrous Tarot prodigy had teamed with Andromeda in the Circus—until the newcomer had demanded more. Meridian had chosen the High Priestess, rendering Andromeda's power useless.

All she'd built, all the people she'd loved in this hellish city, had been lost at the flip of a golden Tarot card. It came back, no matter how hard she tried to will it away…

The cracked doll head rolled back and forth in Andromeda's hand, its unblinking eyes etched with Charonic binding sigils. She lifted the head to her lips and kissed it. Her violet lipstick stained the plastic face. Breathing deep, she gazed into the black sky, trying not to blink against the gentle downpour. Rain beaded on her grease-painted flesh, slid down her reinforced corset.

"Now that your life greets its final wane, I bind you here in Charon's name," she whispered. Out of habit, she glanced at her palms. No tingling sensations emanated from them. The sun, moon, and star glyphs were just reminders of what she'd lost.

Andromeda tossed the head onto Doll House. Every time one of her comrades died fighting the Clowns, she felt obligated to honor them here.

A block away, smoke rose from a steam routing station she and Khyran had just destroyed. Five of their companions still lay among the Clown dead but at least power to the Circus was disrupted. Andromeda made herself stop counting the doll heads. Too many bore purple smears.

"We shouldn't tarry here. The High Priestess has placed the city under martial law and our allies are waiting." Standing beneath a steamlamp, Khyran watched her with crossed arms. His fair hair remained dry underneath his hood. Leather pants and vest hugged his wiry frame.

"I'm done." Andromeda tucked a blonde lock under her cap, its three points damp with rain. "Besides, she won't send her painted freaks here into the Row. Not with our kinkers inciting a riot in the Bazaar."

"Obfuscation and diversion won't fool her for long," Khyran said.

"It'll fool her followers." She touched his chin. "There's no turning back now. Can you do this?"

Khyran's brown eyes darted here and there. "Meridian is feeding my power more than ever. We won't get another chance."

For countless tolls of the Alueryic Clock, they had plotted the downfall of the High Priestess. Gathered allies, laid ambushes, spread anti-Clown sentiment among Meridian's citizens. With the Bone Guild serving less meat, the

Mechos repairing fewer power stations, and street gangs growing in number, the populace wanted a change.

But change only came to Meridian through blood.

"What is the matter?" His arm encircled her waist. Fingers massaged the small of her back.

Andromeda tried to smile but stared at his chest instead. "You have the deck?"

"Right here." Khyran patted a small rectangular pouch on his belt.

She'd stolen it from Boulevard for him, the district where Charon had dwelled. It had taken all her will not to look at those cards. As a weakened cartomancer, the Stygian Tarot might drive her insane. How Khyran managed to view it still amazed her. He really was the Magician, prophesied to change Meridian and usurp the High Priestess.

Many others had come before him, would-be saviors battling the Clowns. All of their heads now resided in the High Priestess's tent. But the cards never lied.

"If I die..." Andromeda stiffened and faced him.

"The cards told me you will live." Khyran smiled.

"If I die, say the phrase and toss a doll head into that pile. Promise me."

Khyran's glowing hands squeezed hers. "Promise."

The Bone Guild kiosk across the street buzzed, dispelling her recollection. Someone had left a copper wire loose after stealing the sign filaments. Sparks plummeted from it, then fizzled and died in the damp street. A reminder of her broken dreams.

Andromeda snatched a rock from the curb and prepared to throw it at the kiosk. Anger, desire, and sorrow crumpled the remnants of her heart. Hovering up from the curb, Khyran watched her.

"You saw your fucking death and faced her anyway," she whispered. "You knew how I would hurt. You pitched that I would love the Magician. I thought it was you, but you knew the take. Goddamn you, Khyran!"

She gripped the rock so hard, her fingers pushed it from her grasp. In reflex, she caught it with her other hand. Andromeda snatched another rock. Standing, she aimed for Khyran's floating head.

"I'll..." Something Georgio had said teased her thoughts.

Instead of lobbing the stones, she tossed them from one palm to the other. Her hands assumed a familiar rhythm. She kicked a third rock up from the street to her chest and caught it in a practiced move. An old tingling filled her as she juggled the rocks.

Khyran jetted steam and flashed his eyes.

Memories of bygone times returned: juggling daggers, cards, balls. Juggling on a tightrope while riding a unicycle. Tumbling through flaming hoops with a mechanis beast. Flinging daggers around the outline of a volunteer. Singing for a rapt audience. Skills she'd since used, then taught the Blades of Charon, in her vengeful quest.

"Aye, I see ya finally took it up again," Saissa said behind her.

Andromeda turned and smiled without interrupting her juggling. "It's been so long." She caught all three rocks and tossed them in rapid succession at the kiosk. Each struck the sign in the exact same spot.

"Nice aim," Saissa said. "Ye looked happy for once."

"How's the clockwork opera going?" Wiping dirt from her hands, Andromeda sat back down on the curb.

Saissa sat beside her. "Jaabir's in his element, ratcheting and tightening everything Georgio wants. Those Gutter Knights Radomir brought round helped mighty fine too, that is." She patted Andromeda's hand. "I know ye ache. I know ye hurt. Maybe we leave 'em Clowns and ride that there airship. Blades' will be sheathed."

"I still owe it to Khyran."

"Aye. But ye owe others, too. Find that smile again, Khyran will forgive ya."

"I…" Their hands touched, and Andromeda squeezed.

"Ye'll do right by us. By him. Like old Emrys once said, ye still smell like the Elysian Gardens. Meridian never took that away."

"Guess I'm the last Harlequin on the Styx." Andromeda gave her a faint smile.

"Aye, but first in our hearts. Love ya, lassie. Love ya like ye my own." Saissa kissed her cheek and entered the Temple.

Andromeda rested her chin on her knees and hugged her legs. What if she left Meridian aboard *Persephone?* Sheathe the Blades, so to speak. Would she be happy?

Would Tagen?

Shivering, she stood and took hold of Khyran. Boulevard had never chilled her like this. Not since her arrival in Meridian. Once, she'd come here to find the Stygian Tarot, hoping it would aid her against the High Priestess. Now she'd returned with another Magician. Another dream. But she hadn't earned her own redemption yet.

"Maybe you've already forgiven me, since you foresaw all this," Andromeda told Khyran. "But I can't forgive myself."

3: Chalice to Chalice

Just one more coupling to install. Radomir turned the wrench and grinned. *Persephone*'s engine would soon be ready for its power source: a copper and gold commutator, with Alueryic terminals. The ancient mechanis device would amplify the ship's boiler output, with the hull itself acting as the router.

Reviewing his work, Radomir smiled. He was among the best Gutter Knights at repair. At least part of his life in Meridian would prove useful, yes.

He paused and studied his three comrades. Together, they'd linked all the conduits to the helm, installed the aft turbines, and sealed off the coils with tar. Georgio's small team would have needed an entire Clock cycle to accomplish the same.

"Hey-o, Radomir, what next?" one of the Gutter Knights asked. "When do we, heh, get paid?" The other two looked up and waited.

"Soon, yes? But finish tasks first. Brag to Lezzek about fat purse later."

The Knights mumbled but they assembled the collapsible gangplank.

As he started on the next coupling, Radomir had no idea what his future would be. He'd never hold Brian again, nor hope to attain such familial happiness a second time.

Lips tight, he turned the wrench and attached thick bronze mesh hoses to each vent. Get lost in the work, yes.

"You could rival Azibar in mechanical affinity." Georgio gave Radomir's handiwork an approving look. "Most of my people don't know the workings of this ship. We only have old charts and a few books to go on. So much has been lost, either to the city's decay, or to those who took it for themselves."

Radomir ceased turning the wrench and pointed at the three Gutter Knights. "Don't do that anymore, yes? Have watched them. Steal nothing."

"That's why I want you to have this."

Georgio produced a silver breastplate and helmet, shiny as Mecho skin. Nomad star motifs flowed over the breastplate's surface in elegant scrollwork. The helmet had a swept design along the ear guards, illustrating clouds and wind gusts. A blazing sun crest topped it. All were legendary weather patterns Meridian had never seen.

Dropping the wrench, Radomir gaped at the armor. It looked like the gear of a Tarot Knight, bent on a righteous quest. He feared to touch it. It didn't belong to him, but a better person, handsome and valorous. Not a stunted scavenger like himself.

Georgio handed him the items. "I think this hails from the days when airships traveled from Meridian to the other cities. Back when there was wind, sun, and clouds. I noticed your own armor is useless now."

Radomir tried to smooth over his dented cuirass.

"You've assembled the most complex parts of *Persephone* by yourself. Even Jaabir doesn't know all the workings, and his skills are impressive."

"Can't." Radomir scooted back, dragging the breastplate on the wooden deck.

"I know who you used to be. Yet now, instead of a Gutter Knight, you are a Sky Knight." Georgio patted Radomir's shoulder and left.

Radomir ran a dirty hand over the breastplate. His reflection stared back at him in the burnished surface. Lips trembling, he unbuckled his own armor and flung it aside. Next, he washed his hands and face in a nearby drain.

For the first time since his initiation into the Gutter Knights, Radomir examined the intricate stitches lining his body. Silver staples held his chest cavity together and his copper heart made his flesh visibly pulse with every beat. He flexed his thick forearms, showing the bronze veins just beneath the surface.

He'd made himself a monster to survive Meridian. How could he be a real knight?

When he finally equipped the items, their balanced weight forced him to stand straight and face forward—like the man he used to be. The man he still could be.

Smiling, Radomir took up the wrench and hurried with the coupling.

4: Copper Synthesis I

Azibar walked past the decapitated heads in the High Priestess's tent. Mannequin followed, nudging a disgusting Gutter Knight onward. Though Azibar recognized a few of the heads, their sheer number surprised even him. How many Clock cycles had passed, while she'd protected her position with senseless amusement and outright murder?

Meridian could not be ruled this way.

"What the hell do you want?" Darwick asked, standing before the High Priestess with dozens of warriors.

Stepping past Darwick, Azibar addressed her directly. Mannequin waited behind him, hands on the Gutter Knight's shoulders.

"As a loyal servant, I feel bound to offer the full services of the Mechos to the cause of reining in this 'Magician'," Azibar said.

Before Darwick interrupted, a vent in Azibar's left side fired hot steam at him.

"Motherfucker!" Darwick stepped close until the High Priestess halted him with a raised hand.

She sat at her card table, opaline loveliness open for all as she propped one leg on the chair's armrest. Sucking from a hookah, her red eyes narrowed to drugged slits.

"This will require more than the maintenance of steamlamps and Bone Guild kiosks. What can you offer? Darwick has already searched Vagrant's Row, Paradise Lane, and the Terraces. Captured heretics have been hung along Gibbet Avenue."

"I have come across a faithful servant of the Clown Tarot who has an interesting story." Azibar gestured and Mannequin released the Gutter Knight.

"What can this piece of refuse know that I would care to hear?" she asked.

Azibar glared at the Gutter Knight. "Speak, if you desire the copper shell I offered you. Tell her what you told me."

The ragtag man nodded and doffed his helmet. Azibar smirked at the figure's amateurish enhancements.

"Name's Lezzek, uh, High Priestess," the Gutter Knight said. "Was looking for loot in Boulevard, when another Knight asked if I wanted to help the Sky Nomads, help the Magician. He's acted crazy here lately. Saw steam rising near the Temple, heard something, sounded like a compressor."

The High Priestess rose from the chair, eyes wide. "What better place to hide from me, than Boulevard? The old abode of Charon himself."

"Georgio's involved, then," Darwick said. "He ain't in Nomad Way."

"Do you know anything else?" the High Priestess asked Lezzek.

"Uh, no, High Priestess. But I can lead you right to them. For a price." Gaping at her body, he licked his lips.

Darwick punched Lezzek to the floor. "You don't make demands of the High Priestess, shitface!"

"I shall compensate your loyal scout, my dear. Yet, a simple party of Clown warriors won't be enough, I'm afraid." Azibar arched a copper eyebrow.

"Bullshit," Darwick said. "Tagen's followers are being served in Bone Guild kiosks right now. I'll find and crush the rest, High Priestess. Can't be many of 'em left."

"How brave," Azibar said. "But foolish. I think Tagen's followers have clockwork weapons. Some Clowns killed by the heretics bore burn marks on their bodies, so the Guild cleavers told me."

"You might've done it, you copper fuck." Darwick raised his sword.

"Then why would I tell you about it? The Magician is my enemy as well. I respect the High Priestess's power." Azibar half-bowed to her.

"Such an act must be total." The High Priestess strutted around Azibar. "If I order this, I want all the heretics destroyed. None saved for your experiments. You already receive enough for that. Meridian must see betrayal as a death sentence."

Azibar nodded. "Of course, my alabaster queen."

"Then gather your Mechos. Darwick will join you in the Bazaar with my warriors. Use this smelly hound to sniff the heretics out." The High Priestess stopped strutting.

"Is there something else, High Priestess?" Azibar asked.

"Never bring that thing into my presence again." The High Priestess glanced at Mannequin, then sat back down. "You may go."

Venting steam from his back, Azibar forced a smile. "I shall return soon."

Chuckling, Darwick scraped his sword's edge along Mannequin's copper thigh.

Ignoring Darwick, he motioned for Mannequin. She followed him from the tent with Lezzek in tow. It took all of Azibar's will not to look at her scratched thigh.

That ivory bitch didn't know what she'd done, permitting him to unleash his Mecho Legionnaires on Meridian. In one swoop he would kill Georgio, take mechanis knowledge, and capture Tagen.

5: Past to Present

As soon as Azibar exited the tent, Darwick spat. "We don't need that asshole to cut up heretics."

The High Priestess motioned for the other Clowns to leave. "I have seen it in the Tarot. One cannot escape what the cards say."

After the final Clown exited the tent, she removed her red cape and crown. She glanced at the sword in his hand and smiled.

Dizziness filled his brain. His fingers numbed. The sword clanged on the floor.

The swaying trapeze lantern showed her stepping toward him. After each instant of darkness, she appeared closer. As if she vanished, then was reborn with the light.

"I want you to destroy Azibar while you're eliminating the heretics. I want his copper face for a chamberpot, I want that bitch of his for a copper Tarot deck!" She pushed him to his knees and gripped his hair. Her crotch enveloped his face.

"Can you do this for me? My King of Clowns, my most faithful servant?"

Darwick slurped and licked while her sharp nails ran bloody furrows along his scalp. Tugging down his ragged pants, he released his iron-hard penis. Everything he'd wanted could be his. He'd fantasized about sliding into her purity. Fucking her virgin deliciousness. She needed it, needed him.

Fingernails brushed his neck scar. Darwick flinched.

Bubbling laughter. Green grass and clover. Crimson tresses highlighted by the noon sun. The steers would be in soon, they could go into town, he'd buy her that dress—

She shoved him away and whispered between clenched teeth. "What is that?"

Blinking, Darwick looked around.

The High Priestess picked something from his pants pocket, then kicked him to the floor. "Is this how you serve me? Is this how you love me?" She loomed over him like a naked, pallid nightmare.

She held a card scrap. The one he'd saved from the Bazaar.

Darwick's heart froze. "No! I swear I serve you, High Priestess!"

"Why do you keep this? Did he show you something, like he tried to show me? What did you see, you piece of filth?" She kicked his face, stomped his chest.

"I was innocent," Darwick said. "I didn't steal those steers. I didn't kill her. I swear I didn't!"

Stopping her brutal assault, she stared at him. Her red hair had loosened from its topknot and dangled over her breasts in matted clumps. "I deserve to see, too. You're no better than I am. I've suffered here longer than you, you bastard. Longer than you!"

Darwick shrunk back and tugged his pants up. He'd never seen her like this. It hurt him. As she wept while staring at the card fragment, he rose and bowed before her.

"We're both innocent. It ain't your fault. It's theirs. They did this to us."

"Who?" the High Priestess asked with genuine interest.

The circle of men, watching him choke to death from a length of hemp rope. It tickled his skin even as his weight pulled against it. All because someone had accused him falsely. Steers mattered more than his miserable life. The sun blinded him but Darwick peeked once more at his murderers before the memory ended.

Each had Tagen's face. Long black hair, blue eyes. Smirking, laughing, hooting.

"Tagen," Darwick said. "But I'll find that asshole. Then we'll both be free."

The High Priestess swiped a hand. Her cape and crown reappeared on her body, her topknot sat back in place. As the golden deck waited in her right hand, she tossed down the card fragment with her left.

"Kill Sveta. Bring me Tagen, alive if possible. But make sure you kill that Nomad whore. I won't have it, Darwick. No one will replace me. I won't be denied any longer." She walked past him and left the tent.

Darwick groped about for the card fragment. The swaying lantern hid it from him every few moments. Finally his hand cupped around it and he stuffed it into his pants pocket. He would bring it back to her with Sveta's blood on it.

"I won't let 'em kill you this time, honey," he whispered.

In his mind, a breeze rustled the red hair lying on the green clover.

6: Copper Synthesis II

Azibar stepped off the railcar in Lotus Station and glanced behind him. To his horror, Mannequin knelt near the platform and beckoned. Several Wretched came toward her. The perpetual smile he'd designed for her grew wider than he'd intended.

"Come along…my dear," he said with flat modulation.

Mannequin laughed while an armless girl with spider-like legs skittered closer.

"Leave those rejects alone. I didn't fashion you into a goddess to cavort with refuse." Azibar waited for her to obey, but Mannequin tickled a boy with a nutcracker-style face, whirring up and down with clockwork precision.

"They are so cute, Azibar. Why are they here in this dark place?" She patted the girl on the head. "I'd like to bring a few back with us. Look at those sunny smiles."

Backed against the wall, Lezzek reached into his armor. "Fuck that. Run!"

Standing over her, fine vapor jets shot from his body. The High Priestess scorning Mannequin still riled his copper heart. That ivory slut doubted his abilities? As he studied Mannequin's friendliness with the Wretched, that scratch along her thigh…he could never share Meridian with her. Mannequin didn't appreciate true beauty, being drawn to cast-offs and trash. His failures.

Whatever had made these cast-offs so friendly? Each bore sickening grins.

"I said leave them alone." Azibar squeezed her shoulder. She groaned as biofluid escaped the rupture in her copper flesh.

"Why do you hurt me? I just want what Tagen showed me. I want to feel air on my real skin, not this." Mannequin's voice fell into modulation as she flexed her copper-sheathed fingers.

He sucked in a steam-scorched breath. "I gave you superior skin. The beauty of progress and intelligence. A mastery over primitivism and entropy!"

"What do you want?" Her voice box creaked into an organic timbre.

"I want you to appreciate it. To revel in it. To love me for it!" Yanking her from the platform, he vented scalding steam from his leg at the Wretched. They shrieked with tinny voices as their remaining flesh popped and blistered.

Mannequin screamed and struck his face, copper on copper producing sparks. Azibar's cheek cracked. Biofluid splattered his hands. Steam hissed out the jagged cavity.

"You're nothing but a brute. I won't be like you!"

Azibar punched her face. It caved in, shorting out her left eye. Wailing, she clattered to the platform.

"True. You are not like me." Azibar straightened. "Stay here with these vermin."

"Hurry, I'll take that copper shell now. She'll do just fine." Lezzek drew a clockwork pistol and pointed at Mannequin.

What a ramshackle fool. Yet, no resource should go untapped… these Knights drank the Stygian waters and enhanced their nasty bodies with mechanis organs. With proper body shells, they could be suitable servants in his new Meridian.

"What if I offer you something more substantial?" Azibar asked. "Gather your comrades into my service. They would all become Mecho Knights, keeping me informed of what goes on in this city. The High Priestess will be powerless soon."

"Fuck off," Lezzek said. "Gutter Knights don't work for—"

Azibar snatched the pistol and fired it into Lezzek's chest. Blood and biofluid plastered the wall. After tossing the weapon to the platform, he tore off the Gutter Knight's head.

"How gracious of you to accept."

With a little biofluid and a copper valve, this wreckage would still lead him to Tagen. He walked toward the hatch leading into the Mecho District. Behind him, Mannequin sobbed in a sickening imitation of a human voice.

XV.

The Devil

1: Those Driven Forth

Tagen rejoined the others as *Persephone*'s dirigible filled with heated air. Fifty adult Nomads waited with their meager belongings to board the craft. Old women holding leather rucksacks. A few young couples sharing excited glances. Hardened Nomad fighters with sword in one hand, satchel in the other.

Brave people, all of them…but Tagen had to turn away from those hopeful stares. Andromeda was right: he was no messiah. He didn't know what he was anymore. Just that he needed to leave Meridian before it claimed him. Before he harmed others again.

Andromeda stood beside Georgio and Saissa as they consulted ancient Nomad charts. Every few seconds, her eyes flicked to him. Sveta refused to look at him.

On *Persephone*'s deck, Jaabir helped Radomir and his fellows double-check the venting system. The former Gutter Knight wore a bright silver helmet and breastplate. He even walked straighter.

Tagen scanned the airship's deck and hull, impressed at Sky Nomad ingenuity and efficiency. He studied the ceiling. How would the airship exit the subterranean chamber? There were so many questions and no answers. Such as, what they would do once they passed over the city docks, over the Styx.

What he would do.

Shifting on her feet, Andromeda looked at him again. He offered a smile and she returned it with surprising shyness. He didn't blame her.

"She gonna fly better than a Clown wig over a Mecho ass vent." Jaabir smiled.

"Fly high, yes?" Radomir adjusted a flap on the portside railing.

"New armor, Radomir?" Tagen asked.

"Gift from Georgio." Radomir beamed and Tagen couldn't help but grin back.

"Volunteers, Georgio? Do they know the danger?" Sveta nodded at the crowd.

"They believe in the Magician—of course they know," Georgio called out. His body now cleansed of grease paint, a fresh blue leather tunic, black vest, and leather vambraces complimented a bright blue sash around Georgio's waist.

"How much time until its ready?" Tagen ran a hand along the bronze hull. Steam capacitor lines stretched across the surface, lending the craft a striped brilliance. He'd like to see it airborne, especially beneath a sun. Such a craft would gleam like a star itself.

Georgio rolled up the chart he'd been examining and handed it to Jaabir. "We're almost done. As soon as we get everybody loaded, we can leave this place."

"Is this what our people need?" Sveta asked. "Or is this for yourself?"

Georgio looked at Khyran in resignation.

"You okay?" Tagen asked.

"A change of view, a sense of waste, a change of residence in haste," Georgio whispered, still staring at Khyran's floating head.

"No more Nomad troupers are coming?" Andromeda asked Georgio.

"I don't know." Georgio cleared his throat. "The Mecho District will be dangerous for us—but I will honor Tagen's request. Until then, I won't load *Persephone* to capacity, or with children."

Shadows darted in Tagen's peripheral vision. *Red cloth drew back from his mind's eye, showing the High Priestess at her table, laying out a Tarot reading. She didn't do it for herself, and no one waited nearby.*

She did it for him.

Images and characters clogged his consciousness, hiding something. The Two of Swords appeared, with the blindfolded woman now coughing up blood. The blades in her hands threatened to sever her neck, while the Styx rushed up in a tidal wave behind her. The rising blackness stole his breath.

A hand shook his arm, dispelling the vision from his mind. Sveta stared into his eyes while the others watched him.

"What did you see?" Sveta asked. "I know it was bad."

Tagen inhaled, struggling for air. "The High Priestess…we need to leave. Now."

The Sky Nomads muttered amongst themselves. Saissa and Jaabir shared a glance, hands on their daggers. The three Gutter Knights whispered in their cant.

"Khyran, check out the street above," Andromeda said. The jack-in-the-box hovered toward the tunnel, eyes flashing.

"What was it, Tagen?" Georgio gripped his sheathed sword. "I'm not…we're not ready."

Steam blew into the chamber from the tunnel. Voices reverberated down from the Temple as Khyran zipped back to Andromeda.

"Get on the ship!" Tagen shouted.

Dozens of Clown warriors burst from the tunnel.

The High Priestess's laughter echoed in Tagen's mind.

A flurry of painted bodies crashed into them, howling like wolves. The Clowns showed no mercy, cutting down men and women with callous indifference. Every Nomad fought with fearless skill, displaying superior swordsmanship against the Clowns' reckless strikes. Both groups fired point-blank at each other with pistols. Blades swished through bodies. Bullets pierced chests and heads.

"Kill these fucking traitors! Kill for the High Priestess!" Darwick shouted.

Tagen punched down an incoming Clown. Muscles flooding with biofluid, he backhanded another. The Clown's neck snapped.

"Come on!" Sveta kicked a Clown in the chest, then elbowed another's throat.

The Nomads formed a defensive wall as Georgio slashed and thrust against the mob, leaving several Clowns at his feet. Those Nomads who couldn't fight raced up *Persephone*'s gangplank.

The wall near the tunnel exploded with a gout of steam. Glowing green eyes shone through the vapors. Bronze bodies marched into the chamber.

The air in the chamber grew hot from so much steam exhaust. Andromeda and Saissa butchered Clowns with their black daggers. Georgio split a Clown skull with his sword and shouted encouragement to his people. Though the Nomad line bucked, it held.

Hulking Mechos formed ranks outside the blasted hole in the wall.

"Tagen, get them aboard!" Georgio yelled.

Tagen helped an older woman board the airship while Radomir raced toward the helm. Jaabir ran from coupling to coupling, activating them in small steam bursts. With a ripple of bulging canvas, the dirigible rose above them, tethered to the deck by thick, bronze-wound cables. Tagen pulled more people up the gangplank, even as the Clowns made headway toward *Persephone*'s hull.

Pushing Sveta up the gangplank, Tagen winced at a fierce hot pain on his left arm. A shot had grazed him. "Tell Radomir to get this thing in the air!"

"Not while my people still fight." Sveta drew a pistol and blew off a Clown's ear.

Saissa sliced one of the ships' ground tethers. Still fighting Darwick's psychopaths, the Nomads backed a step. Soon they would be against the ship's hull.

"We must hold them!" Georgio cried. Several dark stains spread across his tunic.

Azibar appeared in the Mecho vanguard, carrying a Gutter Knight's head. He pointed at the Nomads. Each of his brutish soldiers lowered brass rods. Electrical sparks flew off the devices and burned Nomad flesh. Luggage and tools caught flame. Steel Mecho blades sliced the wounded in half.

Jaabir fired a pistol with precision, while Saissa threw her last dagger into a Clown's neck. She resorted to using her fists and feet. All three Gutter Knights ran about like flies before a spider. Daggers dripping, Andromeda shuttled as many as she could toward the gangplank. Khyran hovered, shooting electrical charges into the Clowns.

"Tagen!" Andromeda sliced a Clown's face, then cut two of the ship's tethers.

Knocking a Clown aside, Tagen pushed Andromeda's group up the gangplank. Two collapsed and rolled off it, shot in the back by pistol fire.

The airship quivered. Radomir had activated the boiler engines. Jets of heated air blew from the hull's sides into the backs of the defending Nomads. Several Clowns pushed through. Jaabir shot down two more, while Tagen kicked one off the gangplank.

Force alone would not save them. He needed the city's help.

Searching his mind, Tagen spread his hands. His palms glowed violet. *Tarot characters flowed from the Stygian mirrors in his psyche, into the minds of his friends.*

The Knight of Swords made the Nomad defenders extra aggressive, striking more by instinct than thought. Clowns fell with sliced necks, blasted faces. The Five of Staves gifted his friends determination and energy but the Mechos remained invincible in their armor. Tagen concentrated harder. Tarot images flowed through his mind, each character offering different advice.

Tagen used the Ten of Swords to turn the Clowns on the Mechos but that only worked with a few. The High Priestess's hold over them remained unassailable and the Mechos cut down any Clown who dared attack them.

Shadows fed into his consciousness as Meridian's power simmered within him. Urging him to do more.

He pulled the trigger. The bullet slammed into Alexis's body. Rather than blood, shadows crept from the wound. Some forced themselves from her mouth. Others ripped out from her chest. Willing to serve him.

Shaking, Tagen clasped his head in both hands. "I won't...I won't!"

Steam haze hung in the air. Blood littered the floor. Sveta used her empty pistol as a club. The Nomads held back their attackers only a few paces from *Persephone*'s hull.

Urging him to do more. Willing to serve him. He could tear them all apart, he—

"I won't." Tagen's face hardened.

With popping noises, the Mechos fired their weapons at those on the gangplank. Nomads fell with burning flesh. Darwick and the Clowns surged forward.

"Come on!" Tagen hauled Andromeda over the ship's railing, then pushed Sveta behind him as three Clowns jumped onto the gangplank. They gutted a young Nomad man and cut down a woman. Palms flashing violet, Tagen pummeled them. The Page of Swords sliced into their personas. The Clowns yelped and staggered from the gangplank. Five more charged him but he tweaked their perception by focusing on the wobbly Two of Pentacles, sending them into a Mecho volley. The Clowns were incinerated.

"Georgio, Saissa, get onboard!" Andromeda slashed painted hands off the railing.

"Take off!" Georgio yelled as he faced Darwick. Their swords clanged with sparks, even as the last Nomad fighters fell to jagged blades and sharp teeth. With deft strokes, Georgio parried Darwick's brutal thrusts, yet his brawny shoulders sagged.

"Forward!" Azibar called. The Mechos advanced in formation and fired an electrical discharge, shattering the gangplank beneath Tagen's feet.

"Son of a bitch—!"

A hand pulled him aboard.

"Ready to fly, yes?" Radomir released Tagen and fired a pistol into the mob.

"We can't leave Georgio!" Sveta threw her pistol at Darwick.

Saissa leapt for the railing and Andromeda grabbed her hands. As she tugged the dusky woman aboard, a Clown stave pierced Saissa's back.

"No!" Andromeda hugged Saissa to her. Blood streaked down her body.

Clowns clambered up *Persephone*'s sides, while Mechos torched the rest of the chamber. Fire devoured the Nomads' remaining supplies. Two Clowns pulled a Gutter Knight overboard and hacked him apart.

Persephone wobbled in the air, still tethered by a single cable.

"Take 'em, you shitheads! None escapes!" Darwick stabbed Georgio's shoulder.

Sveta reached toward Georgio while Radomir fired into Darwick's face. The shot grazed Darwick's temple and the Clown leader jerked away. Shaking, Georgio stumbled back a few steps. Tagen helped Sveta as both their hands touched Georgio's.

"Reach!" Tagen called.

The Clowns regrouped. Mecho eyes glowed through the rising smoke.

Holding the railing with one hand, Andromeda swung herself toward the final cable, ready to cut it. A Clown smacked her with his stave. Jaabir tugged Andromeda's hand as she slipped. She dropped her dagger and slammed back on deck, coughing.

Clasping his sword in a bloody grip, Georgio looked at them with clear, blue eyes.

"Find the path. Khyran revealed mine long ago." Georgio smiled and cut the last cable tethering *Persephone* to the ground.

Sveta screamed, still groping for Georgio as Darwick thrust through the old man's chest. Staring skyward, Georgio's eyes glazed over. His sword clattered to the floor.

Persephone shook and lifted away, leaving wounded Nomads at the mercy of Clowns and Mechos. Tagen yanked Sveta from the railing as the Mechos fired skyward. Two Nomads and a Gutter Knight fell over the side as some of the shots hit home.

"The street!" Jaabir shouted. "We can't escape!"

Persephone's dirigible snapped a thin rope across the chamber's top. Ancient gears turned near the ceiling and a torrent of water rained over them. The dirigible trembled from the impact. Items swept off *Persephone*'s deck. The chamber rumbled as the street above yawned open. Tagen gaped upward. Georgio had housed *Persephone* beneath a clogged drainage pit.

The airship rose above Meridian.

Still holding two smoking pistols, Radomir trembled. Jaabir held Saissa while her blood pooled around them. Tagen wrestled with Sveta, and Andromeda shook Radomir.

"Man the helm! Now, goddammit!"

Radomir dropped the guns and darted to the helm, while Tagen and Andromeda tried to calm Sveta. She wept and gnashed her teeth, cursing the Clowns, the High Priestess, even Meridian itself.

"He's gone," Tagen said in her ear. "I'm sorry, but he's gone."

"It's all gone! All because of you!" Sobbing, Sveta beat the deck with her fists.

Persephone rose further into the air, showing them a panorama of Meridian and the endless Styx surrounding it. Mechos were lined up outside the Temple below.

Fighting the ache gnawing through his heart, Tagen held Sveta and stared down. Smoke rose over Meridian from the hole in Boulevard's street. A funeral pyre for Georgio and so many others. The only path he'd shown was agony and death.

"It should be me down there." He held Sveta so she wouldn't look overboard.

Sveta sobbed against his chest and struggled with lessening strength. Her pain flowed into him and he barely restrained it with his battered will.

It was like killing her all over again.

Wiping blood off her last dagger, Andromeda regarded Tagen with sad eyes. "No. The High Priestess has played this blood opera many times. Georgio and those Nomads are the just the latest kinkers she's put down."

"But I can't lead this ship anywhere!" Tagen released Sveta.

The stink of blood and bowels still fouled his nose. Weakness overcame him and Tagen leaned on the railing. Nausea writhed in his stomach.

He scanned *Persephone*'s deck. Seven Sky Nomads and one Gutter Knight had survived. They still regarded him with hopeful eyes. Jaabir grasped Georgio's paper chart. An older woman clasped a molded tome. Fairy tales and prophecies, all to comfort people trapped in a city gone mad.

"You have to, Jackpot." Andromeda sat beside Saissa, face drawn in anguish.

"Aye, sail." Saissa smiled up at Tagen, though her chest convulsed. Blood spurted onto Jaabir's legs but he kept her head up.

"We will." Andromeda gripped her hand. "But you're coming with us."

"Aye, already awaiting ye, that is. Hurry, lassie—" Saissa fell still.

Tagen gripped Andromeda's shoulder as she smoothed Saissa's hair.

"Charon go with you." Jaabir closed Saissa's eyes.

Persephone drifted from Boulevard on a trajectory parallel with Meridian's docks. Tagen walked to the railing. Several fires burned across the city. Boatman's Corner, Paradise Lane…

"Nomad Way," Sveta said.

Georgio's old district raged with angry flames. Canvas shelters dissolved before the inferno's onslaught. Steamlamps burst from the heat. Brief screams rent the darkness.

"Son of a bitch, no," Tagen whispered.

Mechos gleamed in the blaze, forming a perimeter around Nomad Way. Metal-covered vehicles trundled through Meridian's streets, like tanks. Occasional gunshots and the detonations of vapor grenades echoed down the scorched thoroughfares.

Andromeda glared. "That copper fucker is finally making a power play."

Kneeling at the rail, Tagen shook his head. "This isn't what I wanted."

"I told you this would happen," Sveta said in an emotionless voice. "I warned you all. The cards have never lied to me. Now all my people are dead."

"I'm so sorry," Tagen said. "Sveta…"

"Not even you can deny what the city wants," Sveta said.

"I'm not buying that pitch," Andromeda said. "Show him the other tattoos."

Sveta faced her. "So he can burn the rest of the city down? Go to hell."

"Help us," Tagen said. "Please."

"Leave me alone." Sveta's palm glyphs glowed a sickly green, then she stomped to the other end of the ship. The others shrank back from her.

"Without all her memories…" Andromeda gave him a meaningful look.

He could end it…if he took the High Priestess's place. If he became Charon. What right did he have to redemption? He'd taken it from so many others.

Persephone's steam jets left contrails behind them. For an instant, all Meridian lay silent. The fires continued to burn. A chill sensation made Tagen wonder if the city itself awaited his decision. He gave in to the shadows in his vison for a brief moment.

His mind opened to the Ten of Staves card. The man, carrying the bundle of staves, no longer strained his back. He forged them all into one stave, then pointed it skyward while pointing down with his other hand.

"Radomir?" Tagen asked. "Pilot this thing to the Mecho District. Azibar has something that doesn't belong to him."

Andromeda smiled with relief and thanks.

"What then?" Sveta asked.

The weight of responsibility crushed his heart into his stomach. Darker shadows covered the mirrors in his mind. Everyone onboard waited for his answer.

"*Persephone* will leave this city," Tagen said.

2: Perdition

The Clowns butchered the wounded Sky Nomads with relish. One sodomized the mangled forms while his fellows laughed. Most swiped off fingers and ears for trophies, before ending their victim's pathetic lives. Darwick smiled. Their pitiful screams were a song of praise to the High Priestess.

The chamber's contents burned despite the fresh rain. He wanted all Meridian to see the smoke and dare challenge his goddess now.

Azibar stepped over the mutilated bodies, followed by his tall soldiers. Though the armored brutes were nothing but a collection of hissing cunt vents, Darwick couldn't deny their effectiveness. Not a single Mecho had fallen, while he'd lost over a hundred warriors. Those stupid Nomads had fought hard. By the Tarot, Tagen would pay for this.

"So Georgio has finally met his end." Azibar sneered at the old man's body. "He'll help no more cartomancers now."

Rage boiled in Darwick at Azibar's smug expression. First this copper shitface had been allowed participation in this ritual slaughter of unbelievers, then he wanted to gloat over Darwick's kill?

"Tagen escaped, though." Azibar lifted his green stare to Darwick. "You know you cannot return to the Circus unless you have him, or Sveta's head, with you."

Darwick spat. "You think I don't know? You helped us, now fuck off."

He glanced skyward at the departing airship. He'd never believed the Sky Nomad stories, didn't care what might lie beyond Meridian. With the High Priestess, bloodletting, and the Circus, he had all he needed.

The scar on his neck itched. He felt in his pocket for the torn card. The scent of clover filled his nose. Yes, she gave him all he needed…

"They might sail over the Styx," Azibar said.

"So?" Damn, his mechanical voice was so fucking annoying!

"How will you bring such a ship down?" Azibar asked. "With those toy knives you call swords? With pistols and grenades? You need my assistance. Unless you wish to report failure to your precious ivory queen? Again?"

Darwick brandished his sword in Azibar's face. "Don't fuck with me, copper boy. I'll get 'em."

He itched to sick the Clowns on the Mechos, like the High Priestess had commanded. Once they caught Tagen, he'd wipe out these tin-shitcans.

"Not without me, you won't," Azibar said. "It's time for a change in Meridian. Time for the sun to shine on your little carnival."

The Mechos lined up around Azibar, the flames gleaming off their metal skin.

The cockiness in Azibar's voice jabbed Darwick's instincts. He recoiled as a steel blade whistled past his face. Before he could shout a warning, the Mechos fired electrical discharges into his celebrating warriors.

"Heretic!" Darwick thrust his sword at Azibar but the Mecho leader snapped the blade in two with one hand. Both of them circled the other until Darwick yanked a pistol from a corpse and fired. The shot took off Azibar's left earlobe.

"How feeble." Azibar swatted Darwick aside, leaving him with two less teeth.

The bronze hulks surrounded the Clowns, killing them in droves. Painted corpses burned alongside Nomad ones.

"Traitor!" Frothing at the mouth, Darwick grabbed Azibar's neck.

An electrical discharge scorched Darwick's right leg to the bone, then a blade sliced off his left arm at the elbow. His blood spewed everywhere, popping in the fires.

Hatred and rage dulled these horrid wounds as he clawed after Azibar. He didn't want to see the sun. The last time it had shone, he'd choked to death from a gallows. Watched her be violated and murdered.

Azibar smacked him down to the floor. Darwick's sight blurred into a mirage of fire, blood, and metallic gods.

3: Crimson and Copper

Before the Legionnaire could finish Darwick, Azibar raised a hand. "No. I want this one. He can still serve a purpose."

Kneeling, his right index finger sharpened into a fine point. Azibar stabbed it into Darwick's heart and activated his internal biofluid pump. Some of the black substance entered the Clown's body.

The stump of Darwick's left arm stopped bleeding.

"Take him back to the lab. Have the surgeons repair him." Azibar jerked his finger from Darwick's chest and it reformed into a normal digit. Tiny steam vents between his knuckles scalded off the Clown's blood from his finger.

"Sir, our other units have eliminated their targets," the Legionnaire captain said.

That meant Nomad Way and other rebel hovels were burning. His soldiers had orders to terminate any who tried to flee. And with this victory, the High Priestess possessed only a handful of warriors. Meridian was all but his.

He chuckled and kicked Georgio's body.

"Fool. You should have let me capture Tagen, instead of playing the hero from one of your pointless stories. This time, though, you've given me your cartomancer, your ship, and your life." He ripped the silver medallion from the old Nomad's body.

Azibar stared a moment longer but the confidence in Georgio's dead eyes made his vents hiss.

He stomped Georgio's body, again and again. The old Nomad's eyes lost none of their certainty. With a mechanical roar, Azibar kicked the corpse into the burning piles of supplies. Biofluid rose in his throat. Steam blew from his side vents.

"To think you had this craft all this time! While I tried everything—" Azibar's words slurred together in garbled modulation. Biofluid reserves inside his back pumped through his body. His steam pumps regulated.

Meridian's urges were gaining strength. First that unfortunate incident with Mannequin, and now this…Azibar gently vented steam and calmed himself.

It was almost time for his final transformation. From a hapless waif, then a legless victim, to the demi-god who'd fashioned himself with his own hands, Azibar would defeat Meridian.

"Orders, Azibar?" the Legionnaire captain asked.

No Clown or Nomad in the chamber lived. Flames lapped over the bodies, leaving a morass of scorched bones. Such ugly things. Soon, everything would thus be purged.

"Track that airship and bring it down."

4: Temptation

As *Persephone* neared the Mecho District, Tagen leaned on the railing. Meridian's extent dwarfed what he'd imagined. The Styx stretched in an epic expanse, with no waves traveling its surface. No buoys, islands, or even derelict ships.

The thin gray line remained over the horizon. Is that what Georgio had referred to? Tagen examined his hands. The palm glyphs had solidified, like keloid tattoos.

Beyond the Circus lay a maze-like sequence of lanes: the Barrows. Far in the steam and neon haze, skeletal, metal-beam edifices filled a neighboring district called Gibbet Avenue. A long, rickety bridge spanned a bay between Vagrant's Row and the Barrows, flanked by stone high-rises leaning on each other in precarious decay.

"Fool's Bridge,' Tagen whispered. The black mirrors in his mind told him further details about Meridian. Other districts and factions. People and places he'd not seen.

Would the city let him leave?

Activity hummed in the streets below. Even from *Persephone*'s height, Tagen spotted Magician banners as people rioted or gathered to watch the airship. His cartomantic senses showed him their awe and terror. Smoke ascended from Boulevard. Bodies still lay throughout the Terraces. They must think their reality neared its end.

Turning from the railing, he studied the other passengers.

Sveta tended her people: bandaging burns and cuts, repeating over and over that everyone must deal with their pain. She offered no other comforting words. Manning the helm, Radomir grasped the ship's wheel in tight hands. Khyran helped with the smaller levers, and Jaabir with the gauges and consoles. Andromeda examined the craft's few armaments: a few clockwork pistols and a handful of curved Nomad swords.

Again, Tagen tried envisioning a path from Meridian. Eyes shut, he focused on the red mark he'd made on Georgio's chart. The arrow had pointed at himself.

His mind's eye displayed him walking over the Styx. Sinking beneath the surface, Georgio held a lantern. The Ten of Cups, with him, Sveta, and a dancing Clown. The Stygian cards, exposing mirrored doorways.

Shaking with frustration, Tagen gripped the railing so hard he dented it.

The Ten of Cups, with him, Alexis, and the golden-masked woman. The Ten of Cups, with him, the High Priestess, and a dead body. The Ten of Cups, with...

"Enough," he whispered through gritted teeth.

He didn't have the complete picture. He needed to see the rest of Sveta's tattoos.

Glancing at her, Tagen's brow lowered. There was too much at stake for her to hide the key to all their freedom. Power welled in him. The shadows in his mind formed hooded, rotting figures.

He could take it from Sveta. He could make her—

Alexis flopped off the coffee table as smoke from the gun barrel stung his nose.

"Enough!" he shouted.

Andromeda ran to his side. "Jackpot...?"

"I can't resist it much longer," Tagen said in a rasp.

5: Obsession

Andromeda left Tagen at the railing, unable to watch him struggle with Meridian's power. Unless they left soon, he would be lost to her.

Lips tight, she walked over the deck toward Saissa's body. She'd contained her grief as long as she could. Kneeling over her body, Andromeda pulled back the canvas.

She caressed Saissa's hands, then inserted a curved dagger into her cold grasp. No tears came, just heaving sobs. At least Saissa had died for her own dreams, not another's vengeance. Though she lacked a doll head to complete the ritual, Andromeda clasped Saissa's lukewarm hand to her heart.

"Now that your life greets its final wane, I bind you here in Charon's name."

Andromeda replaced the canvas and stood.

A square shape moved underneath it.

Lifting the canvas's edge, Andromeda's heart spasmed. Her old silver Tarot deck slid the rest of the way from Saissa's bandoleer. How did...well, by Charon. Saissa must have pocketed it before leaving Boatman's Corner. She'd believed in more than just the Magician...she'd believed in Andromeda.

With tentative movements, she rubbed her palm glyphs and concentrated. Tarot images glided through her thoughts before settling on the Magician, her true focus. Perhaps after so long, just this once...

Tagen shuddering at the rail caught her eye. Ceasing her concentration, her hands fell limp at her sides. All she could think about was him, and how long he might have.

Andromeda slipped the deck into her corset. The pressure and guilt he felt would swallow most people. But Tagen had awakened something different in her. Something she didn't want to lose. Should they fly away and leave Khyran's body behind? He had foretold his own death, and Georgio's. He'd known what his fate would be.

Tagen's remained a mystery. She needed to be around...in the event Meridian claimed him. The daggers beneath her skirt chilled her thigh.

6: Damnation

The High Priestess sensed the crowds outside, growing restless and bolder. The airship couldn't be allowed to leave, much less fly for long.

Outside her tent, Clowns stopped writhing in grease paint mud holes and took notice of her. Others in drugged dazes woke with excited moans. Prostitutes in the sideshows ceased copulating with customers and watched their queen. Even while heretic crowds shouted outside the Circus, she forced the Clowns to smile at their deliverer.

"It is time I lifted all Meridian out of darkness. The faithful have paved the way. The martyrs have bled on the streets, combating the Magician's evil." She swept her eyes over them. "Will you cast aside what I have given you?"

All Clowns leapt up and shouted their disagreement. She smiled and sampled sugar-coated meat cubes from a stall. Slurping, chewing, savoring the flesh of a human being. Eyes half-closed, she licked the juice off each finger and moaned.

"I will illumine the true path for you all. I will give you a Sun," she said.

The Clowns gasped and smiled.

While she hand-fed meat cubes to those kneeling around her, others kissed her feet. Panting Clowns gripped her thighs. They were the last of her followers.

She laughed, already seeing the outcome in a vision of Tarot cards and steam vapor. *In her mind's eye, an empty trapeze swung over the Styx. A red blossom withered to black. Thorny vines snaked from it, choking Tagen.*

A black dagger plunged into a Stygian heart.

XVI.

The Tower

1: Labor in Vain

"I can feel her down there," Tagen said. "Working her magic."

The others looked at him sharply. None had spoken since his outburst. His statement did little to defuse the tension.

"But she can't sense you," Andromeda said. "The Magician red lights her divinatory skills."

"The High Priestess will still follow this ship." Sveta ignored Andromeda's stare.

"Then why are we moving so slowly?" Tagen glanced at the helm station, where Radomir stood as if he'd always been a proud airship captain.

"I guess Ratty Boy's still learning how to pilot this novelty." Andromeda approached Radomir. "Which reminds me. Azibar held a Gutter Knight's head during the battle. Weird cheeks, like flaps hanging over gems. Recognize him?"

"Lezzek. Wouldn't help Sky Nomads." Radomir gripped the wheel tight.

"We shoulda listened to him, too," the last Gutter Knight onboard said. "You said the Nomads would pay in gold and copper, if we helped 'em and the Magician."

A hush fell over everyone aboard.

"Oh shit," Jaabir said.

Sveta glared at Radomir. "You what? You son of a bitch. Your friend informed on us, didn't he? Like all Gutter Knights do."

"Nomad Girl's right. What else does Azibar know?" Andromeda drew a dagger.

Tagen stood between them and Radomir. "He's more than proven his loyalty. Radomir is our friend. Haven't you lost enough friends, Andromeda? And you, Sveta? This won't bring them back, or change anything."

"Yeah, Charon's gotten enough loot this day," Jaabir said.

The dagger shook in Andromeda's grasp. Tagen gently pushed it down.

"You can't be angry forever," Tagen whispered.

"You don't know what forever is." She rolled the dagger between her fingers.

Sveta cleared her throat. "How do you plan to enter Azibar's lab without getting every Mecho after us? If we land this ship, they'll overwhelm us at the first opportunity."

"I know." Andromeda shoved her dagger back into its sheath. "We'll avoid them. Jaabir says he managed to install the cling ladders before…before we lifted off."

"That's it? That's the plan?" Sveta shook her head and muttered scornful words.

A blinding blue light shot past the starboard side. *Persephone* shuddered. The surviving Sky Nomads shouted and scurried portside. Scorch marks sizzled along the starboard railing.

"What the hell?" Tagen asked, still blinking from the light.

A jolt shook the airship. Andromeda grabbed a handful of rigging.

"We're being shot at!" Jaabir yelled, helping Radomir with the wheel.

2: Epiphany I

While the clockwork ballista recharged, Azibar stood over its two gunners.

"How did you miss? Tin-skinned fools. You only need to hit the dirigible! I want the ship's hull intact. If you so much as scratch it,

I'll use your bodies to repair the damage." He flared his eyes. The gunners nodded and sat up straight.

The ballista's capacitor vented another jet as the fuse boiler powered up the weapon. Azibar had only tested it in the tunnels beneath his district. In the street behind him, two armored chariots wheeled past, their exhaust stacks belching steam. Both were armed with flechette cannons and vapor sprayers, capable of melting flesh off bone.

With the Clown's martial arm withered, he'd unleashed his full arsenal.

After leaving the Temple, he'd hurried his Legionnaires along a railtrain through Lotus Station, the only such vehicle operating in Meridian. He had worried the airship might escape before he'd have a chance to bring it down, but apparently, its pilot experienced difficulties.

One of the gunners cranked the sight into place over the intended target. "Ready at your command, Azibar."

"Stand by to eliminate all aboard, save for Tagen," Azibar told the Legionnaires waiting behind him. "Wheel the ship into the Spire's maintenance pit immediately."

He glanced toward the Circus, the smoke still rising from Boulevard. Everyone in Meridian could see the airship by now, giving life to the Sky Nomad legends. Once Azibar had the vessel, he'd reverse engineer it and build an armada of them.

"Fire!" Azibar cried.

3: Disgrace

The High Priestess reclined on her sedan chair as faithful Clowns bore her on a course behind the airship. Red silk cushions padded her form, while the chair's grease-painted, bone frame advertised her justice. Two legless, armless Clowns, their eyes sewn shut, lay at her feet, licking her toes. On rare occasions she honored Meridian's populace with such displays. Let them see she did not fear this floating phenomena.

Activity in the city had come to a stand-still. The Bazaar remained closed. People stared from alleys, doorways, and windows. Even the Bone Guild had closed its kiosks.

Mecho vehicles patrolled the streets and their bronze soldiers marched down avenues and even from the sewers. Azibar had kept his word. Yet Meridian wasn't safe.

With sweaty palms, she shuffled her Tarot deck. She sensed Sveta on the ship, as well as Andromeda. Tagen had to be with them. No one had rivaled her power in some time, not since she'd displaced Andromeda at the Circus. Khyran, Emrys…none of them had loomed so large in her mind as that pair on the airship.

"Like Charon and the Gorgon reunited," she whispered. Cards slid from her hands. Perhaps her prophecy about the Magician had been misinterpreted.

"High Priestess!" one of the warriors in her retinue called. Her litter bearers halted.

A heretical mob barred her procession. Fists rose into the air. Stones and garbage struck her Clowns. Magician banners waved over shouting, angry visages of betrayal.

"Why have you stopped? On, you cowards! I fear them less than I would a Gutter Knight's breath." Not even rising in the chair, the High Priestess raised a hand. Her palm glyphs flashed red.

She played on her imagery and glamour: she was the true High Priestess of the Tarot and none could deny their love for her. *In the Circus of her mind, she whispered comfort in hundreds of ears, kissed thousands of lips.*

The mob parted. Some fell to their knees and begged forgiveness.

She rubbed her thighs together. "You see, my righteous subjects? They obey—"

Several people flung filth at her. A few fired pistols at her sedan chair. Clowns shielded her with their bodies but a few shots cracked the chair's bone frame.

"I…I…" Her voice faltered. Did they really hate her this much? Had Meridian's power abandoned her? A dull throb in her mind pulled her gaze back to the airship.

"I will always be your High Priestess, your queen—your goddess. I, and no other!" The magic in her voice knocked heretics onto the curbs. Sheet metal posters of her rattled like thunder. Steamlamps flickered. People crawled away from her retinue.

Sitting up straight, she concentrated more than she had in countless cycles. The sedan chair floated over the pavement without litter bearers. She glared up at the airship and motioned her Clowns on.

More armed heretics greeted her in the next street. Her lips tightened.

Golden cards floated around her, deflecting rocks, knives, and bullets. The crowd's enraged voices still stung her ears.

4: Oblivion

Tagen caught Sveta before she careened off *Persephone*. "Get us out of here!"

Radomir spun the wheel dozens of degrees to avoid a second blast but the electrical bolt still severed one of the bronze cables tethering the dirigible to the airship.

Persephone quavered. A Nomad man plummeted into the cityscape below. Andromeda clung to one of the cables, while Jaabir helped Radomir with the helm's myriad levers. Khyran nudged a Nomad from the portside railing back to the deck.

As *Persephone* righted itself, Tagen looked down. Bronze soldiers waited below, just outside the Mecho District. They stood around a crossbow-like device fashioned with bronze coils and a clockwork stave. A single copper figure stared back at him.

"Azibar," Tagen whispered. *The Emperor card flipped in his mind. Its reverse divulged a hunchback racing toward a stone observatory. Men in plate armor chased the hunchback with barbed whips and thick chains.*

He built a fantastic telescope with careful precision, capable of showing faraway lands, even stars and worlds in the night sky. Spherical, ringed bodies, blotches on the sun, and holes in the moon. Azibar crafted metal wind-up toys for the village children. Transmuted lead to gold in a heated vat. Lanced boils to save plague victims. Most of all, he watched the beautiful duchess within sight of his observatory.

"Bring them down!" Azibar shouted, his voice rising in pitch.

Time and again Azibar studied her through his telescope. The duchess, though beautiful, ruled a place of injustice and dirt. Knights abused peasants, or raped innocent farm girls. Animals were slaughtered for food, then wasted because the duchess didn't want it. People living in hovels. Cracked stone castle walls.

Imperfections far outshining his own.

"Fire...fire!" Azibar wailed with an all-too human voice.

The duchess didn't like being spied on and rebuked him. Her soldiers tormented Azibar, insulting his appearance and deformity. Burned down his lab, defaced his observatory. Marred his flesh with welts, bruises, and cuts... but they never slew Azibar, or forced him to move away. And he remained powerless to change any of it.

He'd starved to death in the ruins of his lab, staring through the telescope.

The telescope was focused on the lovely duchess.

Tagen's vision ended as Azibar screamed. The ballista fired again. A blue bolt zipped skyward.

Dropping, he rolled along the deck, avoiding the bolt's searing path. It struck *Persephone*'s bulging dirigible. The torn canvas emitted a whistle, followed by a jarring, bone-popping explosion.

The force knocked Tagen head over feet. His elbows and knees slammed into the railing. Steam gushed out the torn dirigible, scalding passengers, while others fell off.

Persephone's couplings vented but the craft couldn't stay aloft. Tagen clambered up the deck to Sveta and Andromeda as Radomir fought the wheel. The bow turned down and the last Gutter Knight tumbled off. With an awful hiss, the dirigible floated down toward the deck, draping *Persephone* with burning vapor.

Tagen forced himself through the steam and found Sveta, dangling from a cable tether. Andromeda lay on the deck, coughing from steam inhalation. The dirigible would cover the Harlequin within seconds.

Gritting his teeth, he reached out for Andromeda. The superheated air burnt his arms. They looked into each other's eyes. Something green flashed on her hand as it neared his.

Steam exploded along the deck. White vapor hid Andromeda from him.

"Tagen!" Sveta screamed.

He grabbed her and leapt as the bow plowed through the street. The ear-splitting screech of metal on concrete echoed off buildings, rattling his brain.

Bronze shards and stone slivers flew in all directions. Some thudded into Tagen's back as he rolled with Sveta through a trash-filled gutter. Muck and mildew splattered him. The street caved in further. Pavement crumbled. Steamlamps shorted out. Dozens of bystanders on the curb, as well as the Nomads aboard, fell headlong into Lotus Station below. Many dropped past the rail tracks and into the Styx.

"Andromeda!" Tagen yelled.

A busted gutter leaked a filthy waterfall over them, but Tagen lifted Sveta and jumped to a nearby platform. A massive groan reverberated from above.

He tried to shout for her again. Dust-filled air stole his breath.

Persephone's weight pulled the airship straight down into Lotus Station.

The bow slammed into a sturdy section of track, though the entire rail creaked and trembled. Centuries of dust loosened from the undercity's walls and platforms due to the impact. Steam billowed from all the craft's heatsinks and vents. Sparks lit the dimness with dangerous regularity.

Tagen collapsed with Sveta on the platform. Screams carried from above. Throat coated with dust, he tried to breathe. Smoke rose from blackened blisters along his arms. Moaning, Sveta went limp against his chest.

Had any Sky Nomads survived? He almost called for Andromeda or Radomir—until modulated voices from the street stopped him short. Someone shone light down into the cavity. Saissa's corpse, which had been tied down, now slid from the slanted deck into the waiting Styx. He shuddered and closed moist eyelids.

"Goddamn you, Azibar," he muttered.

With Sveta unconscious in his arms, he hurried to another platform.

5: Epiphany II

Azibar banged his temples with tight fists. The images inside his head wouldn't stop, no matter how hard he concentrated or cursed them. *That hunched monstrosity in the vision couldn't be him! He was Azibar, covered in copper perfection, the conducting metal of industry and progress. The Messiah of Meridian, not a malformed recluse!*

The vision ended with blunt abruptness. His eyes refocused.

Before him, the airship's stern jutted from a large hole in the street. The rest of it had been swallowed by the undercity. Bodies lay in crumpled piles, Sky Nomads and spectators alike. A steam cloud poured from the wreckage. The deflated dirigible lay across three buildings, like a shroud over a corpse.

Azibar trembled with a rage he'd never felt before. Every vent gushed with severe release. He couldn't have lived before Meridian. Tagen toyed with his mind, like the High Priestess did with her pathetic followers. That, and nothing more.

"I told you not to damage the airship," he mumbled while his Legionnaires assembled around the impact crater. Crowds gathered at either end of the street. He turned and hissed steam at the two ballista gunners.

"It crashed," one of them said. "There was no way—"

Azibar crushed the gunner's head and chest with a single downward punch. The other gunner tried to run but Azibar snatched his neck and squeezed. Steam and biofluid burst in a geyser as the gunner's head popped off.

"I won't tolerate such insubordination in my new Meridian." Azibar strode toward the crash site.

As the airship's steam couplings exhausted their built-up energy, he realized the hull remained intact. The sides had been scraped in the crash and the bow had rammed into the rail track in Lotus Station below. Nothing his mechanics couldn't repair.

"Haul it up," Azibar told the Mechos gathered at the crater's edge.

"Now!" he shouted with flat modulation. His followers hurried to obey as three clockwork cranes arrived from his district.

The ship would still take him from Meridian. From the hunchback haunting his subconscious.

6: Knight's Errand

Arms flailing, Radomir fell into the widening impact crater where *Persephone* struck the street. He slammed into a huge trash pile, then slid down a gutter to the rail tracks. The ship's bow smacked into the tracks. Radomir pulled himself up from the edge of a platform and lay on the concrete. Aches erupted over his body.

The wonderful ship he'd assembled with Georgio, Jaabir, and Saissa now stood in a forty-five degree angle of crushed hopes. A huge vapor cloud obscured the tilted deck. Two stabilizer fins flapped against each other. A turbine popped loose and spun off into the darkness. One of the rudders whirred with terminal slowness.

"Magician," Radomir whispered, then recited the others' names. He fought back a sob as he glimpsed limp bodies hanging from the track.

He crawled along the fetid gutter as Mecho voices echoed from above. The concrete scratched his raw, busted knuckles. Pain throbbed in his leg muscles. Knife-like pangs stabbed into his lower back and his mechanis organs clogged twice. Hesitating, Radomir took deep breaths.

On a parallel platform across the tracks, eight Wretched followed him.

He couldn't hide in Lotus Station for long. Even as a Gutter Knight, he'd avoided the undercity, unless he'd been with several comrades.

"Wretched least of problems," he mumbled.

Radomir's hopes of helping Tagen change Meridian and lead the Sky Nomads to a better place were dashed. Tagen and the others might even be dead. Bodies never floated back up from the Styx. No doubt his friends awaited him in those black depths.

After climbing from the gutter, he stepped onto another platform some distance from the wrecked airship. Light from wavering steam lanterns gleamed off Mecho soldiers around *Persephone*. Modulated voices accompanied whirring pulleys.

Recalling past dealings with the Mechos made him nauseous. Lezzek had paid for aiding Azibar. Bartered his life away, yes.

Clattering and hissing noises rose behind him. The Wretched now trailed after him, as well as across the rail. Why did Azibar waste lives and material like this? With the right amount of work, such creatures might become people again.

"Wear new armor now. Won't tarnish with fear." Radomir walked from platform to platform, getting his bearings. The rail track's appearance improved the further he went, and more lamps shone along the platforms. New rivets, no rust. No cannibals in shadowed alcoves. Azibar kept the areas just below his district well maintained.

From the corner of his eye, the Wretched kept pace with him across the track.

"Will exit the next access hatch, yes." If his friends had survived, and Azibar had captured them, he'd find them in the Mecho District.

A quiet anger built up inside him. For Azibar to steal the ship Georgio had built so for long…he owed it to all them, and the ideals of the armor he wore, to do something.

7: Hope

Andromeda rose from the alley where she'd fallen, thanks in part to Khyran. He had broken her fall as she'd rolled off *Persephone*'s deck during its frightening descent. Though loose garbage piles had cushioned her impact, her bruised body protested any movement. She stifled a groan.

"Tagen," she whispered. Right before the crash, their fingers had touched.

Peering over the refuse and burnt scrap metal at the alley's end, Andromeda studied the crash site. Three Mecho-operated cranes salvaged the airship from a hole in the street. Four armored chariots patrolled the area. She shut her eyes as they rolled over bodies lying around the wreckage. Georgio and his people had suffered horribly. Suffered because she had supported a new Magician.

Khyran landed on her shoulder but he weighed her down. Her guilt over him had driven her to involve Tagen with Azibar, to wreak havoc among the High Priestess's Clowns. Saissa, her longtime friend, was lost in the airship's wreckage. Probably Jaabir, too. All so she could revenge herself on that painted bitch and restore her lover's body.

If she even could. It'd been a faint hope all along. One she'd gambled on and lost.

Andromeda slumped in the trash. Fingers numb, she dug out the card fragment from her corset. The Magician. As above, so below.

She crushed the card in her fist. Tears dribbled down her chin. The crumbled paper landed among the garbage.

A gentle flow of warm air caressed her face. Andromeda turned. Hovering beside her, Khyran's glowing eyes dilated, then flared.

"I can't. Sorry I'm such a floss head. I'm sorry you faced your future alone." She closed her eyes and pressed her cheek to his. "I'm sorry my heart isn't yours anymore."

He vented light steam on her neck. Groaning, Andromeda opened her eyes.

"What is it? What are you pitching to me?"

Khyran's eyes flicked on and off. A steel card appeared in the air before him. Its edges were stained black—a Stygian Tarot card. It was the Ten of Cups. On it, Sveta and Tagen faced off in Meridian while an airship flew in the background. A dancing Harlequin and Clown both juggled cards.

The Harlequin's face morphed into hers.

Andromeda sat up straight in the trash. The image warmed her insides as she remembered dancing in the Circus when it still belonged to her. Dancing cards across her fingers like she often did her daggers.

Dancing across the Styx, grasping Tagen's hand before he sunk beneath it.

Gathering all the emotion inside her, Andromeda concentrated. The only image in her mind was the Magician card.

"I need you…" She trembled and focused harder. Surely she could find him, hadn't she felt him enter Meridian? Please, she had to sense him now. Please.

Both her palms flashed green.

Teeth clenched, Andromeda poured her emotions into the image. Caressed the Magician's face in her mind, told him she would do anything for him.

"I'll die for you, if that's what it takes…even if Meridian takes me instead."

Shadows appeared in her sight, then vanished. Palm glyphs thrumming, Andromeda shivered. A shape flew from her corset and spread out before her in seventy-eight cartomantic windows.

"By Charon and the Gorgon…" It was her silver deck. Not even when she'd been a cartomancer, had her deck mirrored the ethereal qualities of the High Priestess's. The physical cards had transformed into spiritual ones.

The Magician card fragment rose from the alley and straightened itself. Andromeda's palms flashed again and the deck stacked into her right hand. After the Magician fragment shuffled into it, the deck disappeared. New onyx daggers appeared from nothing and sheathed themselves under her skirt.

All this time, focusing on the Magician's image in her mind… seeing the shadows again…Tagen had stirred more than her heart. He'd reawakened her very quintessence.

A form dropped into the alley. Andromeda drew a dagger in each hand.

"Shit, thought you'd met Charon, or got captured by that copper sphincter," Jaabir whispered. His leather clothes were singed and his left pincer hung limp.

Andromeda crawled over the trash and hugged him tight. "Like hell I have."

Releasing him, she concentrated. A Tarot card appeared over her outstretched palm. Before she could make out the image, it faded.

"Charon's eyes, Andromeda. You really were a cartomancer." Jaabir gaped.

Tingling excitement flared in her body. "It's a start. Listen, I know Jackpot and Nomad Girl are still alive. Don't ask, I just know. You still want in on this take?"

"Don't insult me by asking." Jaabir chuckled. "Course I'm gonna bust into Azibar's playhouse with you. I gotta repair my left hand anyway. But how?"

Andromeda smirked. "The way a Blade of Charon would: right under his fucking nose. Can you check the situation outside the alley?"

As his clockwork mask shifted, a monocle clicked over his right eye. "I'm on it."

Jaabir clambered over the scrap metal and looked around. The lens focused in and out as tiny gears ticked around his eye. Finally, he nodded.

"*Persephone*'s inside the Mecho District. Looks like they've sealed the entrance. Hell, sounds like a riot's coming down the street." Jaabir leaned back and the monocle shifted from his eye.

"Then we'll try another way," Andromeda said. "Take us in, Khyran."

Khyran hovered from the alley to a large gutter leading into the Mecho District.

Jaabir squeezed her shoulder. "For Saissa."

She gripped his in return. "For all of us."

8: Transmutation

Darwick awoke as small cylinders exited either side of his body. He breathed deep and exhaled. A vent in his right side hissed steam, then his heart thumped with a deadpan rhythm. A metallic taste swam in his mouth. He spat, then sat up on the table.

An expansive laboratory gleamed around him. Steam pistons powered conduits surging with energy. Routers whirred, their terminals aglow with raw electricity. Various Mechos, sheathed in silver skin, walked by with spare parts or biofluid canisters.

"What the fuck?" Darwick yanked copper tubes from his chest.

One of his hands now ended in a metal claw.

Darwick shook. Bumps rose on his flesh. His left arm from the elbow had been replaced with a clockwork limb, powerful yet terrifyingly alien.

"Who did this?" He leapt from the table. "Who did this shit to me?"

The Mechos regarded him with quizzical expressions. Darwick paused, then touched his face with his organic hand. Though his appearance remained intact, his pumping organs, and the air venting from his side, made him snarl in utter hatred.

"Azibar, you fucking cunt! Come and face me!" He'd crush that copper asshole's face, he'd melt him in a vat of fire, he would…

In the lab's corner, a huge golden disc waited. The room's lamps reflected off it, just like the hot sun he'd sweated under while being hanged. While she'd bled to death. His new claw snapped shut as his lip curled.

Why couldn't he remember anything else? They must have shared happy moments, before those riders came with the sheriff. Before coming to this awful city.

He couldn't deny a past life any longer.

Darwick recalled his time in Meridian before his grease paint baptismal. Nothing but razor-edge survival on the streets, fighting over scraps the Bone Guild missed. Lording over Gibbet Avenue's gangs. Killing with more extreme vigor than the rest, just to stay on top of the food chain.

Why should he care? His past life had rejected him. Darwick preferred this world.

Didn't he?

Silver forms entered his vision. "Azibar will deal with you shortly. You must return to the table—"

After pushing his way past the surgeon Mechos, Darwick entered a chamber containing body shells on racks: the form-fitting, flesh-like metallic covering all full Mechos wore. Tin, bronze, silver, gold, and copper. Ranked from the least to the most valued. Once installed, a shell couldn't be removed without great pain or skill.

He studied his new arm. Fuck the consequences of this augmented body. As long as he could still kill, he'd be fine. As long as she still loved him…

Some of the shells made him snort. Several must be extras for Azibar himself, should he need repair. He punched one with his new hand, ruining the molded copper skin. The shells behind it on the rack clanged against each other.

"Yeah, shitface. Like that?" He started to hit the next one when its appearance made him halt.

Captivating face, firm breasts. Sensuous curves and lithe limbs. A shock of filament hair bound into a topknot. Darwick jumped back as he gazed upon shell upon shell molded after the High Priestess.

"She ain't yours." Red heat exploded in his brain. "Azibar, you motherfucker!"

He ripped one in two with his new arm and reached for another. Cold, strong hands clamped his shoulders and turned him around. A huge Mecho soldier held him while the surgeon pressed something into his back.

"Heretics! You can't create her! You can't make her for yourselves! She'll fucking come here and then she'll—"

A socket in his back clicked. Darwick's vision went black. Biofluid surged through him and his anger calmed. His face muscles relaxed from his usual leer.

"You see?" Azibar called. "Even her most prized lap dog can be brought to heel."

Darwick opened his eyes. A headless body hung on a compressor rack in front of him, as Mecho surgeons melded a new copper shell to it. The covering attached with a sucking noise. Biofluid flowed into the cadaver from a pump, while another surgeon coated the palms with copper lining. Rivets, sockets, and gears snapped into place.

"You will be the first convert from her lies," Azibar said. A surgeon carried the Mecho leader's head. "Do you feel it? How the biofluid deadens the primitive emotions she enslaved you with?"

The surgeon snapped Azibar's talking head onto the completed body. The neck clicked. Gears and pumps hummed beneath the copper skin. Steam shot from each vent.

Darwick became nauseous.

"Andromeda was so kind to lend me her old lover's corpse." Azibar disconnected himself from the compressor and stretched his new body. Glancing at his palms, he grinned. There, cast in copper, were the glyphs of a cartomancer.

"You sick fuck." Darwick wanted to rush forward and attack but the biofluid pumped until his temples throbbed. If only he had a sword, a gun…he glanced around for an escape. Lezzek's head, carried by Azibar into Boulevard, stared at him from a table.

"Hey, get my ass outta here and I'll give you a den full of gold apertures," Lezzek whispered. Near the disembodied scavenger, other Gutter Knights hung on racks, their armor now coated in bronze, their fucked-up faces cast in brass.

"Life after death, Darwick. Perfection from decay. The High Priestess can't give Meridian this. I can. With these cartomancer's hands, I'll mold a new goddess from her ivory clay. She will belong to me—not you."

"No!" Darwick screamed. As the lamps glinted off the false sun, he covered his eyes and sobbed.

XVII.

The Star

1: Shining in Darkness

The tunnel branched in two directions: one filled with garbage and discarded clockwork bodies, and the other with mildew and dampness. Holding Sveta close, Tagen looked up and down the platform. No Wretched, no pursuing Mechos. Light from the streets above glittered through sewer grates.

The Styx still waited below. Patient. Unknown.

Continuing down the mildewed tunnel, his boots slapped through puddles. Ancient graffiti covered the walls, faded by water and age. People's names or symbols in numerous alphabets. Accompanying them were numerical totals of the Alueryic Clock. It was the only thing resembling a tombstone Tagen had seen in Meridian.

Sveta mumbled against his chest. Her pink cap had been lost in the crash. Water runoff created furrows in her grease paint.

"Sveta?" he whispered.

She coughed.

Tagen stopped, looked backward, then entered a sluice trough below three sewer grates. Twin gutters poured a steady stream into the trough, powering a large turbine. He leaned Sveta against the wall, where her bottom could rest on the trough's edge.

"Sveta?" He nudged her shoulder.

Eyes opening wide, she gazed around, then at him. "Where are we? What...where are the others?"

Tagen pushed wet hair from his eyes. "I had to get us away from the airship. Mechos were everywhere."

"Damn it, so many have…" Racking sobs ended her words.

He embraced Sveta while she cried. All those she'd known in Nomad Way drifted through his thoughts. *Faces, smiles, quiet times near the docks. Laughter in canvas tents. Listening to Georgio's legendary tales of Sky Nomad exploits. Georgio teaching her mazurka dances beneath colored steam lanterns.*

She'd lived a full life in Meridian before he'd arrived. It seemed he'd lain dormant in that alley…until the city had been ready for him.

As Tagen held her tight, Sveta's shoulder tattoos peeked out from smudged grease paint. *Mirrored doors. Characters from ethereal shadows. Black waters. Charonic words.* The Stygian Tarot saturated his mind with numerous trumps and suit cards but some images remained absent.

"I can't end this until I've studied the whole deck."

They stared at each other.

Sveta swallowed, and with timid movements, removed her ragged corset. Her painted, glistening flesh didn't excite him like it might have in another life. Now, the bullet hole beneath her left breast was a singularity threatening to devour him.

"Help me see them." Sveta stepped under the gutter runoff and washed grease paint off her right breast. "Release this urge I've contained for so long."

"Sveta…" Painful guilt engulfed his heart. "This isn't—"

"Meridian has chosen us both. Don't deny what you feel any longer."

She rubbed water over her breasts, arms, and stomach. With each stroke, Stygian characters coalesced on her flesh. Slowing her ablutions, Sveta focused on him. It wasn't Alexis before him, but her alter ego…one that his cruelty hadn't destroyed.

The ambience of Lotus Station faded in his ears. His fingers brushed her tattooed neck. The secrets of Meridian lay in those images, and with them he could…

"I'm not afraid of you anymore," she whispered, as if to herself.

Sveta tugged him under the streaming gutter with her.

Paint ran off her in pinkish-white waterfalls. Liquid ran down the small of her back as she leaned into him, eyes beckoning him to read her entire body. To behold everything she could offer him.

Shadowy power clawed into his consciousness.

"Tagen?" The fear in her voice stung his heart.

A mirror flashed in his mind. Black vines slithered into his psyche.

Each of her tattoos flexed and writhed.

"No," she whispered. Her tattoos floated off her body in ghostly wisps.

Inky, shadow-like tendrils swallowed them.

"No!" she screamed.

Images slammed into Tagen's consciousness. His hands traced over her body, touching the tattoos. *Characters with tomes, wearing masks, or walking along twisted paths passed in his mind. People either worshipping or tearing down obelisks. Bodies scarred with Charonic sigils. The visions darkened and transformed into the Styx. A brighter grayness than before lurked over its horizon.*

A single star shone in the sky, showing the way to something else besides Meridian.

Sveta cried out and clutched her bullet hole wound. With the eyes of a wounded animal, she stared at him. Black liquid seeped form the wound, from her ears, from her nose. It dribbled from her mouth.

As he reached out to her, Tagen glimpsed recognition in her dark gaze. The hurt, the betrayal in those eyes drove him back as if struck by a physical blow.

"Bastard." Sveta wiped her lips. "You brought me here. It wanted you..."

Black vines snaked around his ankles. Shadows rimmed his eyesight.

"You did this to me! You brought me here!" Her nails dug into his chest.

"I never wanted this!" He jerked away but the vines tugged him to his knees.

Translucent white cloth covered her breasts, wrapping behind her back and over her crotch. Green and violet hues now tinted her tattoos. Each possessed a mirage-like quality, as if alive.

Weeping, she stared at her palm glyphs. "I loved you, Justin… and you did this to me. You did this…"

Sveta's lips and nails blackened. Black petals framed her temple like a crown and thorns stabbed from them into her forehead. Blood pooled at the corners of her eyes and trickled past her nose to her mouth.

"What are you?" Tagen wrenched the vines from his ankles.

"I'm your wife," she said. "The one the city thinks you deserve."

"I never meant…" He simply stared at her, pinioned by the hate in her eyes.

"It's what Meridian wants," she said. "I never had a choice. Georgio tattooed me. You forced me to gaze into the Styx's mirrors. Now everyone's pain rests on my shoulders. Am I to blame?"

"I've changed!" he cried, imploring her with shaking hands. "I can help them—"

"Remember?" Sveta touched the bullet hole and shut her eyes.

"Please, I'm sorry…goddammit I'm so sorry…"

The vines wrapped around his throat as she knelt before him, a dark siren crowned in agony. "You won't do the same to Andromeda. She loves you, Charon help her. She would die for you, I know it. Oh, Justin, why? Why did you do this?"

He hung his head as she silently wept. Finally, she shook her head and stood.

"You fucking bastard. You won't hurt her, or anyone else, like you have me."

Tagen surged with power. "Meridian almost has me, can't you see that? Help me change all this…help me save Andromeda, while I still can."

She studied him with contempt, regret, anguish, and finally, hateful resentment.

"I will make people forget what you've shown them. I will wipe away all that you were, or have ever been. You'll not hurt anyone again." Vines burst from the wall behind Sveta, entwined themselves around her waist, and pulled her into darkness.

"Damn it, this isn't the way!" Tagen snapped the vines holding him and raced toward the ruined wall—but she was gone.

Hanging his head, Tagen shook with fury. All this time, she'd warned him of what she was afraid to become. Now she was his unwilling consort in this horrid city.

And she possessed Meridian's power.

Concentrating again, Tagen faced the mirror reflections in his thoughts. Over and over a light twinkled through the shadows, or within those onyx mirrors.

The Star. It showed a nude, masked woman kneeling over the Styx. In one hand she was pouring blood into it from an urn. From the other hand she poured black water onto a prone figure. A star shone overhead. The starlight reflected in the figure's eyes.

Blue eyes.

"Andromeda." He raced through Lotus Station toward the Mecho District.

2: Optimism

The Wretched's whirs and clicks echoed in the tunnel behind Radomir. Their numbers had grown the farther he traveled beneath the Mecho District. Why didn't Azibar post guards down here, this close to his power base? Perhaps the Wretched kept others away better than mere guards. He quickened his step.

Regularly spaced lamps lit this section of Lotus Station as it might have been ages ago. The stink of mildew and chalk gave way to lubricant smells. Turbines rotated in automated languor along the walls and electrical heatsinks crackled with blue-white arcs under the concrete platforms. He glimpsed stairs set in an alcove ahead and an access hatch above them.

Limbs clacked in sockets behind him. He forced himself not to run for the hatch.

A metallic, gurgling sob came from an alley just beyond the hatch. Radomir wanted to halt. Something might jump out or attack, but with the Wretched following, he didn't dare. Right hand nearing his shiv, he continued toward the hatch.

"Nodule coil single rivet. Kiosk shopper?" Radomir asked in the cant. Those recognizing it would answer whether they were friend or foe.

A copper hand grasped the alcove's corner. Radomir froze. Sure enough, he'd run into one of Azibar's guards. Maybe even a prominent one, yes. Only the Mecho leader and his favorites wore the prized copper shells.

A face peeked around the corner. It had one glowing blue eye. The other was shorted out.

Radomir's breath caught. A Mecho female revealed the right side of her sensuous face, then the bashed-in, bio-fluid stained left side. Bit by bit, she exposed herself until she stood before him. Copper sheathing covered her nude, voluptuous form. Rather than metal hair filaments common to most Mechos, a vent in her cranium billowed steam, as if her hair blew in the wind. Despite the crooked smile on her ruined features, Radomir frowned and backed a step.

"Are you a knight?" Her voice contained silky tones with faulty modulation. Whoever struck her had damaged her voice box. Something about her prompted his mind, as if he'd seen her before.

"Radomir." He was embarrassed at how rough his voice sounded.

The woman neared him in tentative steps. One shaking hand tried to obscure her damaged face. He recognized her demeanor, for he'd felt the same way since Tagen awakened his memories.

She was ashamed of her appearance, yes.

"I am Mannequin," she said.

He tried to peep from the corner of his eye. Small metallic shapes crawled closer.

"Your armor is exquisite. I almost thought you another Mecho." Her single eye brightened as a tittering sounded behind him. "How did you get them to follow you?"

Radomir trembled, rattling his armor. Surely she understood that the Wretched ate or dissected anyone they caught? They must be right at his heels the way she glanced around him.

"Don't know. Exit through the hatch, yes? Keep them here. You escape." He turned and faced them. A boy with metal wheels for legs stared at him. A young woman with four piston legs paced back and forth, venting steam through her ears. Others waited, all horrific results of Azibar's never-ending quest for the perfect organism.

Mannequin laughed, and for once her voice sounded correct. Its resonance soothed him. "You're just trying to be humorous. They won't hurt you. See?"

She walked past him and knelt among the disfigured cast-offs. They clicked and hissed as she patted a head, tickled a chin, or pinched a biofluid-laden arm. For the first time Radomir had seen, a semblance of happiness emanated from the Wretched. Mannequin smiled and vented small jets from her elbows.

What had changed them?

Radomir finally studied her shiny, glistening body. She was as striking as the High Priestess herself…he blinked as Mannequin turned to him. So he'd seen her before after all. Azibar must have fashioned an exact replica of the High Priestess, though in copper glory only. She didn't exude the Clown queen's haughtiness or cruelty, yes.

"Why down here?" he asked.

"I didn't please Azibar any longer. He said I wasn't worthy of him." Mannequin touched her crushed left face. Through that manufactured smile and chiseled beauty, a deep hurt emanated from her.

Scowling, Radomir knelt beside her. "Everyone worth something."

Before, such a statement would have implied trading of parts, selling of commodities. He'd have fetched much for her body and copper skin. Now, though…she was a thinking, feeling, being.

"I didn't want to be like he wanted me any longer. I never thought he appreciated me for who I was, but…what he thought I should be. I was fine living as such, until the newcomer, Tagen, touched my hand." Mannequin's single eye dulled. "I saw these poor things down here and asked Azibar why. He didn't think of them as anything but trash. When I shouted at him, he hit me and left."

The way she cradled a small girl with glowing eyes and clockwork limbs evoked memories of holding Brian. He'd loved his son, and would always love him, no matter what. Mannequin treated these Wretched the same way.

"So beautiful. Not appreciate you?"

"You just see my copper shell," Mannequin replied with strained modulation. "That's all anyone sees."

After a long moment, Radomir removed his silver helmet. "Look, yes? Ugliest in Meridian. Made this face, when Gutter Knight. Feel none sees past. Georgio gave this armor. Dead now, but never forget, yes? Met Tagen. Showed my Brian, old life."

He pointed at her. "Beautiful, because don't judge Wretched."

"You're not ugly, Radomir. No one is ugly unless they choose to be." She touched his cheek.

Radomir's thoughts raced. "Owe Tagen, owe Georgio. Owe friends. Stop Azibar. Help Wretched. Find path, like Tagen."

Standing, Mannequin lifted Radomir up with ease. He wondered, with such physical power, why she hadn't fought Azibar. Perhaps it wasn't her nature, yes. He liked her even more at such a thought.

"We will bring Azibar's lost children back to him." With a pop, Mannequin's lips produced a frown. Azibar must have built her to always smile. Her resistance to fit in someone else's mold strengthened his own heart.

"Mechos kill, yes?" He hated admitting fear to her, but Mannequin waved a hand.

"I know a few maintenance tunnels. Azibar wanted me to rule Meridian at his side, so he showed me many things. I know a route to the Spire. There will be guards."

As Radomir neared the hatch, his foot brushed something on the platform. A familiar clockwork pistol. On the wall nearby, dried blood and biofluid surrounded a small hole in the concrete. A headless body in Gutter Knight armor lay at his feet.

"Lezzek," he muttered, picking up the weapon. The injector coils still contained a few charges.

How proud his former comrade had been of it. Haggling for the best piece. Maybe Radomir would haggle with Azibar in a different way, once they met—after cocking the hammer.

He took Mannequin's copper hand. She flung open the hatch and stepped into a metal shaft. Several Wretched crawled, rolled, and climbed after them.

3: Golden Insight

Andromeda sloshed through the giant gutter into a tunnel three could walk abreast in. Small lights shone overhead. Cool runoff passed in a continuous stream up to her knees. She drew a dagger in each hand and Jaabir cocked his pistol. Khyran hovered at her shoulder, green eyes reflecting off the tin walls. Distant machinery hummed, vibrating the metal under her feet.

"Where do you think this goes?" Andromeda whispered.

"Looks like most of the city's gutters meet here," Jaabir said. "No wonder the Mecho District has so much power. Sure you wanna take this way?"

Andromeda shrugged. "Sure as hell not going to dance through the front door."

They continued in silence, though their legs splashed in the water. The farther they went, the louder the humming became. Vents hissed and the water's sound changed.

"Must be a drop-off," Jaabir said.

The tunnel rounded a corner. Brighter steam lanterns hung from hooks along the ceiling and a metal catwalk ran along the right side. On the left, small gutters spilled into the stream. The water poured into a darker, smaller tunnel.

After scanning the area, Andromeda wrapped her legs around one of the catwalk's support poles. She leaned over backward and pulled up Jaabir. Khyran hovered over the catwalk, watching for Mechos.

"How many shots you got left in that novelty?" she asked.

"Five, judging from the coils," Jaabir said. "Not gonna use them unless I have to."

A hatch down the catwalk hissed open. While Andromeda flattened on the surface, Jaabir aimed the pistol. Green eyes shone from the doorway. The steam lanterns above them dimmed.

"Yes, I know Azibar wants more power for the Spire's maintenance pit," a silver Mecho woman said as she exited the hatch. Her metal-shod feet clattered on the catwalk. "I can't make it rain any more than you can. Blast. Another lighting problem."

A bronze Mecho man came out and stood beside her. "We can fix that later. Did you hear, though? They say the Legionnaires found an airship in Lotus Station. Maybe Azibar's promise wasn't so much smelly steam after all."

Andromeda glanced at Jaabir. Both remained still. By Charon, Khyran better have hidden himself. She focused on the Five of Pentacles in her mind, hoping her cartomancy could still fool others. *On the image, two beggars walked past the Temple, oblivious to the figures watching them from within. Just like these two needed to be oblivious now...*

"I don't know," the woman said. "That curfew Azibar set seems rather harsh. I wonder why Mannequin didn't announce it from the Rostrum?"

"Who knows," the man said. "Though, it will be nice to have our District free of organics for a few Clock tolls."

"I think everyone should share in Mecho greatness, but will we have the materials for more of those aircraft?" the woman asked. "We can't splurge supplies on those undeserving of it. I wish Azibar would salvage all the rails from the undercity. Then we'd have more resources."

"Yes, that and those silly food kiosks. "The man hesitated. "You miss eating?"

"No. Not really. Do you miss...?" Her voice popped as she touched her thighs.

"No, not at all." The man vented steam from his back. "You?"

"Well, no. Certainly not." The silver woman vented a fine jet from her neck. "Let's go. Azibar will just have to be satisfied with the current water levels."

The pair left and the hatch hissed shut.

After waiting a few moments, Andromeda rose. Maybe her magic still worked.

Khyran hovered from the conduit powering the overhead lanterns. Good, he'd crimped it in time to obscure them. She motioned for Jaabir and together they approached the hatch. Khyran spat an electrical charge at the bronze lock and it melted.

They entered a corridor lit with red lights. Machine-like voices came from the left, so Andromeda turned right. The corridor branched in two directions. One led to the street outside; the other into a tunnel filled with cranks, levers, and gauges. Farther on, she spied massive boilers. A steam propulsion station.

"These metal freaks need a good sideshow. Let's do this. And this." She turned a wheel, then pulled a lever. Copper pipes and gold terminals shuddered.

Hands on weapons, they slipped into the street. Few Mechos walked about. Trolley vendors didn't travel the thoroughfares as usual. Bronze guards patrolled in pairs, clockwork rifles in hand. A floating harpsichord blared a triumphant Mecho march.

"Guess Azibar did set a curfew," Jaabir said.

Andromeda nodded. "Shit, no wonder. Listen to the kinkers outside, near the Row. We have to reach the Spire before a riot happens."

Steam whistled from the propulsion station. Jaabir raised his eyebrows at her.

What the hell could they do? There were no more Blades of Charon to sally out and help her now. Two of them against Azibar was madness—

Two Tarot cards appeared in her thoughts and melded together. One showed a falling star above a winged woman. She poured water into a pool. Its reflection showed her as a Harlequin. The other displayed a Harlequin woman and a winged man sitting beneath a Moon. In the distance, an Elysian ivory tower and an Alueryic clockwork tower flanked a winding river.

"The Star and the Moon," Andromeda whispered as the vision faded. The path ahead may be well defended and treacherous, but her heart would show the way if she let it. The tingle of power she'd sensed in the alley after the crash gained strength.

"Jackpot's coming, Jaabir. We have to go. Now."

He grabbed the back of her corset. "Hold it, hungry kitty. Not gonna go anywhere in here looking like that. You need a disguise. Khyran and me, we're good."

"Fine." Andromeda rolled her eyes. "That dome looks like a mechanis boutique. Hurry, before that patrol comes back 'round."

A second patrol walked past. Nervous shudders traveled up and down Andromeda's body. Shit, Tagen needed her! Just a few more moments and these Mecho pricks would enter the next street...

"Now," she whispered.

They rushed over the pavement and under the harpsichord. Jaabir opened the door and they stepped inside the boutique.

Spare parts of every shape, metal, and description hung from racks. Clockwork limbs, golden filament wigs, or geometric steam vents in a variety of shades. Hydraulic oils, syrupy lubricants, and gelatinous flesh liners could be had for a few silver shards. Copper hearts and steel-mesh lung bladders cost much more.

Frowning, Andromeda hurried through another aisle. Interchangeable appendages and organs hinted at what could have happened to Khyran. Each canister of biofluid reminded her of Tagen pushing her aside in the Spire. Saving her.

"I hate Mecho shops." Looking away from Khyran, she bumped into a rack hanging with hands, pincers, claws, and metallic tentacles.

A man with a green Mecho eye and a monocle glared at her from behind the counter. Steam drifted from a large grill in his chest.

"Don't lay your organic hands on those, please. I just polished those a cycle ago."

Khyran hovered near the counter.

Jaabir smiled at the vendor. "She's just nervous. Never been augmented before, you know? Keep telling her it ain't nothing. How much for a pincer replacement? And my friend needs something simple, like a mask, or a chastity gate for her crotch."

Cheeks burning, Andromeda scowled at Jaabir.

The vendor shook his head. "I'm getting ready to close for a few tolls. Azibar's orders. Some unrest going on."

The floor vibrated. Store shelves shook. Outside the window, the propulsion station across the street ruptured in a shower of steam and copper debris.

Six bronze guards ran around the curb, rifles raised. While the vendor gaped, Khyran discharged a bolt into the man's neck. He grunted and collapsed behind the counter. Steam still jetted from his chest grill.

"Let's hurry before he wakes up." Andromeda searched for something she could wear, but not 'install', in her flesh. Jaabir removed his ruined pincer with proficient speed and snapped a bronze claw in its place.

"None of this will work. What if I drape some of this crap over me?" She rummaged through the shelves, chest getting tighter.

Khyran nudged Andromeda's shoulder, then landed on a nearby shelf.

A polished, sculpted, golden Alueryic mask sat there.

Suppressing a chill, she paused. The irony of her former lover, choosing a mechanis covering for her, didn't escape Andromeda. Where had it come from? Not even Azibar could craft Alueryic mechanis.

Khyran's eyes flared. She took the mask.

"Probably won't even fit," she muttered.

Voices rose outside while she put it on. The gelatinous lining suctioned onto her skin, though not permanently. Gears turned, adjusting the mask to her cheeks, brow, and nose. Andromeda shivered. The Gorgon was supposed to have worn a bronze mask. Legend claimed Charon had been killed by that masked woman, wielding a dagger he didn't see. A true Blade of Charon.

"You gonna need more than that." Jaabir held up a filament wig and silver hands.

"Wonderful." Andromeda stood still while Jaabir affixed the items to her. The wig fit over her cap well enough but the hands barely slipped over her own.

"No trouper's going to believe this—"

"Why should they, if you don't?" Jaabir asked.

How right he was. She clasped his hand and faced the boutique door.

In the street outside, the guards left the burning propulsion station and hurried away. As the trio left the shop, a commotion began at the district's main gate.

4: Great, Radiant Star

The High Priestess stepped from her sedan chair onto the backs of subservient Clowns. The Mecho District's walls rose twenty feet in front of her. In the distance, Azibar's Spire challenged her with its gleaming sides and preposterous height.

Citizens gathered at the street's edges on either side of her warriors. A few Magician banners advertised heretics, though many remained curious onlookers. Tagen's escape from the Circus, the fire in Boulevard, the airship in the sky, and now her parade through the streets had forced even the lowliest beggars to come see.

Bronze-skinned guards blocked the Mecho District's entrance: a brass gate reinforced with steel bars. Azibar grew audacious in his rebellion.

As her warriors lifted their weapons, she promenaded before the gate. The Mechos stared with surprise and a little reverence. Not even Azibar's brainwashing and biofluid could dispel her aura.

They lifted brass rods, sparkling with electricity. She grinned as if she would lick all the oil off their sheathed bodies.

"Why do you bar me from my own city? Surely you are still faithful to the Clown Tarot?" She envisioned her words dripping over them like orgiastic juice after a heated coupling. Both Mechos vented steam from multiple vents. One even squirted excess biofluid from his stomach plug.

"No…High Priestess," both said, their mechanical voices cracking.

She waved a hand and the Mechos inside the gate activated the release leaver. Gears turned, injector coils bulged, and the blower vent whistled. The gate opened.

"You see? Everything in Meridian obeys me." She stepped through. A rare breeze stirred her cape, fomenting adoration from Clown, Mecho, and beggar alike.

Over the horizon, something twinkled. She squinted.

A…star?

Thunder rumbled for the first time in Meridian's streets. People jumped back. Golden cards flashed in her hands, reflecting her bared teeth and furrowed brow.

A star? What folly. She barked a laugh, though cold fear grasped her throat. No matter. Let it shine into the eyes of her enemies, then.

Nothing would point the way from Meridian.

XVIII.

THE MOON

1: Reflected Light

Radomir followed Mannequin through the maintenance tunnel. Few lanterns lit it, and the temperature grew hotter. Conduits from the massive boilers beneath the streets ran along the tunnel. A constant drone hinted at Meridian's electrical power source.

"We are almost there." Mannequin's determined stride forced him into a jog.

He didn't jingle anymore in the new Nomad armor. It didn't heat up, either, having been fashioned to resist casual steam bursts. Some of the Wretched had stopped following. He assumed the heat had overtaken the poor creatures.

They stopped before a thick brass door, though Mannequin ripped the lock off and led Radomir into a cooler hallway lit with flashing bulbs. Girders and metal grids comprised the floor and walls. The Styx waited below.

Radomir picked up the boy with wheeled legs and a girl who walked on piston arms. Two dozen Wretched trailed from the tunnel after them.

"Airship, yes?"

"Azibar will have taken such a vessel to the Spire's maintenance pit," Mannequin said. "I'm sure his engineers have already made adjustments to it."

Two tin Mechos in the hall stopped and stared at them. They carried steam torches and wrenches.

Mannequin pointed at her face. "Can you please help? A group of Clowns have made it through Lotus Station! Look at what they have done!"

"What?" one Mecho asked. "What is that behind you?"

Mannequin shook her head. "There's no time for that! You'd better—"

One Mecho activated his steam torch. Blue flame spurted from the emitter.

"Stand back, those things are right behind you!" He stalked toward the Wretched.

Mannequin grabbed the Mecho's wrist and crushed it. Radomir caught the torch and waved it at the other Mecho.

"Burn shell, yes? Back." Radomir waved it again, and Mannequin released the damaged man. Both Mechos fled.

"Good, now they'll search this area instead," Mannequin said. "I hope that one gets his arm retrofitted."

They exited the girder hallway, went through a bronze-mesh flap, and entered a small rail passage. A flat railcar sat empty. Mannequin ushered Radomir aboard, then ensured every Wretched crawled or wheeled onto it. Sitting beside him, she pushed a lever. The vehicle gushed steam and moved forward.

Girders, pipes, and mesh grids zipped past them. Steam blew from grills in the track as the vehicle hovered along the rail. Intense heat radiated down onto the railcar. A few Wretched clicked and popped, their flesh red. Every breath burned Radomir's lungs and throat.

They entered a larger corridor with huge copper cylinders on either side. Each cylinder thrummed with electric power. Rows of boilers lined the walls. Clockwork gears twenty feet in diameter turned as the railcar passed a propulsion station. Hundreds of turbines created an aural wall with their constant revolutions. Water sluiced into heated vats, creating more steam.

"This is a lot energy getting routed to the pit," Mannequin said. "Azibar might have repaired your airship already."

Radomir wondered what else Azibar planned for such immense output.

The railcar slowed and entered a slim passage. Bulbs flashed yellow and green overhead. The track led into a spacious, open-air pit. The walls and floor consisted of riveted steel sheets. Silver-skinned engineers oversaw two dozen worker Mechos. Tool racks and crates lined the pit's sides.

The Spire loomed above them.

"Never seen so much metal in one place, yes," Radomir murmured.

The railcar halted. With the grace of a queen, Mannequin stepped off it. Some Mechos stopped their work and stared at her or Radomir.

Behind them lay *Persephone.*

It had survived the crash much better than he'd hoped: the Mechos had even fixed the blunted, scraped bow. The dirigible had been patched and the injector coils reattached. It still lacked the gangplank. Sections of the starboard railing were absent. One of the cling ladders was unfurled.

"Is that the vessel you described?" Mannequin asked.

Radomir cringed as the Wretched clattered behind them. The engineers regarded them with flat stares. Several workers approached them with large wrenches.

"Azibar shot down, yes?" Clutching the steam torch, he drew Lezzek's pistol. The weapon didn't have enough shots to defeat all these enemies, but Radomir's heartbeat calmed. His friends needed him.

"This place is off limits. Remove yourselves, or I shall have you sent to the scrap bins." The silver engineer's modulated diction was an insult.

"I have Azibar's scrap right here." Mannequin indicated the forms behind her.

The Wretched scurried and rolled toward the Mechos. Girls with grasshopper mechanis legs, boys with pincer gear arms. So many shapes, sizes, and variations. So much exploitation and hurt. For the first time, Radomir realized these particular Wretched couldn't emit human sounds. Only machine-like screeches and clicks.

Though worker Mechos raised their wrenches, the Wretched swarmed over them. Pincers and saws pierced Mecho skin. Steam gushed from torn shells. Biofluid sprayed onto the floor. Wrenches splattered small bodies.

Radomir shot a bronze Mecho armed with a steam torch. "Board ship, yes?"

Mannequin pulled his elbow. "We must confront Azibar first. Please, Radomir."

"Intend to." He cocked the pistol and fired. The shot blew an engineer's hand off. The other workers fled up a ramp leading from the pit, shouting for guards.

Radomir pulled Mannequin along and headed for *Persephone*'s cling ladder.

2: The Abyss Beneath

The Spire overshadowed Andromeda, Khyran, and Jaabir as they approached it. Few residents walked the streets now. Steam whistle alarms rang out in the distance. No one waited at the Rostrum. The disturbance at the main gate had drawn away the Spire's guards, thank Charon.

Andromeda hesitated, sensing a presence inside the structure: a tingle at the back of her mind, familiar but alien. Thoughts of Azibar torturing Tagen made her push past the brass doors.

"Wait, this is crazy. Doors should've been locked." Jaabir raised his pistol.

Inside the lobby, routers hummed and vents jetted from large conduits, reaching to Azibar's throne room. The counters containing Azibar's artifacts had been cleared. An empty steam compressor rack protruded from an alcove she hadn't noticed before.

"Don't like this," Jaabir muttered. "Gorgon's tits, Andromeda. No guards?"

"I know, but I feel him." Andromeda glanced at the compressor rack. Mesh bladders expanded and deflated along its length. A copper tube dripped biofluid. Azibar had rebuilt Khyran's head on such a device. An old dread squeezed her heart.

"Damn it, where could it be? Can you sense your…body, Khyran?" Andromeda crept further into the lobby. The Spire thrummed with more energy than before.

Gears turned inside the Spire's walls. The lobby floor slid open.

Andromeda jumped back, daggers ready. Jaabir aimed his pistol.

A round platform rose from under the floor, bearing Azibar. His wore a different, sleeker copper body. The bronze-mesh toga had been replaced with golden armor. He wore Georgio's silver medallion around his neck.

"How nice of you to visit, my dear Andromeda." Azibar smirked. "I seem to recall that we had an agreement. The new Magician, for the old one."

"Fuck you. What have you done with them?" His arrogance tugged her instincts.

Azibar gestured at Khyran's hovering head. "So he should remain a simple jack-in-the-box? You know what's best for him? What's best for Meridian? You ignorant bitch. If you had kept your part of the bargain and brought me Tagen, the High Priestess wouldn't be destroying the people of this city. Maybe with Khyran's body, though, I will find the path for myself."

Daggers still raised, Andromeda walked behind a counter. "You're no savior. And you won't use Khyran."

"I already have an airship." What was that on Azibar's palms?

Jaabir circled around Azibar, pistol leveled at him. "Not your airship, you copper ass vent. Gonna take you to Charon myself."

"Ah, the Blades of Charon," Azibar said. "We have a common enemy, you two. She's coming closer. I will guarantee a place for you in my new Meridian, if you aid me."

"You'd keep us like whipped slaves," Andromeda said.

"I won't be whipped again." Steam jetted from Azibar's shoulders. "Never again, you hear me? I'll make this place perfect. Maybe I should fix you, like I did Darwick."

An alcove on her right opened, revealing the Clown warrior. A clockwork limb had replaced his left arm. His eyes lacked their old ferocity.

"My new guard dog. Now I need a proper court jester. I think you'll do, Harlequin." Azibar lunged after her.

Andromeda ducked and stabbed, but her daggers scraped off his armor. He swung at her. She rolled away. Rising to a crouch, Andromeda kicked his knee out of socket.

"Pathetic." Azibar's knee popped back into place.

Jaabir fired. The round ricocheted off Azibar's chest.

"I admire your tenacity." Smiling wide, Azibar snapped his copper fingers. "Darwick, if you please?"

Darwick flung one of the counters and Jaabir barely rolled from its path. It crashed against the compressor rack. Steam and shrapnel blew across the lobby. Coughing, Andromeda sidled along another table. Somewhere in the haze, Jaabir fired again. Darwick's claw whirred and clicked.

"Tagen?" she cried out, trying to focus her thoughts on him. Though her palm glyphs throbbed, no visions came.

The steam cloud dissipated. Another alcove opened; a male and female bronze Mecho charged out. They resembled Clowns, with metal-sheathed bodies and wild filament wigs. Jaabir shot the female's face off and drew his own dagger. Khyran seared Darwick's back with an electrical bolt.

As her palms flashed green, Andromeda concentrated again. A card materialized in her mind's eye. "Khyran, find Tagen and—"

Swiping through the steam, Azibar grabbed her throat. As he yanked her close, her feet dangled against his knees. "Yes, find the real Magician. No more pretenders, no more charlatans!"

Choking, Andromeda shoved a dagger into his right ear. Steam scalded her hand and biofluid squirted. Azibar laughed, his grip tightening.

"See this?" Azibar held up a curved black dagger in his other hand. "Tagen will come for you, if you but scream. This will be his beacon."

He shoved the blade into Andromeda's right shoulder up to the hilt.

Gritting her teeth, she stared back at him and tried not to cry out. Her lips trembled at the raw burning in her shoulder. Blood slicked her right arm.

"So beautiful and strong. So charmingly tragic." Azibar twisted the blade in her flesh. Andromeda's resulting shriek made her throat raw.

"I'm not sure if Tagen heard that." Smiling wide, Azibar tapped the dagger. Andromeda gurgled and bit her tongue while agony gnawed her shoulder.

A shot pinged off Azibar's left cheek.

Jaabir aimed again but Darwick flung him against a turbine. A loud crack sounded as its blades flung Jaabir across the room. Jaabir slammed into a biofluid canister, bursting it. The pistol clattered on the floor. The other two Clown Mechos laughed with sickening modulation.

"Goddamn you," Andromeda breathed.

"I found a use for your lover's body. Meridian will obey me, my dear." Azibar flexed his free hand. The palm contained Khyran's glyphs, etched in copper mockery.

Khyran dive-bombed Azibar, who swung at him. It was her only chance.

Andromeda jerked the dagger from her shoulder and stabbed out his right eye.

Bellowing, Azibar tossed her into the two Clown Mechos. Limbs afire with rage, Andromeda shoved a dagger up the male's jaw into his brain. The female slapped her to the floor but the golden mask blunted the strike. Staggering, Andromeda spat blood and reached for another dagger.

Khyran shot Azibar with a bolt and Andromeda sprang up. She severed the coil within the female Mecho's neck. Steam whistled out and the Mecho collapsed. Andromeda cartwheeled backward and aimed her dagger at Azibar.

A metal claw clasped her neck.

"I could've killed Tagen already, except for your bullshit." Biofluid dripped from Darwick's lips. "Look what your meddling has done to me, you fuck!"

He slammed her head against the floor. Blood poured from her shoulder.

Andromeda thought she saw stars over the Styx while she drowned in it. Thought Tagen stood nearby. She reached for his hand.

Darkness took her.

3: Copper Illusion

"You have served your purpose. Allow me to show my appreciation." The fingertips of Azibar's right hand opened. Electrical bolts arced from them over Khyran's disembodied head with satisfying crackles. The jack-in-the-box hit the floor and lay still. Its glowing eyes faded.

Darwick stood over Andromeda, preparing to bash her head into the floor again. Something slipped from her corset.

"Stop. I have a use for her. Wake her up." Azibar's fingertips closed.

Rubbing his neck, Darwick hesitated. Hatred replaced the docile quality in the Clown's eyes. Darwick glanced at his new arm and clenched his jaw.

Steam shot from Azibar's back vent. "Now, you imbecile!"

The lobby doors banged against the walls.

Emotions tickled at his biofluid-drowned brain. Hatred, frustration, fear. Azibar couldn't focus as images of men with whips haunted him.

"I can take them away, Azibar," the High Priestess said behind him. "I make all forget their pain."

Whirling around, Azibar fired steam from all his vents. The High Priestess stared at him, holding a golden Tarot deck. Darwick knelt before her.

Azibar forced biofluid through his limbs. "You make people slaves. You let them live in filth and feast on one another. I am the one who should rule Meridian and all the cities of the Styx."

"You cannot challenge me," the High Priestess said.

"I have the body of a cartomancer now. Your witchcraft is no longer absolute." He lifted his palm, etched with Khyran's old glyphs.

The High Priestess's eyebrows lowered.

He raised a copper fist. "Meridian grants its powers to the one with the greatest will, the mightiest fortitude. The one who resist its urges. I rebuilt the body you ruined. I gave light to your abysmal ghetto of tents. My soldiers own the streets. Now I shall take what is mine."

She made no move as he circled her, reveling in the power surging within him. Sparks popped off his fingers.

"Meridian doesn't belong to me," she whispered. "I belong to it."

"More lies," Azibar said.

"Take my place and discover for yourself." She held up the Wheel of Fortune card; the same she'd shown him before. This time, it showed both of them trapped within the wheel, their flesh melded with the spokes.

"No," Azibar muttered with patchy modulation.

The High Priestess glowered. "I knew you would kill my warriors, you copper fool. I knew you had preserved Khyran's body all along."

He stumbled backward. His exhaust vents sputtered.

"Did you think I wouldn't notice his head's absence from my tent?" the High Priestess asked. "Andromeda underestimated me once. Look at her fate."

Darwick gazed up at her with bewildered reverence. "High Priestess, I killed Georgio and his fucking Nomads for you. You knew Azibar would turn on us?"

Smiling, she cupped Darwick's chin. Azibar tried striking her down but his copper body wouldn't cooperate. Biofluid clotted in his veins. His joints locked up.

"You are still a heretic, Darwick. And now, you're a hobbled Mecho. Yet you served my purposes in the end." She drew a card fragment from his pants pocket. Darwick's eyes widened and he sobbed.

She ran her thigh along his cheek, then shoved him to the floor. He wept like a child while steam spurted from all his vents.

Finally, Azibar forced himself to move. The power inside him soared again. His fingertips opened but the High Priestess regarded him with scorn.

"What can you possibly do to me, Azibar? I have let you plot in this little tower for so long, while you kept all Meridian's machinery running."

White-blue bolts shot from his fingertips.

She avoided his electrical discharge with arrogant nonchalance. The bolts scorched the far wall.

"You can do nothing without me knowing about it. The cards tell me all." Her mesmerizing eyes contained reflections of a hunch-backed man.

Azibar glared at her with impotent fury, though she stood so close, her breath stirred his filament hair. He hated her beauty. Beauty he couldn't have, but had tried to replicate. She didn't deserve rulership or Meridian's love and adoration. Just like the duchess he'd loved from afar.

"These fools may worship you," Azibar said. "You might even force me to do so. Yet, you're nothing but a husk, empty as the golden shells I cast imitating you. I know your weaknesses. I will still light Meridian before this is over."

The High Priestess bared her teeth at him. "You think you're better, because Tagen awakened your past life? Happier, knowing you were a pathetic deformity?"

In his mind's eye, a hunch burst from his copper back. Boils festered through his copper cheeks. He screamed like he had when the soldiers whipped him, mewled until he finally kissed her alabaster feet. Fearing further pain, he lapped up the biofluid he'd slobbered on her perfect toes. So flawless. By all Meridian, so beautiful. The High Priestess epitomized perfection after all.

"That isn't me!" He smashed counters, the compressor, even a large turbine. Finally he came to a new shell he'd cast for Mannequin. Part of the golden face was ripped away. He clasped his temples. "No…"

"Meridian still controls you," she whispered in his ear. "We're its guilty slaves."

"You twisted this place," he said. "Look at what you have made me do…I have crafted something that can resist temptation, that can defy death! That grants freedom!"

"Let me show you how we both can be free." She took his hand.

A look passed between them. She was as frightened and hurt as he was. For the first time in an eternity, Azibar felt relief.

"I don't want to be dead," he said.

She cupped his copper cheek and smiled. "You don't have to be."

They entered the nearest elevator.

4: Drawing the Curtain

"I was innocent," Darwick said while the elevator lifted them to the Spire's uppermost chamber. Conduits along the walls hummed louder. The floor vibrated underneath him.

"I was an innocent man," he whispered to the prone Harlequin lying beside him.

She didn't answer. Blood dripped from her shoulder. His lip trembled, but he cleared his throat and repeated his statement. Still no answer, from anyone.

"Damn it, I'm innocent—"

Darwick paused and considered the Blades of Charon he'd slaughtered, the numberless Magician heretics, all those cartomancers. Men, women, and children. He'd laughed as the bodies burned, cheered as the flesh melted off white bones. White as the High Priestess's skin.

He wasn't innocent at all.

So much torment he'd justified, through his love of the High Priestess. For the supposed truths she spouted from her Circus tent. Giving him a goddess to fill the gap in his soul. In the end, she'd cast him aside like a lame horse.

Lungs inflated with hateful breath, he shouted his rage to the ceiling. Veins bulged with horrendous biofluid. The liquid's deadening effects couldn't contain his feelings. Darwick prepared to shout again but the steam elevator locked in place above.

The sound recalled something from his memory…

The gate of his steer corral shut. The sun warmed his back while he gazed over his ranch. Outside a nearby log cabin, a pretty woman with red braids, wearing a scarlet dress, brought him a pitcher of cool water.

"You working yourself too hard. Leaving me to myself in that stuffy cabin." She arched a mischievous eye. "What have you got to say for yourself?"

Chuckling, Darwick wrapped an arm around her waist. "I love you, darlin'."

She held the pitcher while he sipped from it. The liquid washed the dryness from his throat, then he kissed her forehead. Her hair smelled of lilacs and the almond bread she'd been baking.

"That the only place you kissing on me today?" She laughed.

"Honey, you wanting kids that bad? All these fine ladies wanting my attention, and you out here flirting like that." He gestured at the herd, then laughed as she jerked him down by the shirt and kissed him. Enjoying her touch, Darwick played with her gorgeous red hair. His favorite color.

On the horizon, a band of riders approached, led by the sheriff.

"What they wanting now?" The woman clasped his hand in worry.

Sweat slid down his back. His revolver and rifle were still in the cabin. To hell with 'em anyway. He wouldn't sell 'em his ranch.

Darwick blinked the vision away, afraid to relive his answer to her. Afraid to watch them rape and kill his wife before they hung him for his steers and property. The High Priestess had never replaced that pretty young woman, despite her red hair. Had never parched his thirst, or loved him.

The biofluid slowed in his veins. His lungs relaxed and he shook Andromeda. Groaning, she touched her head.

"I can be innocent again." Darwick stood, flexed his metal claw, and hurried to one of the available elevators.

5: The Light Above

Shaking her head, Andromeda looked around. Across the lobby, Darwick leapt onto an elevator and kicked the lever. Steam jetted and the device pulled him upward. The cool determination on his face belonged to another person.

She scampered to her knees and grabbed her dagger. No Azibar, no Mecho guards. Sucking in a breath, she stood straight. The shoulder wound burned but had ceased bleeding. Fresh bruises marred her neck where Azibar had held her.

Meridian didn't want her to die yet. Her eyes narrowed.

Tagen still needed her.

Reeling on her feet, her shoulder exploded with pain. Andromeda used old cartomantic calming methods and focused. *In her mind, she swung on a trapeze. The air rushed past her body, her muscles stretched, the awed crowd cheered.*

A presence chilled her skin. Familiar laughter from above stabbed her nerves.

"No you don't," she breathed.

Two card scraps lifted from the floor and melded in her glowing palm. Tagen's face on the paper Magician card reinvigorated her body. The paper card shuffled into her Tarot deck and both items disappeared.

She scanned the lobby. Jaabir lay in a pool of biofluid, his steam vent silent. Khyran's head lay a few feet away, blackened and scratched.

"I'm sorry," she whispered to Jaabir's body, then picked up Khyran's head and ran to an elevator.

This time, she would save the Magician.

6: Clarity

Thousands of people filled the streets as Tagen exited Lotus Station via a hatch. Some engaged in brutal fistfights or yelling matches. Vandals busted Bone Guild kiosks, pilfering what they could find. Firearms echoed inside the Mecho District. Smoke billowed from rioter fires across Vagrant's Row, Paradise Lane, and the Barrows.

He clenched his fists and focused. *In his mind's eye, Tarot cards flipped over, revealing a thousand mirrors. Each reflected a different version of what he could be. Gods rising from the Styx, specters with methods, ideas, answers. Rumors of a past life, or the Magician prophecy coming true.*

Leaning back against the hatch, Tagen caught his breath. A great weight crushed his spirit. It wasn't possible to meet the needs of so many.

"The Empress! Pay homage to the Empress!" someone shouted down the curb.

Charonic sigils squirmed at the edges of Tagen's sight.

Sveta stood before him in the street. Dozens of people crouched behind her. Black vines wrapped themselves around kiosks and statues.

"The High Priestess will feed off these people's emotions," Tagen said. "Enslave them with her petty distractions. Not just the Clowns this time. Everyone."

"People need fear. You taught me that, in our previous life." As Sveta walked down the street, the crowds parted for her. The Stygian deck had transformed her into something from the Styx itself. Just like he'd absorbed the biofluid. That's why he didn't die after the execution, and why Sveta had changed.

Meridian owned them both.

"Not like this!" Tagen called.

"Look for yourself." Tarnished cards flew from her hands into the mob. Her eyes held resignation but her voice contained authority. *In his mind, Tagen swam over the Styx. None one could show him his own path. A lantern sunk beneath the water.*

"What the hell did you say?" a man shouted at Tagen from across the street. "I didn't kill that bus driver! It was an accident!"

An elderly woman regarded him with surprise. "How did you know my name?"

"I can't see! I can't fucking see!" a teenage boy yelled, clawing at his green Mecho eyes.

Other people reacted to Sveta's cartomancy in similar fashion. Citizens rolled in gutters or ripped off their clothes. Their past lives were revealed, yet added nothing to their current existence.

Tagen concentrated. His palm glyphs flashed. The people blinked and staggered, then fought among themselves again.

"You focus on the negative. This isn't helping these people!" Cards floated around him, catching the steamlamp light. Flashes of steel brilliance, shifting characters.

"It's horrifying, isn't it?" she asked. "Having your memories ripped between two different lives. Like you did to me."

He'd made her like this. The city played on her fears, her rage, though he was responsible. How could he end it?

The rain ceased. Wind blew through the street, scattering trash. Everyone stopped shouting or fighting and watched them. A Dionysiac man with tattoos of women copulating with wine bottles pointed at him.

"It's the Magician! I saw him come to life, after the High Priestess hanged him!"

"It's Charon himself!" a Mecho woman called.

"Charon and the Gorgon!" a small girl cried.

With roars of approval or loathing, the crowd surged toward them. Tagen and Sveta placed their backs against a crumbling building.

Desperate, he concentrated on the Ace of Cups, once again offering the nourishment of truth to a mob.

The crowd fell over each other and gaped. Some recoiled with horror. Others rejoiced and wept. Memories from a hundred lives filtered into Tagen's mind. The faces on his cards mirrored the crowd, showing who they'd once been. *Carving wooden furniture, raising three children, dying on a muddy battlefield in barbed wire, or expiring in a nursing home.* Tagen couldn't contain them all.

Black vines clogged their minds.

"You're making them your slaves," Tagen cried. "Let them go!"

Sveta moaned as Tagen's mirror of the Styx blinded her psyche with its reflection.

The crowd backed away from them: awed, afraid, or adoring. Their exteriors peeled away, revealing raw instincts.

"I can only handle so much. Don't test me. Don't make me like her, damn you!" Her eyes begged him. Her frown dared him.

The Ten of Cups card had come true in every way so far. *Persephone* in the sky, him opposing Sveta. A woman wearing an exquisite, golden clockwork mask. She danced for him, pirouetting over the Styx. Lifting him above his self-doubts.

"Give me Meridian!" Sveta screamed.

"I can't...."

"Free us, Magician!" The words came from ten thousand mouths.

"I can't—" *His mind's eye opened, showing him two fragments of the same Tarot card, crumpled and bent on a metal floor. Red and white flowers lined it, with himself standing over a table. On it lay a sword, coin, cup, and stave. Tools of ascension. His right hand pointed in the air, his left to the ground. Showing the way. From sky to earth, from life to death. From past life, to his new life in Meridian.*

"I can," Tagen said.

Silence ruled the entire city for an instant. A ripple spread over the Styx. He gazed into the Stygian Tarot's mirror, unafraid of himself.

Taking Sveta's hand, he opened a path. Trails of emotion and thought, like Andromeda had said. Tagen's own instincts opened it for him, to where he wanted—needed—to be. Not at the table with Alexis, not leaving Meridian. To save his friends, and save Meridian. To save himself.

"I won't let you hurt these people—" Sveta gasped and stared at him.

"Ncither will you," he said. "You're coming with me."

A green-violet glow winked around them. Meridian's limitless power touched his psyche for an instant, enabling his desire. One moment they stood in the street. The next, in the Spire's lobby.

XIX.

The Sun

1: Manifest Light

"You have outdone yourself, Azibar. This is perfect."

The High Priestess stepped from the elevator into Azibar's throne room. Taking a deep breath, she sensed the crowds throughout Meridian. The time had come for their judgment. She frowned while Azibar wrestled with the images Tagen had placed in his mind. Steam belched from his body in uncontrollable bursts. What a piteous creature.

Worse, she couldn't remember the transgression he'd accused her of. Meridian was eating away at her, until she was forgetting what had transpired in its very streets.

She had to maintain control.

"See how you fear the darkness inside yourself? Only I can help you." Excitement filled her, though her own emptiness hovered in her consciousness. Like a storm cloud threatening to drown her with emotional rain. It didn't matter. She'd draw strength from others like she always had.

"I despise the night." Azibar's modulated voice rose. "It is the great denier of life; it hides the fruits of our labor, the reasons for our struggles. It is the first enabler of fear."

"What will you do about it?" She caressed his shoulder.

"I can summon the Sun for us." He smiled. "I can dispel the darkness!"

His excitement made her sad. The fool had devised and built all this for her without even knowing it. Manipulation no longer brought her joy. Meridian had taken that as well.

"Yes," she whispered. "You must unleash it, before it's too late."

The High Priestess neared a telescope on a tripod. It pointed toward the Circus. How charming, to think her his beloved duchess, the one she'd seen in his mind.

Azibar rushed to his throne and sat down. Copper tubes extended from it and entered his arms. He grinned with uncharacteristic fervor, then shook as his body hissed and pumped from inside. Vents along the walls shot out concentrated steam. A great hum reverberated from below.

"Together, we will defeat death." Azibar beamed.

The floor mosaic rotated and opened right behind the throne. Pulleys hauled up a golden disc from below. It snapped into place: a halo for the throne's occupant.

Copper conduits lining the chamber flowed with electrical energy. It surged through the floor mosaic until the throne glowed with immense power. Light reflected off it to the golden disc as hatches opened along the chamber's walls. The false sun shone over Meridian with blazing yellow brilliance.

The High Priestess stood before the disc. Electricity flowing along the mosaic did not burn her feet. While Meridian claimed her as its own, she reigned as its goddess. Invulnerable, undying.

"Now...tell me how we break free of Meridian's control." Some of Azibar's will was returning. She sensed her magic fading. But why wouldn't the city let her die?

Maybe it was testing her.

One of the steam elevators opened. Darwick leapt out at her.

She didn't bother dodging. Her golden deck appeared and floated before her. One card darted before Darwick's face: the Sun. It showed a painted, smiling Clown girl riding a mechanis horse through a confetti garden. Over it all shone a yellow sun.

The sun had the High Priestess's face.

"You would not dare harm me," she said. "You love me, Darwick."

"She can help free me!" Azibar's voice popped as he crossed the glowing mosaic. Purple-blue burns marked his copper form.

"You ain't…" Shaking his head, Darwick looked down. Muscles and veins twitched along his body. "You ain't my wife!"

"Leave my duchess alone!" Azibar yelled.

The High Priestess sauntered around the lighted disc. With all people now focused on the Spire, she had everyone's attention. Looking down at her painted, sleek nakedness, she scowled. This was all anyone would ever see. Not who she might be.

She hated Meridian for that. But if she lost it…she would be no more.

2: Naked Child I

Andromeda exited the elevator just as Darwick lunged at the High Priestess. Squinting, Andromeda shielded her eyes from the disc's glare as well as the heat generated by the chamber's mechanisms. The mosaic crackled with electricity. Walking on it would be death.

Tagen wasn't here. Pain shot through her heart. The cards couldn't lie. Not after she'd recovered her dormant sight!

The High Priestess didn't even acknowledge Darwick as Azibar shoved the Clown against the wall. The Mecho leader's functioning eye flickered.

"She will give me Meridian!" Azibar cried, his voice thick with modulation.

Engrossed in her floating cards, the High Priestess smiled. The electricity didn't harm her bare feet.

Dagger in hand, Andromeda crept around the throne room. The Charonic sigils on her blade glowed orange as she concentrated on them.

"You stole her from me, you copper shitface!" Darwick yelled. The brief resentment and determination in his bearing evaporated. Andromeda knew the High Priestess controlled him once more. He walked over the electrified mosaic. Flesh dissolved off his feet. The roasted, bitter stench made her gag.

"Both of you have always loved me…yet I can have only one king," the High Priestess said, still studying her cards.

Azibar and Darwick attacked each other with pure savagery. The Clown pierced Azibar's right cheek with his claw. Venting steam from his wrist, Azibar scorched the flesh off Darwick's chest. Howling, Darwick rammed his claw through Azibar's left side. Biofluid dowsed them both. The Mecho leader ripped off Darwick's clockwork arm, then held him down on the glowing mosaic. More skin melted off Darwick. Andromeda knew steam organs and biofluid kept him alive. It didn't keep him from shrieking.

She searched for a conduit she could slice, anything she could tamper with to disrupt the current. She'd never liked Darwick but no creature deserved such torture.

"Where is your lover, Andromeda?" The High Priestess regarded her with a scornful smile.

Andromeda froze.

"It was feeble of you to keep Khyran's head alive, with Azibar's simple machines. What made you think you could ever revive him? Before you stole his head from my tent, I shared many wonderful times with it." She licked her lips.

Andromeda flung her dagger while circling around the mosaic toward the High Priestess. With a laugh, the High Priestess appeared right before her and slapped Andromeda backward. The mosaic popped and sizzled inches from her feet. Khyran's head flew from her grasp and landed near Azibar's throne.

"You only thought you saw me standing over there," the High Priestess said. "Your perceptions were always so easy to manipulate. In trying to help people, you open yourself to weakness. Just like in the days when you had the Circus all to yourself. Just like when I made you fall in love with Khyran. With Tagen."

"No…" Andromeda raised her fists but the weight of her heart held them in check. Behind them, Azibar slammed Darwick against a router. Electricity flashed across the room.

The High Priestess pinched one of her nipples. "I knew, if you fell in love with a cartomancer, you would use him to destroy me.

Khyran was powerful, yet I never feared him. You helped me eliminate him, Andromeda. Pressured him, convinced him to strike at me, out of love for you. What a fool. By letting you take his head and body, you led me to the real Magician."

Andromeda swallowed and tried to speak as the High Priestess continued.

"I let him enter Meridian through Vagrant's Row, like everyone else. I knew, when he did not give in to temptations, when he did not seek succor in Clown paint, that he was the one."

Andromeda said nothing, knowing that to be true.

"Why else would I have placed Tagen into the Funhouse, instead of executing him?" the High Priestess asked. "Why else do you think I allowed you to fight against me all this time? Residing in that dismal little watchtower."

"I love the Magician." The words sucked all energy from Andromeda.

"You loved a lie," the High Priestess said. "Put your final dagger to the best use, Blade of Charon. Not everyone can dance on the Styx forever."

Pushed by an invisible force, Andromeda's left arm moved toward her right. The dagger's edge touched her left wrist. Charonic sigils burned red on the hilt.

The dagger's tip stopped just before drawing blood while Andromeda fought a deluge of visions. *Tagen aiming a gun at Alexis, after he had beaten her for wanting a divorce. The Tarot cards in Alexis's hands, showing the route to Meridian. A route that Tagen accepted when he shot Alexis…in the same place Sveta bore a bullet scar.*

"Now you know what I saw at Tagen's hanging." The High Priestess caressed Andromeda's cheek. "Meridian chose him because of his inner darkness. Your precious Magician is a murderer. Stop torturing yourself on such a doomed path. End it."

"He's not that person…anymore…" Andromeda glared at her. "He's…"

Tagen pulled the trigger. Alexis sank into her own blood.

"No," Andromeda murmured.

One of Alexis's cards showed Andromeda on the Ten of Cups. Drowning.

Andromeda carved into her flesh with the dagger. Blood sizzled on the mosaic.

"No!" Without looking, she knew the edge had traced the outlines of her palm glyphs, not the veins in her wrist. "I remember who I was. I remember all I've done!"

The High Priestess jerked back.

Green light flashed from Andromeda's glyphs. The cards of her silver deck bridged themselves between her hands. The onyx dagger floated toward the High Priestess's throat…but Andromeda's own white-painted reflection stood before her. The dagger neared her skin.

"You have the mask and the dagger of Gorgon legend," the High Priestess said. "Yet you forgot one thing: you do not have the Stygian Tarot."

Andromeda fell backward as the blade's edge touched her own throat.

3: Attainment I

Bright light emitted from the Spire's apex as Radomir prepped *Persephone*'s steam engines. Yellow beams flooded out open windows near the structure's top. From his memories, Radomir recalled the sun shining over high-rises outside his office window. Though this light paled in comparison, being little more than a lighthouse, it still awed Meridian's populace.

He'd find his friends up there, yes.

Mannequin helped the Wretched aboard and looked up. "Azibar's Sun. He planned to activate it when he ruled Meridian."

"Get airship ready, yes?" He tightened a coupling bolt and grasped the helm.

Shouts echoed from the Spire's summit. The crowds outside erupted in rage and desperation. Mecho guards tried sealing the main gate again but people spilled over them. Standing firm, the guards fired rifles or electrical rods. The mob still overran them. Soon the violence would reach *Persephone*.

"Start boiler pumps!" Radomir yelled.

The Wretched latched onto conduits and couplings, as if feeding their own energy to jumpstart the engines. Mannequin pulled two leavers. Cranking a wheel, he pressed the pedal at his feet to start the combustion cycle. The gauge indicators rose. He hoped the Mechos had repaired any internal damage, yes.

As Mannequin pulled the third pump lever, steam flowed from a compressor near the stern. It filled the dirigible via flexible bronze tubes. The craft's main exhaust vents jetted, and electrical current built up from the commutator to the interior engines…but the dirigible filled at an agonizing pace.

While Radomir waited with Mannequin at the helm, rioters flooded the district. Mechos fired into the crowd. More angry citizens came.

"Force steam into dirigible," Radomir said.

"The heat may be too much on the couplings." Mannequin met his eyes. "You're right. We should do it."

Persephone shuddered as the dirigible filled faster. Gripping the wheel, Radomir clenched his metal teeth. The mob pushed past the last guards, charging for the airship.

4: Beyond the Curtain

Darwick felt every bit of the pain from his burning, melting flesh, but he wasn't dead. The vile biofluid kept him alive through each excruciating second. Could he die again, after the gallows had literally yanked the life from him?

Dying a second time might not hurt as much.

He slid from the wall as Azibar vented steam over his body. They had both been fooled by the same twisted, horrible woman. He had refused to see. Until now.

The mosaic scorched meat off his calves. Azibar shouted something in his face but Darwick stared at his former queen.

The High Priestess's smile sickened him. So many times he'd abetted and aided her tortures, executions. Now, with his mind once again his own, Darwick knew he'd hanged the person who offered release from his grease-painted bondage.

He grunted as Azibar shoved a copper hand through his stomach and lifted him above the mosaic. Though ripped intestines dangled from the wound, biofluid prevented his death.

"You still believe you can best me?" Azibar cried.

Once more her beautiful face entered his mind, framed by red hair and green clovers as they lay on the ground. He'd never been a heretic for keeping the card fragment, or for loving her all along. Not a blasphemer for remembering who he'd really been. Strength built in his chest. Calmer than a well-fed steer, he faced Azibar.

"I believe in me."

5: The Light of the World Past

Fierce heat emanated from the Spire's inner walls. Conduits and pipes throbbed with current. Tagen winced as Sveta wrenched her hand from his. A black thorn stuck out of his finger, then turned to ash.

Sveta backed from him toward the last elevator. "There is nothing for you to do here. This place will finally be your tomb—"

"Not yet." Tagen extended both arms. One moment he stood in the lobby with Sveta. The next, in Azibar's throne room. No boundaries could hinder him, no barrier keep him out. Meridian was open to him. Everything stood still, as if time had stopped.

The throne and mosaic glowed with electrical power. Tagen shielded his eyes against the bright golden disc behind the throne. Windows in the chamber's walls stood open, showing all Meridian the false sun. Azibar stood on the mosaic, holding Darwick over his head. The Clown had been augmented, yet burns and scars covered his body. Nearby, Andromeda faced the High Priestess. Cards filled the air around them.

Tagen gaped at Andromeda's golden mask. The face he'd seen from the beginning. The one who'd guided him through Meridian all along. Doubt and guilt had always shaded Andromeda's eyes. Now, love for him saturated them.

Time returned to normal in a whip-crack of thunder.

Azibar dumped Darwick on the mosaic and pointed at Tagen. Electricity arced over his copper skin and his remaining eye flared.

"Meridian belongs to the strongest, to us who have mastered our emotions. With your death, there will be no more rivals." He extended his hand. Copper fingertips opened. A dozen alcoves along the wall unlocked, each releasing a golden Gutter Knight.

"You are a better man than those who whipped you." Tagen summoned steel cards that floated before him, ready to deflect the attack.

Sveta walked around the mosaic toward the two painted women. Steam gushed from the windows on Tagen's right as a shape hovered outside the Spire. So much was happening at once, the city urged him to crush it all—

"Who holds the whip now, Magician?" Bolts from Azibar's fingers lashed Tagen's body. Tagen screamed as flesh sloughed off his bones. He tried to concentrate.

Sveta smiled at his agony and touched herself. Just like the High Priestess.

"I will burn my own path through the darkness," Azibar said. "Through you."

The electrical bolts arced at Tagen again but the steel cards reflected the current to all twelve golden Knights. Surging cerulean power blackened their shells and cracked their metallic skin. Biofluid and lubricant evaporated in oily, tar-smelling puffs. The bulky forms clattered to the floor.

Filled with power, Tagen focused on the High Priestess, but black vines coiled around his ankles. Two bolts grazed Tagen's left arm. "Sveta, stop—!"

"You won't take Meridian away from me." Electricity from the mosaic sparkled along Azibar's body. His arms glowed blue-white as he raised them.

More vines crawled over Tagen, pinning him in place. Sveta smirked at him.

Darwick jerked Azibar around as the energy blasted from his copper hands. Electricity struck the throne. Coils popped and whistled. Gauges burst. The bolts arced over Sveta, knocking her to the floor. Black vines caught flame and withered. Bolts ricocheted off the High Priestess's cards and struck the sun disc. It moved, focusing the light energy against the chamber walls, which overheated the routers. Excess electricity conducted from the mosaic and into Azibar.

Darwick smiled. "I can see her—" The mosaic's current burned him to ashes.

Azibar screamed as his copper hands melted. Slag dripped from his steam vents.

Two conduits blew open from the disc's reflected heat. One of the chamber's walls gave way and a tremor shook the Spire. Sections of the floor sunk outside the mosaic. Tagen ducked as another conduit burst overhead. Clockwork gears strained, then popped off. Two turbines blew apart. Chunks of heated metal sliced through the fiery air. Tongues of electricity lashed out from the mosaic and throne. The stench of burnt ozone and metal made him cough.

Through the smoke, he spotted Andromeda. She screamed, clutched her throat, and fell through the floor.

"Andromeda!" Tagen ripped the vines to shreds. Desperate power engorged his legs and he leapt over the mosaic. Electricity arced over him but his mind's eye sent it into a Stygian mirror. He landed on the other side, unscathed.

The High Priestess appeared before him like an apparition from the smoke. "Like I saw in the cards, I summoned you with a Harlequin's cries."

Tagen tried to focus but losing Andromeda crushed his will. Her golden mask blinded his mind's eye as much as the disc behind the throne. The light magnified the golden cards into a beacon of lies and servitude.

"Bow to me one last time, Magician," the High Priestess said. "With me above, and you far below."

He knelt.

6: Attainment II

Leaping from *Persephone*'s railing and through the Spire's ruined wall, Radomir fired his pistol. The shot merely dented Azibar's copper flesh. Mannequin and the Wretched jumped after him. Electricity arced all around, frying two of the Wretched. Cocking the pistol, Radomir aimed for the High Priestess. Tagen knelt at her feet.

Azibar kicked Radomir aside and he slammed against the throne. Only the silver breastplate saved him, though his body numbed from the blow. The red bloom fell from inside his armor. It floated on the steam filling the chamber.

"It's time I corrected my mistakes." Azibar stomped the girl with grasshopper piston legs. Flesh and biofluid splattered him.

Her blue eye flaring, Mannequin shoved Azibar backward.

"You can never be her, do you understand? You were just an experiment!" He swung a melted fist at Mannequin, snapping her left arm off. Biofluid splashed the mosaic and hissed.

"You are the mistake." Mannequin ripped a vent from his left side. Steam and electricity shot out, scorching their copper bodies. Azibar squealed with sickening modulation. Shaking like a doll, Mannequin forced him toward the throne.

Radomir shot one of the coils running from the mosaic into the throne. The throne started reshaping into a copper sarcophagus. Gears beneath him pushed Radomir toward the mosaic.

The Wretched formed a bridge with their bodies and caught him. Before the mosaic's raw energy melted them, they shoved Radomir onto the floor. He rolled over just as Mannequin pushed Azibar into the sarcophagus.

"Seal it, Radomir!" she yelled. Azibar punched through her abdomen, spraying biofluid on the sun disc. The sarcophagus snapped shut, with Mannequin's torso wedged in the opening.

"Seal it," she repeated in a slurred, deeper tone.

Blinking away tears, Radomir cocked the hammer and shot a conduit behind the throne. Electricity raced over Mannequin's form, melting her copper flesh. The molten metal clumped in the sarcophagus's opening. Her perpetual smile creaked wider and her single blue eye flickered.

"We did it. We did it…we…" Mannequin's voice became a series of mechanical whistles and clicks. Radomir turned away as her face liquefied. She had locked away Azibar with her own body.

"You cannot take Meridian from me!" Azibar's voice vibrated through the sarcophagus. Steam jetted from dozens of vents and the mosaic flared white hot. The golden disc glowed brighter as a silhouette loomed over Radomir. A tattooed hand snatched the flower from the chamber's steam clouds.

"I feel the pain Tagen caused you, Radomir. Don't let it consume you." Sveta's eyes glowed green. The thorns sticking in her forehead, the blood, her writhing tattoos…she chilled his blood, yes. The flower turned black and withered in her hand. She reached for him as Azibar's sarcophagus rotated and blasted steam.

"Memories hurt, yes? But Brian cheers. Mannequin cheers. Won't let go." Radomir cocked the pistol.

Sveta's tattoos moved with ethereal animation. "He corrupted you, like he did me. I can fix that." Horrid faces screamed at Radomir from within her tattoos.

7: Naked Child II

The rush of air filled her ears as Andromeda gagged, clawing at her throat. The blade of vengeance had been turned against her. Silver cards plummeted along with her from Azibar's throne room. She'd failed Tagen. Failed herself. She tried pulling the dagger out. The Charonic sigils stung her skin.

"Tagen, I'm…"

Her back slammed into something hard and flat.

"Charon didn't wanna see me yet." Jaabir stood over her, holding a lever.

The elevator lurched to a stop just below the throne room. By chance, it had caught her fall. More debris rained down. Steam burst over them as Jaabir crouched beside her. Biofluid leaked from his steam vent.

"The dagger, get it—" Andromeda released her throat.

No dagger protruded from it. The High Priestess had fooled her with a cartomantic illusion. She sat up, her back protesting with sharp aches. Her lungs struggled for air after such an impact.

"Huh? We gotta leave. People are beating against the Spire outside. Tagen ain't here." Jaabir groaned and rubbed his chest.

"You okay?" she asked.

"Filters are busted and my vent's clogged. Won't be long for me." He smiled.

"Bullshit. We're still Blades of Charon." Concentrating, Andromeda gestured, and the silver cards flew up toward the throne room. Strength swelled in her limbs and she pulled Jaabir along with her. Her cards spiraled up and Andromeda stepped onto them as if they were stairs. Meridian fed her magic in ways it never had.

Ways she'd never wanted.

"Your outfit," Jaabir said as they neared the top. "It's different."

Andromeda hauled him into the throne room. "I know."

She now wore her blue outfit from Meridian's original Circus: stockings, corset and diaphanous skirt, gloves, and a matching cap. All three points ended in a gleaming sapphire star. Her body paint was white and flawless—like the High Priestess's.

The city was still deciding…but she'd had enough of its game.

Radomir backed away toward *Persephone*'s railing, just outside the Spire's wrecked wall. He aimed a pistol at Nomad Girl, who had changed into something dark, sensual. Azibar cursed from inside his sealed sarcophagus. On the other side of the chamber, Tagen was on his knees, glaring up at the High Priestess.

"Jaabir, get on *Persephone*. Don't look back."

Before he could question her, Andromeda tossed her deck into the air.

8: The Light of the World to Come

The High Priestess glanced at the others and laughed. "You think yourself a prophet of these weak fools. Azibar wanted to be their messiah, too. Look at him. A slave of his own perceptions and desires, just like the rest. What can you give them, Tagen? You only remind them of their pain, their sadness."

"And you?" A Stygian card appeared in Tagen's hand. "Should I remind you?"

Her palms flashed red. "I am the High Priestess. I have no past life."

"The people of Meridian do." Shadows, mirrors, and Charonic sigils crept into his peripheral vision. Meridian's dark energy clawed at his willpower. He didn't have long.

Torment shone in the High Priestess's eyes. "Why do you tempt me with it?"

"Who are you?" he asked in a voice not his own.

The sarcophagus spun to a fever pitch, then white-hot bolts and vapor shot out from it. Azibar screamed. Something slammed into Tagen's chest and he slumped over.

There, melted into his flesh, was Georgio's silver medallion. He keeled over.

"Who are you?" someone asked. Time slowed again.

"Tagen…Justin Tagen," he breathed. Everything around him washed out to gray, as if bled of all contrast and life.

"Not anymore," a voice said in his ear. "Don't you remember who you are?"

He quivered, clutching the medallion as it seared deeper into his chest. "I'm…"

"Charon," the voice said.

Above him, the golden disc blinded him with its dazzling, lifeless light.

Tarot cards lay scattered in Alexis's blood, though all were now face-up. They formed a panel by panel conspectus of Meridian. Brass routers, gaudy tents. Black water, decayed buildings. Nudity obscured only by grease paint. Crimson-spattered gutters.

"Is this what you want to feel?" The High Priestess's voice came from Alexis's stiff lips.

Paramedics hurried in and lifted Alexis onto a stretcher. She was still alive, though his life had already emptied from his wrists. Outside, her parents wailed.

Meridian would soon have him and Alexis. The apartment window became stained glass, showing figures in violet and green. The colors of the Stygian Tarot.

"Is this what you want to remember?"

Tagen flinched as the apartment faded into the main Circus tent interior. The ivory beauty watched him from her high-backed chair, laying out Tarot cards on her table. Instead of the condescending sneer she always wore, compassion ruled her beautiful features.

The High Priestess roved her fingers over his palm glyphs. Her skin looked so pure, so milky white. The epitome of virginity, ready for him to savor and enjoy, as long and as much as he wanted. His lips neared her red-painted ones.

"You must love me, always. You must never leave me, or hurt me. You must belong to me, Charon." She spoke with a thousand different voices.

Tagen jerked back.

Meridian tempted him through her. All of its previous rulers had been absorbed, using its magic until it consumed them. The High Priestess, like all those who came before her, could not recall a past life any more. It was as if they had never been.

Something else rose from the Stygian depths in his mind. A hand holding up a lantern. A silver ring adorned one finger.

The hand holding the lantern rose further from the Styx. Images on the ring glowed, then stamped themselves into Tagen's psyche. Moon, star, sun. A cartomancer's glyphs, or Sky Nomad navigational symbols. Divination, emotion, perception. All shot from his hand and went over the horizon like meteors.

Lighting a path.

Tagen shielded his eyes as the vision ended. Azibar's sarcophagus spun in place, jetting steam. The entire Spire trembled. Angry voices rose from below. The golden disc flared and the mosaic sparked electrical bolts in all directions. Radomir and Jaabir raced for *Persephone*, which floated just outside the Spire's summit.

They wouldn't make it.

He concentrated as the High Priestess drew a flaming card. Andromeda's cards deflected blue-white bolts from the mosaic while she somersaulted to the High Priestess, dagger raised.

Sveta glared at him from across the mosaic. "You can't save them."

Shaking, Tagen focused harder. The Ten of Staves, a bundle of staves...a bundle...

Persephone's cling ladder wrapped around Radomir and Jaabir in a bundle as the throne room's walls blew apart. Electricity and steam burst in a concussive cloud. The golden sun disc toppled over and shone skyward.

The High Priestess's card grazed his cheek as she tumbled from the Spire, then Andromeda slammed into Tagen. They plummeted together. He wrapped his arms around her. Air whooshed past them.

The street below raced up to them.

XX.

Judgement

1: Trumpet Call

Radomir rose from *Persephone*'s deck and peered over the railing. Hundreds of people waited in the street below, silent and unmoving. The Spire's summit burned, even as the false sun shone skyward. What had happened? He tapped his gauntlets together.

Another chance might not present itself, yes. He helped Jaabir to his feet.

"Get more aboard, yes? Climb up ladder and vines."

Coughing, Jaabir pulled out Georgio's map and handed it to Radomir. "Not gonna make it without this. Think you can outrun Charon in this thing?"

The red arrow remained on the chart. The blood of the Magician. The Path.

"Still owe friends," Radomir said. "Still believe Magician."

Jaabir wheezed and nodded. "You get this thing ready, and I'll bring them in."

Radomir checked the couplings and pressed the pedal beneath the helmsman's wheel. Activated the boilers. Gripped the chart. Stared over the Styx. Georgio had entrusted him with the armor and thus *Persephone*. Mannequin had confided in him. Leader or not, he would fly this ship from Meridian, yes.

As he pulled a lever, several people clambered aboard from the cling ladder: a Gutter Knight and three Clowns. From a vine, two

Sky Nomads and a Mecho came up. The woman in pink rags, then the Dionysiac wine salesmen he remembered from before. The boy who'd handed him the Magician banner. All looked at him with hope.

2: Prince from the Inner World

The Judgement card flashed in Tagen's mind: a masked woman and a winged man rose from Meridian's depths. A Harlequin blew a trumpet above them.

"Tagen?" Andromeda squeezed him tight as they continued to fall.

He concentrated on the card's imagery. The masked woman, the winged man. Red, feathered wings. Focused all his need, his emotion, into the mental image.

Something sprouted from his back.

Red-feathered wings.

The wings righted them in the air, flapping with vigor and certainty. Tagen carried Andromeda as people in the streets milled about with stupefied expressions. *Persephone* sailed toward them.

As the wings disappeared, Tagen landed near Doll House. His body scuffed over the pavement but he shielded Andromeda from any damage. Gasping, he lay on his back in the heap of doll parts.

Andromeda gaped and touched his cheek. The graze from the High Priestess's flaming card had healed. The damage done by Azibar, the melted flesh around the medallion—all whole again. Before his eyes, a deep cut sealed on Andromeda's shoulder.

"I can't hold on much longer," he said. "Andromeda...I murdered my wife."

She smoothed his hair as more explosions rocked the Spire. "I know."

He wanted to say more but all he could do was hang his head. She gently nudged his chin up to meet her eyes. Clad in a sleek blue outfit, she was every bit the Harlequin he'd see on the posters at Femur Tower.

"Get on that ship and leave, before Meridian takes me," he said.

"I'm not going anywhere." She showed her palm: the glyphs glowed green.

He sat up. "I mean it."

"Me too." She kissed his lips and the sweet ecstasy of that moment made his torments all the more painful.

Persephone hovered overhead. A single black vine dangled where the cling ladder had been. Crowds gathered and watched them, their collective expectation suffocating. A force welled up inside him.

Andromeda kissed him again. "Meridian wants me, too. But you must—"

A black vine shot from a sewer gutter and wrapped around Tagen's throat. Thorns bit into his skin. Andromeda sliced it with her dagger but another vine slapped her aside.

Walking through the crowd, Sveta appeared more striking than before. Her braids had lengthened. Each strand contained black thorns.

"I won't allow this." Sveta's brow furrowed. "You'll do no more harm!"

Vines rose from the gutters and tethered *Persephone* to a steamlamp.

"Let go, damn you!" Andromeda leapt through the air, slicing the vines.

"He will betray you, too." Cards slid from Sveta's tattoos and flashed in her hand. "The Magician is a trickster…and Justin tricked me for so very long."

"Justin is dead." Andromeda ignored Tagen's anguished stare.

Sveta's jaw tightened. "I know every image, every face, of the Stygian Tarot. None of them belong to him. He can't rule Meridian, he couldn't even control himself…"

"Who are you?"

Tagen held his head in his hands as Sveta's words branded his conscious.

"In coming here, he let you go," Andromeda said. "He's no longer a sideshow. Meridian bound you both here…to see who would become its new ringmaster."

Sveta hesitated. "The Styx is the final mirror. He will drown in it. I have seen it."

"Everything's not etched in copper," Andromeda said.

"Why do you love him?" Sveta asked in a tight voice.

"Because the man he became here—that man gave me hope again."

Tagen's heart burst as he met Andromeda's eyes. Her ardor for him smoldered.

"The city is mine! You don't understand it as I do, you can't give them what I can!" The High Priestess lay on the curb beside Doll House, sobbing and quivering.

It wanted them all.

If he drew on the city's power…maybe he could drain it away from the others. It was their only chance to escape. The only path to his redemption.

Turmoil churned in his mind as Tagen concentrated. Magician faithful knelt in the streets, while others swayed and held their heads. People saw loved ones again, or recalled their final moments. Some died with dignity, surrounded by friends and relatives. Others perished in murders, wars, and suicides. So many lives, so many stories. A library of intimate selections he thumbed through like a book.

Mirrors emblazoned with Charonic sigils glimmered with insight. Stars, moons, and suns shone from every one. Reflecting one's greatest fears back at them.

"I know," Tagen murmured, the words a statement rather than an answer.

Masks protecting inner strength or hiding sinister evil. Tomes imparting knowledge, or instilling dogmatic lies. Obelisks of achievement or monoliths of terror. Pathways to paradises unimagined, or to levels of degradation beyond horror. The Stygian deck's Minor Arcana flowed through him, finally revealing the Major Arcana. Much to Tagen's surprise, the shadows remained, the ambiguous characters morphing from one face to another.

The street returned to Tagen's sight. Black vines enveloped the buildings around them. Some looped around bystanders, thorns breaking through flesh in red droplets. Other vines wrapped around ancient statues of Charon or the Gorgon.

"They don't want to see." Sveta beckoned more vines from a sewer grate. "I can take it all away, relieve them of their burdens. Let the dead have peace."

"I can give you peace," Tagen said.

Andromeda juggled silver cards, her lips tight. "Tagen…don't."

"Isn't this what I was meant to do? Why else have I come here?"

"Because the cards foretold you." Andromeda's eyes glistened.

Sveta glared. "Because you brought me here!"

The vines snapped after Tagen but he didn't move. They enveloped him, thorns ripping his skin off, abrading away all he'd ever been. The black tendrils smashed and squeezed him as Sveta screamed her rage, and he was dimly aware of Andromeda, slicing through the hellish jungle, trying to reach him.

"Who are you?" the voice shrieked in his ear, like a banshee in a hurricane.

From his chest, Tagen produced a pomegranate seed. It sprouted into a red flower. "Andromeda…Sveta…get away as soon as you can."

"Tagen, no!" Andromeda yelled.

Sveta lashed him with all her power until the tattoos faded from her skin, one image at a time. He absorbed all her pain, the thousand agonies he'd put her through in this existence, and their previous one. The faces in her tattoos shrieked and howled but her shoulders stiffened with one last gasp of willpower. "Meridian has all but claimed me. Please…shatter this final mirror…"

He recalled her smile on their wedding day. Her laughter when he'd locked himself outside their house, in his underwear. That time the camel spat on him at the zoo and she teased him about it for days. The way she always slept close the nights after he returned from a mission. The utter trust in her eyes, before he'd broken it.

Each tattoo reminded Tagen of good or bad moments from their past life together, until nothing was left but brittle vines and Sveta's prone form on the street.

In her apartment, Tagen—gray-skinned, palms glowing—knelt over Alexis's body. Blood and Tarot cards surrounded him in an ocean of anguish. He held a cup filled with pomegranate seeds. He gently put one in her mouth.

"Who are you?" the voice asked.

"What you need me to be," he said.

Meridian's power filled him. His flesh regrew; his wounds sealed. Fighting its power, he managed to kneel at Sveta's side and lay the blossom on her chest.

He would remember her as she was. Not what he'd made her become.

Her face softened. The flower was heavy with dew.

"Justin…?"

Before he could speak or touch her, Sveta—Alexis—faded from Meridian.

Tagen couldn't smile, even though she was free. He couldn't do anything now, because the city owned him.

"You fool! Can't you see what will happen? Chaos will rule Meridian!" The High Priestess's golden cards flew at him like dozens of flaming missiles.

With a wave of his hand, Tagen snuffed the fiery cards from the air.

Andromeda ceased her juggling and drew a dagger. "You're not Charon yet."

A commotion erupted behind them as people rushed toward *Persephone.* Over three dozen already stood on deck. Radomir and Jaabir helped others aboard.

Black, spidery veins bulged from Tagen's flesh. Charonic sigils appeared all over his body, much like Sveta's tattoos. The ends of his hair curled up into black thorns.

"Go," Andromeda said. "Lead the ship from Meridian. It won't have us both."

"No!" He touched the blue diamonds, painted under her eyes.

"I've loved the Magician long enough. You must help others now."

"No, I did this for you, too—"

Andromeda jabbed her dagger straight into his heart.

A mirror in his mind showed a woman in a bronze mask, her hair coils of steaming snakes, stabbing a black-clothed man with gray skin in the heart. Pomegranate seeds spilled from his hand.

The Gorgon slaying Charon.

Tagen's heart broke while it struggled to pump with Stygian steel piercing it. As he staggered back, all minds in Meridian closed to him once again. Clowns, Mechos, and others fought anew. He keeled forward and fell on his knees.

Meridian's dark magic emptied from him.

"Why?" he managed from a raw throat. Fat raindrops beat down on him.

"Go!" Tears didn't mar Andromeda's face paint this time. "Your path is open!"

"I won't let you do this!" He tried to stand. "This is my burden, my fate!"

Andromeda touched his lips, then faced the mob.

The next instant, he stood beside Radomir on *Persephone.*

Tensing, he gripped the dagger in his chest. It vanished in thin air. It had been an illusion. Only Andromeda's willpower had allowed it to fool him. Charon slain by a masked woman: a myth repeated to spare him from this horrible city.

Instead of a dagger, he held a pomegranate seed. A promise of life in a wasteland.

He tried using magic, tried telling Radomir to stop the ship, but all he could do was stare at the woman he'd come to love, the one who believed he was something better.

"I love you," Tagen whispered.

3: Resurrection

Andromeda didn't turn for a final glimpse of Tagen on *Persephone*'s deck. She didn't let any more tears fall from her eyes. No onyx daggers appeared in her hands, or a curse on her lips. Instead, colored balls materialized in the air. She juggled them.

The mob continued fighting, their minds on the precipice of realization or damnation. Meridian's power made her feel their emotions, see their memories. Tempted her to take it all for herself. Stab every one of them in heart with Charonic steel.

Andromeda had lost faith in the people of Meridian long ago. The murder, rape, cannibalism, and cheapness of human life had inured her to happiness. With the man she loved leaving her behind, she had every reason to let it continue. Every reason to allow Meridian to take control of her.

She whistled as she'd once done to alert other Blades of Charon. Some people stared at her. Balls and pins appeared in her hands while she juggled. Pieces of candy, Tarot cards, simple cloth masks. These Andromeda tossed to the crowd. An old song came to her lips. Its notes floated over the street and filled the ears of everyone. She loaded each phrase with emotive inflection. With love for the one she'd just stabbed.

People smiled at her. A few hugged each other.

Dark shadows still rimmed her sight. Rain drizzled.

"Such a selfless sacrifice," the High Priestess said. Clowns rallied behind her. "Too bad it won't save Tagen."

Andromeda faced her. "Jackpot is beyond your blood opera now."

"Not while Azibar's fools serve me." The High Priestess smirked as an electrical bolt shot from outside the Mecho District toward *Persephone*. It missed it, but the airship shook and lost altitude.

By Charon, not when Tagen was almost away!

"You always loved a lie," the High Priestess said. "Now you will die for it!"

Focusing, Andromeda leapt forward. Golden cards grazed her skin, burning her. The High Priestess appeared on the curb, then behind her. Sarcastic laughter drowned out other sounds. Andromeda didn't falter or flinch. A dozen jack-in-the-boxes bit at her, a hundred Magicians lost their heads. None of the phantasms distracted her focus.

Charonic sigils flashed on a black blade. A greater strength than any she'd ever known rose in Andromeda's heart. Her dagger slashed the High Priestess's chest, just below those ivory breasts. No blood spilled forth.

"I...I am..." The High Priestess's lower lip trembled. Yellow-white maggots seeped from her wound. They spattered and wriggled on the street.

Shrieking, the High Priestess covered herself with both hands.

Clowns thrust and slashed at Andromeda but she cartwheeled backward and tossed a single Tarot card at them: the Queen of Swords. Their weapons snapped or melted. Several more fired pistols at her. She caught every bullet, then juggled them all until each vanished in a puff of steam. The remaining warriors fled.

"You're not invincible anymore. Meridian has already chosen." Andromeda raised the dagger, but those ruby eyes held pain and confusion. The same expression the High Priestess had shown so long ago, when Andromeda took her in.

The naked woman shivered as Andromeda lifted her from the gutter. Young and lovely, she stared about with the typical fright of a new arrival.

"Are you okay?" Andromeda glanced at the three bodies nearby. The other thugs had fled before they could finish with the woman.

"You...you killed them. For me." She touched Andromeda's corset, then her painted face. "You are like an angel."

"This mud show isn't heaven." Andromeda removed her red cape, worn by the ringmaster of the Circus. "Here, this will keep you dry until I find something better."

The cloth draped the woman in vermilion folds—the same color as her hair.

"Let's get itchy feet and go. Georgio makes excellent mushroom soup."

The woman smiled and Andromeda returned it. They walked toward the red and white striped tent a few blocks away, where Andromeda's friends awaited her next show.

Andromeda lowered the blade as the memory ended. Revenge washed out of her heart and into the gutters with all the blood and grease paint.

"This isn't what I am." The High Priestess sniveled and beat the pavement. "I am your goddess, not a maggot-filled whore!"

The white grease paint, always sleek on her perfect body, now flaked off. Red smears marked the corners of her cracked lips.

Andromeda stepped back from her. The rain fell heavier, thicker.

"Take me to the Circus!" the High Priestess screamed. "Take me now, you dogs!"

Clowns scampered from the alleys and surrounded her. Grease-painted limbs hauled the limp queen into her sedan chair. Moments later all they held were her red cape and ruby crown. The rest of her was gone.

"A whisper of love, a whisper of fate," Andromeda said. "Lay her heart at the Circus gate."

The rain ceased. Confetti drifted by in the gutter. People watched in silence.

Another ballista bolt passed below *Persephone*'s hull. Andromeda huffed and turned about. She'd not make it there in time.

Meridian's raw power flowed around her in rippling waves of invisible energy.

She found Tagen's image in a Stygian mirror, then dove through it.

Andromeda blinked. She no longer stood outside Doll House. Now Meridian's docks surrounded her, with *Persephone* floating overhead, almost clear of the city.

A steam ballista hummed nearby, preparing another charge.

4: Prince from the Next World

Throat tight, Tagen studied Georgio's chart, handed to him by Radomir. The navigational symbols and smudged arrow meant little, but he couldn't face the three score passengers Radomir and Jaabir had aided aboard. Old factional politics and hatreds had been forgotten as they watched his every move.

What could he tell them?

"Never thought Andromeda would do something like that." Jaabir's voice sounded strained and he ran his organic hand over his chest. "Hell of a brave woman. Don't think I'm gonna make it, though. Looks like I got your old problems, Tagen."

"Where are we going?" a woman in pink rags asked.

Tagen tried tuning out the sounds of rioting behind him. The woman in the golden mask remained behind. Leaving Meridian was a defeat now. "Georgio said other cities could be found in the Styx. I think he expected my cartomancy to show a path."

"You mean you don't frigging know?" a Gutter Knight asked. Several passengers grumbled and crossed their arms.

"Magician know." Radomir stared the doubters down. "He find—"

A bright flash passed *Persephone*'s stern. The vessel shook and dropped altitude.

Tagen turned toward Meridian. On the docks outside the Mecho District, a steam ballista reconfigured its firing trajectory.

"That copper shitcan doesn't know when to quit." Jaabir staggered to the helm as Radomir took the wheel. The other passengers gawked around like trapped rats. Stretching out with his mind, Tagen calmed them.

"Latch onto something. Use that cling ladder and tie yourselves to the railing." Tagen didn't enjoy playing the captain but they all expected him to save them.

What did he expect now? Most of his power was spent. So was his heart.

Another bolt whizzed under the hull. *Persephone* vibrated from the near miss.

Passengers screamed and shouted at one another. Trying to make the airship a more difficult target, Radomir turned the wheel back and forth. Jaabir pushed every lever. Coils along the deck shook with fresh steam.

They wouldn't make it. He didn't know the ballista's range and the airship had only just cleared the docks outside Vagrant's Row. Another shot scorched the bow. Radomir decreased altitude.

Examining Georgio's chart again, Tagen concentrated. His palms glowed violet. The hopeful commuters stared. A familiar voice passed in his thoughts.

"The knave's tongue, the sting of lies, beyond dark waters are blue, blue skies," Tagen whispered along with the voice.

His mind's eye opened. Georgio waited in the Styx, holding aloft a steam lantern. Stars, moons, and suns illuminated the path in the sky. In his heart.

The Moon gave him divination to know. The Sun allowed him to understand his emotional drives. The Star gifted him the perception to see in the darkness.

The grayness on the horizon flared. The darkness gave way. Fog drifted over ivory towers. Airships floated above them. Polished streets and elegant, white buildings hung with colorful banners. All qualms about finding another city faded. Georgio's tales had been vindicated.

"Radomir, follow the horizon," Tagen said.

Radomir and the others gawked at him.

"The gray streak, just under the horizon. Don't you see it?" The chart floated from his hand to Jaabir's. "The stars, the sun, the moon? Open your eyes, people! It's there!"

Steel cards flowed from his hands and touched every passenger. With the last vestiges of his magic, Tagen imparted his vision into their minds. "Follow the path in your heart. The one no one can steer you from."

He stepped to the railing and pointed.

Fog lurked just beyond the city's steamlamps. Tagen's palm glyphs glowed bright violet. Everyone aboard gasped.

A path parted itself though the mists.

A ballista shot rocked *Persephone.* Tagen flailed overboard. People yelled. Radomir shouted after him.

The Styx rushed up to him, having been patient since his arrival. He'd learned its Tarot, used its magic. Even possessed its fluids in his body. This moment had always been inevitable.

Tagen closed his eyes and crossed his arms over his chest. His fingers brushed Georgio's medallion, seared permanently into his flesh. "Andromeda…"

His mind's eye went dark.

XXI.

THE WORLD

1: As Above…

Andromeda ducked a Mecho blade, then stood on her hands and kicked. Gears snapped under her feet and the Mecho's knee caved in. An electrical discharge seared the wooden planks beside her but Andromeda rolled and lunged. Her dagger slashed through armor and bronze organs. The Mecho fell off the dock.

Two tin Mechos operated the ballista while eyeing her with dread. Steam blew from the weapon's vents as they readjusted its aim.

After tumbling past a Mecho solider, Andromeda vaulted over the ballista. Her right foot squashed a gunner's face. An electrical bolt grazed her right shoulder. She gritted her teeth and balanced herself on her palms along the ballista's stave. With a second kick, the other gunner's neck folded as he pressed a lever.

A steel blade nicked her corset but Andromeda flipped from the ballista and summoned her cards. Tarot images confused the Mechos as they fired their arc rods. Cartomantic vigor fueled her body, heart, and mind. A perception and grace she'd not possessed for some time accentuated every step.

Electrical bolts shot toward her. The ballista fired one final time.

Focusing on the paranoid man on the Nine of Staves, Andromeda made the soldiers think the ballista was their enemy. They fired in crackling unison.

She sprung behind a busted steamlamp as the weapon exploded. Armor, gears, and shrapnel rattled off the steamlamp post. Some stung her right thigh and left shoulder. Mechanical voices groaned.

"Charon's eyes," she breathed, scanning the air over the Styx. A bank of fog had appeared. Light twinkled through it. Stars? *Persephone* flew toward the fog as the last ballista bolt rushed by its hull.

A figure fell from the railing.

Her heart stilled. Silver cards faded from her hands. Andromeda knew who splashed into the black waters. No one ever escaped them.

"Tagen!" Andromeda shouted.

Not him, not like this. She'd accepted Meridian's burden so he could leave. She—

Her feet balanced on sheer darkness. Without realizing it, she had jumped from the dock after him. Onto the Styx itself.

Fear shackled her mind as shapes formed beneath her. Faces stared up at her: Saissa, Georgio, Pixie, Khyran. Other friends or lovers she'd known gazed upward, many of them false Magicians. Men shot the tightrope she'd been walking on.

"I thought I was strong enough to let you go," she whispered.

Sorrow weighed down her mind. She spread her arms for balance as one foot sunk beneath the black surface. Muscles tensed. Sweat slid down her brow.

Closing her eyes, Andromeda recalled her old dances. Silver cards floated around her. As she'd once balanced daggers on her fingertips, her toes and heels poised on the water's surface. Her mind's eye directed, while her heart buoyed.

Andromeda spread her arms again and pirouetted over the Styx.

With an unburdened heart, Andromeda danced as she'd done on the tightrope in the old Circus. Free, exultant. Alive. Opening her eyes, Andromeda marveled at the stars above her. Twinkling like the ends of her cap.

She reached down. The lukewarm water suggested she keel over and enter it. Like the Queen of Swords, though, her throne hovered in the air above her fear.

"Though sorrow come with parting pain, he shall come back to Meridian again," she murmured.

Andromeda's fingers closed around a wrist. She pulled up, by his right hand, the one she'd waited for over immeasurable time.

Stars reflected on the Stygian waters as *Persephone* entered the fog.

Andromeda cupped the Magician's face and kissed his lips. They embraced over the black waters. Radomir and Jaabir waved at them from the airship.

"I love you, Tagen."

She held a paper Magician card, similar to the one Darwick had torn. The figure on it had Tagen's face. Charonic sigils burned around it for a moment, then fizzled out.

"Tagen...?" Grief dragged her down to the Styx but her knees struck a solid surface. A pier now extended from Meridian, with her kneeling at its end. The city had created it to protect its chosen cartomancer...while allowing Tagen to fall into the abyss.

She concentrated on his face, his image, she drew all she could from the city's immeasurable power. Nothing brought him back from those depths. She cursed, she screamed, she carved angry lines into the pier with her dagger.

Finally, she wept.

"Though sorrow come with parting pain, he shall come back to...he shall..."

Andromeda clutched the card to her chest and gazed at the graying horizon.

"Come back to me."

2: The Way Revealed

Radomir waved with both hands as *Persephone* departed Meridian. He could only smile while Tagen held Andromeda on the Styx's very surface. They were beautiful together, yes. Across the docks, many celebrated the Magician's true arrival. Over the Mecho District, Azibar's steam-powered sun still shone upward. If

Radomir ever returned to Meridian, maybe the light would serve as a beacon.

Clutching his chest, Jaabir stopped waving. "Shit, not gonna see much longer. Should've cast me aside and took somebody else." He spat up a wad of biofluid.

"Everyone worth something." Radomir lowered Jaabir to the deck as several gathered around. The woman in pink rags wiped Jaabir's mouth while the wine salesman held up his head.

"Just glad I saw the Magician. Saw Andromeda finally get happy. Saw Meridian finally change." Jaabir coughed and drew his last onyx dagger. With a cold hand, he gave it to Radomir.

"Toss this over the side. Not gonna need it, where I'm going."

Radomir wanted to reassure his friend, but his mechanis knowledge told him Jaabir would be dead soon. He raised the dagger and neared the railing.

Fog enshrouded the airship. Stars twinkled overhead. Meridian's steamlamps, Azibar's sun, Tagen and Andromeda—all were gone.

"Hey, what's that ahead?" a Sky Nomad man asked.

"Hey-o, looks like a lotta steamlamps," a female Gutter Knight mumbled.

Radomir turned and gaped. The fog before *Persephone*'s bow parted.

Soft, warm light bathed the deck and passengers. Soaring white walls, minarets, towers, and palaces jutted from an island in the Styx. The scents of Nomad spice, fresh rain, and flower petals wafted among them. Four steam-powered dirigibles floated nearby. A large clockwork bird carrying Harlequins flew past the portside railing.

The dagger in Radomir's hand changed from black-stained steel to shining silver. He tucked it inside his armor, his steel shiv having disappeared.

Jaabir slowly stood, then examined his left claw and poked his chest. "My biofluid pumps have stopped. How the hell am I still breathing?"

A copper-skinned Mecho woman turned to Radomir. "Yes, my organs run much more smoothly now. Why do you think that is?"

Her face and body matched Mannequin's in every detail, save for a silver-mesh corset and skirt covering her nudity. Her eyes glowed a soft blue.

Gulping, Radomir stared at her. Finally, he held up Georgio's chart, stained with Tagen's blood. "Magician showed path, yes?"

The Mecho woman laughed naturally, without modulation. "Yes, I suppose he did, but you piloted this vessel. That armor really suits you. I'm Kore. Who are you?"

"Radomir." It seemed the friend he'd known for a short time had been reborn. At least one of Azibar's High Priestess replicas had escaped, yes.

"Then, perhaps upon landing, we can tour this place together?" Kore asked. "I don't know anyone else aboard."

Taking her hand, Radomir led her to the helmsman's wheel. Jaabir followed, breathing with ease. As Georgio had wanted, some of his people had traversed the Styx from Meridian. Maybe they originated from this city.

He sensed that more than just Tagen had led them here. Radomir knew, in his heart, he could venture across the blackness if he obeyed his instincts. Feeling a strange urge, he glanced behind the stern. The fog and stars had disappeared, but Meridian couldn't be seen.

A breeze blew over them. Chimes tinkled in the city ahead. Violin mazurka music drifted up to his ears.

The wind rattled the chart in his hand and Radomir glanced down. The red arrow pointed at him. Smiling, he took the wheel. Jaabir operated the levers, while Kore stood at his side, hand on his silver-armored shoulder.

In Radomir's mind, Brian giggled and smiled. He had made his son, and his friends, proud after all.

3: So Below…

Blackness dominated Tagen's sight. His limbs swirled in liquid, depthless and perpetual. After a few moments, he calmed. One cannot stare into oblivion and avoid being devoured by it. He'd already given up hope for himself. Now it belonged to others.

A hand broke the surface above as yellow light stabbed through the darkness. A lantern bobbed in the distance. His mind's eye stared wide.

He could stay here and wallow in what he'd lost. Up there would be pain, evil, and suffering. Utter darkness.

There would also be light and all that came with it.

"Andromeda," he said.

He grasped the hand and rose from the Styx. Soft lips crushed against his. The path in his mind became real.

Tagen embraced Andromeda while standing atop the Styx. Their bodies trembled against each other. He tugged off her cap and stroked her blonde locks. After they kissed again, Tagen pressed the clockwork mask's release pins. The mask morphed around her neck as a torc.

"This is the face I want to see," Tagen whispered.

Andromeda grinned.

Beneath the Styx, Tagen had sensed variant paths across the water. The Tarot was all about interpretation and his perceptions stirred it in different ways. The cards didn't show the future. They revealed possibilities based on desire.

He had risen toward Andromeda's hand as much as she had pulled him up.

On a distant pier, Andromeda held the paper Magician card, made whole again. Just like him: no longer torn between worlds, lives, or memories.

He blinked. Tagen now floated out in the Styx. Meridian's lights faded.

"Andromeda!" He swam back to where he'd seen the pier and steamlamps. His powerful limbs slashed through the water, stroke after stroke. Yet all was black, still water. An opaque ocean.

Concentrating, Tagen used what little power remained in him. As the Magician, he could show the Path to any who wanted to see. Now he was blind, in need of aid.

He thought about the city he'd left behind. The woman who'd sacrificed herself to save him. Closed his eyes, mumbled Andromeda's name, over and over.

His mind displayed a card of a naked woman floating in the air, holding a small obelisk and a tome. A wreath of masks surrounded her. Unlike other Tarot decks, she had her back to the viewer, gazing at a path over a hill in the distance.

The World. Everything he desired.

Something wet rushed over his legs. Tagen opened his eyes.

He lay on the shore of a small rocky island. Harsh yellow light came from a rectangle on the island's other side. It took him a second to realize that it was a window.

It was attached to a long, flat vessel. Blackened seaweed hung from the railing. Bones and filthy doll parts lay scattered on the deck. Turbines were clogged with grime. Steam coils were caked with rust.

"Hello?" he called.

Stepping onto the vessel, he felt a surge of power. His palms thrummed.

The window looked into a simple piloting cabin, where a single steam lantern burned. A clockwork helm and rows of gauges filled the space. A ragged, black cloak was draped over a rusty chair.

Standing in the light, he glanced down at his body. The Charonic sigils and black veins had vanished, yet he still possessed the bio-fluid's power. He made use of it, cleaning the vessel's turbines and other machinery. It was a large craft, at least three hundred feet long. Tagen had no idea how long it took him, but he remained focused on where he wanted to go…who he wanted to see.

As he entered the piloting cabin, he stopped short and stared.

The helm bore an embossed silver compass in the center, resembling the one on Georgio's medallion. He touched it, thinking of that old Nomad's proverbs.

"If Charon's heart you fix, it is your luck to go over the Styx," he whispered.

The ship's gauges came online. On the deck, the steam coils filled with energy. The floor rumbled with the churning of internal engines. The turbines whirred to life.

Tagen gripped the helm and turned it to starboard, away from the rocky island. Peering through the blackness, he spotted ivory towers. A hint of blue sky.

Shutting his eyes, Tagen shook his head. He'd not enter some wondrous paradise, while leaving her behind. He stared around the cabin until his eyes fell on a deck of cards, laying behind a row of steam sensors. Though his palm glyphs no longer glowed, Tagen drew the top card.

It was the Ten of Cups, with Tagen kissing Andromeda on a neon-lit pier, extending over the Styx. A pier reaching into paths yet to be tread or discovered. A bridge spanning lifetimes and dreams, still under construction.

His right hand thrummed. He opened it. The same pomegranate seed lay there.

Eating it, his heart swelled with emotion. It tasted like life, felt like pure joy.

"Andromeda," he murmured.

The helm jerked and turned on its own. Tagen grabbed it. Teeth gritted, it took all his strength to regain control. Black waves crashed against the vessel. The hull creaked and he pulled to starboard as something green flashed to the left in his peripheral vision.

A pier stretched along portside. A golden lighthouse shone over a familiar-looking skyline…

The vessel shook slightly, like something had jumped onboard.

Tagen rushed from the cabin and ran up the deck. He smelled gardenias.

Turning round a capstan, he ran into Andromeda. They both collapsed onto the deck, with her straddled atop him.

"I—"

She kissed him before he could say anything else.

Nothing mattered in that moment but her touch, her breath, her joyful whispers. They shared tears, laughter. Made silly promises with desperate breaths. Couldn't stop touching each other. Only when she kissed his glowing hands did she sit up.

"You're…you're still…?"

He sat up beside her, examining her palms. They glowed green.

"Meridian chose us both," he said. "It needs us."

"But what happened when I pulled you from the Styx?" she asked.

"I think the Tarot showed us what the future might be," he said. "But we still have a choice."

"So you came back to me…you silly floss head." She ran fingers through his wet hair. "A twilight kiss and a dream of bliss…A Harlequin's lips will lead you to this."

They smiled and kissed again.

Footsteps clomped over the pier. A few at first, then dozens. Hundreds.

Tagen and Andromeda stood. Hundreds of people waited on the pier. Clowns, Mechos, Orphans, even a few Wretched. He knew, from the look in their eyes, that they remembered who they were. Meridian had released them, too.

"Are you the one who will take us over the Styx?" an old man asked.

Tagen clasped Andromeda's hand. She squeezed it back.

"Yes," Tagen finally said. "Come aboard. There's plenty of room."

While he readied the helm, Andromeda entertained the passengers with songs, juggling, and some of Georgio's old Nomad tales. Smiling, he watched her, until she turned and winked at him. He sighed and restarted the engine. The boat left the pier.

After focusing on his course, Tagen piloted the vessel away from the steam-lit metropolis and into the darkness. While he worked the valves and gauges, Andromeda kissed his cheek and leaned on his shoulder.

"Will we ever return?" she asked. "What about all those other kinkers?"

One hand on the helm, Tagen wrapped the other around her waist and smiled.

He'd found Meridian once. He could do it again.

The grayness brightened on the horizon.

About the Author

Tony Peak is an Active Member of SFWA and an Affiliate Member of HWA. He is represented by Ethan Ellenberg of the Ethan Ellenberg Literary Agency. His debut novel INHERIT THE STARS was published by Penguin Random House in November 2015. His interests include progressive thinking, transhumanism, and planetary exploration. Residing in southwest Virginia, he has a wonderful view of New River.

About the Publisher

This book is published on behalf of the author by the Ethan Ellenberg Literary Agency.
https://ethanellenberg.com
Email: agent@ethanellenberg.com

9 781680 681789